This Book Belongs

NIGHT
OF
DEMONS

By Tony Richards

NIGHT OF DEMONS
DARK RAIN

NIGHT
OF
DEMONS

TONY RICHARDS

An Imprint of HarperCollinsPublishers

EOS

An Imprint of HarperCollins*Publishers*
10 East 53rd Street
New York, New York 10022-5299

Copyright © 2009 by Tony Richards
Cover art by Don Sipley
ISBN 978-1-61523-847-7

Printed in the U.S.A.

This one's for Alan Beatts, Jude Feldman, and all the gang at Borderlands Books, San Francisco.

ACKNOWLEDGMENTS

I would like to thank the following people for their invaluable help in the completion of this novel: Alan Beatts, Mike Abramov, Ann Crimmins, Diana Gill, Patrice Silverstein, Emily Krump, Will Hinton, Leslie Gardner, Darryl Samaraweera, and, naturally, my biggest fan and best helper, Louise Richards.

PROLOGUE

Dammit, he was nearly out of gas.

Cornelius Hanlon—known across the nation as the Shadow Man—glanced up from the dashboard, squinting through the darkness. It had just begun to rain. Fat drops were smacking up against the windshield like translucent bugs.

He fumbled around until he found the wiper switch—he was unfamiliar with this model of Chrysler. And when he finally clicked it, the glass in front of his face turned out to be greasy, obviously unwashed for weeks. The rubber blades, scything noisily across it, made such a blur that he could barely see where he was going. He wished that he'd stolen a better car, a newer one. But there had not been time for such refinements. Cornelius craned forward to get a better view.

It had been a couple of hours since he'd fled Boston. But he was still in Massachusetts, he felt sure. He was on a dead straight road with barely any lighting, that ran like a needle through the heart of the New England woodlands. Dense, tangled shadows were the only things he could make out.

He'd practically been caught back in the city. His heart thumped when he thought about it. The cops had turned up without any warning, and he'd barely gotten away by the skin of his teeth, vanishing into the sewers underneath the basement of his home.

They'd been going through his stuff by this hour. He hated the thought of that. All his copies of the Bible, with the passages in Revelation underlined. Hell, even his diaries, which were numerous and complex. Did any of those idiots have the sense to read between the lines, and understand the basic truth behind what he'd been doing?

How had they found him at all? He'd thought he was invulnerable to human interference. But the voices in his head kept telling him that he ought not to worry. The Old Ones were still watching over him, and he would come through this safely.

The point was proved a short while later. A bright rectangle of light appeared ahead. As he got closer to it, he could see it was a gas station. Cornelius slowed down and pulled in, drawing up to a pump.

He stared in through the storefront window as he filled the tank. There was only one teenaged boy on duty—stubble-chinned, sporting a ponytail—who hadn't even seemed to notice he was there. His gaze was fixed on a small portable TV. His mouth was slightly open and his eyes looked glassy, reflecting the images.

Unawares. He preferred catching people unawares. Just perfect.

The noise from the set washed over him as he walked in. He recognized this show. It was a rerun of *The Simpsons*— Homer was falling, with multiple yelps, down Springfield Gorge. Cornelius cleared his throat. The ponytailed kid glanced across at him, looking slightly annoyed to be disturbed. Then he seemed to remember what his job was. His expression became milder.

"Hi, there." He peered at the readout on the till. "That'll be seventeen-ninety, dude. Need anything else?"

Dude?

"Just the gas and I'll be on my way, young man."

Cornelius handed him a credit card. Not one of his. It belonged to the owner of the Chrysler. Who, presumably, was still lying in that alley in the South End, with his throat slit open like a second mouth.

"Okay, then—" and the kid glanced boredly down at it. "Mr. Mackie."

Cornelius just smiled and nodded. The transaction was being rung up, and this whole business seemed to be going fine, without the slightest hitch. When the cartoon voices abruptly stopped.

"Tonight's big breaking news," a woman suddenly announced. "The Shadow Man—the killer who's been terrorizing the Boston–Cambridge region for the past eleven months—has finally been identified as one Cornelius Caldwell Hanlon. A statewide manhunt is underway tonight, with police convinced that he has left the city. They are advising the public not to approach the man, and anyone spotting him should notify the authorities at once."

Cornelius looked over at the little screen. And there, squarely on it, was a photograph of him—his driver's license photograph, in fact, which was not a particularly good one. His flat, bald scalp reflected too much light. His jowls looked thicker and more pendulous than was actually the case. And there were such dark shadows underneath his eyes, they seemed like holes punched in a mask.

When he turned back, the kid was gazing at him very strangely, the color disappearing from his face. Cornelius's grin grew wider.

"Sorry to have deceived you, young man. Very impolite of me. Apparently, I am not Mr. Mackie after all."

Then he started to make his way behind the counter. He did it casually, in no great hurry. There was nowhere for the kid to go.

"Identity theft is such a dreadful problem these days, isn't it?" he pointed out.

The narrow blade appeared in his hand,

"Especially for you."

Ten minutes later, he was back on the same road, still wondering where it would take him. Across the state line, hopefully. The rain had stopped, and the moon had come out. The shadows around him looked even more profound under its warmthless light, the woodlands like a series of mazes folded across each other. The kind of place where some primeval beast might dwell.

But then, more circles of light appeared. A pair of headlamps, in the distance behind him. As they drew closer, he could see that they belonged to a patrol car. But no beacon came on, and there was no siren he could hear. It was doubtlessly simply a trooper, going about his usual rounds.

Cornelius bit his lip all the same. His hands grew clammy on the wheel.

You are already in the process of becoming invincible, the voices in his head assured him. A higher breed of being, capable of doing anything you want.

That calmed him down a fair way. Although not completely. The cruiser trawled along behind him, keeping a safe distance. But there was no way to be sure how much longer that would last. The cop might already be checking on his license plate, or even calling in for backup. It would be better to get off this goddamned road, and fast.

When a ramp appeared a minute later, Cornelius took it without hesitation. The patrol car didn't follow him. It simply stuck to the main drag, and went humming on by. So all that panic had been for nothing. He let out a depleted breath and then scolded himself. He had to trust the Old Ones more.

This was a far narrower road. And the forest seemed to be even more thickly tangled than it had been earlier on, if that was possible. And where might he be on his way to? There hadn't even been a sign.

He was surprised, then, when he crested the next hill and a good-sized town came in sight. Rows of streetlamps sprawled below him, illuminating the roofs of hundreds of clustered houses. There was a river running through the middle of the place, and a big square to the north of that. Which was surrounded by some rather larger buildings whose function he could not make out. He could even see a park with a huge lake in it, its surface reflecting the moonlight.

Cornelius pulled over and rummaged in the glove compartment until he found a map, which he spread out. No town of any size was indicated here. So where on earth had he wound up? Maybe he'd become confused, and had not been headed where he thought he was.

No matter. This seemed as good a place as any to hole up for a while. So he put the map away and then continued on. He would find out where he was soon enough. And—who knew?—maybe he could even perform some more of his ceremonies here. A warm tingle ran through him, at the thought of that. What he did, yes, was vital and sacred. But enjoyable as well—and he was not ashamed to admit it.

He even had a name for that whole aspect of the work that he engaged in. Special Fun. His anxiety melted away and he beamed suddenly, as happy as a child.

Oh yes, yes. Watch them try to beg against the pressure of the gag. Watch them clench their jaws on it, then try to scream. Their eyes became so wide—at that point—it was almost like they were in love with him.

Special fun. It might be breaking man's laws, but the Old Ones approved.

An ancient-looking signpost went by, but Cornelius was too lost in his own thoughts to even notice that.

CHAPTER 1

There'd been nothing much happening the last few days that genuinely required my attention. No spells gone wrong, nor the wielders of them going berserk. No monsters or such appearing from the ether. No real crises of any kind, in fact. Although, in a town as peculiar as Raine's Landing, a lull like that usually means there's serious trouble waiting just around the corner. And I'd already been warned, hadn't I? The Little Girl had told me. Something new and very bad was headed here. She hadn't been able to be specific. So the real question was . . . what?

But waiting for it ground me down. I felt bored and twitchy at first, and then strangely numb. I'd gone for several walks. I'd spoken with Cassie on the phone—she sounded all keyed up, with nowhere to dispense her energy. I'd even considered going fishing on the Adderneck to try and calm myself down. But without Pete—my son—around any longer to go with me, all I finally did was shy away from that idea.

Darkness had closed around my neighborhood. It's called Northridge, and is a friendly, unassuming place. We were right at the tail end of summer. The air was cooler than it had been a couple of weeks back, far fewer bugs in evidence. Across the street from me in Roger Lym's backyard, a plume of smoke lifted for a while, I could hear voices back there. It was his traditional late summer cookout. But then the skies started to drizzle gently, and the smoke and chatter died away.

My porch was covered, so I stayed out on it all the same and drank another beer. More time passed. Lights started going out in the windows around me. In another half an hour, almost every house was darkened. In the distance, I could hear the chiming of the clock on the Town Hall.

I felt becalmed. The beer had filled me with a floaty, weightless drowsiness. So I finally headed back indoors, pulled off half my clothes, then flopped down on my bed. It's something I never like doing because I always have the same unpleasant dreams when I sleep. All of them centered on the same subject. The day my family disappeared.

And it was precisely that way tonight. I wanted to wake up but, as usual, couldn't seem to manage it.

Jason Goad, a stage magician from Las Vegas, had some-how found out about this weird, dysfunctional town of ours. How the real witches of Salem had fled to this place shortly before the trials in 1692. How they'd blended into our com-munity, gradually taking it over. Until the entire place had gotten all filled up with the arcane and the bizarre.

Goad had managed to get in past the curse which keeps us separated from the outside world. He'd moved into the loft room of the house right next to mine. There he'd taught himself genuine magic. The strongest adepts are born to it, but anybody who lives here can learn.

But he'd done something else as well. He'd coveted my family. My wife especially. Alicia . . .

I drifted partway back to consciousness, and took in the fact that I was tangled up in my damp sheets. Struggling feebly to get free of them, but I couldn't get a proper sense of where to go. And my eyes would not come open more than half a crack. I sank into the dream once again. The events in it raced to their terrible conclusion.

They were standing in his room, completely motionless, transfixed. Pete, Alicia, Tammy. He had put a spell on them and drawn them there. Still a cop back then, I was trying to get in through the door. But Goad had conjured up a bar-rier, and I could not get past it. I beat against it helplessly, the whole while that he rambled on. They were his now, he proclaimed. His family. And he was going to turn them into gods.

That's the thing with magic, and part of the reason that I genuinely detest it. It partially comes from what's inside. And if your psyche's messed up, then it can go very badly wrong.

The light in the room changed, growing so bright that it was painful to look into. My family became reduced to ghostly silhouettes. Then the glow started filling up their bodies. But that didn't last for long.

The brilliance took on a deeper hue, like bronze. And this was definitely not supposed to happen. Tammy, three years old, let out a shriek. The room went black. And when it cleared . . .

They were all gone.

The anguish of it had never diminished, despite the fact it had been over two years ago. It never got a tiny bit easier. The dreams were always very painful, horribly intense.

It was partly my fault it hurt so much, and I understood that. Not once had I tried moving on. I hadn't watched them die, you see. I'd only seen them vanish. And perhaps they were still out there somewhere. That was a hope I constantly clung on to.

I came half-awake again. And the self-same words went through my head that come to me every night. Still out there? But if so, where?

Then I dropped into a deeper realm of sleep, where no more dreams were possible.

A different light was waiting for me there. Not searing white or bronze this time. This one was a pale, electric blue. And at its heart revolved the Little Girl.

This wasn't any kind of dream. It was a visitation. Because the Little Girl is perfectly real, existing in the here and now. She inhabits the nursery room at 51 Bethany Street, in the Marshall Drive area of town. And she is one of the Landing's most mysterious denizens.

What she is or how she got there, I couldn't tell you. I

have tried to find out, and can't. The things I genuinely know about her? She only looks like a small child, about five years old, fair-haired and tiny. No one's certain what she really is. But—despite the fact she always keeps her eyelids closed— she sees most things that happen here, and some things out beyond our borders. She has enormous powers of perception sometimes, and has helped me before. Since I quit as a cop, I've been what you would call a freelance, fighting everything that's bad about the supernatural. And in that role, quite frankly, I need all the help that I can get, whatever source it comes from. I just wish that some of them weren't quite so peculiar.

Her tone was rather echoey, as usual. As if several different voices were overlapping every time she spoke. And you could see her eyeballs moving underneath her delicate lids, the lashes shivering gently.

"Hello, Mr. Ross," she said.

She always calls me that, and will not be corrected. Ross is actually my given name. My surname is Devries.

I heard myself murmur, "Don't you ever sleep?"

Her edges became blurry, and she sounded slightly distant when she answered back.

"I'm not really sure, but that's beside the point. I'm here to warn you."

"Okay, then. Do that."

"Something new has arrived. I told you it would."

I felt the bedsheets tighten around me.

"What exactly?"

"A very bad man indeed, for the moment. He is headed for the center of town, but has his eyes on Sycamore Hill."

Which was where most of the richest folk here lived, a great deal of the power in the Landing being concentrated up there. Gaspar Vernon, Samuel Levin, Kurt van Friesling, many others like them. But it didn't worry me too badly. They could look after themselves for the most part.

The Little Girl had used the strangest choice of words, though. "A very bad man . . . for the moment." What precisely did she mean by that?

I could have asked her, but already knew that she could

read my thoughts. She understood what the question was before I even voiced it. So I simply let her carry on.

"He will still be very bad in a few minutes' time. But not a man any longer, Mr. Ross. Something far more dangerous than that."

"In what way?"

Her face became rather strained, and her voice dropped to a rasping hiss.

"It's difficult to tell. I'm not sure what he'll become. It is all bound up with secrets, you see. And secrets are such personal things."

She often spoke in riddles, and tonight seemed to be no exception. So I was left struggling to get the gist of what she was trying to convey to me.

It didn't take very long to realize that was pointless. She seemed to be rather confused herself. What was going to happen from this point on? She didn't even know.

Which was unlike the Little Girl, and that worried me badly.

"I didn't think there were any secrets," I pointed out to her. "At least, not from you."

She turned that over carefully before replying.

"Oh," she whispered. "You'd be surprised."

The blue light started to fade, and she diminished with it until she disappeared. After that, I hung in pure darkness for a while.

And then I woke up sharply. Because the phone beside my bed started ringing.

It was Cass.

CHAPTER 2

About an hour earlier, Cornelius had been heading in.

Voices had been sounding in his head for quite a while. And they were not the ones that he was familiar with, those heavy, breathless murmurs. For a start, these were mostly female. Their accents were strange, old-worldly. And they did not try to comfort him or reassure him, the way the Old Ones usually did. They were hostile, hissing at him in an urgent tone.

"Stay away from here, you fool!"

"This is no place where you are welcome!"

"Turn around!"

"Go back! Go back!"

He wasn't sure whose they were exactly. But they didn't really bother him. He had been hearing people speaking in his mind since he'd been eight years old. They were as unremarkable to him as the sight of his own hands. And the fact that these voices were brand-new ones made no particular difference.

As for what they kept on telling him . . . well, they were talking to precisely the wrong person. Thanks to the ceremonies he'd performed, he was becoming very special, and could do almost anything he wished. He'd be transforming before too much longer. Becoming something more than human. Just a few more sacrifices ought to do the trick. So he wasn't going to be scared off by any vague warnings.

Cornelius chuckled, shaking his large head. And, after a couple more minutes, they simply faded away. He had already driven well inside the town.

The rain had stopped a while ago, leaving everything around him shimmering with damp. The streets were broad and empty, with nothing to slow him down. A sleepy place, which was what you would expect in this part of the world. He passed through suburbs, mostly filled with wood-built houses, not special in any way. Except . . . his gaze kept flitting to a high, bumpy hill that rose against the night sky on the western side of the town. There seemed to be some much larger residences on the crest up there. And that intrigued him.

Ahead, some slightly taller buildings came in view. The avenues grew narrower. There were more stores and restaurants than there had previously been. He kept on heading in, ignoring the stoplights. And finally wound up at the central square.

"Union Square," a sign informed him. It was pretty large for a community of such apparent insignificance. And was full of shadows, in spite of the way it sprawled.

It was surrounded by globe-shaped lamps, shining like little amber planets. At the center was a huge bronze statue of a stern-faced man. By the way that he was dressed, he'd lived a very long time back. Some hero from the Revolution, maybe?

Cornelius didn't stop. He cruised around the square's perimeter. Most of the buildings surrounding him, on closer inspection, turned out to be offices, all their windows dark. The river that he'd spotted flowed nearby, a sturdy metal bridge running across it.

At the north end—dominating the whole place—was an edifice that took up that entire side of the square. It rose four stories, and its stonework was ornate. There was a flight of wide steps leading up to the front door; a matching pair of statues, seated lions, were on either side of it. And a massive clock hung above them. He was in no doubt that this was the

Town Hall. There was a motto carved above the doorway—
VALOR IN EXTREMIS. But no indication, still, of where he had
wound up.

Directly to the south of it, there was another large building with Doric columns on display out front. A theater apparently, by the posters on the wall. The play currently on
show was *The Crucible* by Arthur Miller. And there was a
matinee this weekend. *Brigadoon*.

A street to his left had some gaudy neon signs, for eateries and bars. And there'd be people there, for sure. But
not the kind that he was seeking. He preferred clean-living,
decent folk for his ceremonies. Homebody types, for whom
a glass of eggnog was a sinful pleasure. The spilling of their
blood—after all—pleased the Old Ones so much more.

He found himself cruising by a post office. And, by the
sign beside its shuttered entrance, finally discovered where
he was.

Raine's Landing? Cornelius had never even heard of the
place. But there were so many towns dotted through this
part of Massachusetts, hidden by the woodlands from the
outside world. And so he shouldn't be surprised.

Special fun, though? Fun, fun, fun? Where could he go to
find him some?

Back in Boston, he had favored the well-heeled districts for
his little visits. The Back Bay and Beacon Hill. He preferred
to visit educated folk. They were better equipped, surely, to
appreciate the subtleties of what he did. The clever classical
references, especially when he carved the symbol into them.
But where did such people live around these parts?

His gaze lifted to the hill again. It was not too far away.
And this time, when he looked at it, he seemed to feel a
tugging deep inside of him. Almost as if something were
drawing him that way. It was not simply an instinct. The old,
familiar voices, they were talking to him once again.

Cornelius swung the car around, and headed off in that
direction.

The weirdest thing happened, a couple of minutes later.
He had found the main road leading to the hill, and was

about to start climbing the gradient, when a bus went by. It was painted green, and brightly lit inside. And there were a couple of drowsy-looking passengers on board. But he couldn't see the driver. How could that be?

He had obviously not been looking properly, or in the right direction. His pulse bumping faintly, he continued up.

Plymouth Drive, this street was called. And it got so steep in some places that the motor of the aging Chrysler growled. There was a succession of hairpin bends, some of them giving him superb views of the whole township, lit up in the darkness like a Christmas tree. The size of the place struck him all over again. This ought to be some dinky little burg but, for some reason, wasn't that. Then he was among the massive residences that he had seen from below.

Disappointment started to worm through his bulky frame. The folks up here seemed to be terribly particular when it came to the matter of security. Each of these places had big, high walls or dense, towering privet rows protecting them. The gates were firmly locked, and in most cases you could barely see the actual dwellings. Trees got in the way.

But the couple that he could make out . . . they genuinely made him gasp. One was a vast, sprawling pale stone manor, Grecian pillars—not unlike the theater's—around its portico. And another—quite bizarrely—was an exact reconstruction of the Taj Mahal. How crazy was that? For Pete's sake, how much money did these people have?

Looming high above him, at the crooked peak, was another mansion that looked—if anything—even stranger. Caught in silhouette against the moon's glow, it was the last word in brutal, ugly Gothic. Its grounds were overgrown, the branches of countless trees twisting against the night sky. And the place had a huge spire, like a cathedral. Insane!

Even crazier, instead of a crucifix, there was a massive W on top. It had to be the owner's initial. That was taking ego to its very furthest limit, wasn't it? Cornelius felt pretty sure he didn't want to go up there.

But he was still being drawn as if by a magnet. The instinct was tugging at him from the left hand side. So he turned at the next corner, found himself on a much smaller lane. There was no sidewalk. The pavement was ill tended and broken in parts. Bushes scraped against the body of the car as he progressed. The branches of sprawling elms and oak hung overhead, and were dripping from the recent downpour. It was as dark in here as a coal mine. The white tail of a rabbit flashed in his headlights before vanishing.

Finally, he reached another pair of wrought-iron gates, much smaller than the ones he'd passed. They looked slightly rusty. And a chain and padlock hung there, but not fastened. This homeowner, apparently, was not as careful as the rest.

Cornelius grinned, killing the engine and the lights. And without making a sound—he was so very good at that, despite his size—he clambered out.

There were a few small conifers beyond the gate, and then a broad, rolling lawn that glistened moistly. He moved across it swiftly, lightly, silently. That was why the newspapers had all dubbed him The Shadow Man. The only thing that witnesses had ever seen of him? A brief glimpse of his silhouette, in somebody's backyard.

He'd been getting tired of Boston anyway, he thought to himself. It was time to spread his work to regions new.

And this seemed an excellent place to start.

CHAPTER 3

The house itself was far more compact than you would imagine for such large grounds. No grand residence like the others that he'd seen on the main drag. It only qualified, if anything, as a good-sized cottage. It was covered almost entirely in ivy, wearing the stuff like a big fur coat. A tall brick chimney pot protruded from the sharply angled roof.

There were silken drapes with oriental patterns on the leaded windows. And, by the number of lights on in the place, somebody was definitely home.

Cornelius snuck around to the rear. His breathing had sped up a little. The lawn squelched underneath his tread, letting out a musty odor. He skirted past some rosebushes, their petals and leaves beaded with rainwater. Then, rounding the corner of the building, a conservatory came in view.

The glass was lit up very brightly, shining like a diamond. Inside, at the center of the tiled floor, was an antique-looking bureau with a roll-down lid. What a curious place to put such a thing. There was no other furniture except a wicker couch, and a load of plants in big glazed pots with Chinese characters on them.

Standing in front of the bureau was one of the most peculiar figures he had ever seen. A man, in his eighties at the very least. He was painfully thin, his back severely hunched. But he was smartly dressed, entirely in black. His shoes. His shirt—he wore no tie. His dapper suit, which had an overly long jacket. The darkness of the clothing made his lengthy mop of pure white hair all the more striking. It seemed to sprout in every direction before flowing in thick, tangled locks down his back.

The fellow seemed engrossed in something, with his head tucked down. So—reasonably sure that he would not be seen—Cornelius ventured closer.

The man's face was unusual too. The nose was hooked. The chin was sharply pointed. The eyes seemed sunken, lost in gloom. Cornelius could see, the nearer he got, that the jacket wasn't merely too long. It was an actual tailcoat.

As he watched, the man reached into the top of the desk, and began fingering something inside it. But the angle was wrong, he couldn't make out precisely what.

There was a back door to the house, a few yards from him. Cornelius moved across and tried the knob. It turned easily, and that pleased him. Like the front gate, it had not been locked.

His breathing became harsher, and his heartbeat increased. This was promising to be very special fun indeed. He'd not had things so easy in a good long while.

He went into some kind of pantry, stacks of foodstuffs and crockery on the shelves around him. The floor was hard, another tiled one, and he slipped his sneakers off before pressing on. By the time he reached the inner hall, the narrow blade was gleaming in his fist again.

When he reached the staircase, he could see lights on above. But no one seemed to be moving around up there. There was not the tiniest creak or murmur. So—with luck—perhaps the old man lived here on his own.

The artwork on the walls around him looked extremely strange. He studied it warily. It depicted fire-breathing dragons, and even more peculiar beasts. Chimeras, he thought they were called. Griffons, Gorgons, a Hydra. Cornelius felt slightly anxious as he took it in. What sort of twisted mind collected stuff like this? Maybe he had come to the wrong place.

But the rest was regular enough. A cabinet with porcelain

figurines neatly lined up on display in it. More plant pots, and an umbrella stand. That made him feel a little easier.

He worked his way through to the back, still getting the strange sensation he was being guided there.

The bright lights of the conservatory filled his vision. The old man's back, turned to him, was a solitary dark column, like an exclamation mark. The guy was mumbling something, maybe reading from a book. If so, it had to be a foreign one. He didn't recognize a single word.

Everything seemed to be hurting Cornelius slightly, as it usually did by this point in the proceedings. The intense electric glow, pressing at his eyeballs. And the unfamiliar murmured phrases banging at his ears. His lungs were getting painful, and his ankles ached from his own weight.

He had to stop this. This discomfort and uncertainty. And there was only one way he knew how.

The old coot still hadn't noticed he was there. And so Cornelius raised the blade a little higher, then continued to creep up on him.

"Partez!" the old man shouted suddenly. *"N'existez pas!"*

Cornelius jerked, then cast his gaze about. Who was he talking to? They were completely alone here. Blackness pressed at the conservatory's panes, so that they might as well have been in outer space. Only the distant stars were looking down. Except Cornelius knew the word "alone" was not entirely true. The Old Ones were still watching him. Expected certain things of him. And he'd not fail them.

"Un oeil invisible!" the man chanted.

"An oily" . . . ? What was the old fellow yammering about? He'd met some strange ones in his day, but this guy seemed to be out dancing with the fairies.

Shifting his weight again, he didn't test his footing carefully enough. His toes came down on a loose section of tile. Which rattled.

Finally, the old man turned around.

This happened occasionally. Cornelius had gotten used to it, and knew what to do. He beamed at the man hugely. And spread his arms to display himself.

You see? Aren't I beautiful, so close to transformation? Aren't you glad I came into your home tonight?

But the old man, just like all the others, didn't seem impressed by that. His gaze darted to the knife instead.

Viewed up close, his face had even more irregularities than could be picked out from outside the windows. One of his irises, the left, was cataractous, milky. The other was a shade of turquoise that Cornelius had never seen in human eyes before tonight. It put him in mind of a cat. There were two large moles on the guy's cheek. And his eyebrows sprouted like white crabgrass, beetling.

The aged face filled up with startlement at first. But then, to his surprise, it blazed with anger.

And that was when Cornelius saw the man was holding something in his own right hand.

He thought, at first, it was some kind of weapon. But it didn't seem to be that. It was a rod, for sure. But not large enough to do any harm. About a foot long, and as narrow as a pencil. A pure matte black, like the man's clothes. So dark it almost seemed to draw the light in very slightly. Except that there was something shining at its upper tip.

What had he been doing with something like that? And more importantly, Cornelius wondered, what was he planning to do with it now?

The man wasn't reacting in the way that the folk who he dropped in on usually did. There was no apparent fear. He didn't try to back away. Instead, he simply stood there, almost casually, working the stick between his wizened fingers. And he still looked angry, certainly. But a puzzled air had blended in with that. There was a question in his one good eye.

Then he pursed his lips, and voiced it.

"You are . . . an outsider?"

His voice crackled like a pile of leaves. But . . . what exactly did that mean?

The old man looked him up and down.

"You shouldn't even be here. How on earth did you get in?"

Which was a stupid question. Cornelius felt bored, answering it.

"The back door was open."

All he got was an offended look, as if he'd just said something genuinely dumb. Or maybe they were talking at cross-purposes, somehow?

"No. I understand which of my doors are locked and unlocked. How did you get into the Landing? How did you get past the curse?"

Past what? This made no sense in the slightest. Maybe the coot was insane, or senile. It would be better for everyone concerned if they got to the business in hand.

Cornelius took another step forward, and announced, "I'm here to teach you Special Fun."

And those words normally sent people on a fast descending spiral. They'd start begging him. Their eyes would fill with tears. But this fellow simply held his ground. And then, to his surprise, grinned nastily.

"Now I see why you are here. You're one of the disturbed ones, aren't you? The destructive ones. Like Saruak. Like Jason Goad. You're so messed up in here"—he tapped his forehead—"you ignore the voices, and the curse has no effect on you. We have dealt with your kind several times before, my boy. Do you seriously imagine I'm afraid of you?"

This was the first time—ever since he had become the Shadow Man—that anyone had spoken to him in such a way. Cornelius could scarcely believe his ears. A tremor ran through him, mostly indignation. He was the one with the power, the knife. Who did this elderly degenerate think he was?

He reached into a pocket of his baggy sweatpants and produced a roll of duct tape.

"I have to bind you first," he said. "And gag you. I realize it's uncomfortable, but I need to have your complete attention."

The nasty smile remained in place. "Is that so?"

"I won't lie to you. There's some actual pain involved after that. But it's necessary. A means to an end, you see?"

The good eye glinted with sarcasm.

"Yes? And what might that be?"

"The End is coming soon. The End of Days. And to survive it, I must do the Old Ones' bidding. If I do it properly and well, they will allow me to transform, become a higher being. I'm already most of the way there."

The fellow simply shrugged.

"As I first suspected, you're completely crazy. Listen to me carefully, now. It would be far better for you if you left here right away. Nothing good will happen to you otherwise."

Which left Cornelius's head reeling with astonishment. What . . . was the old man planning to fight him off with only that little stick? Or was there something else? He could see no bulge beneath the tailcoat or in any of the pockets. So the fellow didn't seem to have a gun.

But something happened, the next instant, which utterly astonished him. The old man's face abruptly glowed, a startling pure white. His massed wrinkles were flensed away by the stark brilliance of it. He suddenly looked forty years younger. His body filled out, and he held himself completely straight.

The cataract had gone too. Both of his eyes glinted with a turquoise sheen. He looked very vital and alive. He bared his teeth and snorted. Then he threw his right hand—the one holding the stick—back across his shoulder, a motion like a coachman drawing back his whip.

And when he brought it cracking down . . . ?

Panic tore into Cornelius. He felt sure he was in danger, though he wasn't sure exactly how. A startled yelp came from his throat. Then he went rushing at the man, as quickly as he could.

The tip of the rod was shining brighter. Maybe it was a taser of some kind? It began swinging down at him. The figure wielding it looked thoroughly triumphant.

But he wasn't so smart, really. People always made the same mistake. They looked at him, the doughy mass of body. And they never guessed how fast he really was.

The rod was barely halfway down when Cornelius's blade reached its target, pushing in through the fabric of the coat and plunging deep into the old man's body. And Cornelius didn't stop at that. He turned the blade in its bed of flesh, then dragged it up until a rib bone stopped it.

The transformation was immediate. The old man's wrinkles all came back. And his expression changed one final time, despair replacing triumph.

Until finally, even that was gone.

The corpse was lying crumpled by his feet, blood spilling out across the floor.

Cornelius felt disappointed. Thoroughly let down, to tell the truth. It had been enjoyable, yes, watching the old man understand that he was beaten, for all of his superior airs. But it had been so very quick. Over and done with in less than a heartbeat. And where was the special fun in that?

It was like expecting a banquet, and winding up with a bag of potato chips instead. Cornelius pressed his eyes shut, feeling beads of sweat run down between them. Then he started to think more clearly.

There were certain things that the Old Ones expected him to do. Certain rituals. He was obliged to carry them out.

He crouched over the figure. Unbuttoned the tailcoat, and then ripped away the black shirt underneath. And, working diligently, he began to carve into the loosely withered flesh.

Once that he was satisfied, Cornelius stood back up and looked around again.

The stick the fellow had been brandishing had rolled away, and was lying against one leg of the antique bureau. He gazed at it. It looked like the blackest thing he'd ever seen, a bottomless strip of shadow on the patterned tile. Except for its tip, which was still subtly gleaming.

Wiping the blade and pocketing it, Cornelius went across. He stooped, examining it more carefully. It was not smooth, as it had first appeared. There were dozens of small symbols carved into its rounded surface, none of which he recognized. They made him feel anxious again. What precisely did they represent?

But symbols could not harm him, surely? So he picked it up.

He almost dropped it immediately. Because, when his chubby fingers touched the rod, he felt a mild charge run through them. The tip gave a shimmering flash.

There was one simple reason that he held on to it, in the end. The stick was so light he could barely feel it. Scarcely heavier than air, in fact. What, in the names of the gods . . . ?

No more pain came. So he held it up to eye level, gazing at it closer. Might it be a pointer? A baton, like a conductor might use?

A . . . wand? Could it possibly be that?

Cornelius answered to many descriptions, but "cynic" was not one of them. He already believed in magic. How could you explain the Old Ones' existence otherwise? He knew the world was full of things that science could not possibly account for. But an actual embodiment of sorcery?

Standing back up, he held the rod the way the old man had. And shook it gently. Its tip released a few sparks, and they lingered several seconds before vanishing.

He chortled. Oh, this might be even more fun than the special type he usually had. The real question was figuring out how to make this work.

"What do you do, huh?" he asked the rod.

He shook it a little harder, letting out a few more sparks. And nothing more than that.

"I represent the Old Ones, you know. So you'd better reveal your secrets, or they'll be mad at you."

He lashed it back and forth, but that got no reaction whatsoever.

"Whatever that old fool used you for, I own you now! So do the same for me!"

He swung it around in a broad circle. What little weight there'd been between his fingers disappeared completely. Cornelius could still see the thing. Except its shape and color were changing.

As he watched, it ceased to be so very dark. The wand became pale gray. Then its edges started breaking up.

It turned to smoke before his startled gaze. Cornelius lurched back, trying to let go of the thing. But it would not drop from his grasp.

Looking down, he could see why. He let out a shriek. It was not simply the wand that was dissolving into vapor. The same was happening to his fingers. They had turned a similar pale gray.

It spread out right across his hand. There was no pain, but terror overwhelmed him. He shook his wrist furiously, turning around in circles, making small, horrified gibbering noises. Nothing that he did made any difference. His wrist turned to gray smoke—then his upper arm.

And that was when a new idea occurred to him. Maybe this was supposed to happen. Maybe this was what the wand actually did. Cornelius stopped moving, trying to calm down. It wasn't easy, but he forced himself. Because . . . perhaps this was part of his destiny. What the Old Ones had wanted for him all along.

He watched as his whole arm dissolved. His body broke up the same way.

He felt his head begin to fade, and peered at his reflection in the dark, surrounding glass. There were only his eyes left. They let out a glint, then vanished too. His entire frame was lost from view, just pale mist by now. He tried to move around, and found that it was easy. He just had to will himself in a direction and he drifted there.

High in the conservatory, a single panel was propped open. Presumably for ventilation, since it was still warm, despite the rain. Cornelius wafted up toward the opening, spilling out through it into the night air. He swept across the grounds in the direction of the rusted gate. Went by the abandoned Chrysler.

Floated back to Plymouth Drive, then headed back the way he'd come.

Lord, so many lights below him. So many dwellings filled with people, drowsy, unaware. And there would be no stopping him in this new form he had assumed.

Those newspapermen, back in Boston, had been right about him without even knowing it.

He really was the Shadow Man.

CHAPTER 4

"Ross, are you up?"

I pressed the receiver against my cheek. A thin, pale shaft of moonlight was streaming in between the drapes, casting the bedroom's furniture into shadowy relief. The full-length mirror. The dim outlines of the dresser. The bowlegged stool in front of it. I seemed to inhabit a world of shadows a lot of the time, these days. More than any sane man would reasonably want. And I could see Alicia sitting there a moment, applying brief touches of makeup. It's the first thing I remember, every time I wake.

And then I blink, and she is gone again. The flat, empty normality of my bedroom returns. Her perfume, the smell, faded a long time ago, and I missed that.

"Well?" Cass asked.

"I am now."

"Then you haven't heard?"

I sat up sharply. Hadn't the Little Girl just warned me something bad was going down?

"Heard what?"

"Lucas Tollburn's been murdered."

And Lucas Tollburn was the oldest, most respected adept in the Landing. So I pulled myself together pretty quickly after that.

* * *

One of the rarest sights on Sycamore Hill is flashing lights up there. The pulsing red of police beacons cutting through the expensive gloom. As I've said, it's where the very richest live. And rich—exactly like in any other town, I'd suppose—means cosseted, aloof. Means powerful. Except that word has some very different connotations, in the Landing.

When the genuine witches of Salem arrived here—fleeing the trials back in 1692—they were single to the last. Men and women both, they'd lived that way their entire lives. But, having only narrowly escaped an ugly death, they saw they needed to change their ways and blend in better. Some of them had married into the few well-heeled families of that era. Others had chosen bloodlines that were not rich yet, but would be one day. Gaspar Vernon and Judge Levin were both good cases in point.

Whatever, people here are careful not to mess with them. So there is little in the way of robbery or violence on the Hill. But I was still thinking of what the Little Girl had told me. This was someone from outside, who didn't know the usual rules.

"A very bad man indeed, for the moment."

And now I was in my aged Cadillac. It had started drizzling gently again, damp smearing my windshield. The lights up ahead looked unreal, like a glow from a television screen viewed through a blurry pane of glass. I fished out my cell phone, speed-dialed Cass, and started talking to her again.

"How did you get in on this?"

"I was out for a ride, just cruising around. And then I spotted some patrol cars heading up here, so I followed."

On a night like this? Hardly the time for joyrides. Cass lived over in East Meadow. She'd been a good long way from home then, to spot anything on Plymouth Drive. But Cassandra Elspeth Mallory ranks among the walking wounded, the same way I do. She'd lost her family to magic too, in equally grim circumstances. And so when she's not busy helping out, she kills time any way she can.

But there's something else as well. She has the keenest nose for trouble that I've ever come across. Almost like she's born to face it. That is something that I always try to keep in mind. It stops me from acting like her boss, which I am not. She backs me up of her own choosing.

"Tollburn lived alone, didn't he?"

"Ever since his wife died, yeah."

"Then how—?"

"Your friend Levin simply got this feeling. Spirited himself over here. And that was when he found the corpse."

And the judge was one of the few adepts who I really trusted. He had a code of honor, at least, which made us similarly inclined.

"He still there?"

"No, he was too upset. Tollburn and his father were close friends, apparently. There's only Hobart and his men, a medical examiner. And me of course. How long are you going to be?"

"I'm almost there," I told her.

Then I hung up and turned onto the darkened lane at the end of which the Tollburn house stood. Three patrol cars and Saul's dark blue Pontiac were parked by the front gate. And there was a fifth car in among them—an aged, grimy Chrysler—that I didn't recognize.

At first, I thought that everyone had gone inside. But I was wrong. Matt Chalker's face appeared out of the tree-filled darkness, seeming to float weightlessly above his navy uniform. I knew him well, from my own time on the force. He'd always been a decent guy. But Matt rarely looked at ease these days. His best friend, Davy Quinn, had been killed not long ago by Saruak, another interloper to this town.

When he saw me climbing out, he scowled. Maybe, when he looked at me, he simply saw more disaster coming. Which wasn't my intention in the least. But you cannot help the way that other folk perceive you sometimes.

"Hey, Devries," he mumbled. "I kind of guessed that you were on your way—that weird broad's already here."

Which meant Cassie again. She's not exactly on the department's list of favorite people. Rather too contemptuous of the rules for that. I spotted her bright red Harley.

"I'm not supposed to let you in," Matt told me when I started heading for the grounds. "You're not on the payroll anymore."

Which was nitpicking, since he'd just admitted that Cassie—who had never been on the payroll—was already in there. Besides, every cop knew what I did these days. I seemed to have developed a real talent for facing down problems of the supernatural kind. And it wasn't just a knack. I'd found out recently that there was something more than that involved. Higher powers watching over me. I didn't understand that fully, and I wasn't sure I wanted to. So I tried to forget about it, simply get on with the job in hand.

Matt was making no real move to stop me.

"Saul inside?" I asked.

"Where else would he be?"

"See you later, then."

I reached across when I went past him, giving his shoulder a firm squeeze. I was trying to show him that I understood. So many of us have lost people that we care about to magic.

He simply looked away, then reached up and yanked at the peak of his cap, and that was all I got from him.

Once through the gates and past the conifers, surprise struck at me. I'd only been here a couple of times. But I didn't remember the Tollburn place being quite as small as this. He had been very old. His wife had passed away. He didn't need a larger dwelling. Perhaps, it occurred to me, the house had once been bigger, and he'd used his powers to hive it off into a space where he felt comfortable. I'd known adepts do stranger things to their homes, Woodard Raine for instance. But then . . . no, don't get me started.

The lawn was dense with moisture. A couple more uniformed cops were out there, playing their flashlight beams across the wet turf, looking for signs of anything that shouldn't be there. This entire area was surrounded by trees, I noticed, giving it a closed-in look.

"I can see footprints going in," I heard one of the guys say. "But none coming out. What the hell is that about?"

I had to admit, it didn't sound exactly promising.

With most of the lights in the house on, the leaded windows made it look partway like a cage. But the door was wide open. There was another patrolman, Hugh Williams, stationed by it. He stepped back and let me in. I wiped my shoes on the mat and then, finding no one in the living room, went through to the back.

When I saw the corpse, I felt my frame twitch. Lucas Tollburn was the last person that you'd expect to see this way. Such a massively respected figure in the town, an adept of almost legendary power.

He was lying faceup in a pool of blood. But there was more than that. He had apparently been mutilated. I'd met the man several times. He had seemed amiable and charming. So . . . who'd do such a thing, and for what reason? Why?

The examiner was crouched over the body. He was new to the team, a small, yellow-haired guy called Troughton, and I didn't know him very well.

Saul Hobart and Cass were standing at opposite sides of the conservatory, their backs propped against the glass, watching the man do his work. I could make out silhouettes beyond them, the trees I'd noticed and a higher section of the hill, a few other lights shining in the distance. Their heads came around when I walked in, and both Hobart and Cassie nodded to me. Cassie looked like she wanted to favor me with a brief smile, but then thought better of it. She is used to death and tough that way, but understood she ought to be respectful.

The detective lieutenant, Hobart, was smartly dressed as usual, in a plain navy suit, a blue shirt, and a knitted woolen tie. He was, above everything else, a family man. He had a wife and three young daughters up in the northern suburbs. And they defined most things about him.

Massive, sometimes lumbering, he was no soft touch—don't get me wrong about that. But he was generally slow and thoughtful, sizing up the consequences of his actions. The sort of cop—in other words—who thinks first, hard, and only shoots if he has to.

Cassie, my de facto assistant, was the precise opposite of that. Her black hair cropped closely to her skull, she stood nearly six foot tall. She had on a sleeveless beige T-shirt, and the same ripped jeans and biker's boots she always wore. The faded tattoos on her arms stood out in the room's stark light. There was a 9mm Glock strapped to each of her hips, as usual. I sometimes imagine she sleeps with them on.

As I've mentioned, she used to have children too. So, when she peered at me, there was a spark of pain in her dark eyes that never really went away.

She looked pretty sickened. Both of them did. I took a closer look at the corpse. Cause of death had been, without any doubt, a stabbing to the abdomen. An exceptionally savage one, it looked like. The blade had been dragged about with expert cruelty. Lucas here had either bled out, or had simply died of shock. But his shirt had been ripped open. And some kind of symbol had been carved into his chest. An oval, with a horizontal line running across it.

I didn't recognize it.

"It's postmortem," the examiner told me, seeing where my eyes had gone.

There were no ligature marks, so I'd already figured that one out. No one simply lay there and let someone else do this to them.

"He went quick," Troughton added softly. "Barely felt a thing."

"Anyone know what this is?"

I looked across at Saul. The big guy nodded, his bald head glinting faintly as it caught the light.

"I spoke with Levin, then got on the phone to a few other adepts. This is not a symbol any of them use." He worked his heavy jaw uneasily. "Gaspar Vernon knew what it was, though."

Vernon was, among other things, a classical scholar. I didn't get on with the man particularly well, but I respected him for that.

"It's a theta," the lieutenant continued. "Eighth letter of the Greek alphabet. A 'tee-aitch' sound, as in 'them,' 'those,' 'that.' But it can signify something else as well."

I waited, the night's silence closing in around me.

"It can sometimes stand for *thanatos*. Which means 'death' in Greek."

At which, Cass let out a snort.

"Someone kills this guy, and then writes 'death' on him? So . . . we're looking for someone with a knack for stating the obvious?"

Saul peered at her annoyed.

"More like, whoever did this has a weird mind-set, and maybe an agenda."

I could see what he was driving at. The more I thought about it, then the more it dawned on me we might be heading down a path we'd never gone before. You see, Raine's Landing might be a pretty weird place. But folks here are generally peaceable. They've learned, down the centuries, to get along with their neighbors and make the most of their tenuous lives, largely because there's no option. We're all stuck here. No one born inside the Landing can ever get out.

We call it Regan's Curse. And because of it, nobody from our town can wander off into the outside world. No one visits here for very long either, save for the occasional lunatic. And now, Hobart was suggesting . . . ?

That someone might have killed old Lucas merely for the sake of killing. For the pleasure and the thrill of it. In which case, he might strike again. Serial, I knew they called it in the outside world. And we'd not had one of those before . . . not human anyway. The thought of it made my blood run cold. This was something none of us was used to.

"Found a pair of sneakers next door, definitely not the old man's," Saul went on. "Whoever was here left them behind."

And what exactly did that indicate? The only thing it did was leave me puzzled.

Troughton finished up and left. A couple of forensics guys moved in. One began dusting for fingerprints. The other went across the flooring with a pale blue light. I was still trying to sort this through my buzzing head when a commotion out front brought my attention swinging back around.

Someone else had turned up. A woman, apparently. Her voice was raised in anger, and it wasn't anyone I knew. She was trying to get past Hugh Williams. He was trying to reason with her, but wasting his breath.

"I have to get in there, you idiot!" Her tone was supercilious, shrill. "Do you have any idea who I am?"

She must have simply shoved past him, next instant.

Her heels made a staccato clattering as they came down the hall.

CHAPTER 5

The house was fast asleep. Darkness and silence hung about it like a pair of overlapping shrouds. There were not even any ticking clocks. Stephen Anderson had always hated those, and made it his habit to buy only electric ones.

His was a two-story home, painted white and with a green-tiled roof, in the area of town known as East Crealley. With small variations, the other houses around it looked pretty much the same for block after block. There were two cars on the driveway, since both adults worked. An aluminum swimming pool out back—little more, in truth, than a large hot tub without the benefit of any heat. And beyond that, an old apple tree, a swing hanging from one of its stouter branches. There were a few scattered balls and other toys. And a kennel occupying the rear corner of the yard, sitting empty.

There'd been a dog until two weeks ago. But Rusty, a friendly but rather dumb Labrador cross, had taken badly sick this summer, and had had to be put down. It was the worst tragedy this family had ever known. Both kids, as soon as they were awake, would whine about it constantly, and their parents were looking for a suitable replacement.

In the smallest bedroom, at the front of the house, slept Joe. He was six, liked comics and superhero TV shows. His sister, Aggie, next door, cared for neither. She was two years older, and already displaying a notable musical talent. There were a flute and oboe in her room—she practiced the whole time. She wanted to move on to alto sax, and was dreaming about playing a solo in the Liberty Theatre on Union Square, which also doubled as a concert hall.

In the largest bedroom, at the back, Stephen Anderson lay slumbering next to his wife, Christine. They were not snugglers, which did not mean that their marriage was emotionally lacking. Nothing could be further from the truth, in fact. They simply needed their own space to get a good night's sleep, and so had bought the widest bed that they could find.

Stephen worked for one of the Landing's few insurance companies. There were only two, if the truth be told. It wasn't a popular business to be in around these parts, for obvious reasons. Both companies had pages of disclaimers attached to their simplest policies. But there'd been a fire recently, at one of the warehouses in the commercial district. And it had not been caused by supernatural forces. Stephen was still trying to crunch the numbers properly, the claimant's attorney arguing with him at every turn. It had been a rather trying week.

Christine was a high-school teacher. She was good at it, but got far too involved in her students' lives. Their problems became hers as well. And one of them, a bright thirteen-year-old girl with a promising future ahead of her, was suffering from depression and had even threatened suicide. It had affected Christine badly. She had poured herself a glass of Scotch this evening, before turning in.

Her mouth dropped open, and she began snoring faintly. So the silence in the room was broken, just a little bit.

And then—as if summoned by the noise—there was sudden motion at the window.

One small pane had been left open. Neither of them slept well in a stuffy room. There was not the slightest breeze outside, so the drapes didn't tremble. But a portion of the darkness directly outside their window . . .

Seemed to detach itself from the rest, revealing itself as a much paler gray. It moved to the opening.

Wafted in, tendrils of it spreading out across the ceiling. Formed a thick pall of vapor, the same color as a heavy fog. Parts of it would swell, come boiling outward, then shrink back again. Once that it had entered completely, it hung over the couple like a canopy, expanding and contracting gently as though it were breathing.

Christine gave a gentle grunt, then her lips pressed together and her snoring stopped. Her husband's mouth dropped open instead. They always did everything that way, one picking up where the other had left off.

And that seemed to be the signal that the gray mist had been waiting for. It coalesced abruptly, drawing itself in tight. And then started funneling down in a thin, dank stream.

It went into Stephen's throat, until every last scrap of it had disappeared.

The man coughed. Then his jaws clamped shut, the muscles in them going very tight. His whole body went rigid for a second.

It relaxed again. He sat up on the mattress in one smooth motion, the quilt dropping away from his chest. His face was completely blank. His eyes came open, very wide. Their normal blue was gone. There were gray from lid to lid. The color swirled before becoming solid.

Stephen smiled—but there was no humor in his expression. Then he murmured two words, in a tone far deeper than was normally his own.

"Special fun."

He peered around carefully. Being careful not to wake Christine, he climbed out of bed and started heading down toward the kitchen, where the sharpest knives were kept.

CHAPTER 6

The owner of the heels—they sounded like pretty high ones—finally came to a halt bolt upright in the conservatory's doorway. And that was when I recognized her. Or rather, realized that I'd seen her from a distance a couple of times. It had been at the big garden parties thrown by Raine's distinguished father, back when I had been a cop.

I'd never spoken to her, but knew a bit about her history. This was Millicent, Lucas Tollburn's sole surviving grandchild. The man had had two children, a son and a daughter. The latter had never married, and was a reclusive type. But his boy, Tremayne, had continued the bloodline with three kids of his own.

One had fallen to a childhood illness. The second had died in an accident when he had been fifteen. Millicent here was the last one left. It wasn't exactly the happiest of sagas, but that's often the case with wealthy families.

There was something else I knew about her too. Not so long ago, she'd married into the Vernon dynasty. It had been Gaspar's nephew Todd. She'd stayed with him for barely a year, and word had it she'd done very well for herself out of the divorce.

These days, she'd reverted to her family name. She had to be in her midthirties, not the slightest crease or shadow on her expertly made-up face. At this hour? Where'd she been?

And she was dressed from head to toe in designer clothing, all of it the darkest shade of blue. Her hair was a lustrous brown, and was tied back in a ponytail. Her eyes were the same peculiar turquoise as her granddad's. She wore a silver pendant with one large diamond in it—not a magical device, so far as I could tell—and a few narrow but expensive-looking rings. And she stood about five foot seven, very slim. She might even have been attractive save for one small adjective. The word for the way she looked was "pointy."

Her nose and chin had plenty of that quality. And her ears were rather that way too. Whoever had carved her cheekbones had overdone it with the chisel. And when you saw the way she held herself, the angle of her limbs, you quickly understood that this was someone who was sharp all over. Even her bright gaze, which swept across us quickly as if summing us up. You could cut yourself badly on Ms. Tollburn—I was left in very little doubt of that.

I also knew that she was just a minor leaguer in the hierarchy of adepts. Lucas must have taught her some tricks—that went without saying. But she seemed to prefer using other means to get the things she wanted. Judging by the way she'd prospered, it was a reasonable guess that she was pretty good at that.

The look on her face was haughty, her eyebrows lifted like a distant pair of birds in flight. And then she looked down at the floor, and her whole expression changed.

Although . . . I wasn't really certain what to, during those first few seconds. Her face didn't seem sure what shape it wanted to take. As if a dozen different emotions were clashing across it, disbelief and denial at one end of the scale, fright and anger at the other.

Partly she was confused, and I gave her that. But it seemed to me like she was trying to choose what to show the rest of us.

She finally decided. Her mouth contracted and her eyes grew very wide.

"Poppy!"

She came hurrying forward with tears welling up in her eyes. And was practically touching the corpse, when Saul grabbed her gently by the shoulders.

"Let go of me, you imbecile!"

She lashed out at him, catching him on the cheek with her long fingernails. But Saul hung on, moving his grasp down so that her upper arms were pinned to her sides.

"This is a crime scene, Miss," he told her. "I'm genuinely sorry, but you can't do that."

She seemed to think it over, and then quieted down. Her chest was going like a bellows, but no more tears came spilling out. Looking at her carefully, I could see her cheeks were barely wet.

The forensics guys were both watching the scene unhappily, as was Hugh Williams, who'd come stumbling along behind her. Cassie hadn't even moved. She was still standing by the glass, her arms folded in front of her. And by the steadiness of her gaze, I could see she wasn't impressed by the woman either. But then, Cass generally has little time for wealthy folk and their petty antics.

Millicent stared around at us.

"Who'd do such a thing?" she blurted. "He was such a well-loved man."

Saul let go of her and straightened his tie. A spot of blood had appeared on his cheek, but he just ignored it. In fact, he looked as solemn as an undertaker. People tend to forget that dealing with not merely death, but bereavement, is a major part of a cop's job.

"I know," he nodded quietly. "And I understand how you must feel. We're going to do everything we can to get to the bottom of this."

Which didn't seem to reassure her even a tiny bit. Her eyes took on a fiery glitter, venom creeping back into her voice.

"You're treating this like a normal case?"

It was the first time in ages I had seen Saul look so flustered.

"We're giving it top priority, Miss Tollburn. You have my word."

"And where are the others? Vernon? The McGinleys? He was one of theirs! Why aren't they here?"

Which was not police business, but Saul still felt obliged to answer.

"The judge was here earlier. He alerted us, in fact. You know perfectly well—Miss—that we have an understanding with the adepts in cases like this. If there's nothing supernatural involved, then it's up to my department and to no one else. And there seems to be no magic here."

"You're treating this as commonplace? The death of the most revered man in this entire town?"

"I know. Again, I'm sorry."

She took a step back, something happening to her features once again. Softer quivers played across them, the small muscles working by themselves. And I thought I saw a strange glint in her piercing gaze. Then her face rearranged itself until it gave away precisely nothing. The dampness of her stare was like a pane of opaque glass. And when she spoke again, her tone was mollified.

"All right, then. I understand your position and respect it. But can I stay a little while, at least?"

I saw Cass jut her lower lip out. And Saul looked extremely doubtful.

"To be honest, it would be much better—"

"Yes," she cut him off. "I know what the procedure is. But my Poppy and I were very close, and his death has been so sudden, unexpected. Could I simply spend a little time here, simply to say goodbye to him?"

She was exploiting Saul's good nature, and I knew it. But he didn't seem to have it in him to refuse the woman, she sounded so sincere.

"Just two minutes," he replied quietly. "And you can get no closer than about four feet. Please don't disturb anything."

She nodded. "Certainly. Of course."

Millicent stepped up to her grandfather's body. Folded her hands in front of her and bowed her head a couple of inches. Then she looked around at us again.

"If I might be allowed a little privacy?"

"Right," Saul muttered.

He turned away, closing in quickly on Hugh Williams, and I followed him. I could see by the set of his shoulders how angry he was. Not that it was my place to interfere.

What Saul does with his people is his concern—I'd known that ever since I'd quit.

"What the hell is wrong with you?" he hissed at his subordinate, once we were out of earshot. "How did she get past you? You have to be twice her size."

Hugh looked like someone who had trodden on a kid's pet hamster and was trying to hide it underneath his shoe.

"I'm sorry, Lieu. I tried to, really. But she made like she was going to cast a spell on me."

"And you're not used to magic yet?"

"You should have seen the look on her face."

Saul was about to answer that, when a yell from Cassie brought us spinning around. Millicent was no longer standing reverently by her granddad. She had crossed over to the roll-top bureau at the center of the conservatory. Was crouching down in front of it, and rummaging through the drawers.

"Miss Tollburn?" Saul exploded.

And he lurched at her.

Cassie looked like she wanted to join in, and I felt the same impulse. But we both hung back. This was police business too. Although the look on Cass's face spoke volumes. She'd known from the outset that we couldn't trust this woman.

"Miss Tollburn, what the hell d'you think you're doing?"

Millicent took no notice of him, and kept on searching for whatever she was after. There was a clattering as her narrow fingers scrabbled through the second drawer. I could see a huge cluster of magic implements in there. It was a pretty even guess, given who her granddad was, that some of them were pretty powerful devices. But her hands went past them. Kept feeling around like busy spiders.

Saul ran across and grabbed her by the shoulders again, rather more roughly than before, and hauled her off. By that time, she'd already reached the bottom drawer. She pulled it back with her as she was dragged away. There were a load of small black books in there. But apparently, they were not what she'd wanted.

Her face was slightly flushed, her brow damp. But other than that, she looked perfectly composed when he let her go and she stood back upright. I watched her carefully, trying to figure her out. Didn't like just being a spectator in this fashion, but what option was there? This was still Saul's show.

"What the hell were you looking for?" he demanded.

The briefest hint of a smile flicked across her narrow lips.

"That's entirely my concern."

"Not if I arrest you, it ain't."

"Should I call my lawyer?" she inquired.

Which amounted to an open threat. Since, if she did that, it would be a terribly expensive example of the breed who'd turn up at the station house. We each knew that. Hobart took a step away and looked her up and down, seeing her in a brand-new light, his face creased up with apprehension.

"How can you behave like this with your grandfather lying there?" he asked her. And then he gave up on politeness altogether. "Exactly what kind of vulture are you?"

Millicent did not look in the least embarrassed. If she disliked being called a name like that, she didn't let it show. The expression on her face got milder, her thin eyebrows riding high again. But I could see that peculiar, faraway gleam in her eyes a second time. And I didn't like the look of that one tiny bit. It seemed to add up to some kind of madness.

"When he was alive," she told Saul, "I was welcome here any time I liked. Poppy always told me I should treat it as my home, and make use of anything I wanted. That was all that I was doing, to be honest. And actually, part of this place is mine now. Legally, I mean."

She could have at least waited for the will to be read. Saul glanced across at me, an open question on his face. Should he cut her some slack, or start reaching for the handcuffs? Me, I had my own ideas. I gave my head the tiniest of shakes. He took a breath, and rounded on her.

"I don't give a damn whose property this is. For the next few days, it's under my jurisdiction. And I'm having tape put up, the kind that reads, very clearly, 'Do Not Cross.' I want you on the far side of it from this point onward. Understood?"

"With perfect clarity."

She turned smartly on her heels, and marched out of the

room again. I noticed one more thing when she did that. When she'd first come in, her attention had been pinioned to the body on the floor. But—leaving—she didn't even glance in that direction, not for a split second. Like her granddad's death was already forgotten. Like . . . the grieving of before had been nothing but an act.

The sound of her heels retreated. We were left with each other and our reflections to stare at. A few more spots of rain hit the roof of the conservatory, but it didn't seem like that was going anywhere. Cassie let out a slow breath, and Saul peered at me warily.

"Explain to me?" he inquired. "Why did I just let her go?"

I was glad that he had taken my hint. We'd have gotten precisely nowhere if he had arrested her.

"She was looking for something," I pointed out.

"But couldn't find it," Cassie added.

As is usually the case, she was already on my wavelength.

"She knew exactly where to look, but it wasn't there. Which probably means whoever killed old Lucas took it. That's our lead."

Saul's face went a few degrees more slack.

"Okay?" he grumbled. "So . . . this is your case now?"

I'd run into problems like this with him before. And knew that the best way to deal with it was simply to push on through. Our town's only detective lieutenant is a reasonable man, and puts getting results before matters of protocol. So that generally works.

"Whatever she was looking for, there has to be some kind of sorcery involved. You know I've got a gift for stuff like that. And if you'll excuse me for saying it, I was always better at tailing a suspect. You stand out too much."

The big guy thought that quickly through, then acquiesced and nodded, staring at me wearily.

"I've still plenty of work here, I guess. See you later?"

"Count on it."

"How about me?" Cassie asked.

I knew she didn't like inaction. There was nothing I could do about it at that moment, though.

"I'll bring you up to speed as soon as I know more."

The set of her mouth got slightly anxious.

"You be careful. I'd say that one's capable of turning pretty mean."

But that was a place I'd been to plenty of times before. So I just headed back outside.

CHAPTER 7

It turned out that Miss Tollburn drove a powder blue Jaguar convertible, an XK, barely six months old. I caught up with it a minute after I had swung back onto the main road. But then I hung carefully back, a good distance behind it, with my lights switched off. Like I pointed out, I'm better at this than Saul.

It kept on disappearing behind bends, then coming back in view again. Millicent had the hood down, in spite of the weather. And her tires were kicking up a good deal of spray, sending it into the air behind her in corkscrewing plumes. She'd untied her hair, which played out in the wind. But there seemed nothing carefree or relaxed about her. She was heading further uphill, taking the wet curves at a reckless speed. My old Caddy was pretty stable, but I still had trouble keeping up.

Plymouth Drive straightened for a while, the streetlamps showing half a mile of it at a continuous stretch. A dense wall topped with spikes flashed past and then, shortly after that, we went by Judge Levin's handsome residence. Up ahead of me, there was a momentary gleam of yellow light. I thought at first that she might be using magic, but she'd only lit a cigarette.

Then the road described another huge bend, climbing ever steeper. And by the time we'd crossed the final intersection, there was little doubt where we were heading.

That made me a lot less happy, and I hadn't been too cheerful in the first place. We were going to the very summit of the hill. And there was only one house up there. My least favorite in town. Raine Manor.

The Jaguar finally drew up to the front gates, which had rusted open long ago. You couldn't even see the place, its grounds were so chaotically overgrown. You'd need a Sherman tank to make your way down its long, gravel driveway. Roots and saplings were pushing out through it everywhere you looked. Some of the latter were becoming full-blown trees. The only part of the house you could properly make out was the spire that Woody had added about a year back. It belonged on a church really, but that hadn't seemed to have occurred to him. There was a huge capital W at its apex, standing like a second Cassiopeia against the night sky. N for "nut" would have been more appropriate.

By the time she was climbing out, I had parked back at the last bend in the road and then stepped up behind a tree trunk. Water was still dripping from it, but I ignored that. I watched while Millicent headed—at a brisk, stiff pace—in the direction of the mansion. And let her disappear into the gloom before I followed.

Once past the gates, a chill descended around my shoulders. It seemed to get worse, the further in I went. There'd been no coldness to the air the last time I had been up here. So . . . was Woody's frame of mind affecting his environment even more pronouncedly than usual?

The grounds had gotten even more shambolic since I'd last walked through them. No one ever tended them at all. The spindly, leafless branches of the trees on either side of me had grown longer and meshed together, forming a wide canopy. I could barely make out the stars any more. And something rather large was on the move up there, making the twigs shake and rattle. I tried to get a look at it. Caught a glimpse of an unusual shape with wings, then took in the fact that it had two heads. It had spilled, in other words, out of Woodard Raine's insane imagination. I'm not sure he even knows it, but he keeps on doing things like that. My heart missed several of its next few beats. But the creature moved away from me, disappearing quickly.

Which was what passes for something good happening, in this neck of the woods. I swore, and kept on heading through the clustered shadows.

A cloud of mosquitoes, with bodies the length of cocktail sticks, descended on me, whining dismally around my ears. A few of them tried to land—to feed presumably, which made my flesh crawl. But I could still hear Millicent's crackling footfalls up ahead. So I batted at them and pressed on.

Finally, the mansion came in view. The moon had come partway out, catching the building at a curious angle. Traces of mist hung around its corners. The wind chimes that he'd hung around it last time I'd been here were gone. They'd never chimed when they were supposed to anyway, so he had probably grown bored with them.

The gargoyles on the roof were all asleep, mere hunched, darkened shapes by this hour. I knew they sometimes moved around. One of the place's countless windows had no glass left in it, and was expanding and contracting like the mouth of a big fish. I stared at it bemusedly. What the hell was that about? But with Woody, as usual, there was no real way of telling.

His family had founded this town. Theodore Raine, his illustrious ancestor, was the face on the big bronze statue down in Union Square. And I often wondered. If they'd known how their bloodline was going to end up, would they even have bothered in the first place?

They had practiced magic regularly since the early seventeen hundreds. You'd have thought they would have got used to its strange twists and caprices. But in Woody's case, the use of it had turned him—at first—agoraphobic. And then totally deranged.

Nothing could be seen beyond the windows. They were ordinary glass so far as I knew, but didn't let light in or out. So the panes appeared completely black, like they'd been painted that way. The front doors were shut when I approached the porch. Millicent had already gone inside. I'd no clue what she had come here for. I'd been unaware, until this point, that Woody entertained visitors in the normal sense. But the kind of work that I find myself mixed up with often involves a lot of waiting. And so that was what I did.

Did Raine know that I was here? In spite of his madness, he was still extremely powerful. An awful lot came to his attention. He was the first person who had warned me of Saruak's arrival in our town. But the trouble was you could never genuinely tell what he was going to do with the knowledge he collected, or even how real he thought it was. In a mind as warped as his, it might all be regarded like some kind of weird illusion. I scuffed at the mud and gravel at my feet, then wandered around to the mansion's west side.

Something heavy began rustling about in the undergrowth near me. I tried to ignore it as best I could. But I really hated being out here. There was no anticipating what was roaming through these grounds. All kinds of bizarre things come out of Woody's mind. When you're around him, the impossible can become a living fact, with texture, form, and substance.

I stopped in front of the west wing. The soot stains were still there above the shattered windows. And the roof, already weakened by the fire that had gutted it, looked like the rain had damaged it even more. It was hanging inward like a long stretch of damp cardboard. This part of the mansion hadn't been touched since his parents had both died here, more than six years back. Except that nature had now started playing its part in the equation, ivy winding thickly through the broken panes. Dandelions were sprouting in the gutters. If he didn't do something about it soon, this whole section of his house would fall apart.

It was possible he didn't even notice it enough to care. Woody had always been a spoilt, unruly brat. But the night his parents died had marked the onset of his plunge into dementia. For all I knew, he'd blanked the whole thing out by this time.

This was one of those occasions when I thoroughly agreed with Cass. The inner workings of the very rich could be extremely tiresome.

About ten minutes passed before I heard the front door come back open. I returned to the corner and then ducked into the shadows there. I could see Millicent moving away from me along the drive, the fragmented gloom gathering her up. And waited until she was gone from sight before walking quickly to the porch.

My presence had been noted. Because Hampton—Raine's manservant—was waiting for me just inside. He had on his dark blue uniform, but was wearing a pair of maroon carpet slippers too, which didn't exactly set the outfit off very well. A massively round man, his skin tanned a light brown color, he was walleyed, one iris green, the other yellow.

He was not such a bad guy really, considering who his employer was. But he didn't look overly pleased to see me, and I wondered why.

"I've been asked to tell you, Mr. Devries"—his voice was high-pitched for a man that size—"that you're trespassing here and you should go away."

Which was not the kind of reception I had been expecting. The last time I'd been up here, I had been in Raine's employ. And he had even tried to help me, in his own disoriented way. But "changeable" is one of his numerous middle names. I tried not to look too taken aback.

"Seriously?" I asked him. "I thought me and Woods were on good terms?"

The big fellow glowered at me.

"I'd thank you not to keep on calling Master Woodard 'Woods' or 'Woody.' He doesn't like it, and neither do I. He's expressly instructed me to see you off the premises, if that becomes necessary. And be assured, I'll do it."

Or he'd at least try. His bulk was fat, not muscle, so it didn't sound like too much of a threat. I'm six foot two, I used to be a cop, and I had a Smith & Wesson tucked inside my coat.

But this show of animosity—it seemed like an act on behalf of his employer. I saw that almost right away. He actually looked uneasy, talking to me in this fashion. Hampton had even saved my life one time. But—given the straight choice—he would always choose to be on Woody's side. The man was a loyal employee to a considerable fault.

I thought it best to try and reason with him.

"Look, I understand that your boss has these little mood

swings. All of us get that. But if you knew what'd been going on, you'd see that this isn't the time for stupid games."

"No game, sport," came a taut voice from the darkness behind Hampton. "I know why you're here. I've got your number, you might say. And I'm not having it, not in the least bit. No."

I craned my neck, trying to make Raine out. But he usually dresses in drab colors, which makes that a problem in the dark. So I let my head drop back and shoved my hands into my pockets, trying to appear relaxed.

"Not having what, exactly?" I inquired.

I almost flinched as his fruity tones washed around me a second time.

"Not having rudeness, interference, prying. Learn your limitations, Mr. Private Spy. Ms. Tollburn is a friend of mine."

I didn't know he had any of those. But then I remembered something. Back in their wild youths, she'd run with his crowd several times. I'd no idea how thick she had been with him, but it seemed that she was cashing in on old connections.

The fact that she counted as an acquaintance of his made me trust her even less. And I hadn't trusted her that much in the first place.

"She came here," Raine went on, "to speak with me in confidence. To impart certain, private, things. And do you really imagine you can just walk up and ask me to divulge them, like some fishwife in a Laundromat? I think not, sport. I really do not."

It wasn't simply his house that he kept on changing. He had altered himself physically in several ways down the last few years. Didn't even look like a normal human being any longer. Most notably, his eyes were twice the size they had originally been. They now had slitted pupils, like a cat's. And they shone like bright gold beacons.

So . . . right at this moment his eyes were shut, I guessed. That was why I could not see him. He often did that, even while talking. Another indication of the state his mind was in. I was reduced to staring where I thought he might be, which did not feel very comfortable. Pretty much like talking to a disembodied voice.

"You're always telling me how much you care about this town," I pointed out.

"Of course I do. Of that there is no doubt."

His own bizarre take on reality again. And if I hadn't been used to it then it would have annoyed me. The fact was, most of the time he remained totally aloof, even when the Landing was under dire threat. But there was no point trying to argue with him. Any action like that was a waste of breath. The only thing I could do was pretend to believe him and press on.

"Its oldest adept is dead, murdered, as of tonight. And something from his place is missing, probably something magical. By the way your *friend* went after it, important too. A stone killer's gotten hold of it. How good does that sound?"

A pair of huge eyes suddenly sprang open beyond Hampton's shoulder. I practically lurched back. It wasn't just the sheer abruptness with which they'd appeared. When I had last met with Raine, they'd been a golden yellow. Now, they'd turned considerably darker, practically a glowing bronze. And the pupils, although still slitted, had shrunken to a smaller size. As if they were diminishing into the distance. Physically retreating from our world.

A shudder ran through me. There was no use trying to hide it. What had brought about this change? Whatever, I was pretty certain he was getting worse, his madness devouring him and growing more intense.

He didn't move. The twin orbs hung there in the dimness. Then his voice came oozing out beneath them.

"This is not a matter for the general public's gaze, Devries. Whatever has happened is the sole concern of those involved. And we can deal with it perfectly well, without any help from your sort."

My what? He might have always been a self-important little S.O.B., but he'd never spoken to me that way before. Even Hampton looked embarrassed.

But Raine's attitude was catching my interest far more

than offending me. The way that he was behaving made one thing pretty obvious. Whatever might be going on, it was something major. The fine hairs prickled on my wrists when I realized that.

"Go away," he snarled at me.

But I just stood there, waiting to see how far he'd take this.

"Go away before I make you go."

Which was the first time that he'd ever really threatened me. He'd always been a stickler for old values like hospitality. But it seemed even that was gone. Those incandescent eyes of his were not even blinking. I had no doubt that he could do something pretty awful to me if he got a mind to. But I've always stood up to adepts, and wasn't about to let him brush me off like this. I wanted the satisfaction, if nothing else, of having the final word.

I tipped my chin.

"Your property, your rules. Okay. But knowing you, Woods, if you're taking charge of matters, things are going to get out of hand pretty fast from this point on. When that happens, you know where I am and how to contact me. You understand?"

He made a faint hissing noise. And I have to admit, I tensed up slightly when he did that. But it turned out to be his only response. His eyelids slid back down, so that to all intents and purposes he disappeared again. And then, the heavy doors swung shut, apparently under their own steam.

I got one final glimpse of Hampton's face, still looking decidedly unhappy. And then, I was staring at blank panels of wood, and nothing more than that.

A rattling noise from high on the roof told me one of the gargoyles had woken, and was scuttling about on the tiles up there. I'd never seen any of them climb down, but there was a first time for everything. So I went back to my car, still wondering what the big secret was.

I was sure that I would find out soon enough, though. And a little knowledge can be a dangerous thing, especially in a place like Raine's Landing.

CHAPTER 8

My mind was buzzing by the time that I got home. But then, it often is. Living where I did, and doing what I do, tends you keep you more mentally active than is sometimes comfortable.

The street was silent around me when I pulled up on my drive. A black diorama of surrounding houses, with no lights on in any of the windows. And once inside, it was even worse. Without my family there, the place had the echo of a crypt.

The silence wormed into me, stopping me from pondering the whole thing for a moment. But then it came rushing back insistently. Exactly what was going on? I'd become so used to that question the past couple of years, though, that it didn't have the power over me it used to. I managed to ignore it, threw myself out onto my bed, still fully clothed, and tried to grab a few more hours' sleep.

I sank into oblivion rapidly enough. But the darkness quickly faded to a blurry gray. And then new features started making themselves obvious. A matter of sound and scent, at first. I could hear a murmuring somewhere in the distance. And I thought I could smell woodsmoke.

Everything came sharply into focus. I was on open ground, a huge plain of some kind. A vast outcrop of jagged rocks could be made out near the horizon. The sun was low and red above them. And there were deeper shadows across their surface, which I thought might be the openings to caves.

I jerked slightly. But I wasn't totally surprised. This wasn't any dream either . . . it was a vision. My mind had traveled to this place, briefly, once before. I wasn't quite sure where it was. But I knew it was connected to the spirit-woman in the gemstone I'd once owned.

She was called Amashta. When her voice—flat in tone and creaky with age—came drifting to me, I was already expecting it. She was some kind of very ancient shaman. And she'd helped me before, back when I'd been fighting Saruak. Although to what ultimate end, I still had no idea.

What I had real trouble grasping was the title she'd bestowed on me. She used the word in her very first breath.

"So, Defender? You find yourself at the start of yet another battle."

I had no idea why she called me that. It felt like something that I didn't even want, a heavy burden pressing down on me like a ten-ton weight.

I cleared my throat, which felt very dry.

"Are you here to help again?"

Her power had flowed through me the first time I'd encountered her. It hadn't been enjoyable, and I wasn't looking forward to the prospect of it happening again. But here we were once more, so it seemed reasonable to ask.

"It is better not to, on the whole. You are the Defender, and your purity must be intact."

My what?

"As I told you earlier, it's a matter of free will. Massive strength derives from that. One of your modern mystics said it well. 'That which does not kill you makes you stronger.'"

I was familiar with the quote. But personally, it had never been my experience. That which didn't kill me generally left me bruised, exhausted, and wishing I lived somewhere else. Besides which, she was avoiding the main point.

When we'd first run across each other, she had implied certain things, and pretty startling ones at that. A whole bigger picture to our lives here in Raine's Landing. A struggle underway here that went well beyond the everyday perils that we faced. I seemed to play some kind of vital role in it. I had some kind of destiny. And I still wasn't overly delighted about the prospect of that.

If I could only get a clearer picture. What was this whole thing about?

Amashta seemed to sense what I was thinking. And her voice became far milder, filling up with empathy.

"Yes, I see your point, Defender. Blind faith does nothing to enhance free will. And so of course you need to know a little."

She paused, then told me, "Go to the shaman you call Willets."

How much did she know about this town of ours? Everything?

"Say one word to him, and he'll explain."

"That word being?" I heard myself ask.

"T'choulon."

There was suddenly a shrieking noise, like a massive blast of cold wind rushing through my head. It swept away everything. Her voice. The smell of smoke. The scene around me.

And it woke me up, very sharply.

Dawn was brightening my drapes. A car went by outside, and then a baby started wailing in a nearby house. I took in my surroundings, and then clutched my forehead, groaned.

I felt even more tired than when I'd fallen onto the bed. And little wonder. First it had been the Little Girl. And then the spirit-woman. And since when had denizens of the supernatural world begun using my head like a bus station waiting room, ducking in and out of it whenever the fancy took them?

I tried to stay down for a short while longer, clutching at my pillow. But the intensity of the late-summer daylight forced me to let go of that. There were plenty of sounds outside my house. Mine is a modest but respectable neighborhood, one that has no truck in the slightest with late risers.

The house seemed fairly cool around me. And the chill clung to me like a clammy second skin, in spite of the fact I was still dressed. I wasn't in the mood for a proper breakfast. There was a leftover slice of pizza in the fridge, and I decided to settle for that. I went through into the kitchen, fished out a small saucepan, and then heated up some coffee that I'd brewed the day before.

The living room had become a little more untidy since I'd last looked at it properly. I hadn't thrown out any copies of our newspaper, the *Landing Ledger*, in the last two weeks. And there were certain things I never touched. The checkerboard off in the corner of the room, for instance. There was still a game on it, half played. There were half a dozen shelves of books—Alicia and I had always been big readers. A large stack of records, which included classical and jazz. The paintings on the walls were all by local artists and, obviously, were of places inside town, or else the edges of the forest.

Mounted over the mantelpiece was the first fish Pete had ever caught, a little bass.

He had been five years old when he had disappeared. I felt angry and lost as usual, thinking about that. I cleared myself a space on the couch, and switched on the TV to our local station. Marlon Fisk was on a sidewalk in front of somebody's front yard. A microphone was clutched in his grasp, and he was halfway through his report.

". . . still reeling with shock at the murder of the town's oldest and most respected adept."

But it wasn't the Tollburn house that he was standing in front of. And that took me by surprise. Behind him was an ordinary residence with white walls and a green-tiled roof. So apparently, something else had happened.

A small crowd of people had gathered around the man. Each of them looked anxious and disturbed. His face dropped for a second, then he peered at the camera again.

"A night of tragedy grew even worse when, here on Hutton Avenue in the East Crealley district, insurance adjuster Stephen Anderson butchered his wife and both of his children before taking his own life."

Some coffee slopped from my mug and scalded my fingers, but I kept on watching, listening.

"People who knew the family are describing them this

morning as 'happy and normal.' So whatever caused Mr. Anderson to behave the way he did remains a total mystery."

I recalled my feelings last night, when Saul had suggested a serial killer. The plain fact is, the Landing is no stranger to tragedy. It happens all the time, in various ways. But most of it is down to witchcraft, either gone wrong or plain misused. No one around here committed murders out of spite, or for the hell of it.

It was like the whole dynamic of the place had altered overnight. And that made me as edgy as the people on my TV screen were looking.

I got Saul on his cell phone. As you'd expect, he sounded quite harassed.

"There's stuff even the press doesn't know," he told me. "The whole thing's worse than it already sounds."

I sat up a little straighter. "How so?"

"This is strictly between us, Ross. The Andersons? They had that same symbol carved into them."

"The theta?"

"Yup. I don't understand how, but this one and the Toll-burn case are linked."

The Little Girl had told me something new was here in town. But I didn't mention it to Saul right away, since the danger was too indefinite as yet.

"We should talk this over in more detail," I suggested.

"Absolutely. There's this place—it opens early. Harriet's Pantry, on Maynard. Know it?"

Yes, I did. It was barely three minutes' walk from the office I have on Union Square.

"Meet you there in half an hour's time?" he suggested.

And I could see nothing wrong with that.

CHAPTER 9

I called Cass and told her where we'd be, because I wanted her along. She needed to be in on this. And it turned out that she'd already heard about the Andersons. The fact that there were children involved had shaken her up. We both have that particular Achilles heel. But I tried to remain as calm about it as I could. I showered and shaved, dragged some clothes on, then went out again.

The town sped by as I headed for its center. Its sidewalks were only very lightly populated by this hour. Most people would be indoors having breakfast, getting ready for work or school. And catching up with the morning's news, which wasn't going to be an awful lot of fun. Except it would look, to them, like nothing more than an unpleasant coincidence. Nobody would have a clue, as yet, that something really bad might be descending on us once again.

The place looked as fresh as a daisy in the early morning light. At first glance, you'd think that nothing ever happened here. I went past an empty schoolyard, then a small pond with some ducks. The shoe store on Kent still had its sale in progress. And just beyond the stoplights there, a fellow in coveralls was hauling a wheeled tin-can kind of device along the pavement, refreshing the white line down the middle of the road.

I parked in the alley behind my office building, and went the rest of the way on foot.

Rounding the corner of Maynard, I practically bumped into Hoyt Dinsmore. He owned a store nearby, and was on his way to open it. We nodded, acknowledging each other, but he looked surprised to see me. And a little nervous too, his eyes widening behind their glasses. Like a lot of folk in town, he knew the kind of stuff I got involved in. And it makes them jumpy when I look like I've got something up. He seemed faintly relieved, to be quite honest, when we went our separate ways.

The drizzle of last night was gone. Most of the puddles had dried up. It was growing brighter, sunlight flashing on the windows around me. The air was a touch crisper, but by no means properly cool. Summer was still hanging on by the ragged edges of its fingernails.

I reached the eatery and sat down at an outside table. I didn't come here much, favoring a different diner. Either Harriet's Pantry had never changed its décor since it had been opened, or was going for a retro look. The awning above me was a candy-colored, stripy one. The tablecloth in front of me was checkered, red and white. There was a candle in a holder made out of a pinecone, unlit at this time of day. And posters for old musicals on the walls inside.

A waitress—too young to be Harriet herself—took my order, bringing me another mug of coffee. Then I leant back and watched the world go by for several minutes.

There were a few more cars than there had been before, and more pedestrians in evidence. Folk were starting to head into work. Everything looked the way it should. A fire truck went by, although slowly and without its siren on. And then a small blue-green car drew up to the far curb. Something about it captured my attention.

I'd seen its kind on TV ads. It was called a Focus, and apparently it was a popular model in the outside world. Except that I had never seen one in this town before. Most people here drive large vehicles like my own, or station wagons, pickups. There was not much call for compacts.

A woman got out whom I didn't recognize. But the sight of her set off an immediate, gentle twanging in my nerves.

The first thing I noticed was she looked exhausted. Why

was that? Her bright blue eyes were red rimmed. There were squinty creases under them.

The second thing was, however haggard she might be, it didn't conceal her essential attractiveness. She looked to be in her early thirties, a couple of years younger than me. Stood five seven or maybe eight. Her hair, cut to shoulder length, was slightly curly in a tousled-looking way. And it was pale blond, shining in the sunlight. Her figure was slim and shapely, with plenty of emphasis on leg.

Her face was a narrow heart shape, her features on it delicate, and she didn't seem to be wearing any makeup in the slightest. Her lips were a natural pale rose color, like my wife's had been. Her small nose even had a slightly upturned tilt to it.

Just like . . .

Watching her, my heart began to ache. She looked so similar to Alicia that it hurt.

She didn't dress as casually as my wife used to, and had less of her calm manner. She was dressed in a charcoal-colored pants suit, which was rather badly creased. A crisp white shirt was buttoned to her throat. She had on sensible black shoes. There was no jewelry in evidence, but a large patent leather purse was slung across one shoulder.

The third thing I noticed? She looked rather lost. A touch off balance, dazed. Her head kept wandering around as though a blow had mildly stunned her. And I couldn't help but wonder what was wrong with her. People in the Landing get a variety of strange expressions on their faces from time to time. But this wasn't one of them.

I was starting to think she had actually been hurt. And was about to go across and help, when two things stopped me.

Saul's Pontiac came around one corner of the street. And, as if on cue, Cassie's Harley appeared at the other end, cruising along noisily.

The blond woman's eyes went to the motorcycle, drawn there by its twin-cam rumble. But then she reacted in the last way I'd expect. Her shoulders drew up, and her eyes came open wide. The weary glaze I'd seen there earlier dropped away completely.

Cassie hadn't even noticed. She was drawing up to the café, nodding to me.

As she came to a halt, the blond woman stepped off the curb. And—reaching underneath her jacket—pulled a handgun out.

The only thing that I could do was stare at her amazedly.

And Cassie did the same.

"Step off the bike! Do it now! Keep your hands where I can see them!"

The woman took a couple of steps in closer without her eyes leaving Cassie for a second. She had her piece aimed with a double-handed grip. Looked like she knew exactly what she was doing, and I wondered how that was.

My own hand started going for my Smith & Wesson, but didn't make it the whole way. Cass was directly in between us. Unless she moved, there was no clear shot. And besides, it didn't look like anyone was going to open fire immediately. I wanted to find out what was really happening before I acted.

Cassie seemed confused more than alarmed. Never good at taking orders, she kept her hands in view, but remained firmly where she was, still straddling her Harley.

And everything got even crazier after that. There was the clack of a hammer being pulled back. My gaze leapt a little further. Saul had got out of his car and crept up behind the blond woman, pointing his gun at her back.

This, I believed, was called a Mexican standoff. I'd never seen one in real life before, and it made my stomach tighten. I eased myself carefully out of my chair and started edging around, my mind working quickly. But the blond woman noticed that and swung her aim in my direction. If I put her under too much pressure she might fire out of panic, so I stopped moving.

"Put the gun down, lady!" Saul barked.

The blonde stiffened and her face tensed up.

"Put it down by your feet and then kick it away from you!"

She looked slightly frightened, but she didn't move. Then a thought seemed to occur to her, and her head tilted slightly back.

"You a cop?" she asked in a tight voice.

"Damn right I am."

"Then what the hell d'you think you're doing? Look at me, then look at her."

Her eyes went to Cassie's weapons. And I thought I saw what she was getting at. In addition to the twin Glocks on her belt, Cass had the usual Mossberg 590 pump-action shotgun strapped to one side of her bike, and her Heckler & Koch assault carbine on the other. But the fact was, they were always there. We needed them a lot of times that trouble came knocking. The sight of Cassie kitted out this way was such a regular sight around the Landing that it barely drew the slightest comment. So which neighborhood exactly was this woman from?

Something else struck me, and I glanced over at her little car. There was a sticker in the back window. I'd noticed it when she had first turned up.

And now I stared at it more closely. It read "New England Aquarium." Which I'd never heard of. There was no such establishment around here.

The standoff, though, was still in progress, with the Focus's owner at the center of it. And I couldn't tell how it was going to end.

"Stand down!" Saul was shouting at the woman. "Lower your weapon!"

But instead of doing as she was told, she came back with another question.

"And you are?"

"Detective Lieutenant Saul Hobart."

The woman's expression slackened slightly and she changed her grip on her gun, a Walther. She freed her left hand, and then held it up with the index and middle fingers raised.

"I'm going to reach inside my coat, okay? With just two fingers."

We watched her closely. When her left hand reemerged, there was a plastic wallet in it.

And when she flipped it open, I could see the flash of a bright golden badge, although it wasn't in any shape I recognized.

"Lieutenant Detective Lauren Brennan," she announced loudly. "Boston Homicide."

CHAPTER 10

"Look, I realize I'm new here," she was explaining to us a few minutes later, although it felt like a good deal more than that. "But can I be blunt? What kind of community allows anyone to go around in plain view armed like that?"

She jerked her head toward an angry, scowling Cassie, who was propped against her bike and had no plans to join us.

"I mean, I thought she was going to go postal."

Our weapons had been put away by this stage. Everything had calmed down. Or, at least, to outward appearances anyway. I didn't know about the others, but my brain was racing, trying to figure all this. An outsider? One who was a normal human being, and who didn't seem to mean us any harm?

The three of us were seated around my original table, me and Saul both trying to hide our absolute bewilderment. There was almost a feeling like we were being played by some kind of trick. No one just walked in here in this way. Once again, it was Regan's Curse, cast by a witch named Regan Farrow.

A few years after the Salem witches first arrived here, back in the late sixteen hundreds, she'd managed to overstep the mark. Annoyed a lot of people, got herself burned at the stake for it. She'd begged to be released, to no avail. And, as the flames climbed up around her, she had yelled out the words that had altered this town's destiny right up to the present day.

"If I cannot leave, then none of you ever shall. And you shall dwell alone here."

Which meant not only that we could never leave. It meant the outside world practically never intruded. Supplies came in, and we still managed commerce. How could we survive otherwise? But human visitations were a very fleeting thing. People arrived and quickly left, without so much as a backward glance. The only types who stayed for long periods—Willets apart—were either totally insane or terminally evil. And this Lauren Brennan didn't seem to fit into either category.

I stared into her gently colored but attractive face. How the hell had she got past the curse? There was no direct way to ask that question, so we stuck to the subject in hand for the moment.

"Erm, Cass is . . . how best to put this?" Saul was mumbling, trying to get his own thoughts in order.

There were even more people walking past, and some of the stores were beginning to open. None of the café's staff would come outside to serve us, though. They'd seen what had been going on, and were staring at us anxiously from behind a counter. And some folk, as they passed by, were glancing at us oddly, like they sensed that something genuinely unusual was happening. It made the way they walked a touch unsteady, like their own balance had been thrown off.

"She's my assistant," I put in quickly. "I'm a security consultant."

The woman took another look at Cassie's heavy weapons.

"Who do you consult for, Delta Force?"

The only response I could think of was a shrug. So I did that.

"Perhaps you could tell us," Saul asked warily, "what it is you're doing here? You've no jurisdiction outside Boston."

Which was a good way to approach this. But she didn't even seem to hear him straight away. Lauren Brennan pulled a troubled face, then raised her head—her neck was long and slender. And she peered around as if she were caught in some mild kind of trance.

"I'm still trying to figure out where this is," she murmured. "It's not exactly tiny, so why can't I find it on my map?"

Then something slightly peculiar happened. She appeared to forget the question, almost as soon as she had asked it. Maybe that was the curse taking partial effect.

"You've heard of the Shadow Man killings, right?" she went on evenly.

Me and Saul both shifted in our chairs. However isolated we might be, news did still reach us from the outside world. In the normal course of things, incidents beyond our borders had very little impact on us. But we'd picked up on this item practically a year ago, and understood the murders she was speaking of were pretty awful things. Entire families had been killed, and their deaths hadn't been quick exactly. So we knew about the Shadow Man.

But if she was here because of that . . . ? I cast a darting glance at Saul, remembering our conversation of last night.

Then, rather more gravely than before, we returned our attention to our brand-new guest.

"Go on," Saul muttered.

"It was my case. I saw the first bodies." When her eyes dropped and she shook her head, I could see that it was something she would never manage to forget. "Of course, not long after that, the Feds took charge. They spent ten months getting absolutely nowhere. But then, finally, we got a break. We tracked him down."

She pursed her lips.

"Cornelius Caldwell Hanlon. Didn't you see the TV reports? But it's almost like the guy has a sixth sense. By the time we got to his apartment, he was gone. We found out when we tossed his place that he's obsessed with the Apocalypse."

"Beg pardon?" I asked.

"He thinks the End of Days is coming. So far as we can tell from his diaries, the murders are some kind of ritual."

Saul bent his head in and inquired, "To achieve what?"

"To turn himself into a higher being, who can survive the world's end. Have you ever heard of anything crazier?"

I had, but it still sent a cold chill down my spine. If she was hunting down someone like that, then I was definitely on her side. I studied her more sympathetically.

The last time I'd seen anyone so tired and frustrated, I'd

been staring in a mirror. But Lauren seemed a pretty hardy type. She ran her fingers through her hair, gathering her thoughts. Then she continued.

"News came to us of another killing. A gas station attendant, about fifteen miles from here. Then a state trooper told us about a stolen Chrysler, headed up in this direction."

I recalled the grubby old car parked outside Lucas Tollburn's place.

"So here I am," she finished up.

"You came alone?" I asked.

That same muddled expression drifted across her face again.

"Some Feds were supposed to be on their way up here. I've no idea where they've gotten to."

Which doubtless meant that the curse had driven those guys back. But the question remained—why not her?

"Um, did you have any problems, getting here?" Saul asked.

She stared at him, the bridge of her nose crinkling.

"How d'you mean?"

"Did you feel that there was anything . . . holding you back?"

His words puzzled her, as well they might.

"I got this creepy feeling driving in, if that's what you're referring to. But I usually get that out here in the sticks. And I've not got any sleep for the past forty-eight hours, so I'm kind of jumpy, I suppose. How's this relevant, exactly?"

There was no way we could tell her. But I finally had a grasp on what was happening. I had no doubt that Lauren was a good cop. But more than that, she was an awfully determined woman, and was on Hanlon's case like a pit bull with its teeth sunk in. She probably had been that way ever since those first few murders. And so, not even our ancient magic had been able to divert her from her goal.

She had ignored its effects and just come steaming in here. That must have been quite a feat, and I started to feel a growing respect for her.

"So you reckon this Hanlon might be here, in our town?" Saul was asking her concernedly.

It certainly wasn't a comfortable prospect. And seemed

to dovetail with what the Little Girl had warned me of. But something else occurred to me at that point.

"Serial killers often have a signature," I pointed out. I'd read about it in a book. "Did Hanlon have one?"

Faint disgust lit up her eyes. So it seemed that I was right. Lauren let her face tilt, so a lock of pale hair dropped across her brow. It was obvious she saw us as provincial types, inexperienced in matters of this nature, and was wondering how far she could trust us.

"Well, we've always held that back," she told us. "I'm not sure that you guys need to know."

"No offense," she added, quickly and rather unconvincingly.

Which was not nearly good enough. I knew that, and so did Saul.

"We had four, possibly five murders in this town last night," he informed her.

And that changed her attitude instantly. Her pupils flared with stark alarm. She hadn't even known about that. Hell, there was no reason why she should.

"One an old man. One an entire family," I put in, picking up the thread. "Need to know, lieutenant? I think we have the right to know."

And this new information certainly seemed to force her to revise her opinion of us.

"Okay, then." She threw her hands apart and slid back further in her chair. "Hanlon carved a symbol into each of his victims, on the chest. Do I need to say any more than that?"

Even Cassie, over by her bike, went rigid.

"A theta?" Saul asked. *"Thanatos?"*

Which was obviously correct. There was no other confirmation needed. Lauren looked like she was being pulled apart by two separate emotions. Anger, that there'd been more deaths. And relief at the knowledge she was firmly on the scent.

"Haven't lost me yet, Cornelius," she murmured into the thin air around her. "Man, I'm right behind you."

CHAPTER 11

"Looks like I might be staying awhile," she announced, once she had come to a decision. "Where can I find a half-way decent hotel?"

Which—you have to understand—is the kind of question that we'd never been asked before. Saul ducked his head. Even Cassie looked away. So it was left to me to tell her.

"Er—we don't have any."

Her expression phased through to astonishment. Or maybe she thought that I was kidding her.

"There has to be something?"

"'Fraid not."

"A Best Western? Or a Holiday Inn?"

I only had a vague idea what those might be, and shrugged again.

"My God, I really am in the back of beyond." Then Lauren started looking faintly aggravated. "I don't want to drive the whole way back to Boston, just to shower and change."

By the look on Cassie's face, that wasn't such a bad idea. But my take on this was rather more fair-minded. Boston's problem had become our own. Our community was under threat. I had no real idea what had become of Cornelius Hanlon. But his behavior seemed to be unchanged. And we might need this city cop. So it made very little sense if she was forced to go away.

"Someone could put you up for a couple of nights," I suggested.

I tried to look at Saul again. But he'd already seen what was coming, and wouldn't meet my gaze. He had a family of four, his wife included, and his house was already full to bursting.

When I glanced around at Cass, it was like staring at a block of wood. The set of her mouth told me everything that I needed to know. There was plenty of room at her place on Rowan Street. But she wasn't offering an inch of it to this outsider, not after the way that they'd been introduced.

So it appeared there was only one option left.

"I've a spare room," I heard myself say.

"Thank you. It's appreciated," Lauren Brennan answered.

We agreed she'd leave her car here. She could pick it up later. Saul would get her from my place and take her to the crime scenes in another hour's time.

She went to her trunk, and got out a small round blue case that she told me she always carried with her.

As we headed off to my place, she produced a narrow pack of gum.

"Want some?"

I shook my head. We pulled up at a stoplight, a bunch of college kids heading across in front of us, clutching books and chattering. Yes, we have our own college. It was founded by Raine's great grandfather. I've always rather envied them myself, the casual air they have. And the way they're always talking, happily more often that not. But Lauren stared at them uninterestedly. There were plenty of their type where she came from. I understood that.

As we moved off again, her head kept leaning at slight angles, taking in the sights around her. The town had come fully awake. There was quite a lot of traffic in the center this particular day. Folk were filling up the diners. And the sidewalks were becoming fairly busy, bustling. The truth is, the Landing is a bigger and more heavily populated community than it genuinely ought to be. That's because, unlike other provincial towns in New England, no one ever gets to leave.

"A lot of people here dress pretty old-fashioned," she told me, apropos of nothing. "I already noticed that."

I hadn't before—I had no reason to. Clothing's hardly a big issue in a place like this.

"The dress sense round here?" she went on. "It's almost like stepping back into the fifties. I keep expecting Fonzie to appear."

Was that how we genuinely looked, I wondered, to someone normal from the outside world? Had we been isolated so long that we'd fallen out of step?

But I wasn't sure I liked her manners. Were city folk this blunt the entire time? Although I had to admit that, at close quarters, she smelled just as pleasant as she looked. And it had been a good long while since I'd had someone this attractive sitting next to me.

We got clear of the center, still heading north. The traffic became a good deal thinner, just us and a push-bike sometimes. There were wider sidewalks with grass verges. Rows of elm and maple trees. Well-tended front yards. And then finally, we were into an area of single-story houses, all extremely well maintained. Not a crooked shingle, nor a broken picket in a fence. Everything was looked after meticulously. I'd grown up here, and it had always been this way.

"My neighborhood," I told our visitor.

"Looks okay." Lauren turned the gum around in her mouth. "This isn't exactly what you'd call a small town, is it? So how come it doesn't show up on my map?"

"A printing error?"

Which, even to my ears, sounded pretty lame. She stared at me oddly and I couldn't blame her.

"No. I don't think it's that. You got Area 51 round here or something?"

She cracked a grin. Then got her cell phone from her purse, and dialed a number far longer than any I was used to. One which had a city code. I couldn't help but watch her, fascinated.

Someone picked up at the other end. Her whole manner went stern and businesslike.

"Jeff? It's Lauren. I've found Hanlon. I'm in a place called . . ."

Then she tailed off, her expression growing puzzled.

"Jeff?" she asked, rather more loudly. "Hey? Can you hear me?"

The line apparently went dead. She peered at the phone, then tried redialing. And didn't even get an answer, this time. I had been expecting that. She had no way of knowing it . . . but when you're in this town, there is a real serious problem attached to communicating with the world beyond its borders.

"What the hell is going on?" She jabbed at the keypad a few more times. "It was working before."

"We have trouble with reception," I explained. "The woods."

"The . . . ?"

"We're so deep in them. They mess up the signal sometimes."

She squinted at me awkwardly, then stared out through her side window again.

"This really is an isolated place, huh? I couldn't imagine living anywhere like this."

"Oh," I assured her, "it can get pretty interesting here from time to time."

"What, you have a swap meet twice a year?"

Which should have annoyed me. But I was getting used to her attitude, and didn't let it bother me. In spite of her appearance, she carried a hardness with her, like a shaft of steel inside a velvet coating. She had either been born with it, or it had formed. But there was no doubt that she needed it. I found it hard to even imagine what her job was like. All those gangsters. All those junkies. Jesus Christ, a city cop.

She'd obviously been places and done stuff I could only dream of. I was learning new things, the whole while she talked. And so the best course of action, I finally decided, was to simply go along with the flow of this, and hope she never found out how different a place the Landing really was.

"We're an inward-looking community," I told her. "We live our lives our own way, and keep ourselves to ourselves."

She munched at her gum, then pulled a face.

"That's Massachusetts for you, I guess."

On the whole of Kenveigh Street, there's only one home that shows any slightest sign of neglect. And it's mine. The lawn out front is a little too tall, and has crabgrass. Some moss has formed on the concrete in front of the garage door. And none of the windows have been cleaned in quite a while. But people around here understand my history, and know that I'm kept busy a lot. So they're polite enough not to comment on any of it. Which doesn't mean that they necessarily like it.

When we pulled up, Lauren looked renewedly puzzled.

"You live here alone?"

This was a family-sized house. What could I tell her—that a would-be demigod had spirited them away? I opted for a simpler explanation.

"Divorced, I'm afraid. Two years now."

"And you got the house?"

I was forced to think quickly.

"My wife left Massachusetts. Headed down to Florida. She took the kids with her."

Sympathy began to creep into her gaze. "That must be rough. You ever see them?"

My jaw hardened of its own accord. "No."

Lauren put her gum in the ashtray. "That sucks."

"You get used to it," I told her.

"People can get used to anything. Doesn't mean it doesn't suck."

Fortunately, none of my neighbors were outside to see this. No curtains moved. I carried her case for her. It turned out to be very light. We headed up the front path. But as soon as we were inside, Lauren spotted the phone and asked me, "Do you mind?"

She headed to it without even waiting for an answer.

I already knew what would happen. But it gave me enough time to clear a few things up, ahead of her. I went into bathroom. Alicia's nail varnish and makeup were still there, and there was a robe of hers on a hook on the door.

I bundled them up and hid them in a cabinet. Then I went into the living room and did the same.

I could hear her dialing a third time, rather angrily, by the time I'd finished.

"I still can't get through," she called out.

"Same problem?"

"How can it be? This is a landline."

Which was a good point. I was going to have to watch my step.

"Maybe the switchboard's down. It happens sometimes."

"What?"

I changed the subject hurriedly.

"Let's get you settled."

I gave her Pete's room, which had a larger bed than Tammy's. He had been into all kinds of fearsome creatures, alive or long dead. There were dinosaurs depicted on the bedspread, snarling at each other. And a variety of large predatory cats on the wallpaper and drapes. An alarm clock in the shape of a T.rex sat on the nightstand. We had let him choose it all himself.

"Where's your computer?" Lauren asked.

Goddamn. Here in the Landing, there was little point in owning such a device. A computer will do some of the things that it's normally supposed to, for sure. But we cannot reach the outside world by means of one. We've tried sending out emails. And we've tried going on message boards. Our communications simply get ignored. And without that facility, the machine is just a box that pushes largely useless information at you. Our libraries have a couple. But I was forced to admit I didn't have one.

She looked suspicious all over again.

"So how do you run a business?"

"All my work is local."

"Wow!"

Wow indeed. I fetched her my bathrobe, and then showed her where the shower was.

She closed the bathroom door behind her. Water started

hissing after that. I walked back into the living room. And, I have to admit, something clenched up hard inside me, listening to that retreating sound. How long had it been since anybody else had used the shower in this house?

My heart was thumping gently. And my mind felt slightly muzzy. I went to the mantelpiece, and stared at the photo of my family I keep there. Time seemed to turn to a gray blur and drifted by.

The hissing and spattering noises had stopped again, by the time I came around. I heard the bathroom door swing open.

Lauren padded, barefoot, past my doorway. She was toweling her hair, and didn't even seem to notice I was looking at her. But I found it hard to breathe, for a while after that.

My robe was far too large for her. She'd rolled the sleeves back, but was tripping over the hems. Her face was turned away from me. And considering the way that I was staring, thank heavens for that.

It could have been Alicia. Same build. Same height. Almost identical coloration.

She was gone a moment later, back in Pete's room. But she didn't seem to close the door. I thought I heard the bedsprings creak.

It's not her, I kept on telling myself. It's a stranger. Although something in me didn't want to listen.

No more sounds were coming from the room. I went back into the hallway. Reached out cautiously and rapped at her door. Then waited until I got no answer before peering cautiously inside.

It was apparent what had happened. She had only meant to sit down on the bed a while. Her bare feet were still on the floor. But she was sprawled out on her back now, fast asleep among the dinosaurs. Exhausted from the start of this, she'd gone out like a light.

I gazed at her for rather too long. Then I went back to the front door. Got out my own cell phone and called Saul, keeping my voice low.

"Wait a couple of hours before you come and get her," I told him, describing the way things were.

"Which is to miss the bigger picture, Ross. What the hell are we supposed to do with her?"

"I'd say we'd better find this Hanlon quickly, since she isn't going back without him."

"And if she begins to suspect . . . ?"

"She's already started to."

Saul grunted.

"Show her our provincial side, as much as you can," I suggested to him. "She already thinks this place is weird, but only because—so as far as she's concerned—we're a bunch of hicks. Anything that strikes her as off-center? She'll put it down to that, most likely."

"Sounds like a plan, although a fairly stupid one," he grumbled. "What are you going to do now?"

"I need to consult with someone."

Which made him grunt again.

"I could ask who," he said, "but I'd honestly prefer not to. Let me know what you find out."

CHAPTER 12

I left a brief note by the side of Lauren's bed. Then I drove to the commercial district, which is hidden behind a strip of parkland with a double row of fir trees, at the northeastern edge of town. There were a couple of older structures in view, the lumber mill, the brick-built smokestack. But most of the buildings had gone up between the fifties and the modern day.

I was heading past office blocks before too much longer. Warehouses and light-industrial factories. A truck went by that was from out of town. I could see the driver's face behind the windshield. He looked rather anxious. That's the way the curse usually works on folk who were not born here. They don't like visiting this place. They want to leave as soon as possible. And once gone, we've come to the conclusion that they simply forget about us, all knowledge of our town dissolving from their minds.

I watched the trailer in my rearview mirror. It was moving away from me at quite a speed. Then a forklift truck piled with wooden crates came rumbling out from a factory door, yanking my attention back.

It stopped for me, and I continued on. I was driving to the very outer edge, where the township gave way to dense forest. Dr. Lehman Willets lived out there, if you could call it living.

"Sanderson's Supplies" read the big sign painted near the top of the building. There were three stories of it and a basement, all of grimy, crumbling brick, the mortar interlaced with moss. The windows were dusty, lightless. Some were broken. And you would have thought it was abandoned. But everyone knew who inhabited the place.

If you don't count Raine, who at least has Hampton, then Lehman Willets is this community's best-known hermit. And he has another distinction as well. He is the only person living here who was actually born in the outside world.

He'd been here for a good few years. And the fact that he could walk out any time he liked? . . . Let's just say he has his reasons, and they're not exactly happy ones. Most people are afraid of him. So far as I know, no one ever visits him, except for me.

He'd set his home up in the lower sections of this place. And so I headed for the metal door around the side. There was a wasps' nest in an air vent higher up, the black dots spiraling out from it rather sluggishly by this time of the year, distracted by the cooler air. Dimly conscious in their tiny minds of the approaching winter, their own End of Days. That had put them in a bad mood, which was understandable. One of them hummed angrily in front of my face until I swatted it away.

I was about to turn the handle, when a window swung open above me. I must admit, it made me jump. I'd not been expecting anything like that. When Willets's head came poking out, it was in silhouette against the sky. My surprise leveled off to puzzlement. He was somebody who almost never altered his routine. So what was he doing up there?

I could just make out his pupils from this distance. They were tiny specks, a searing shade of red. And I supposed that he was scowling at me, since the man never had much of a cheerful demeanor. He's African-American, and looks much older than he really is, gray-haired before his time.

"Oh, it's you, Devries!" he called.

As if he'd been expecting someone else?

"What are you doing up there?"

"Been here since midnight," he told me.

"Why?"

"Felt something creeping around, late last night. Something pretty weird, on the night air. Can't tell you what it was. But . . . something we're not used to. So I spirited myself up here—it just felt safer."

Then he seemed to remember that I couldn't move around that way.

"You'd better use the fire escape."

Everything he'd told me came as a surprise. I knew the kind of magic he could conjure. What was capable of making him that nervous? I thought about it on the way up, and didn't like the answers that I got. Willets might be an outsider, but he'd taught himself the use of magic in his first months here. He'd turned out to have a natural aptitude for it. And by this time he was, for all his shortcomings and foibles, one of the strongest sorcerers in town. Most adepts can't cure injuries or wounds, for instance. But Willets could.

Whatever had spooked him, it had to be something really serious. If he'd felt obliged to alter his habits, then everyone had cause to worry.

He had been, back in the normal world, a researcher of the paranormal. That was what had brought him here. The curse had not deterred him. And once he had arrived, he had learned witchcraft so quickly that—for a while—it had sent him on a downward spiral into pure dementia.

He was no longer that way. Dotty, yes. Unpredictable, sure. But insane, like in those early days? It was better not to think about it.

I reached another door at the top. And when I let myself through, trumpet music washed around me. It was very dim in here. Not that he had covered up the windows. He'd simply made them go opaque. The holes in the glass too, which seemed impossible. But not for Willets, apparently. I hung back while my eyes adjusted.

He'd lived underground for so long that he couldn't abide direct sunlight. He seemed to have left most of his possessions downstairs. The big leather-bound volumes on the subject of arcana. And the old-fashioned iron kettle that he

usually kept on the boil. His folding bed was here, though—
he'd already sat back down on it. And at the center of the
room was the source of the music. A matt black plinth with
a turntable on top, the one thing left in the whole world he
really seemed to care about. There was no other equipment,
not even speakers. The chords lifted straight off the vinyl
and then floated up into the air.

You could feel the power rising off him. As he came into
clearer view, I could see that he was dressed in his habitual
serge pants and tweed jacket. He didn't even look at me.
His chin was resting on his knuckles, and his features were
intense and furrowed as he drank the music in.

"When there's something genuinely bothering me," he
told me, still not looking up, "I always find myself going
back to Miles. He soothes me like no one else can. This
was recorded at the Blackhawk Club in San Francisco, April
1961. I went there once. A lovely city. Probably still is."

He came from South Carolina himself, although he'd been
a lecturer at Boston U. But it was rare for him to mention
the outside world at all. So he was in a peculiar mood this
morning.

His eyelids slipped shut, and he waited for the final chords
of "Love, I've Found You" to slip away. Then he raised his
right hand slightly, gave a gentle click of his fingertips. The
turntable and plinth both vanished. And a canvas chair—for
my benefit—appeared on the same spot.

As I settled down, I noticed something else. He'd only
been up here a few hours. But small creatures had already
started gathering around him. Spiders were spinning brand-
new webs off in the corners. A few mice were watching him
over by the skirting board. A pigeon had got in somehow,
and was eyeing him from a rafter. That was the way it was,
with the good doctor. His power was so massive that it captured everything's attention.

It has to be pointed out, he used it very sparingly these
days. When he first became deranged, you see, he'd tried to
spread his newfound powers to the other people in this town.
An act of charity, to his mind. Twelve had died as a result.
Which was why he now lived where he did, completely on

his own. He couldn't bear to face the world beyond these walls. Guilt gnawed at him, every single day.

He finally peered at me with that unnervingly bright gaze of his.

"I know why you're here," he told me. "It's about Lucas Tollburn, right?"

I looked him straight in the carmine-centered eye.

"Of course. Was it Hanlon who killed him?"

In addition to the red ones, Willets had a powerful inner eye that had a habit of fastening on anything remarkable that happened in the Landing. And he gave a cautious nod.

"I saw him approach Tollburn's house, but not what happened after that. Circumstantial evidence, then. But this is not a court of law, so I'd suppose that it'll do."

I felt bemused. His gaze normally penetrated almost anywhere. Why hadn't he seen more? But he seemed to understand what was concerning me.

"Ever since I first developed my powers, I've been aware of certain things regarding Tollburn. Firstly, he was a far more complexly talented adept than anyone ever suspected. His maternal grandmother was Erin Luce, one of the great dowager-witches of Victorian times, and he learned his magic at her knee. So I suppose that should have been predicted."

He was right. I waited for him to go on.

"Secondly, for most of his life, he had not one but two Spells of Shielding set in place around him. One around his home, and the other around his actual person."

"Stopping him from being watched?" I asked.

"Exactly."

"Which is why you didn't see the murder."

Willets looked pensive and troubled.

"Tollburn was a mystery to me. Despite the fact I could not see him, I could sense him sometimes. And often, come nightfall, in places where he ought not be."

Which was a completely new one to me. There had been no hint of that before. I felt my eyebrows rise.

"Other people's homes, for instance," he continued. "While they were asleep."

But we were talking about a man in his eighties. What exactly was the doctor suggesting?

The pigeon on the rafter rustled its wings and then stopped again. Powder from them floated downward through the gloom, making it sparkle slightly.

"This was recently?" I asked.

He nodded. "Almost up until his death. I could feel him skulking around. But, no . . ."

He could see what was bothering me.

"Not physically, you understand."

I didn't. But I didn't press him either. Willets took his time about explaining things, and it was usually worth the wait.

"More like his undiluted spirit. He went all over town that way, and stopped in certain places, just watching and listening."

"But you said the people he visited were asleep."

His head came up a few inches. "Watching and listening to their dreams, perhaps?"

And altering them to his benefit? A chill ran through me, at that thought. I had heard of some pretty weird power games being played by the Sycamore Hill set. Influence and status were like food and drink up there. But this capped almost everything. What exactly had the man been doing?

"You want to hear my theory?" the doctor asked, breaking across my train of thought. "I think Lucas Tollburn had some form of spell, maybe some kind of magic instrument, that rendered him invisible and let him move around that way. He always was near the top, hierarchy-wise. Maybe he used those powers to maintain his position."

And we'd always had such a lofty opinion of him. I swore to God, when it came to the dealings of our upper echelons, it was like the court of Caligula sometimes. I struggled to make sense of what I'd just been told.

"So if Hanlon killed him, then he might have gotten hold of the instrument in question."

Willets pursed his lips. "It's more than likely."

"And you've no idea what it might be?"

"None. But there's one person who definitely will know."

I got that one straightaway.

"Millicent?" The way she'd scrabbled through those desk drawers. "What can you tell me about her?"

"Again, Devries, practically nothing. She has the same two Shielding Spells in place. I've no idea what she's been doing. I can feel something about her, though."

His face became even unhappier than was usual. He drew in a breath and held it, and then let it out.

"Beneath that outward polish, she is very deeply twisted. There's a blackness, like a canker, at the center of her soul. Someone hurt her, once upon a time. And all she's dreamt of, ever since, is hurting someone back. Make sure it isn't you."

Cass had sensed pretty much the same, hadn't she? The second warning on that subject, so I told him I'd bear it in mind.

"And that's the entire sum of my knowledge on the matter," Willets finished up. He brought his narrow hands together. "We won't know how much danger we're in till we find out what Hanlon stole."

But I was already starting to get a clearer picture. That second set of murders, last night. Anderson butchering his family, then killing himself. Did this thing Hanlon had stolen merely make a person like a ghost? Or was there more to it, far worse than that? I didn't feel too optimistic about the way that things were starting to unravel.

I reminded myself that it was still a bright day outside. This place was even worse than the basement, the unnatural darkness pressing in on me. The doctor was looking slightly impatient, which was odd for a man with so much time on his hands.

"You've something else to tell me?" I asked.

"Something I've noticed, yes."

"About?"

"You, man. Usually, you're straight out through the door once we've finished talking. Yet you're still sitting here."

My thoughts were half elsewhere.

"Excuse me?"

"I sensed things about the Tollburns, and I sense them about you as well. You've another question, haven't you? On a completely unrelated subject?"

There was a scrabbling noise from the corner of the room, but it didn't bring my head around. There wasn't much that I could hide from him. I'd resigned myself to that a long while ago. And so, my mind went back to the vision that I'd had last night.

I remembered what I'd been told by Amashta. So I asked him, exactly as she'd advised, "What does the word *'T'choulon'* mean to you?"

He looked utterly dumbstruck. His eyelids narrowed, making the pupils burn even fiercer. And the permanent furrows on his brow grew more pronounced.

His head gave a shake, like he couldn't quite believe what he'd just heard.

Then he said, "It's not a word, Devries. It's a name."

He peered at me gravely.

"Where exactly did you hear it?"

A squirrel had snuck in and joined the pigeon on the rafter by the time I'd told him everything I knew . . . which wasn't much. The two creatures took no notice of each other. They merely perched there, side by side, gazing down at Lehman Willets. I was staring at him too.

The bright red in his pupils seemed to dance and flicker slightly.

"It came to you in a dream?"

"Maybe something more than that," I said. "A vision."

"You're a visionary now?"

I didn't particularly care for the hint of dark sarcasm in his tone.

"Who or what exactly is T'choulon?"

See, I hadn't mentioned Amashta yet. And he seemed to understand that I was holding something back from him. I'm not sure that he liked that very much. But this seemed to be a matter of importance, and excited him. His fingers wrapped themselves around each other nervously for a few seconds. And his head went down and swayed from side to side a little. He looked utterly consumed in thought.

Then, at last, he got himself calmed down. He put his

palms on his thighs, and then straightened on his camp
bed.

"Early on in my researching days," he told me, "I got a
notion that was unusual at the time. That if I tried to plan
everything, do everything to schedule, then I wouldn't get as
far as I might, simply because the supernatural doesn't work
that way. Better, I decided, to surrender myself to the vaga-
ries of tide and time, and let them deposit me on whatever
shores they chose."

I thought I could see what he was getting at. He'd had a
whole wide world to choose from, after all.

"So I allowed myself to drift around a couple of years.
Hitched rides on a whim, took random buses. Walked down
certain streets because I felt I ought to. Got on trains because it just felt right. And it worked, to an extent. You'd be
surprised how much you can find out, that way, about the
world we live in and the other ones we barely know."

I was trying to be patient. Willets, as I've mentioned, took
his own sweet time getting to any given point, and it was no
use trying to hurry him. He had become even more intense
and serious than usual, his face a heavily lined mask of con-
centration in the gloom.

He wet his lips before continuing.

"One time, I wound up in Nebraska. I was walking on my
own, near dusk, cornfields all around me. And I thought at
first I was alone . . . until I came across a very old medicine
man, settling down by the roadside for the night. He invited
me to join him. A peculiar-looking fellow."

Willets paused yet again, digging back into his memory.
It seemed to be very important to him that he got the details
right.

"It was difficult to tell his age precisely, but . . . he was
very old. Very skinny. Hooked nose, slightly bulging forehead. Eyes as dark as any I had ever seen. Whitish hair, like
straw. And he had this—"

One of the man's hands came up.

"This scar cut into the side of his neck, just under the left
ear. Like a hash mark."

Which made my mouth go dry. The rest of the room

seemed to fade away. The only time I'd seen Amashta, there had been a scar carved into the exact same spot. In her case it had been two parallel lines, like an equals sign. But I was pretty sure that it was no coincidence.

"He wouldn't tell me his name," the doctor continued, "or even what his tribe was. Told me stuff like that had no importance in the true order of existence, which was odd. But he let me share his campfire for the evening, and we talked. He told me stuff. He claimed to belong to a family that went back almost to the last ice age."

I sat up a little straighter myself. That couldn't be true, could it? Someone claiming lineage the whole way back to times like those? I kept on listening anyway, holding my tongue and nodding.

"According to him, they'd passed on tales, purely by word of mouth, relating to that era. Stories six thousand years old and more. An astounding claim, and quite absurd sounding, I'd suppose. Except—you had to have been there—he was utterly convincing. And in several of the stories, that same name cropped up."

He looked straight into my face.

"T'choulon. A city. The world's first, older even than Eridu in Sumeria. He referred to it as a 'city in the rocks,' so I'd imagine it was based on caves."

His pupils fastened on my own.

"But many shamans gathered there. And then, there was a war between them."

CHAPTER 13

Millicent Tollburn's residence—she'd had it built to her own
design with part of the settlement from her divorce, and
called it Millwood House—was square and largely featureless on the outside, with a flat roof. The place was built of
pale brick and was ostentatiously large, with fourteen bedrooms. Odd, for somebody who had few visitors, no live-in
staff. It looked out onto Plymouth Drive, about halfway up
the gradient. The grounds behind it descended the slope for
more than half a mile before they gave way to a tree line.
There was a pond halfway down, overgrown with algae.
And stables too—she kept four horses And a wall around
the entire place, some ten feet high, with iron spikes at the
top.

Her Jaguar was sitting, with its top still down, on the
sprawling gravel drive, where it had been most of the night.

Millicent was standing by a window at the rear, gazing
out across the town. The embroidered silk drapes that she
was leaning against were just a façade to show the outside
world. The interior of her place was minimalistically furnished. Very modern, exactly the way she liked it. Nothing cluttered. Nothing a mess. She even emptied her ashtray
every time she smoked a cigarette.

She'd gotten no sleep last night, but was not in the least bit
bothered about that. Too much occupied her mind. Some-

where out there in that seething anthill of a town was the most valuable part of her inheritance. Her blue-green gaze narrowed with anger at the very thought.

She'd earned it, in the hardest way you could imagine. She deserved it. Damn, the Wand of Dantiere was hers!

She watched as a tiny-looking green bus rumbled to a halt on Brent Street. The passengers started getting out. They looked like bugs from up here, but it wasn't just the distance. She'd despised the people of this town ever since . . .

She shuddered, then tried to close her mind to the memories. No.

She was clutching something in her right hand. Woodard Raine had given it to her last night. He knew about the wand, how Lucas had used its power to spy on his peers, even influence their minds. Most people would have been shocked. But Raine was different—a moral law unto himself. He lived so distantly from the real world, stuff like that amused him. To his mind, it was a merry game. And he'd offered his help—enthusiastically, in fact—as soon as she had told him it was gone.

She opened her hand a little wider, and the object she'd been given glittered in the filtered sunlight. It was called a Thieftaker, a very rare and special magical device. There'd been one in the Raine family for generations, or so she'd been assured. At first glance, it looked like a solid jewel, roughly the size of a hen's egg. But when you took a closer look, you could see that it was more than that.

There were gaps between the facets. And the entire thing was hollow. It was made up, in fact, of hundreds of much smaller jewels, all linked together in continuous strands, crisscrossing each other in the most intricate fashion. When her palm quivered slightly, they shifted a touch, a motion like tiny cogs in the belly of a pocket watch.

Raine had told her which words to use, and the ones to emphasize. The spell was in Latin. And, like the device itself, was a complicated thing. But if anyone had stolen something from you, this would get the object back. And—so she had been promised—it would bring the perpetrator along for the ride. Revenge, you see, was part of its purpose.

It could not be used in daylight. She would have to wait until nightfall came slipping down again. But, simply holding it, she felt its influence reach out. She got a definite sense of the man who had killed Poppy and taken the wand. He was not from around here—that was the biggest surprise. And his thoughts seemed to go flying off at tangents even more bizarre than Raine's.

The dirty piece of thieving scum was extremely pleased with himself, right now. For the moment, he was laying low. She wasn't sure quite where, but it seemed to be a very dark place. Murky. Fetid. Not in the least bit pleasant. But that didn't seem to bother him. He was chortling quietly to himself.

"Shadow Man" were two words she got off him. And then "special fun."

And that word—'special'—brought the memories tumbling back. She could not stop them this time.

"This will make you special, Milly. This will make you strong."

Her grandfather's face, both eyes clear back then, loomed up in front of hers. The most venerated adept in the Landing, yes. Except that was not the entire truth. When she'd been a little child, he had insisted on spending time alone with her. Hours alone.

She clenched her teeth, trying to fight against the images flooding through her head. It did no good. She couldn't stop them.

He'd use his magic on her, doing dreadful things. Turning her into awful creatures. Sending her under the ground.

"But I don't want to!"

"How do you expect to be a powerful magician if you don't understand all the darkness in the world?"

And if she kept protesting, he'd cast spells on her that made her hurt.

"I'll tell Mom and Pop!"

"You can tell them anything you want. I'll sneak into their thoughts and change them. It will make no difference. This remains our special secret. You will thank me later on."

The scene suddenly changed. She was at a garden party at

the Vernon house. The occasion . . . her grandfather's sixty-fifth birthday.

The broad, sprawling mansion with its Grecian pillars lay off in the distance. She was standing on a perfectly clipped lawn, surrounded by topiary cut in the shape of mythic beasts. A huge satyr crouched like it was stalking her. A Minotaur stretched out its arm. She knew that they were only plants, but they frightened her, and she was trying not to show it.

There were hundreds of people around her. Everybody who was anybody in the town was here. And it was not just adepts. There was the mayor, Edgar Aldernay. There were men from the police department, and the fire chief and his assistant. There were representatives from the Board of Commerce, ministers, folk from the PTA.

It was a brilliantly sunny day, the sky a startling shade of blue. A constant thrum of chatter rose toward it. Folk were getting to know each other, and old acquaintances were being renewed.

Waiting staff carrying large salvers were circulating. A string quartet was playing nearby. Millicent stood frozen on the edge of all of that activity and sound.

At the direct center of it was her grandad. Everyone seemed drawn to him. Everybody smiled. His hand was being shaken constantly. And people were respectful, deferential to him. When he spoke, they hung on his every word, and smiled, and even laughed.

What were they laughing about so loudly? Was he telling them about his secret games, and what a helpless little fool she was? Millicent watched the whole thing numbly. Didn't they know who he really was? That evil man. Why were they treating him this way?

It finally occurred to her. They had to be in on the secret. And they either didn't mind, or simply didn't care. Her dismay turned to simmering anger, although she took care to hide that too.

Another half an hour, and photographs were being taken. People started gesturing to her. She was obviously expected to be a part of this.

"Come on, Milly! It's your turn!"

Everyone was looking at her. She quaked furiously inside.

"Don't you want a picture with your granddad? He's a very special man."

And she wanted to come right out with it. Tell everyone exactly what kind of cruel filth he was. But there were hundreds of eyes fixed on her. Hundreds of faces, beaming expectantly. And she realized, in that instant, they'd despise her if she told them that.

Finally she walked across, a smile fixed tightly on her lips. It didn't even falter when his arm settled across her shoulder, although revulsion uncoiled through her gut.

He moved his cheek so close to hers that their faces were almost touching.

"Look into the camera, dear."

"Yes, Poppy," she heard herself reply.

The flashbulb blinded her—once, twice, three times. And her head was spinning so much that she thought that she was going to faint. But when her vision cleared, everyone was chuckling and applauding. So she was a joke to them. And they were all in on the secret, weren't they?

It was hurting her face simply to smile by this time. Just as well they couldn't see past it. It was lucky for them they couldn't hear the thoughts now running through her mind.

I hate you. All of you. This entire town.

And one of these days, you'll pay for this. I swear it. You will all pay dearly.

CHAPTER 14

The FBI had taken over Shadow Man after the first few killings, naturally. But it had been her case in the first place, and
Lauren had stuck with it in her spare time. This particular
month, she had been delving into the plethora of crazy things
that had previously inspired serial killers. Lunar cycles, as-
trology, the motions of the planets. Sunspots, for heaven's
sake. And, going through the files, she'd noticed something
that she hadn't been expecting. Never in a million years.

The weather . . .

She was woken by the noise of someone ringing on the
doorbell. And it wasn't like the buzzer in her own apartment
on the edge of Chinatown. It was heavier, a clanging sound.
Lauren felt disoriented at first, not at all sure where she'd
wound up. But then she remembered some of it. The boo-
nies, for heaven's sake. She struggled up into a half-seated
position on the edge of the small bed, rubbing at the gunk
that had formed in her eyes.

She found her watch in a pocket of the robe that she was
wearing, squinted at it. Damn, she hadn't meant to fall asleep
this long.

She still felt out of kilter, squinting at her new surroundings.
This room reminded her of Tommy Valentine's on Dartmouth,
back when she had been a little girl. Then the whole of it came
back to her. Raine's Landing, yes. Ross Devries's home.

The bell was still ringing, and no one seemed to be answering it. She noticed a piece of paper on the nightstand, picked it up and read it. Then she went to the front door.

When she yanked it open, Lieutenant Hobart was standing on the porch. He stared at her, looking quite surprised. She realized why, and pulled the robe a bit tighter around her. What did the man think was going on?

The street was washed with sunlight behind him. Birds were singing in the trees. Hobart stared down at his massive shoes, then said, "We agreed I'd pick you up and take you to the murder scenes."

Straight to business, then.

"Give me five minutes. You can come in, if you like."

But he looked wary and mumbled, "I'll wait by the car."

As he lumbered away, she was struck once again by how ungainly he seemed. She knew it was unkind, but she'd already given him the nickname Herman Munster. An odd sort of man to be a detective, although he seemed to suit this particular town.

She thought it through again as she scrubbed at her teeth and got her hair untangled. No computers. Not so much as a boarding house. What kind of place was this? Talk about back of beyond.

Still, these were not the kind of mysteries that she was paid to solve. She had been determined to catch Hanlon ever since she'd seen what he had done to his first victims, a family on Fairfield. She had sworn to get the man, in fact. She went back through into the bedroom, got a change of underwear and a fresh shirt out of her little case. Caught a glimpse of herself in a nearby mirror as she put them on. She had a black belt in jujutsu, and she swam a lot, and felt pleased with the way her body looked.

Which got her thinking about her host. She already knew how she felt about Hobart. But what did she think of Mr. Ross Devries?

He'd seemed too controlled and unforthcoming when she had first met him. And she'd thought initially that he was a cold fish. Although as it turned out, he wasn't exactly that. He'd been hurt emotionally, that much was for sure. And he held himself at a slight distance from the world because of that. But she'd begun to like him, on the drive back here. He was intelligent, a little wry. Reserved certainly—but what the hell. She hated men who talked too much. Tall and narrow, with his blond hair and his pale gray eyes. He was certainly attractive.

She pulled her suit and shoes on, checked her Walther, then returned to the front door.

Saul Hobart, true to his word, was waiting by his Pontiac. As she approached the man, he peered at her again with an inquiring expression. And it wasn't anything to do with the robe this time. He was staring at her like she was some kind of total mystery.

People didn't normally react to her that way. And she wasn't quite sure why, exactly. But Lauren got the strangest feeling he was hiding something fairly important from her.

Saul drove her up Sycamore Hill first. As they neared the top, she got some glimpses through the gates of the enormous, sprawling mansions here. Wow, this was genuinely impressive. Who'd have thought so many wealthy people lived in a town no one had ever heard of. It occurred to her that—just maybe—they had sufficient influence to keep it this way, keep the place anonymous. Was that the explanation for the odd things she had noticed?

They pulled off onto a narrow lane and drew up to a smaller gate. Saul led her across a broad front lawn and past the yellow tape at the doorway of a cottage, and then took her through to the conservatory. It was washed in yellow light as well. What was a bureau doing there?

Lauren walked around carefully. The scene had been processed to a good standard, she was pleased to see. There were chalk marks, and numbered tags all over the floor. By the amount of spatter, it was just an ordinary stabbing. Except that, in the dried-up pool of blood where the body had been lying, someone had left a knee-print. She'd come across the same at other killings. That had been Cornelius, crouching down to leave his signature.

Other than that, there was nothing more she could turn up than what the local cops had found.

"Let's take a look at the Anderson place," she suggested.

It turned out to be most of the way across town. And that struck her as very odd. Why'd Cornelius gone so far to find a second set of victims, when he'd constantly returned to the same districts, even the same blocks, back in the city?

The town sped by them as they left the hill behind. They headed down a road called Sandhurst Avenue, then turned east onto a wide, straight thoroughfare the signs told her was Greenwood Terrace. And, gazing at her surroundings, Lauren felt a nagging sensation, not for the first time. She could almost hear a little voice whispering in the back of her mind. Telling her that she did not belong here. That she ought to leave.

She'd heard it several times already. First when she'd been heading into town. And then when she'd been wandering around it, before she'd met Ross.

And the appropriate word was "huh"? She'd been to towns like this before, and this one looked pretty much par for the course. Some quaint older houses thrown in among the newer ones. A variety of rooftops, weather vanes on some. They went past a schoolyard. It was midmorning break. The kids were playing with Frisbees and brightly colored balls in the sunshine. Older folk were outside too, mostly tending their front yards. A phone company van rolled by, although it was no company that she had ever heard of.

But all this normalcy seemed lost on her. She felt her heart bump over quickly. Go, right now! the voice inside demanded. But it couldn't be real. She simply ignored it. It was just a vibe that she was picking up. She remembered what Ross had told her—this was a place that minded its own business. Little wonder she felt out of whack here.

The plain fact of the matter was, she was determined not to leave without Cornelius Hanlon. She would turn her own gun on herself before she contemplated that.

Saul swung the Pontiac around a corner again, heading north this time. She caught a flash of the river in the distance. Then they were going past a massive park, with a huge blue lake at the center of it. There was a rowboat out on the water. Folks were fishing on the banks.

See, it was all perfectly okay. The voice died away in her mind.

They stopped outside the Anderson house, which looked as utterly mundane as everything they'd passed. But Lauren had to steel herself before she went in, all the same. Family homes, with children involved, were the mentally the toughest crime scenes she'd ever had to deal with. She had never gotten used to it, even after month after month of the Shadow Man. Recollections came surging back.

The weather.

On four separate occasions, the Shadow Man had returned to a city block he'd previously visited, entering a different house. He'd done it completely at random, so there was no way of predicting it. But—to her astonishment—she found that several days before the first killing on each block, there'd been a storm or a strong overnight wind. So she'd begun canvassing those areas again.

"Sure, we had a few tiles loose. We called the insurance people, and they sent this guy around."

She'd found a ladder, climbed up on the roof herself. And from there, she could see the back of every house on the far side of the block. There was the Nevills' overly large cat-flap. And there were Mrs. Sommer's windows with their rusted-open locks.

The route to Hanlon had been very simple after that . . .

They both went in. The wallpaper was a slightly garish yellow, but otherwise this was a normal family home. She could see framed certificates for musical achievement on one wall of the living room. The couch was yellow too. These people seemed to have really liked the color. A small plastic model of the Hulk was lying at the foot of the staircase.

It was best, she'd always found, to get the worst part over right away. So she asked if she could see the kids' rooms first.

The sight of blood on child-sized bedsheets made her tighten up.

"What were their names?" she asked, as calmly as she could manage.

"Joe and Aggie," Saul responded quietly.

He looked angry, and his big face had gone gray. There was dampness in the corners of her own eyes, but she didn't let it overwhelm her. If she couldn't act professionally, she had no business being here. Lauren drew herself up straight and went through to the girl's room. Damn, there were the instruments. This was the kid who had earned those certificates downstairs.

Both rooms were in the same state. By the pooling of the blood, there had been no struggle in either case. They'd almost certainly died in their sleep. Son of a bitch! She never ceased to be amazed at the sheer depth of Cornelius's evil. Lauren felt her hands begin to shake, and clasped them together to stop that happening. She took note of what she needed to, and then moved on.

The main bedroom was a completely different story. There had been an obvious struggle, an attempt at flight. She scrutinized the muddled red smears on the vivid yellow wallpaper.

"This was all . . . Christine Anderson?"

Saul fingered the loose skin at his throat and nodded.

"And what was her husband doing? Was he restrained?"

Her opposite number squinted at her.

"We found him lying on top of her body, with his throat cut."

Which was not Cornelius's style at all.

"Ligature marks?"

The big man shrugged.

"Tell you the truth, we had it down as a murder-suicide, at first."

Why'd they come to that conclusion? Lauren frowned. But, looking at the evidence around her, none of this made any sense. She worked it over in her mind, then came to a new decision.

"Okay. I'd like to see the bodies."

The morgue was precisely the same as you found anywhere in America. An unreal-seeming place, except that it was too real. An environment where everything was kept as businesslike as possible, to avoid the word "macabre."

They went down a wide corridor. The fluorescent lighting was harsh and robbed everything of its color. The paint on the walls had once been white, but had faded to a tepid, neutral blandness. And the whole place reeked of carbolic, in a vain attempt to cover up the lingering smell of death.

The coroner, a bearded man with hair down to his shoulders, had the husband on the slab and was cutting into his chest cavity when they walked in. His name was Leonard Furbellow, Lauren could see from the plastic nametag on his stained white coat. Anderson was a medium-sized man who had kept himself in reasonable shape. Handsome in a slightly dull way.

"I think there's something in his lungs," Furbellow said, looking up and nodding at Saul. "Was this guy a heavy smoker?"

Lauren hadn't noticed any ashtrays. But considering there were kids in the house, maybe Stephen Anderson had taken his habit outside. Saul, apparently, thought the same.

"I'll get back to you on that," he answered. "Mind if we have a private moment with the vic?"

The coroner frowned, then set his scalpel down and went outside.

"Hold on," Lauren said, the instant he was gone. "Where is it?"

"Where's what?" Hobart asked.

"The symbol on his chest. The theta." She stepped forward, peering at the corpse. "If this was Hanlon, then there ought to be one. Where are the other bodies?"

Hobart led her across to a row of oversized steel cabinets on the far side of the room. She watched as he slid several of them open. They had already been examined and then tidily stitched up again. The sight of grade school kids in that condition frankly made her want to hurl. But she was too confused for that. Each of these had the *thanatos* carved into their chest.

She peered back at the body of the man of the house.

"So how come he has nothing?"

"That's why we thought it was a murder-suicide. He had

his family's blood all over him. What other conclusion would you like us to come to?"

Her head spun slightly. She could feel her face draining of heat. This wasn't what she'd been expecting. Lauren tried to take a step back. And then had to reach out for the nearest solid object, to steady herself.

Could Hanlon have somehow forced the guy to murder his own family? But that didn't ring true. She'd read his profile several dozen times. The Shadow Man took massive pleasure in the act. It was both high art and entertainment, to his fractured mind. He wouldn't delegate it to anybody else. In which case . . . ?

She had no idea. Her head was rotating even worse. And those strange voices had started up again, far more loudly this time. Everything seemed to tilt abruptly.

"Lieutenant Brennan?" she could hear Saul asking. "Hey, are you okay?"

She felt hands grip her shoulders. Normally, she'd be affronted . . . but right now, she was glad of it.

"We'll go outside for a while, okay?" she heard him saying. "This place gets to me sometimes too. Perfectly understood."

Except he didn't understand. Not the tiniest bit. She wasn't fainting here.

No, she was completely lost.

As they hobbled out, a thread of pale gray vapor emerged from one of Stephen Anderson's nostrils. It hovered above his lip for a few seconds, then went sucking back inside.

The right hand of the corpse twitched. Then it lifted slightly, and began edging its way toward the scalpel that the coroner had left behind.

CHAPTER 15

Halfway out into the corridor, a little of her independent spirit reemerged. Lauren tried to hold herself upright under her own steam, forcing her legs to work properly. But they wouldn't cooperate. They felt like hollow tubes made from the thinnest rubber. And her whole body seemed to be out of kilter. She could barely catch her breath.

This wasn't just surprise, confusion. No, in her job those were common enough things, and you learned to deal with them quickly enough. It was more like she had completely lost her inner sense of balance, and was no longer connected to the normal world. And that alarmed her badly, sending tremors through her. She had never experienced any feeling of that kind before.

The hallway was as dead of energy as it had been the first time she'd passed through it, one of the fluorescent strips flickering slightly. The smell of the place kept trying to overwhelm her. The shaggy-haired coroner was standing with his back against a wall, his hands thrust in his pockets. When he saw what was happening, he made an attempt at looking sympathetic. But she could detect a slightly mocking gleam in his reflective eyes.

"Looks like your friend has a bad dose of the corpse-town queasies," he remarked to Hobart.

Again, no. It wasn't that. She'd been in mortuaries a thousand times before. The voices in her head kept pounding at her, as if they were trying to split it.

"She'll be fine," the big lieutenant told the man, a touch sternly. "A rough day, is all."

"Looks like it, from where I'm standing. Mind if I get back to work?"

"Knock yourself out."

Hobart propped her up against the same wall, then gazed at her concernedly and murmured, "Try to breathe. Just concentrate on that."

He studied her eyes, checking them for focus, and then gently felt her pulse. She managed to gulp down some air. Then she got out, "Sorry. I don't know what came over me."

His attitude was far more relaxed than hers would have been under the circumstances. A homicide cop who couldn't deal with a few dead bodies? But he seemed to understand that there was more to it than that. He just looked pleased she was recovering. And was about to speak again, when two loud noises broke across him.

First, an ear-splitting howl, half pain and half terror, from beyond the double-doors. And then a massive crash on the tiled floor in there, metal instruments going everywhere by the sound of it. Had the coroner slipped?

Saul let go of her, his frame tensing.

"Leonard? You okay in there?"

Footsteps started to approach the doors. But they were shambling ones, uneven. So maybe the guy had hurt himself.

The left door started to push open. Lauren tried to make out what was going on.

It wasn't the hirsute Furbellow whose face emerged from the examination room, though.

It was the guy from the slab. Stephen Anderson.

Lauren thought she was hallucinating, at first. Then she took in the fact, dizzily, that what she was seeing was real. The shock slammed at her like a wrecking ball. Her stupor left her, and she flattened herself against the wall, her slender body tightening up. Her chest felt like it had filled up with concrete.

Oh my God! Her lips dropped open, but no sound came out.

Then she glanced over at Saul Hobart, expecting him to be the same. And that was when she got another shock.

He looked surprised, certainly. But his body didn't even twitch. He simply took in what was happening, then squared his shoulders, his chin lifting. Like he'd faced this kind of thing before.

Anderson's eyes were still glazed over. His lips were the same shade of blue they had been when she'd seen him on the slab. The structure of his cheekbones stood out very starkly on his bloodless face. He stepped out fully into view.

There were some ugly purple patches where the blood had settled. His flesh matched the walls out here, a pallidness pretending to be white. It looked like there was a second mouth across his throat, the severed edges curling back. And his chest cavity gaped redly where the coroner had sliced into it. But there was not a single drop of blood that she could see emerging from the wounds. And so his heart was still not pumping.

Lauren tried to make herself smaller, but couldn't move a muscle. She could barely think.

Which made what Saul did all the more amazing. He just muttered quietly to himself.

"Aw, dammit."

Then he drew his piece and aimed it.

Which seemed inhumanly calm.

She noticed something else red, and her attention dropped to Anderson's right arm. The hand was covered with fresh, dripping blood, splattered the whole way to his elbow. And there was a scalpel, equally drenched, in his right fist.

So now she knew what had happened to Furbellow. Except . . . her mind couldn't take it in. She couldn't quite accept it.

Lauren wanted to run, but couldn't. The strength had rushed out of her body as though somebody had pulled a plug. She felt her legs beginning to give way completely. She was sliding down against the wall, and there was nothing she could do to slow her descent.

Anderson took another step forward. The big lieutenant told him, "Stop right there."

The fellow did as he was asked, at first. But then his milky gaze slid past the man and his gun, and settled on Lauren. His stare on her felt ghastly. She pushed herself back into the wall.

The corpse smiled. It was like watching latex being tugged out of shape, a humorless, unnatural thing.

"Why hello, Lieutenant Brennan," its voice came hissing out. "I've seen you on the TV several times. Good to meet you in person at last."

She felt like she was going to pass out. Was this thing claiming to know her?

"It was awfully nice, having somebody so very pretty searching for me for a while," the dead voice went on. "It made me feel loved and wanted. What a shame the FBI took over."

Hanlon? Another fierce quiver ran through her.

Then the corpse's smile completely vanished.

"Although you did say some nasty things about me in those early days, dear. Pervert? I'm not that, sweet pea. What I do is spiritual, not sexual. The killings weren't 'brutal' either. They were merely to a prescribed plan. And I always thought, back then, how appropriate it would be if you became one of my sacrifices. And now you're here. Just how much luck is that?"

He took another step toward her. She finally heard a sound come out of her own mouth, though she was not sure what.

"Hold it!" Hobart bellowed.

The corpse swung its faded gaze back at him.

"Or you'll kill this body? Hate to point out the obvious, friend, but it's already dead." It jabbed at its chest to emphasize that. "I'll make a deal with you, okay? Leave now, and you'll survive to see another sunrise. Attempt to defend the little lady here, and you'll die alongside her."

The only thing Saul did was grunt and hold his ground. When the corpse moved again, he fired twice, grouping both the shots near the heart. The impact made the body rock, but it showed no sign of doing any more than that.

The corpse's voice had become gloating. "That's no use. I told you."

Then it kept advancing, trying to go around the man. Saul placed himself directly in between them. The corpse's right arm swung back. Then, the scalpel came lashing at him. The big lieutenant stepped away from it just in time, and fired another shot into a bare knee.

The thing started limping when it tried to move again. So it could be damaged. But apparently not halted.

It suddenly occurred to her that she ought to be defending herself, not letting someone else do it. That would have normally been her first instinct. But she was still having trouble even thinking straight. She pushed a hand inside her jacket, got hold of the Walther's grip. But her fingers were so nerveless that, when she tried to pull it out of its holster, it clattered away to the tiles below. She couldn't even see where it had gone, because her gaze was still fixed on the corpse.

"Get out of my way," it was saying to Saul.

Lauren watched, horrified. Hobart was still looking far more composed than he ought to be under the circumstances. He seemed to be trying to think this through.

And then he came to a decision. Aimed higher than before.

And put one shot each into the corpse's murky eyes, leaving only ruined sockets there.

The scalpel dropped and rattled as it struck the floor, bright red flecks of blood appearing around it. The only thing that she could do was wait and see what happened now. It felt like time had stopped completely.

"It's gone all dark. What the hell did you just do?"

If it was Cornelius Hanlon in there, using Anderson's cadaver like a crab inside another shell . . . ?

"This body's ruined!" Hanlon was shouting angrily. "You big dumb ape! That was a lousy thing to do. But it won't stop me. I'll be coming back."

Without any warning, the corpse tumbled to the ground.

Its arms went out to either side. Its mouth dropped slackly open.

Gray vapor came pouring out. And even Saul jumped back at that. It spread across the ceiling. And at first, she was afraid it might attack them too. But it just went streaming off, billowing away in the direction of the entrance.

Saul watched it go, then put his gun back in its holster, wiping some perspiration off his face.

"That was pretty close," he murmured, turning back to her.

He walked across, looking worried and apologetic. Crouched down and reached out a big hand.

But she simply couldn't help herself. Because by this time, panic was exploding through her like a fireball. Everything inside her seemed to be collapsing in its wake. Her bones. Her organs. Sanity itself. None of this could be real. But she'd seen it!

So Lauren pulled her knees up to her chest, cringing away from his touch.

"What's going on?" she could hear herself start yelling, almost as if from a gaping distance. Body and mind were that far separated. "Who are you people? What the hell kind of a place is this?"

CHAPTER 16

I was coming back down the fire escape, my head still pounding from what Willets had told me, when my cell phone rang, bringing me to an unsteady halt. It was Saul Hobart. And I could tell, merely from his tone, that something new had happened.

"Where are you?" I asked him.

"With Lauren Brennan, at Sam Scott's."

Which was a bar. At this time of day?

"What are you doing there?"

"Trying to calm her down." His voice sounded tired, defeated, with a strong ring of inevitability to it. "She knows, Ross. You'd better get over here."

I took that in carefully. Saw that we'd been swimming against far too powerful a current, trying to keep the truth from her. There was too much going on that was unusual, even by our standards. And she wasn't stupid. Was in the same line of work that we both were. But apprehension seized me all the same.

See, we'd had interlopers several times before who'd found out the real nature of this place. They had been evil or deluded beings almost to the very last. Never someone genuinely good. So we'd never once been in a position like this. How were things going to pan out, from this point on?

That's another thing about the Landing—it is always

throwing up brand-new surprises. Far too many of them, in fact. And very few of them are welcome ones.

I told Saul I'd be ten minutes. Then I went the rest of the way down.

I drove back into East Meadow. It was Cassie's neighborhood, and sprawled out around me in all its shabby glory. I hadn't heard a peep from her since the incident outside the cafe, but there was no time for an impromptu visit. If there was one certainty about Ms. Mallory, it was that she could take care of herself. She'd been doing that since the age of seventeen.

I headed for Crealley Street, the fastest route to the center of town. But my mind was slightly elsewhere. Willets's voice was still causing percussive echoes, deep inside my head.

He had described to me this war he'd mentioned, many thousands of years before the birth of Christ. The first war between adepts, as it turned out. They were called shamans back then.

"Not with clubs and spears, you understand. No, this was a war with magic, a far more terrible thing."

And his red gaze battened on me in the dimness, seeing how I'd react. To be honest, I wasn't quite sure how I felt about this. How could anything so old be relevant to us today?

"A war about what?" I asked the doctor.

He looked thoughtful for a few seconds.

"The guy was pretty vague about the cause of it. I'm not even sure he fully understood. All he could really tell me was that it had to do with 'free will.'"

Which was precisely what Amashta kept on mentioning. But what on earth did that mean? It was a term that conveyed very little, without being put in context.

I had to swerve to avoid a stray dog that had wandered out across the blacktop. Then I reached Crealley and started speeding up.

"He was more specific about the 'who' than the 'why,'" Willets continued. "There were two factions. One styled themselves 'the Elite.' The other? The closest he could tell me was . . . 'the Liberators.'"

Which—like "free will"—raised an unanswerable question. If they called themselves that, then who did they liberate, and from what?

"There were many deaths on either side, and some atrocities, apparently. As in all wars, terribly cruel things were done. But it ended, so it seems, with an impasse. Neither side completely won."

"Which might mean it's not over yet," I pointed out.

Willets's head jerked up at me, his features becoming twisted. Like he hadn't even thought of that. And then he seemed to figure out that I knew more than I was letting on. So I decided it was time. I told him the whole story about Amashta and the gemstone pendant. I had never known him listen to anyone so closely and carefully, motionless as a dim painting.

The lights were red at the Colver Street intersection, and I drew up to a halt. There was only some light crosstown traffic, a patrol car among it. Jenny Pearce was at the wheel, her white-blond hair clearly in view. She noticed me and gave a brief wave as she passed. I nodded back.

Then the lights changed, and I was heading on a couple more blocks of plain-looking houses before turning right.

"But what does such an old war have to do with us?" I asked him.

Willets favored me with a warmthless smile.

"Few things in magic are permanent. The nature of it, after all, is constant flux. If there's still a conflict taking place, then the best way to win would be by altering the rules. The problem is, both sides are capable of that. The battle would constantly evolve, in other words. Who knows which direction it might go? As for 'old,' well, magic is a cosmic thing. And a few millennia count barely as a heartbeat in the time frame of the cosmos."

Which was not the kind of thing I really liked to hear about.

"So why this town? How come we got involved?"

"If the war's not over, if the issue's not resolved, then what better place to settle it than here? Raine's Landing is, let's face it, the most magic-imbued place on this entire planet."

I took that in uncomfortably, seeing he was right. Then we talked about the gemstone pendant that the woman had been sealed in. It had broken in half when I'd freed her. The pieces were, at present, off at Gaspar Vernon's place.

"Regan Farrow owned it, and the curse came into being," Willets pointed out. "Jason Goad owned it and . . ."

He faltered, embarrassed. Hadn't meant to bring my family up.

"But I think the upside might be this," he went on, his voice rather quieter. "Once you'd freed her, her first instinct was to help us. At a guess, I'd say that you can trust this woman, whoever she is."

Something else was nagging at me. I decided to voice it too. So I told the doc what Amashta had dubbed me when I'd first encountered her. He peered at me slightly askance.

" 'Defender'?" He shook his head. "It's not a common title, Devries. There've been Defenders of the Faith before. Defenders of the Realm. But merely plain Defender? Against what?"

He looked brooding, something confounding him. And when he stared at me again, was he seeing me in a new light?

"I really don't know what it means. So I can only tell you what I think again. To hold such a title . . . that sounds like a pretty hard thing. Dangerous, and lonely too."

He let his head tilt to one side.

"But if I had to choose anyone to hold it, then I wouldn't hesitate, not for a second. I'd choose you."

Sam Scott's Tavern, on the corner of Pine and Logan, was well known as a cops' hangout. At this hour of the morning, it was usually empty. So there were only the thin redheaded barman standing behind his brass-topped counter and two figures on stools in front of it. Saul was slightly hunched, as usual. But Lauren was slumped the whole way down, almost like she'd fallen asleep.

It wasn't that. All three faces swung around when I walked in. Her head came up a few inches. I could see her features were as white as a sheet, her eyes shining like glass. But then they tipped away from me again.

The lighting in the place was turned low. Shadows swallowed half of it up. The air smelled faintly of stale booze and age-dried woodwork. A long row of bottles glinted behind the counter, and the brass on the beer taps had a ruddy sheen. There was an engraved mirror back there too. It was six feet long and had a gilded frame, and was probably quite valuable.

On the back wall were photographs of cops who'd died the past few decades, Davy Quinn right in there among them. Below each of them was a pewter tankard, suspended from a hook. Cops have weird traditions, and those in the Landing are no exception. Even though you'd bought it, you were still a drinking buddy to their minds. That was what the tankards represented. Guys even poured a little liquor into them from time to time.

Saul seemed exhausted, and had a mug of coffee in front of him. But Lauren had a shot glass in her grasp, and a bottle of bourbon propped in front of her, half empty. I could see, even from this distance, that the hand holding the glass was shaking.

Saul came across and quietly explained what had been going down. And I was thunderstruck.

"You're sure it was Hanlon?"

"It recognized our friend here. So I'd say yes."

Lauren Brennan didn't even seem to notice we were talking about her. She was finishing off the rest of her drink, then reaching for the bottle again, the barman watching her unhappily.

I told Saul about the doctor's suspicions regarding the Tollburn family.

"A magical device?" His eyes got wider. "Couldn't he be more specific?"

"Afraid not. But if Hanlon's gotten hold of it, we're in a big, fat mess."

But we'd been in that place before. The main thing was to hold our nerve, and both of us knew that.

Except that Lauren didn't understand. And you could scarcely blame her. When she poured herself another shot, half the whisky missed the glass. The barman went to get a cloth.

It had to be terrifying for her. Those who had been born here—we had grown up our whole lives with strangeness. Fact was, we'd known nothing else. I'd never claim that it felt normal—human beings aren't wired that way. But they can adapt to most circumstances, which was precisely what we'd done.

But what did it have to be like for her, everything she'd ever known being turned completely upside down? When I walked across to her, she stared at me like I was some kind of creature from an old movie. One from outer space, perhaps. I reached out, but she only flinched away. And I should have been expecting that. So I took it in my stride and shoved my hands into my pockets, where she didn't have to worry about them anymore.

And told her, "Sorry you had to find out this way."

She shivered. Took a swig from her glass and almost choked. Her eyes went damper.

"'This way'?" Her voice was much lower and hoarser than it had been. "As opposed to what other way? Crazy is crazy, any way you look at it."

And wasn't that a fact?

"It must be pretty hard, taking it all in at once like this."

"Hard?" she echoed.

Her hand gave a sudden twitch, slopping a bit more of the liquor. The barman left it alone this time. He had a thin red moustache and olive eyes, and was peering at her anxiously.

"Yeah," she went on. "I'd say a corpse walking toward you with its chest cut open is a pretty awkward situation. What next, fire-breathing dragons? Got any vampires wandering around?"

Well, we'd never had any actual vampires. Saul had joined me, standing quietly by my side.

The woman wiped a hand across her pale, wet features, trying to rearrange her thoughts.

"You know what really gets to me? Saul told me this has been going on for—what?—more than three hundred years? Are all you people nuts? Why don't you just get out?"

"He didn't tell you about Regan's Curse?"

Her jaw dropped.

"There's a curse as well? Well, naturally there is! How could there possibly not be?"

So I explained it to her. Lauren looked less drained and far more nervous by the time that I was done.

"That means . . . I'm trapped here?"

"No way," I assured her. "It's only people who were born here. You can get out any time you like."

Which I half wished she would, despite the fact I'd come to like her. We were wasting time here, when we should have been out looking for Hanlon. I asked Saul what he was planning to do in that regard.

"I've spoken to Judge Levin," he assured me. "He's alerting all the major adepts. Maybe they can figure out some way of finding him."

Perhaps the Little Girl could help as well. It was an avenue I'd used before.

"Other than that," Saul was telling me, "the only thing that we can really do is wait for him to show up again."

Which was a dismal prospect, since it might involve more people getting hurt. But I couldn't see any other way to take it. My focus went back to Lauren.

And I was freshly surprised, because she seemed to have quieted down a bit. She'd been listening to every word we'd said. A crease had formed across the bridge of her nose, and her gaze was more perceptive than it had been.

She seemed to be coming around to the realities of her new situation. I reminded myself how tough and determined she had struck me from the very first. This still had to be genuinely hard for her. But she seemed to be made of sterner stuff than most folk.

"If you want out," I offered, "I can drive you back to my place and collect your things."

But a flinty look had come over her bright blue gaze. And when she gave her head a shake, there was nothing spasmodic about it.

"No," she murmured quietly.

The word fit uncomfortably between her lips, but she pushed it out anyway. She seemed to have arrived at a decision.

"Nothing's really changed," she told me. "I came here after Hanlon. And he's still the same psychotic asshole, whatever he looks like now. Still out there, hurting people. If you're going to stop him, count me in."

"You're quite sure about that?" I asked.

She looked away for a few seconds, then stared at me and nodded.

"Okay then," I smiled. "Welcome on board. In which case, we go to Plan B."

"Which is?"

I could see that she was wobbling slightly on her stool.

"We get several pints of coffee down you, pronto." I turned to the barman. "Hot and strong, and keep it coming."

Watching her down the first mug, I saw a flush returning to her cheeks. She was going to see this through, no matter what. She'd been so scared and confused a few minutes back, but had the strength of will to fight against it. I was reminded of a quote—Eleanor Roosevelt—about standing up and facing down our worst and deepest fears.

Hobart's cell phone began ringing in his pocket, and he snatched it out.

"What's that? Where?" It sounded like a dispatcher on the other end. "Jesus Christ, we're on our way."

CHAPTER 17

Treated like a criminal! By an outsider, no less! In front of her own friends! In her own town! In front of Ross!

Cassie had been bristling like a porcupine all morning, ever since she'd got back from Maynard Street. She was in such a foul mood, in fact, that Cleveland—her big tabby cat—had been avoiding her completely, scampering away whenever she got close. And the state of her place didn't cheer her up any. She didn't usually even notice it, but had now become self-conscious. It was clean enough. But not exactly tidy, to understate the case. She had a tendency to leave things wherever was easiest. The furniture was all cheap looking, and the whole apartment had needed redecorating a long time back. She knew that. Except normally, it was of scant interest to her.

Not today. She felt vulnerable and on edge today, and everything seemed wrong. The only things that—even remotely—calmed her down were the framed photographs of her three children, which filled every spare corner of her living room.

Kevin. Angel. Little Cassie. God, she missed them so much. Captured on film, and frozen in the moment, their smiles were bright and unafraid. Their faces glowed with happiness. They'd no idea, back then, what fate had in store for them. No one did, when she thought about it. Fate just hit you from behind, when you weren't even looking.

Her apartment made up one half of the wide, single-story building that she occupied. Out front was the diner that she had run for the past eight years. It was still the way it had been, but abandoned, with its front door padlocked. Had been that way ever since her kids had disappeared.

"You be careful with that thing."

She could still recall, with perfectly clarity, the day the bum that she'd been living with—not the children's father—had brought home a talisman with a black stone at the center of it. He'd stolen it, more likely than not. And there he'd sat, slumped on the couch, fiddling with it while the kids played around him.

"Don't let the little ones touch it," she'd admonished him.

Then she'd had to go out front again. The diner was busy that late in the morning. Two weeks before Christmas, and there were customers waiting. The place felt really warm on a day like this, the windows steamed up, and she'd been joking with her regulars about how they'd become that way.

"All the heavy breathing I do every time I see you, handsome."

Except a bare few minutes later, in the middle of pouring someone coffee, a prickling instinct had overtaken her. She'd rushed back in. Tom Larson and her three kids had vanished into the ether. Magic had taken them away from her.

The emptiness of the place hung around her, the quietness so profound that, when she stopped still, she could almost hear it like a subcutaneous murmur. Like the rushing of some invisible tide. There were days she felt as if she were drowning in a vast ocean of silence. There were even days she wished it would all stop, for good.

What was she, without her family? She had been in that position once before, back when she was seventeen and her parents both died in a road accident. She'd run wild for a few years, falling in with a bad crowd, a motorcycle gang. And had done a lot of crazy things back then. Helped rob stores and burgle houses. Had got in a load of fights. But she had done all that to fit in with the rest and stop herself from feeling lost and helpless. Once she'd started her own business, and her kids had come along . . . ?

These days, she still had a sense of purpose. And real friends, which those guys in the gang had never been. There was a town to save. And there was always Ross to count on. They were more than merely friends—there was a real connection between them. Not amorous, but a definite spark. Except, the way he'd looked at this new woman . . .

The phone next to the couch started ringing. She was so confused, Cassie just stared at it for a few seconds. Then she pulled herself together, leant across and snatched up the receiver.

"Cassie!"

The voice was extremely strained and high-pitched, but she recognized it all the same. It was Ginny Graves, one of her small coterie of girlfriends. Their kids had gone to the same school, and they'd been close for several years. Ginny lived on the edge of East Meadow, where it gave way to the rather more respectable neighborhood of Pilgrim's Plot. Normally, she was soft-spoken. But now, she was yelling like she had the devil on her tail.

Cassie stiffened, coming around quickly.

"Gin? What's going on?"

"It's Karl!" Ginny shrieked down the line at her.

That was her mild-mannered and rather boring spouse.

"I don't know what happened, but he's gone berserk! He came at us with a kitchen knife!"

"Us" meant Gin and her two daughters. Cass froze with shock, her grip around the phone tightening.

"Where are you now?"

"We're locked in the bathroom! I'm on my cell! Karl went crazy for a while, trying to hack his way in! But he's gone away! I think he's gone for something bigger than the knife! And there's something really weird with his eyes!"

Which meant what, exactly?

The woman let out several sobs. And then she choked those down and gasped.

"I can hear him again! He's coming back!"

Cassie's heart was thumping, and her instincts were pulling her toward the door. But she'd been in violent places loads of times before. She knew the first thing that she had do was to inject some common sense into the situation.

"Ginny, listen to me carefully. Hang up right now, and then call the police. Promise me you'll do that?"

She heard a loud thud in the background. And it did sound like an ax on wood. Gin let out a broken gurgle. Both her daughters started wailing, and the sound of that near broke Cassie's heart.

"Please, Cassie! Please get over here!"

"I'm on my way! But call the cops!"

And she'd make sure she called them too.

The blocks went by, no more than streaks. She skidded up outside the Graves house. Cass leapt off her Harley without bothering to kick the stanchion into place. The bike crashed down behind her as she began to run across the front yard. But to hell with that. Her boots kicked up large flecks of mud. There were poppies of all colors in neat rows around her.

The front door was shut. There wasn't time to check around the back. She'd normally never even think of using guns with any kids around. But they were upstairs, weren't they? Gin had said so. This was a two-story house, with only one bathroom. She had been here many times.

Without even slowing down, she yanked both of her Glocks from their holsters and fired two rounds into the lock.

Reaching the porch, she drove the sole of her boot, hard, into the door. It burst open easily. She got a brief impression of pastel-painted walls, vases full of dried flowers. Several of them overturned. But there was no sign of any blood, thank God.

Then she heard the thudding from above. A heavy blade cutting into wood again. And after that she was pounding up.

She drew to an uneasy halt, once she'd reached the upstairs landing. Karl Graves—in his usual blue plaid shirt and faded jeans—was standing with his back to her at the far end of the hallway. The man was hard at work. He had already carved a ragged hole the size of a pumpkin in the bathroom door, and was swinging back the ax again.

Cass immediately slipped the pistol in her left hand back into its holster. She felt rather shaky, by this juncture. This was not the kind of situation that she usually had to deal with.

Whatever was wrong with him, this was still Ginny's husband. So this wasn't a matter she could settle with a fatal shot.

"Karl?"

He stopped what he was doing, and then turned around. Cassie twitched when she saw what had happened to his eyes. There was no color left in them. They were pale gray from lid to lid, iris and pupil no longer visible. But the man apparently hadn't gone blind. So this was something supernatural.

He looked perfectly normal otherwise, his usual short and rather tubby self. The same dumpy features and untidy brown moustache. Except the muscles in his face were very slack, the way that people looked when they were sleeping. Like he was no longer in control of them.

In which case, this was not his fault. She held out her free hand with the palm spread wide, indicating it was best that he stayed where he was.

"Why don't you just stop this, huh? You're frightening your kids."

Their shrieks could still be heard from behind the ruined woodwork. And a second later, Ginny yelled out, "Cassie?"

But Cass ignored that, concentrating on the man in front of her.

He seemed to be doing the same. Studying her evenly. Trying to size her up. He didn't look like he even remembered who she was, which also indicated there was someone else in there. His shoulders were heaving from his earlier exertions.

Finally, the slackness left his mouth. He smiled, and then he spoke to her.

"Oh my, you look like really special fun."

And it was Karl's voice, sure. But not quite the same. The lazy drawl was mostly gone. There was sharper enunciation. Who was this really? Cassie felt her neck prickling when she wondered that. But she knew it was important, now, to stand her ground.

One of the lightbulbs up here had been smashed. The hall was darker than it should have been. Karl took a step in her direction.

"I don't want to hurt you!" she yelled.

His smile grew broader.

"You can always try."

And then he threw caution to the wind and lurched at her, coming down the hallway as fast as his legs could carry him. Cassie tried to think straight. She could see no other choice. She didn't want to kill the man. But wounding him was another matter.

So she tilted the Glock at an angle, and pumped a round into Karl's shoulder. She tried to avoid the bone and simply leave him with a flesh wound. It would hurt like hell, but with luck it would stop him.

She saw the shirt rip. Saw the flesh beneath it tear. A bullet hole and a spatter of blood appeared on the wall behind him.

But he did not slow down.

"Can't hurt a shadow!" he roared as he closed in on her.

What?

She was still holding the gun out, struggling to think what to do, when he swung the flat edge of the ax blade at it. Pain blazed through her hand. The Glock flew from her grasp. She stumbled back and hit a banister. Her knuckles were stinging like hell. But why wasn't he feeling any pain, from the slug she had put into him?

She'd never seen Karl move so quickly. He was all over her before she could recover, slamming into her. She almost went over the railing but tensed her legs, stopping that in time. They swung around, and her back hit another wall. Gripping the handle with both hands, the man shoved the ax against her throat and pushed hard, trying to throttle her.

Cassie's reaction was pretty well instinctive. She brought her knee up into his groin.

Although—exactly like the bullet wound—Karl did not react in the slightest.

"Oh, fun-fun-fun," the man was muttering between clenched jaws.

Who was this? Someone crazy, and strong too. She put both palms against his chest and tried to shove him off. Could scarcely budge him. The contours of his body shifted slightly, but his feet would not go back. His pressure on the haft grew even more intense. It was cutting off her windpipe, and she felt her head begin to pound.

Then a few words spoken long ago came rushing back to her.

"That's it, Cassie. Use my own strength against me."

That had been her father, Gus. In his off hours, he'd taught her how to defend herself. How to shoot, and a few judo tricks he knew.

So she let Karl continue bearing down on her. And then swung her own weight completely to the left.

And it worked. He abruptly went crashing past her, banging his forehead on the wall. Although it didn't seem to hurt him any more than had the other stuff.

Cassie snatched at the ax and caught hold of it below the metal blade. Karl's face swung at her again.

"Let go, you stupid woman!"

But that was the last thing she was about to do. She tried to wrench the thing out of his grasp. Fresh beads of perspiration sprang up on her brow, and she felt her face go red with the effort. She could not budge the ax in her direction, not even a little bit. And the strangest thing was, for his part, Karl barely seemed to be making any effort.

She kicked at him again, his shins this time. The only thing that happened was . . . his misty gaze seemed to laugh at her.

"Oh, but you play nasty, don't you, little girl?"

His gray eyes appeared to gleam.

"You really want this thing? Well, have it!"

He suddenly let the ax go, with Cassie still pulling at it as hard as she could. And that got the drop on her, taking her completely by surprise. Its metal head shot at her, catching her a glancing blow on the right temple. She let go of the thing, brilliant lights flashing in her head.

She tried to right herself. But the blow had been much harder than she'd thought. Her vision swirled, and she began to lose her footing.

Karl was moving in on her again.

That was when she heard a siren pulling up outside, and tires screeching. The cops had finally arrived.

Footsteps were hurrying this way. But would they be in time?

CHAPTER 18

I had to hand it to him—when it came to policing this town, Saul was the last word in experienced preplanning. He knew the Landing back to front. Understood the kinds of curves this place could throw you. And so—following on from the strange turns the business with Anderson had taken—he had ordered his people to get in touch with him immediately if there was another instance of domestic violence. Which was what they'd done. They'd called him right away.

His vehicle, mine, and a patrol car pulled up almost simultaneously outside the house on Clore Crescent. I could see immediately the front door had been busted open. But I wasn't sure what sense that made, until I spotted Cass's overturned Harley.

I'd been thinking about her only recently. But what in God's name was she doing here?

We ran for the porch. I managed to outstrip them, and reached it first, my weapon drawn. The moment that I stepped in, I could hear that there was shouting coming from above.

"Leave her be, Karl! She's our friend!" rang out a woman's voice I didn't recognize.

And then I heard one that I did.

"Get back inside, Ginny! Please!"

She sounded like she was under a lot of pressure. And

we've always looked out for each other. So I started heading up, taking the stairs three at a time.

"I'm not letting you exchange your life for mine! He's my husband!"

"No!" Cassie was yelling. "He's possessed! It's not him!"

I finally came to a halt, tilting my gun backward slightly, unsure what to do with it. This was a bewildering scene. I felt my insides tighten.

At the far end of the corridor, a brown-haired woman was standing in an open doorway. There was a full-length mirror on the wall back there, and so it had to be a bathroom. I thought I'd seen her several times before, back when Cassie's Diner had been open. The blood had drained from her face, and her narrow frame was shaking. But she looked defiant all the same. The screams of children were emerging from inside the bathroom, and that made my gut tense up even worse.

Cass was hunkered on the floor midway to me, with her back pressed against a wall. One of her Glocks was lying on the light brown carpet. Why wasn't it in her hand?

There was a bruise emerging on her temple. Otherwise, she looked okay. Except . . . not for too much longer.

A short man in a plaid shirt was standing over her, an ax drawn back across his shoulder. I immediately took aim.

Cass noticed me and held an arm out.

"No! It's not his fault!"

The others had come up the stairs behind me. Not only Saul. There was Hugh Williams again. A rookie called Colin Trent. And even Lauren, who must have ridden here in Hobart's car. She'd sobered up extremely quickly. They all aimed their weapons too.

The man turned his face to us. Took in the fact that there were five guns pointing at him, and then snorted.

Blood was oozing thickly from his shoulder, from a bullet wound. So he had no right to look that smug. His eyes were the same shade as a misty morning in the fall, a gray so bottomless it seemed to go on forever. Saul had already described this, but it was the first time that I'd seen it. And it was slightly difficult to hold my aim steady under such a penetrating gaze.

"Go ahead boys, fire away," he laughed. "Do your worst. You'll only hurt poor Karl."

Then he looked directly to my left.

"Did I say 'boys'? Excuse me—that was not exactly PC, was it? Why, hello again, Lieutenant Brennan."

I glanced quickly around at Lauren. Her face looked like it had been fashioned out of clay. Her upper lip had gone wet, her blue eyes squinting slightly. She was reliving the nightmare from the mortuary, I knew. And it had to be torture for her, going through the same thing twice in a few hours.

But she didn't back off. She stayed right where she was, trying to do her job the best way she knew how.

My attention went back to Hanlon, or at least the body he had occupied.

"The Old Ones have truly smiled on me," the figure with the ax was telling us. "I've finally got what I wanted."

"And what's that, Cornelius?" I asked.

"Invulnerability, until the End of Days, and then beyond them. You see, the Shadow Man can't be hurt anymore. But he can still hurt you!"

The muscles in his arms bunched. The ax head flashed when he did that.

And then he brought it swinging down on Cass.

I suppose I fired without thinking very much. Except that I was shooting at wood rather than the man

The ax handle blew apart. The head went flying off, embedding itself in the wall about a yard above Cassie's head.

She was back on her feet in a flash. She shoved the guy away from her, as hard as she could, then raised her knee and drove a boot heel into his solar plexus. At which point, he should have doubled up. But he didn't even seem to feel it. His grip tightened on the broken handle, and he slammed it into her chin. Cass went flying back again.

And then he did something that astonished and appalled me. The man simply turned his back on us, as if we were not even there. And began advancing on the woman in the doorway.

She shrank back inside. But in her panic, she'd forgotten to close the door.

I pocketed my gun, and started running. Threw myself on the man's back. It should have been easy to bring him down—he was stocky, but much shorter than me. But the experience turned out to be like riding one of those rodeo machines. He bucked savagely, swinging me around like I weighed nothing.

Saul came in behind me, adding his considerable bulk to the fray. He got his arms around the fellow's neck and then bore down with every ounce of his might, trying to wrestle the guy to the floor. The other three had got hold of his legs, trying to yank them out from under him.

He still wouldn't go down, at first. Like we were running on steam, and he was nuclear powered.

Cassie jumped onto his back behind me. The man struggled a few more seconds, teetering under our weight, then finally collapsed. We grabbed every limb and joint we could, and pinned him down.

He leered at us with contempt. His eyes were genuinely startling this close up.

"Okay, you've got me," he snarled. "But who—Cornelius Hanlon, or Karl Graves? And what if I decide to stay in here?"

I could see it from his face in the weak light. He knew what our dilemma was, and was reveling in it.

"What would you do then, huh? Lock poor Karl away for life?"

I was acutely aware that the guy's family was listening to this. But I'm afraid that seemed to be the plan, at least for the time being. Saul already had his cuffs out. And with the uniformed guys' help, was getting the man turned facedown with his arms twisted behind his back. It was an effort, but the lieutenant managed to snap the first bracelet on.

Hanlon burst out laughing.

"Oh good heavens! You're arresting the wrong man— can't you see that?"

Tears of mirth began spilling down his cheeks. That infuriated me—I could hear one of his daughters crying. What ground at me worst was the knowledge that the man was absolutely right. But I couldn't see any other way to go with this.

Which was when Lauren reached in past me. She still had her Walther out. To my surprise, she jammed it into the man's face. His eyes went very narrow when she did that.

My God, was she going to . . . ? I started to reach for her, but then had second thoughts. She looked levelheaded, in control. So I decided it was best to trust her for the moment.

"I know you, Cornelius," she snapped.

To emphasize her point, she shoved the muzzle of the gun firmly against his right cheek, so that the flesh puckered around it.

"You like to play your little games, don't you? But you can't do that in jail. You're seriously going to languish behind bars, simply to spite us? What sense does that make? Let this guy go."

"What if I killed him first?" he grunted. "I could make him swallow his own tongue."

Lauren's tone grew even frostier. "Doesn't work. I know first aid."

That made him blink with confusion. I think I saw, in that instant, how detached from reality Hanlon was.

"You're in a no-win situation here, " Lauren insisted. "Better to make yourself scarce, don't you think?"

I knew how determined she was to catch the man. But this wasn't the time for it, and she had the common sense to see that.

He became very still, his body going slack. And you could almost hear his crazed mind ticking over.

Then, without another word, his mouth stretched open wide. And pale gray vapor came rushing out of it. The color started bleeding from Karl's eyes at the same time, his normal brown shade coming back.

The cloud billowed up against the ceiling, making us duck. Then it went churning down the stairwell to the front door of the house, disappearing through it.

Other shapes were moving toward us, next instant. The woman of the house and her young daughters, who were practically hysterical with fright. They threw themselves on their knees beside Karl, their hands going to his face. I backed away, and everyone else took my lead on that.

He was in a good deal of pain now, the wound in his shoulder finally making itself known. He squirmed and moaned. I didn't enjoy watching that.

"What's happening?" he yelled.

Then he jerked alarmedly at his tethered wrists, noticing the cuffs for the first time. So he obviously remembered nothing.

Saul undid them and then we backed off another couple of yards, giving these folks some privacy. I think it was Hugh Williams who called an ambulance.

I was deflating with relief, like everyone around me. Cass was rubbing at her chin, but seemed otherwise fine. Looking across at Lauren, I could see that she was shaking and perspiring. But she'd done good, and I told her that.

"So where do we go from here?" she asked.

Well, this whole thing had been down to magic, hadn't it? And when it came to that particular subject, there were plenty of experts that we could consult.

It was time to go back to Sycamore Hill.

CHAPTER 19

Samuel Howard Aldous Levin—Judge Levin to most people in town—walked up to Lauren, adjusted his rimless spectacles, and then studied her as if she were an exceptionally fine and fragile statue made of crystal.

He was a short man, slightly built. But perfectly turned out, as always. A tailored dark brown suit was draped immaculately around his narrow frame. His shirt was a much lighter shade of the same color, as was his tie. Gold cufflinks gleamed at his wrists. His shoes were handmade and looked brand new, but then they always did.

Me and Saul had both been here before. But Cass had never been inside his house. We were in his study, which was tucked under the gables of his tall, picturesque residence. And it was not the kind of environment she was used to. She kept gazing around like she'd wound up on a different world.

This was nothing like her own home. Everything was very neat and orderly, from the huge four-panel cherrywood desk, which had only his big leather diary on it, to the collection of scrimshaw in the cabinets along the walls. The furniture was American Classic. Hers was chain store cruddy, and she knew it, and it showed.

"Remarkable," the short man breathed. He started reaching gently for our new visitor's face, but realized that was not appropriate. His hand withdrew. "The first outsider that I've ever seen who isn't bent on harming us. Precisely the opposite, in fact."

Lauren stared back at him blankly, unsure how to react to this much scrutiny. But that didn't faze the judge. He turned to the rest of us with a quiet smile on his features.

"Who knows? Things here in the Landing might be looking up."

Except it didn't feel in the least bit like that, not to the rest of the people standing here. He hadn't been through what we had. Hobart looked uneasy. As for myself, I made a point of clearing my throat loudly.

"Ah, yes," the judge took note. "This Hanlon."

Who was far more the type of visitor that we were used to. Levin went back behind his desk and sat down in the big green leather swivel chair. Light was coming in weakly through his windows, since he had the maroon drapes closed most of the way. Adepts always prefer the shadows. But at least he'd switched his desk lamp on.

"I've consulted with the others. And the problem we keep running up against is this. If Lucas had some kind of device that turned him into this"—he seemed to be struggling with the concept—"this . . . living vapor, then he managed to keep it a secret completely. We never had the first inkling that it existed."

He glanced at me, sharpness in his gaze.

"You say Lehman Willets was aware of it?"

"He sensed something. He wasn't exactly sure what."

"Which is a good deal more than we can claim. I do so wish," the judge mused, "that the doctor would rejoin our community. He'd be such an asset."

I wasn't sure how most people in town would take to that. You try to persuade him, I thought. But I didn't say it.

"Anyway," the judge continued briskly, "what's done is done. You say, when Hanlon's in that form, he can take over other people's minds?"

I thought about Karl Graves, the way that he'd not even known what he'd been doing. But there was more to it than merely that. When it came to Stephen Anderson, there had been no mind to take over. The second time he'd brandished a knife, the guy had been dead.

Hanlon had become a puppet master on a grand scale. I explained that.

"It makes me shudder to think about it," Levin murmured. "But the salient fact is this. We weren't able to detect this device before, when Lucas owned it. And now that it's in the hands of this interloper, little has really changed. We've already tried Locating Spells, Revealing Spells, and nothing works."

Kurt van Friesling had a black stone compass with a golden needle that detected supernatural forces. I suggested that.

"Already attempted." Levin pulled a face. "It was no use. Whatever it was that Lucas owned, it seems to contain a power way beyond the reach of our own."

And I didn't like the sound of that even a tiny little bit. Magic might cause genuine problems in the Landing. And the major adepts were a bunch that I was always wary of. But they were our main line of defense against serious attacks. If they were at a loss, where did that leave the rest of us?

"If only we could find out what it was," the judge pondered, tenting his fingertips under his chin.

"His granddaughter certainly knows," put in Hobart.

"Little Milly?"

"Not so little any more. And she couldn't wait to get her hands on the thing."

We told him about the angry scene she'd made last night, in every distasteful detail.

"I must say I'm shocked," he blurted. "And she wouldn't tell you what she was looking for?"

"She maintained her right to silence."

The judge peered at him. "You arrested her?"

At which point, Saul glanced across at me annoyedly. "Not yet."

"But you'd like to?" Levin asked him. "Haul her down to the station house? Let her sweat under some nice bright lights?"

We both knew the man's reverence for due process and

the Constitution. It almost amounted to a religious belief. And Saul had been expecting this, but wasn't in the mood for backing down.

"Maybe. It's an option."

The judge favored him with a tight, humorless grin.

"I hope you're not turning into a cruel and unusual man, Lieutenant."

Hobart looked completely unbothered. And I stood firmly by his shoulder, trying to back my old boss up. Levin relaxed his fingers and then laid them on his desk.

"There've been rumors about her, now I come to think of it. That she left Todd Vernon in a pretty fragile state. And the family did pay her off extremely handsomely. They don't usually dig so deep into their coffers."

Had they done that because they'd been very anxious to get rid of her? What Willets had said came back to me, about that genuinely twisted darkness in her soul.

"But I can't imagine why," Levin murmured, still trying to think things through and taking his sweet time about it. "Her parents were charming people. And her grandpa, of course, was an exceptional man."

Exceptional in what way? I couldn't help but wonder. How charming a habit was it to go sneaking around at night and rummaging through other people's minds? If Millicent Tollburn was a twisted sister, it might be something in her background, although I wasn't sure quite what.

"We're going to need a warrant to search her place, at least," Saul was pointing out, trying to take command of the situation and failing.

"I'm afraid that you won't get it," Levin told him.

Saul frowned, mystified. "Why not?"

The judge didn't like his tone, apparently, because I could see his pale eyes flash behind his glasses. And his shadow, on the wall behind him, seemed to actually swell, becoming taller and more threatening. It reminded me how powerful he could be, in spite of his small stature. I'd watched him turn himself into a massive eagle once.

But then he got a handle on himself again, and his shadow— like some strange reflection of his temper—settled down.

"We know that she doesn't have the device, man. Hanlon does. You told me so yourself. There's no clear connection between Millicent and anything that's happened, so how can you show me probable cause?"

A little of the air went out of my lungs. I should have been prepared for this turn of events, and so should Saul. You see, the judge worked to a very simple principle. In a town where anything was possible, you had two choices. You either lived in total chaos, or you stuck intently to the rules.

I could see his point, even though it was damned frustrating sometimes. But I also knew that there was something else involved. This was the Sycamore Hill set closing ranks, the way they always did. The town's elite looking after their own. They did it almost instinctively. And the judge, for all that he liked to present himself as a prudent and impartial man, was really no exception. It's just the way that they are brought up, I suppose.

Saul looked exasperated, working his jaw angrily. His eyes had become hot. I thought it best to butt in, before he said something he regretted.

"But Millicent is connected to Raine," I pointed out. "She visited him right after Lucas's murder. Doesn't that point to a conspiracy?"

"Woodard Raine is quite beyond my remit," Levin came straight back at me.

Which was another standard mindset up here on the Hill. The Master of the Manor was so crazed and unpredictable, they did their level best to ignore him when they could. They certainly would not attempt to involve him in any kind of legal process. Once again, they had a point. I tried to imagine Woody in a witness box, and couldn't.

The judge gazed around at us, seeing nothing that appeared to impress him. Lauren seemed to sympathize with Saul completely, but was out of her depth and holding her tongue. And Cassie looked like she was wishing she had not come with us.

Satisfied that he was fully on top of the matter, Levin tipped back in his chair.

"Bring me some real evidence, people. Bring me hard

facts, something I can grasp. Before I decide what to do, I have to understand where this is heading. And—as of this moment—do any of you have the first idea?"

And he really did have the upper hand here. Because none of us replied.

We gathered quietly outside, on the very neat front lawn. This was probably the most beautiful house in the whole Landing, wood-built and three stories tall. It had a conical turret in the roof. The weather vane up there was in a classic cockerel design. There were numerous eaves and gables, and the roofing tiles were scallop-shaped. Flower baskets hung around each window. In the borders, huge rosebushes grew, and there was honeysuckle draped around the porch.

Beyond its outline, the sky was a pale blue, a dusting of white clouds across it. Down below, the town was trundling gently toward noon like a big old machine with several thousand moving parts. Traffic wandered in and out of Union Square. And I could see that a few youngsters were flying kites off in Crealley Street Park.

You would have thought it was a normal day, except for the tension between us.

"Something he can grasp?" Saul repeated angrily, taking a few heavy steps across the turf. "Has he ever tried grabbing hold of smoke?"

But the fact was, we had very little choice. If magic couldn't pin down Hanlon, and the law couldn't be used against dear Millicent, then regular procedure was the only course we had. We'd simply have to do our normal jobs, and pray that something turned up. Griping wouldn't help.

"You need to put your guys on alert for anything unusual," I told him.

"Define that, in this town?"

Which was a point, but I just turned to Cassie. "You too. You know what to look for."

She gave me a nod.

"And me?" inquired Lauren.

"Saul?" I suggested, looking back at him. "Okay with you?"

He seemed to trust her fully, by this time. "I'd be glad of the company."

"And yourself?" Cass asked me.

"I thought that I might stake out Millicent's place for a while."

She looked surprised at that, her dark eyes widening sharply.

"Trying to catch her up to something? Or do you think that Hanlon's going to show up there?"

The truth was, I'd been mulling it over ever since this whole thing had started. Why, straight after the murder, had Ms. Tollburn gone to Woodard Raine? The man wasn't exactly known for giving good, level-headed advice. So what had she wanted from him?

There was one explanation I could think of. One small fact that I had dredged out of my past. And as to Cassie's question . . . ?

It might prove to be the case that Hanlon had no option but to go there. He may have made himself extremely powerful.

But there were other kinds of strength in this town, some of them even more bizarre than the type that he'd acquired.

CHAPTER 20

I took a back route to Millwood House, avoiding Plymouth Drive, which I'd easily be spotted from. And wound up parked in the uncultivated space between a couple of smaller residences, behind a narrow row of trees across the main road from the mansion. I could see the top edge of the flat, brick-bordered roof through the branches. Otherwise, it was just high, spiked walls, and a gate woven into iron curlicues as thick as your wrist. Something could be going on in there, and I'd be none the wiser. But I suspected nothing magical was going to happen yet.

One of the most important things to understand about witchcraft is that it works much better in the dark. Nighttime is the natural element for that stuff. So if anything was going to happen, it would most probably be at dusk or beyond.

The days were growing shorter by this time of year, but it was still a good long wait. What was I doing up here so early, then? I wanted to get a feel for the place Millicent lived in. People's homes tell you a lot about them. And I'd never examined this particular one.

A stiff, cool breeze had sprung up. And it made the branches around me rattle, worrying at my hair as I got out. The edges of the leaves were already turning yellow. We'd be in the fall before too much longer. The sun was still visible, and bright enough, although it appeared very slightly distant. A flotilla of small clouds had started drifting across.

I made my way between the trees, and then slipped quickly over Plymouth Drive. And wound up underneath the front wall. There was nothing to be seen from where I was, so I made my way to the gate itself. It wasn't padlocked. I took note of that. Then I peered through, trying to keep out of sight.

The house was rather plain-looking, in spite of its size. The windows were leaded, like at her grandfather's place. Matching cages, was the thought that came to mind. There were a few trellises on the front wall, creepers hanging from them—their summer blooms had mostly dropped away. The portico had Grecian columns, just like Gaspar Vernon's. And there was an iron weather vane on the roof as well, this one in the shape of a crow. I could hear it creaking faintly.

The drapes had to be silk, since they had that kind of sheen in the clear light. But there was no movement at any of the windows. She had to be home—her car was parked outside. Except that there was no way to tell what she was doing.

So far as I knew, she had no servants. She lived in the place alone. Kept it clean by magic, doubtless. Not the first time I'd encountered that.

I doubled back, heading for the northward corner of the wall, then went around. The ground began to slope unevenly from that point onward. Where it dipped, it was still boggy from the previous night's rain. So I did my best to avoid those spots.

I'd never even been back here. Because of the surrounding trees, you couldn't see it from the road. The wall descended, in graduated stages, almost half the way down Sycamore Hill's gradient. It had those iron spikes at the top the whole distance along. There were no other entranceways that I could make out. No slightest interruption to the high brick-work. God, the place was like a fortress.

Most folk on the Hill valued their privacy. But this was something more than that. This was somebody who pre-ferred—needed?—to shut the world out completely, keep-ing it at a very far remove.

There wasn't any point that I could see in walking the whole way down, so I halted, gazing at the scene below me. I could make out the commercial district from here, its Victorian smokestack like an exclamation mark. Closer up, the entire town kept moving languidly. The flags on top of the Town Hall were being lifted stoutly by the breeze, and I could even see part of the massive, ornate clock above the entranceway.

When I turned around and looked back, I got further glimpses of Millwood House. It was still largely feature-less, as plain as a length of bone. The home of someone who couldn't decide exactly what she wanted out of life. How much, I wondered again, had her grandfather to do with that? What kind of childhood had she had? Lucas had been a respected figure in this town for decades, sure. But me . . . I simply wasn't certain.

I remembered what Cass had said to me a while back. "You always were a good cop. But these days? There's this tight focus, this clarity, to everything you do. You notice things that other people don't. You're attuned to everything that's going on around you."

And was that the case right now? I needed to have more to go on than just instinct.

I started heading back. And as I did that, the wind changed direction by a few degrees, bringing a new odor to me. That of stables. So she kept horses back there. That was some-thing else I hadn't known before. Some folks like animals because they are softhearted, I reflected. Others? Because they can't stand being around people.

When I finally got back to the car, my stomach had started rumbling. Nothing seemed to be happening at the moment. So I came to a quick decision and turned the Cadillac around, headed quickly back into town.

I got some takeout from a place I knew on Hawthorn Street, then drove back up and waited far more comfortably.

Don't remember falling into a doze. But I suppose I must have done.

No dreams or visions came this time. And when I awoke it was with a sharp jerk, wondering why I was sitting up. Then I remembered where I was, and peered wearily around me. The windows of my Caddy had steamed up slightly.

My surroundings had been drained of color. The sky had

turned a leaden gray. I glanced at my watch. Evening was approaching.

Staring at the distant woods beyond the edge of town, I could see a final shaft of golden sunlight cling to the horizon, and then shrink and vanish. The clouds went dark carmine. The shadows around me immediately grew deeper. I got out again, and walked through to the front edge of the tree line, although I didn't step out into view this time.

The stiff breeze was still blowing, making a low thrumming sound. Thin twigs lashed at me, driven by it. A raven landed on a higher branch, then noticed I was there and flapped away again.

It was colder than it had been. But I was used to this kind of vigil, so I simply buttoned up my coat and remained where I was.

A car went thrumming by. It was a big gold-colored Lexus. And I didn't know to whom it belonged. There is never much traffic up here. The long, winding drive leads nowhere really, save the Gothic mansion at the very top.

It's not only the major adepts who have made their homes up here. There are several important lawyers—although only important, I'd suppose, in provincial terms. People whose families own tracts of land in town, commercial blocks. Business folk of every variety. Nearly all of them practice magic to some extent. Most folk in the Landing dabble with it sometimes.

But the major adepts are a different prospect. They don't merely do magic. They live it. They were mostly born to it, and have it in their blood.

That included Millicent here. I'd do well to keep reminding myself of that.

I edged along until I could see through the iron gates again. No lights had come on in the house. Its windows were murkily reflective, and then deepened until they were rectangles of black. But that proved nothing. She could be around at the back of the place, where there was no risk of being overlooked. The weather vane up on the roof made another grating sound.

Lights were coming on in other houses around me. The

nearest was about eighty yards away. Coach lamps gleamed in a couple of porches. And I could make out the edges of a chandelier through the window of a stone-built place on Privet Close.

I glanced to my left again. Another shape was coming up the hill. The wind was blowing in the wrong direction, so I couldn't hear what was approaching. But I assumed it was another car. Then I saw it had no headlamps. It was hard to tell in the gathering dimness, but the shape seemed to be wrong as well.

As it drew closer, I took in the fact it had no proper outline. It was shifting constantly, amorphous. And it looked like a heavy pall of smoke, although the breeze was not affecting it. The thing was actually heading against the wind. I sank back a little further back into the trees. This was what Cornelius Hanlon had become. And if he noticed me?—I had no particular desire to wind up like Karl.

The vapor continued on a dead-straight course. It moved up to the front gate, slipped in through the twisted metalwork, then headed for the front door. I already had an idea what had brought it here.

It reached a keyhole, funneled in, and disappeared through that.

I waited until it was completely gone before making my move. Hurried across to the big iron gates and shoved at them. They did not budge, despite the fact there was no padlock, nor a bolt. I could only imagine they were being held in place by sorcery.

Climbing them wasn't any kind of prospect. The ironwork was too tortuously woven. Which left the wall.

I peered at the spikes on top. They were closely grouped in sets of three, and looked genuinely sharp at their tips. Not simply there for ornament, in other words. Like everything else about this place, they were designed to keep humanity out.

I speed-dialed Cass as I jogged back to my Caddy.

"Where are you?" I asked, as soon as she picked up.

"Turling Street."

Which was in Clayton, a short way southwest of here.

"Hanlon's shown up. I need you here."

Which got an approving "On my way." She sounded relieved to have something to do.

I knew how fast she was on her Harley. She'd be here in a bare couple of minutes. I went around to the trunk and got two objects out. One was the old thick blanket that I always keep back there. The other was a sturdy six-foot towrope.

I was recrossing the asphalt when a solitary headlamp appeared on the gradient below, then came hurtling toward me with breathtaking speed. Cass drew to a halt and killed the engine. And she did look energized, eager to get moving. Her dark eyes were gleaming, and the muscles of her bare arms bunched.

The truth is, she is pretty damned attractive. A whole string of men had fallen for her hard-nosed charms. I'd had moments of temptation myself, the last couple of years. But there was still the matter of my missing wife. My conscience wouldn't let me.

As usual, she was in tune with me from the very outset. Seemed to understand what I was thinking. She looked at the objects I was carrying, then glanced at the wall and nodded.

"I'm going first," she said, keeping pace with me as we hurried over.

"Like hell you are."

"You haven't been up against this thing yet. But I have."

"And you've got the lumps to prove it," I pointed out.

But this wasn't the time to stand around arguing. So we ended up doing as she'd asked.

The rope went up ahead of her. She got a loop of it around a set of spikes. Then dragged herself halfway up on one arm and, with the other, pushed the blanket over her until it rested at the very top. It wouldn't protect us completely, but reduced the risk of getting stuck.

Cass hauled herself the rest of the way up. She spent only a second finding her balance before jumping down the other side.

And I didn't like watching her disappear from sight like that. Not under these circumstances. So I followed her over, as quickly as I could.

CHAPTER 21

She was still in the drawing room at the rear of her house. Had been there almost the whole day. Had not eaten, nor drunk a drop, such was the level of her anticipation. She'd smoked a few cigarettes, but that was all. Their odor lingered.

As the last light fled, Millicent Tollburn went to the narrow glass and chrome desk at the back of the room, and picked up the object she had placed there. The Thieftaker. She returned to the darkened window, cupping the device between her palms. Its facets shifted very gently as she moved, making the softest humming. There was a faint rasping motion on her skin. The thing seemed more like a machine than a jewel.

Everything beyond the glass panes was reduced to a series of vague silhouettes. She could see thousands of small lights when she looked down at the town, but her gaze dropped from it. She was concentrating hard now. Woodard Raine had told her precisely what to do. She had memorized every action, every word, even the emphasis on certain syllables.

She bowed her head. And held the Thieftaker as high as she could.

Latin, he had told her. But no. This spell covered both the taker of the object, and the stolen thing in question. It would be better to address the wand in its own tongue, the way her grandfather always had.

In French, she decided. And then she began.

Thief, you are discovered.

"Voleur, vous êtes découvert."

The hundreds of tiny facets shifted a bit more. And a small surge of energy seemed to pulse out from them, rushing through her hands. Millicent was not wholly surprised. Her family's magic had always been mighty, and the sorcery of the Raines was notoriously strong. Combined, who knew what they might achieve? This was merely the start of it—of that much she was certain.

Thief, there is nowhere to hide.

"Voleur, il n'y a pas de lieu pour se cacher."

Return to me my property.

"Rendez à moi ce qui m'appartient."

Your fate? The gods can then decide.

"Votre destin? Les dieux puissent décider."

The shining, overlapping strands of the Thieftaker started to turn slowly, crisscrossing each other in patterns so intricate that she could not begin to make sense of them.

And it wasn't just a mild pressure against her palms, this time. Hold on any longer, she realized, and the miniscule facets would start to cut her. And so Millicent let go of it.

It didn't fall. Didn't drop so much as half an inch. It simply floated in the air, precisely where she'd left it, remaining aloft like a hummingbird and letting out a grating sound.

She was so beguiled she practically forgot the next few words. And had to struggle to remember them.

You have no choice. There is no option. In chains you are bound. Appear before me now.

"Vous n'avez pas de choix! Il n'y a pas d'option! Vous êtes enchainé! Révélez-vous maintenant!"

The room abruptly shuddered, like it was vibrating to the heartbeat of some giant. And there was a brilliant flash of light. So intense that—if she'd not been warned by Raine to close her eyes—it would have blinded her.

When she opened them again, the Thieftaker was glowing furiously, a huge white fire seeming to churn within it. In fact, the thing had grown larger. Was the size of a softball by this time. And the facets were rotating even faster, clacking, whizzing as they turned.

As she watched, the individual gems seemed to lose their substance. They became simply revolving flecks of light. Were following the same complex orbits as before, but their trajectories were widening.

In less than a minute, they had spread so wide they nearly touched the floor and ceiling. They had formed a cage of spinning brilliance, which continued to clatter and fizz. About eight feet tall and five feet wide—large enough to contain any man.

There was one more sentence remaining to complete the spell. She raised her right arm, and jabbed at the whirling brightness with her sharply pointed index finger.

Thief, despair, for you are trapped.

"Voleur, perdez espoir, car vous êtes attrapé!"

The instant she said that, she felt a tremor run through her. It wasn't a vibration on the air, this time. No, it was an instinct. She had shuddered. The cloud of vapor was very close. She could sense it!

Her flesh turned clammy. Yes, she knew it was inside the house. She turned toward the drawing room door. Thought she saw it shudder in its frame, the instant before the pale gray smoke came seeping underneath it.

It reformed into a ball in midair, hanging there as if it was unsure which direction it should take. Millicent tensed up. Had the spell gone wrong, so that she'd brought it here but did not have any real control over it?

But the strands of brilliance were churning even faster, lighting the whole room up like a strobe lamp gone berserk. The sounds they were emitting had grown to an intense, fragile whine that set her teeth on edge.

The pall of vapor tried to drift away, but then gave up and submitted to the magic. A few of the bright strands opened for it, and it floated in between them. Then they closed behind the cloud again. It hung there at the center, passive and immobile.

The noise died down, although the lights continued to re-volve. Millicent felt the tension dropping from her body. She drew in a breath, then stepped up to the thing. There was no need for French, any longer. So she spoke to it in flat, plain English.

"Finally!"

Her top lip curled. Her eyes flashed.

"You're the one who robbed me! Let's see who you really are?"

Trapped in there, the thief had to obey her. It was part of the spell too, and there was no way to defy it. The smoke reformed until it was in vaguely human shape. Then it resolved itself more clearly.

My God, he was fat wasn't he, whoever this was? Disgustingly so. And bald as well. Men looked so vile, the older they got. His features began appearing.

Lifeless eyes. Jowls all stubbled. And a thick-lipped mouth that had an ugly tilt to it, like he was smirking at some obscene joke.

The man was wearing a polo shirt, old enough that it had holes in it. He had on baggy sweatpants, fastened loosely with a drawstring at the top. And on his feet . . . stained white socks, with larger holes in them. No shoes, oddly.

He was breathing heavily, his beady gaze fixed on hers. In his right hand was a small knife, the blade glinting sharply.

And in his left?

There was no left hand. That part of him had not been revealed. It was still a ball of vapor. And hanging from it was a darker, thinner strand. She immediately knew what that was. The Wand of Dantiere itself.

Millicent could see what had happened. A fresh shock went through her as she took it in. The wand had bound itself to this man. Had become part of him, their essences fusing. And because of that, the Thieftaker hadn't managed to do everything it was supposed to. It could apparently control the human being, but not the magic instrument.

In which case, could he still get out? How much danger was she in? She took a step away alarmedly.

The man seemed to pick up on that, with the keen sense all predators have. His grip tightened around the blade. He lowered his head slightly, peering at her through his bushy eyebrows. Grinned. Then started to move forward.

It took an effort, but he began to pass right through the strands of light. They ought to have held him just as solidly as iron bars. But the wand was helping him. He pressed himself against them, and they bulged out slowly under the pressure. Then gave way finally, parting. And by this time, his smile had become savage, feral, almost like he was already tasting blood.

Millicent felt the urge to run, but fought it. If she only knew who this man was. Understood what drove him, what he really wanted. While he was still closing the distance between them—and he was taking his time about it—she muttered a Spell of Linking.

There was no sound this time, no bright flashing lights. But their minds became connected instantly. She could see his thoughts, his memories. And drew in the information that she needed.

Yes, now she saw it. This was no one to be genuinely afraid of, whatever the rest of the world might think. A lowly and pathetic creature really, even more wretched than most normal men. She could see his one real weakness. What this Shadow Man genuinely feared. And she could control him with that knowledge. She was quite certain of that.

So, raising her arms slightly, she started changing her appearance. It was not real. Her own dark witchcraft was not strong enough for that. She was simply bending the light around her, so that anyone who looked at her would see a different person.

But it looked genuine enough. She seemed to grow shorter. And her hair became gray and tangled, rubbing at her brow. Her face expanded, growing rounder. There was even a double chin.

She glanced across at her reflection in the window. Her eyes were now piggy, exactly like the man's. Her stubby nose was noticeably red, and dimpled like a strawberry. And a flush had extended itself across her newly flattened cheekbones. Years of drunkenness had been the cause of that.

Her hands were precisely the same as his, like those of a massive, pudgy baby. The clothes she wore were old ones, very cheap. Her thick legs had blue veins running down them, the tops of her stockings furled around her knees. And there were battered, fluffy green mules on her swollen stubs of feet.

Her lips parted, showing rotten teeth.

"Cornelius!"

She spat the name out like a curse.

He halted. Stared at her, aghast. His ugly grin vanished, like it had never been there in the first place. Then he shrank away from her, actually cowering. It was the bizarrest thing, watching a man so large—and with a knife, and murderous intent behind it—behaving this way. Almost comical, though she was careful not to show it.

His expression was horrified. He couldn't seem to fathom what had happened. But he believed that what he was seeing was real. There was little doubt of that.

When he finally found the courage to speak, one solitary whimpered syllable came trickling out.

"Ma?"

"Cornelius! What in the blue blazes do you think you're doing with that knife?"

Her voice rang out like a thunderclap. It had a strong Irish accent, and the words were all a little slurred. But she pinned him with her gaze as if he were a bug. The man quaked. The whites of his eyes showed clearly.

"Who are you planning to harm with that, you halfwit?"

It dropped from his grasp, glinting as it fell. Cornelius was shaking furiously by the time it hit the floor.

"No one, Ma." And then he added, "I'm so sorry."

"You're a sorry excuse for a human being, that's what you are!" She took a heavy, wobbling step in his direction. "What's that in your other hand? You can put that down as well."

His left arm came up, but it had not changed above the wrist. Was still composed of vapor, and the wand as well. He shook at it, but it remained in place, all part of the same structure.

"I can't do that, Ma." He gazed back at her helplessly. "It seems to be stuck."

She lurched at him suddenly, and cuffed him around the ear. Cornelius let out a piteous wail, and crouched lower in front of her.

"Stuck, is it? Do you know what you're holding there? It's been in my family since the Norman Conquest."

She was so anxious to get at it that she'd forgotten herself, dropping out of character. Cornelius squinted up at her, and Millicent stopped dead.

"What, Ma?" His expression, though still terrified, had grown slightly puzzled. "I . . . don't understand."

She saw she had to keep up the momentum. The man wouldn't dare to question her if she only went at him hard enough.

"That's because you are an utter moron! An embarrassment to the family name! Hand it over to me, or I'll fix you good and proper."

He shook his arm even more furiously, but the slender line remained intact.

"I can't do it!" He began to panic. "Can't! I can't! I can't!"

He covered his bald crown with his right hand, expecting another blow.

But Millicent paused thoughtfully, the Thieftaker still casting flecks of light around her. Some of her original shape returned. Her eyes became turquoise again, her mouth thinning and her nose regaining something of its slender sharpness. And yes, she was getting a clearer idea of precisely what had happened. The wand was vastly powerful, hugely varied in the functions it performed. And—like any such magic object—it had a mind of its own. A will. A sense of purpose.

It had, quite literally, grown attached to Cornelius here. She remembered the old stories regarding its origin. Its creator had been completely mad. And so perhaps one distorted intellect had found sympathy with another.

She linked with him again. Saw the intention of the wand itself, through the medium of the man's thoughts. And she also saw what they'd been doing since Cornelius had gotten hold of it. Her sense of understanding grew.

The wand had enjoyed the killings. Blood, and pain, and death? It wanted more.

A momentary surge of jealousy ran through her. She regarded the thing as her own. Her rightful inheritance. What business did it have, attaching itself to such an awful, unclean misfit? But she was forced to recognize two facts.

She simply had to accept matters the way they'd turned out. The wand was far too strong for her to countermand its wishes. And—the more she turned it over—then the more she understood how this might go to her advantage. With this killer by her side, she could genuinely wreak some bloody vengeance on this town.

The real point was this. Cornelius had been working at a very simple stage of magic, up until this point. He had no idea what the instrument he was holding was capable of. So it was up to her to show him.

She brushed her fingertips together. The Thieftaker stopped moving, and the sparks of brilliance disappeared. When she reached for his head again, he made a small keening noise. But she did not hit him his time. Merely stroked his scalp. The sensation was repellent to her, but she continued with it. There was no other option, since she needed him completely on her side.

"Silly boy," she murmured, in a voice far gentler than before. "You don't understand much of anything, now do you?"

He didn't seem to even notice the changes that had come over her, the reality of his situation lost to him completely. Perhaps his mind had shrunken back, and he was only seeing what he thought was there.

His next words seemed to confirm that.

"No, Ma," he murmured. "I'm so sorry."

She shushed him.

"Don't you know what that wand can really do?"

He tried to think about it. "No."

"Taking control of merely one person at a time?" Her tongue clucked. "What a waste, Cornelius. It's not a toy."

"Sorry, Ma . . . I'm really sorry." Tears started dribbling down his face. His voice had grown extremely nasal. "But I just don't know what else to do. I'm pretty ignorant, I guess."

"It's easy," she explained to him. "I'll show you. Hold it out toward me."

"But I can't let it go."

"Did I ask you to? Do as I say."

He obeyed without any further protest, stretching out his arm. Millicent took hold of the strand of vapor. Felt her fingers start to tingle. When she looked at them, they had turned gray, translucent. Then her hand started to fade.

Cornelius gawped at her, his shoulders heaving.

"What are we going to do now, Ma?"

She grinned savagely. "We're going to have some extra-special fun, my boy."

She already knew about that from the Linking Spell.

"We're going to rip this town to pieces, from the inside out. The Old Ones would approve of that, wouldn't they?"

Cornelius's mood began to brighten and he nodded.

"Yeah . . . I guess they would."

Something broke across them at that point. Faintly, from a distance, she could hear her horses whinny in their stables. Something had disturbed them. Had they caught an unfamiliar scent on the air?

Millicent cast her senses out. And yes, there were intruders. Two of them. She recognized their auras from the night before. A glance at the window revealed nothing. It was practically pitch dark out there. So she returned her attention to the task in hand, her manner becoming urgent.

"You must repeat these words, Cornelius. They're foreign and complicated, so you'll have to listen carefully."

He looked apprehensive, but he nodded all the same.

"Deux yeux invisibles," she said.

He muttered it back at her. His accent was atrocious, but he got the wording right.

"Deux êtres au noir, inaperçus et sans bornes."

Which he fluffed the first time, and her teeth ground with impatience. Devries and his assistant were already at one of the back doors, planning to burst through it. But she held herself steady and repeated the sentence, just a few syllables at a time.

"Sans bornes," he mumbled.

He looked and sounded like a fat little boy being taught his catechism.

There was a sudden crash. The door had been kicked open, and the two intruders were through.

Millicent grabbed Cornelius's shoulder.

"Three more words, the same, repeated! Are you ready?"

He knew what the noise had meant as well. The possibility of being caught. And looked very anxious when he nodded back.

"Partez! Partez! Partez!" Millicent snapped at him.

"What?" he blurted.

"Say it!"

He sucked in a breath, then spat out the word three times, exactly as he had been told. Disappear, disappear, disappear.

They both turned to gray vapor this time, one ball of the stuff far larger than before. And they were lifting through the air next instant, drifting to the window, a pane of which swung open for them.

The door to the room came open as the last of the mist filtered out.

The vapor headed down into the main part of the town again, going south this time.

CHAPTER 22

It turned out that a lot of the lights in the back of the house were on. Room after room of them. So we had no real idea where Millicent was. Cass and I split up. I began opening one door after another, taking note of how sparse and empty the place looked. There was no paper—the walls were painted in matte, neutral shades. The large rooms were bare save for a few items of expensive but impractical-looking furniture. There were a couple of Modigliani-like statues—you couldn't buy stuff like that here, but she could easily have conjured them up, using magazines for reference. A couple of paintings that looked like Braques, doubtless acquired by the same process. Otherwise, it didn't look like a real home, a place where you lived and relaxed. More like someplace where you drifted and existed. Which confirmed my earlier opinion of this mansion.

"Ross, in here!"

Cassie sounded urgent, but not like she was in any kind of trouble. I went quickly in her direction, wondering what she had found.

And walked into a drawing room. There were some stunning views from here. The windows looked out over the whole center of town, most of the north and some of the eastern suburbs. The house's grounds stretched away until the darkness swallowed them. I could make out the dim shape of a long wooden building that I supposed was the stables. But most of the rest was lost from sight.

Cass was peering at an object on the floor. It glimmered like a diamond in the soft electric light, but I could see immediately it was not that. She didn't seem to want to go near it, but I didn't have the same kind of problem. I picked it up, since I'd been half expecting this.

"What is that?" Cassie asked.

Woody's father, August Raine, had shown me a device like this years ago. I'd still been a cop back then, and he'd thought that I'd be interested.

"It's called a Thieftaker," I told her, holding the thing in my open palm.

I took note of how warm it felt, almost like it was alive. And had no doubt that Millicent had been given it at the Manor. Now I knew what she'd been doing up there.

"I think that it's been used," I added. "Recently."

The fact that Cassie never finished high school doesn't mean she isn't smart. She was quick to catch on, putting her hands on her hips and staring at it.

"She used it to draw Hanlon here?"

I nodded uncomfortably, slipping the thing in my pocket. It might turn out to be useful later.

"So where are they?"

Now that was the question, wasn't it?

When we looked around, we couldn't find the slightest sign of any struggle. So whatever had gone on here, it had either happened very quickly, or had somehow turned out amicably. And I didn't care to think about the latter option too much. Hanlon and Millicent combined?

Frustration seethed through me. We'd arrived too late. No one but the two people involved knew exactly what was going on. And they hadn't hung around to answer any questions.

Cass blurted, "Do you suppose they came to an agreement?"

Which told me she'd arrived at the same conclusion. And it was a pretty frightening concept, any way you tried to cut it. I struggled to think how we could react to that.

"Hey!" I heard her say, a bit more loudly. "What the hell is going on?"

Which sounded like a pretty big non sequitur, until I glanced where she was looking. Her eyes were tracking something out beyond the windowpane. And I couldn't make out what it was, at first. It all looked normal, Union Square illuminated with its old-gold glow, a couple of the streets running from it shining with bright neon signs. The rest of the Landing sprawling away, double rows of street-lamps marking out the wider routes.

Then a red flash caught my attention. Held it, repeating itself. A patrol car with its beacon on was heading southward, moving really fast. Which would not have been too remarkable. Except I looked across and saw another, heading in from Pilgrim's Plot and turning in the same direction.

Then a third appeared.

I got on the phone to Hobart. By the sound of it, he was in his car as well.

"The switchboard's jammed! Reports of some kind of creature!" he yelled down the line at me. "It's tearing up an entire block in Garnerstown!"

One of the least prosperous suburbs in the Landing, Garnerstown had suffered quite enough already. Saruak had struck there on two consecutive nights when he had first arrived. Nobody had moved back into Cray's Lane, so far as I knew. As for St. Nevitt's—they weren't even planning to repair that stricken church. They'd simply shut it down.

The word "creature" could mean a very wide variety of things in a place like the Landing. The fact that Saul hadn't been specific told me what? He wasn't sure?

I'd reached Sandhurst Avenue, the gas pedal pushed down through the floor. The red taillight of Cassie's Harley was visible about a quarter of a mile ahead. She could have easily outstripped me. But when there's trouble going down, we prefer to stick together, back each other up. And trouble with creatures . . . that can be the very worst kind.

Sometimes—either willingly or by mistake—people conjure the things up. They pop into existence. Other times, it is the conjurer who gets transformed. Fear and madness quickly work their way into that particular equation, and that's usually when all hell breaks loose.

As to which type we were facing? Well, we'd soon find out.

I hit the intersection at Greenwood Terrace, swinging to the left and going across town a couple of blocks. Then I was turning right and heading south again, down Keane Street.

Halfway along it, five squad cars had been pulled up, forming a tight barrier. Saul's Pontiac was in there with them too. And Cass was already off her bike, sprinting over swiftly.

The cops were kneeling. Most of them had their revolvers drawn, and a couple were holding riot guns. I skidded to a halt behind them, got out, and surveyed the scene. Which was fairly difficult, because a lot of the streetlamps were out.

Four wooden houses had been torn apart almost completely. Broken walls and shingles, and pieces of furniture, were scattered everywhere. The top of a chimney pot was lying in the middle of the street. A power line was down as well, the cables jumping and sparking furiously.

Their intermittent glow lit up Lauren Brennan's face. I'd not supposed that she'd be here. She was crouched down with the uniformed men, had her gun out the same way they did, and was looking drawn. But not nearly as frightened as she'd been at Sam Scott's Tavern.

Then I noticed there were corpses lying in a few front yards. None of them looked like they'd died easily. One body was almost ripped in half.

I was about to go across to Saul, and ask him what had done this, when a massive shadow moved out there, behind another wooden house. Lights were on, but the front door was wide open. So whoever had been living there had fled.

Everyone around me stiffened and took careful aim. I went so completely still that I could hear my own heart bumping. A bead of moisture started trickling across my lip. Whatever had shifted off in that direction, it had been enormous.

Then I heard the weirdest noise, a loud sharp clattering that seemed to go on for longer than made any sense. The echo of it, even after it had stopped, went ringing down the street.

It was followed by an abrupt, scaly grating sound, like two pieces of huge shell being rubbed together. Out where the streetlights didn't reach, the shadows took on an extra density and began to bulge. I tried to follow the movement, but it was far too quick. Too fleeting to make out a proper shape. The only thing registering was that the body I was catching glimpses of appeared to be jet black, darker by far than its surroundings. It had disappeared behind the broken houses before I could take in any more.

It was something long, although not in any form I recognized. I thought I'd caught a glimpse of spines, but knew I could be wrong about that.

Something very fast and huge, and obviously deadly.

I hunkered down a few more inches as the first noise I'd heard, the prolonged clattering, started up again.

CHAPTER 23

The strange sound went right through me, grating at my nerves. I had my own gun drawn by this stage. Every weapon swung in the noise's direction, even Lauren's. I could see how badly her hands were shaking, but she was staying put and doing her part.But none of us could tell exactly where it was coming from. It was so loud it echoed up and down the street, rebounding.

It stopped for an instant, and then started up again. And . . . I thought I recognized it. It seemed to be a hugely amplified version of a sound that I had heard before. Although I couldn't recall from where or when. And this wasn't the moment for guessing games.

The next instant, it died away completely. And the shadows up ahead of us lurched again. One of the cops fired. That seemed to have no effect. Whatever was out there, it was circling back the way it had first come, still clinging to the darker areas. It struck me that we should have been able to make out more than this. The moon was high above us, almost full. But whatever this thing was, it seemed to absorb the best part of the light that touched it, making itself practically invisible.

It had gone behind a clump of low trees in between the ruined homes and the abandoned one. Cassie—both her Glocks drawn—started edging forward. But I reached across and caught her elbow, staring at her and shaking my head. And she took notice of that, thank God. We had to know what we were dealing with before we tried to confront it.

The clattering did not come back. Nor did any of the scraping sounds. I almost wished they would. It was better than the silence that had descended over us.

My insides felt rigid. Staying hunkered down actually hurt. And there was a fine second skin of moisture on my face. Everyone around me was the same, excepting Cassie. We knew there was some kind of terrible danger out there, but we couldn't even see it properly.

When the hush was finally broken, it was not by what I had expected. The sound that came to us this time started softly, but then lifted to a high-pitched wail.

I felt my shoulders jolt with shock. It sounded like a child in pain.

My first instinct was to start moving toward it. It was a safe bet that was Cassie's too. We'd both had families of our own, even though they were not with us any longer. But, impulsive although she can sometimes be, Cass just stayed put. And we exchanged puzzled glances. Could this be some kind of deception, to fool us?

Except that hadn't occurred to everyone. A young sandy-haired cop called Gregson suddenly stood up and began heading forward, mumbling something. Then we heard, "It's got hold of a kid!"

His voice was choked up with emotion, and I understood exactly why. He had twin baby boys at home.

Everyone was watching him. And Saul began shouting at him to come back. But no one tried to follow. Gregson was apparently too caught up in what he was attempting to notice the lieutenant's voice. The only thing that we could do was aim into the darkness up ahead and try to cover him.

He was going at a slow jog, keeping low, his head darting around. His service pistol, at the ready, gleamed beside his shoulder. Gregson knew the risk that he was taking. That did not deter him for a second.

And I thought at first that he was going to be okay. What

if he was right, there was a child out there? There had been ordinary families along this entire block, let's face it.

But then the shadows seemed to coalesce, and started moving faster than I'd possibly imagined.

There wasn't time to fire. Not even Cass managed to get a round off. It was over and done with between one blink and the next, so that you only got a brief impression of it, like a sudden bright light on your retinas. Except . . . no, not bright. The opposite of that.

Something vast—with a blunt, triangular head—came surging out. And slammed into Gregson's chest, knocking the man over.

He'd barely hit the pavement before jaws sprung open, clamped around his leg. And he was dragged away in a split second. There was a brief shriek.

Then silence closed across us again, like a wall of blackened water.

A terrible coldness began to fill me up. And it seemed to seep through every pore. I wasn't even sure that I was drawing proper breaths. The only thing that I could do was stare at the empty space where the man had been standing.

I heard someone mutter an oath. Hobart whispered, "Oh my God."

What had I just seen? I tried to piece the fragments I had glimpsed together. It had been . . . a long shape. Uniformly wide along its body. I could remember no colors. It had been a massive silhouette. But a serpentine shape, I felt sure of that.

A snake? A rattlesnake, by the noise it had been making? We have no such creatures around these parts, but even if we did they wouldn't be that size.

This was making less and less sense the more that I thought about it. And my head was whirling slightly now. If it was a reptile, how'd it made that childlike wailing?

I got my answer to that next second, when a creaky, rather demented-sounding laughter started ringing out behind the trees. Which told me that we weren't dealing with any kind of real animal. This was either Hanlon in a brand-new incarnation, or something else that was sentient and vicious.

The reaction of the cops was instantaneous. They'd been holding back in the hope that Gregson might still be alive, but the laughter seemed to indicate he wasn't. So they opened fire on the trees. Cassie joined in. I did too. Twigs and leaves, and then whole branches, started flying everywhere, a cloud of splinters swelling up ahead of us.

You'd have thought that nothing could withstand a storm of lead like that. But the only things we'd damaged were the natural shapes up front. The unnatural one came surging out again as the noise of our shots was still dying away. Swifter than lightning, it slid across the road in front of us and disappeared behind another house.

I could see spines along its back. I was pretty sure of that, this time. A cop next to me blurted, "What the hell?"

And there'd been something like a leathery frill around the part of its body where its neck ought to be. So this wasn't just a snake. Far more like some kind of basilisk, or a reptilian demon. I didn't have the first clue where it might have come from.

Then I saw something else moving in the house that it had gone behind. A small head bobbed up in a first floor window, followed by a larger one. The lights might have been switched off in there . . . but the family who lived there hadn't managed to get out.

Cassie saw that too. And her response was instantaneous. She holstered her Glocks, sprinted across to her Harley, and came back with her Mossberg in one hand and the Heckler & Koch carbine in the other. She handed the latter to me. It didn't look quite as scary as the shotgun but its bullets had a similar impact, and she had it set to triple bursts.

She leapt up on the hood of the nearest patrol car, and then stepped onto its roof. And from that vantage point, she began stamping on the metal, yelling at the point where she'd last seen the creature disappear.

"Over here, you asshole!"

When nothing happened, she stamped even harder, leaving dents in the car's roof.

"Wanna meal? Well, come and get it!"

None of which would have made much difference to an

actual reptile. I'd seen rattlesnakes on TV, and knew they didn't work like that. But that laugh we'd heard. That trick that it had used to bait poor Gregson? We were dealing with something that had a mind, an ugly sense of humor, and malign intent. Which made me all the more convinced that it was supernatural. Although for the moment, it was staying put.

Cassie started jumping up and down with both feet like a big kid on a trampoline. Several of the cops around us stared at her like she was crazy. But I'd seen that kind of bold behavior in the face of peril plenty of times before.

"What's the matter? Scared of me? You frightened of a girl?"

And for some reason, that seemed to do the trick where nothing else had. The deeper shadows in front of us drifted together, then came boiling out again. I saw that I'd been right about my first impressions. But I noticed something else as well. The thing wasn't entirely dark. Its eyes were such a pale gray that they almost seemed to be glowing. The same shade as the vapor we had previously encountered. So this was connected.

Except with one big difference. We were ready for it, this time. We both had our weapons to our shoulders. And we opened fire immediately. Cass wasn't even using regular shot. She loaded the Mossberg with BRI saboted slugs, chunks of ammunition that could punch holes through a solid concrete wall. And she pumped one round after another straight into the creature's face. I drilled it intently with the carbine.

But I thought at first we still weren't going to stop it. My heart turned to a rock inside my chest. Its great triangular head kept on expanding in my vision, its jaws coming open as they got nearer to Cassie. But she didn't even flinch away. Simply stood there, firing mechanically.

Then—without any preamble—the whole head burst apart.

Although it didn't turn out to be flesh and blood. Its entire body lost its structure, then began to fall apart. And in another second, it had transformed into a vast, elongated plume of vapor.

Which started drawing back in the direction of the house again. None of it dispersed. It churned gently as it moved away, retaining its general shape.

Just before it disappeared around the corner, I saw it turning denser, darker. Getting more compact. So it was probably returning to its solid state once more.

At least Cass had given the trapped family a chance to run. As I watched, the front door burst open and they came dashing out. A couple of cops sprinted across, and started hustling them away.

When I looked at the backyard again, something was still on the move in the deepest shadows out that way.

We hadn't hurt the thing in the least little bit. We'd only, momentarily, slowed it down.

CHAPTER 24

Insubstantial one moment, solid the next. How could we fight against something like that? But I couldn't understand why Hanlon—or was it Millicent?—had chosen to turn themselves into that kind of creature. It honestly didn't seem to be in either of their natures.

The great shape was still clinging to the deepest shadows, slithering over to the next backyard along. Cassie kept after it with her shotgun, but it didn't take much notice of that. It was hard to be certain, but it seemed to be altering its appearance. And none of what I could make out was good. Its head seemed to be changing, its mouth splitting ever wider. I thought I might be imagining it at first, the darkness playing tricks on me. But . . . the whole top section of the thing appeared to be dividing, splitting the way an amoeba might. And as it came open, it was revealing rows of curving fangs the whole way down.

It disappeared around a wall. Then it suddenly lashed out at us with terrifying speed. In fact, it came straight across the barrier of blue-and-whites. And it was definitely solid again. Metalwork groaned and crumpled. Windshields splintered. Thank God, we stepped back in time. And then, before we had time to do anything more, it withdrew into the gloom, so swiftly that there was barely time for conscious thought.

Off to my side, I could hear Saul Hobart swearing brutally.

The creature was moving again, changing position, so fast it was practically impossible to track. Which direction would it strike from next time? I chanced a rapid glance behind me. And got another big surprise. When I'd first arrived, there had been no one apparent on this street except the cops. The usual inhabitants had presumably been hiding. But some of them had now emerged.

They were gazing at the whole scene from a healthy distance, watching it unfold with utter disbelief. Some had had the presence of mind to arm themselves—rifles and shotguns could be seen. And one burly fellow was even clutching a sledgehammer. But not one of them moved toward us. They were waiting to see how this played itself out. And they were absolutely right about that, so I couldn't blame them. As things stood, there was no way that they could help.

One of the cops near me let out something that was half a word and half a frightened yelp. And that brought my attention back. The serpentine shape had moved again, as fast as a winter wind. Had gotten in between two of the nearest houses. And it coiled up tautly for a second. Several people opened fire, but that did no good.

Then it came squirming across the pavement at us, with the velocity and power of a locomotive. It lunged at the nearest car. Its head slammed at it like a battering ram, lifting the vehicle clear of the ground. At which point, the windows shattered. Safety glass came raining down on us.

The car landed so close to Cassie she was forced to jump away from it. But this time, the beast did not retreat again. It went behind one of the other cars and stopped there, furling up. It had put itself within easy striking range of every person trying to stop it. So there was no choice. We began falling back.

It seemed to like that, growing bolder. Two of the patrol cars groaned, then shifted on their axles as it nosed its way between them. As its head emerged, I could see that my original impression had been right. It had mutated, the top of it splitting. It had become less like a snake, and more like something shapeless from a nightmare.

No one turned and ran. They rarely do, and I'm proud to

say that. But we kept stepping off, the whole while we were firing. Cassie's shotgun pounded like a jackhammer. The carbine jerked and sputtered as I fired off triple bursts. The creature up ahead of us came apart again for a few seconds. But then it funneled back into its original shape.

A crawling instinct made me glance across, and I saw something that concerned me badly. Lauren Brennan, looking pretty dazed, was moving back too slowly, getting separated from the rest. When that bisected head came lashing out again, it was in her direction. And she wasn't halfway used to stuff like this, the way that me and Cassie were. And so she did entirely the wrong thing, and froze. I saw her mouth drop open.

I started reaching out for her, painfully aware she was too far away. That was when a speeding blur rammed into her, knocking her to the ground. A band of pure darkness went sweeping through the empty space where she had been, and then retracted.

It was Cassie who had jumped in. They both hit the pavement together. But Cass didn't even pause. She rolled, and was back on her feet in the same fluid motion. Then she grabbed Lauren by her suit collar and hauled her away to safety.

Her expression—when she did that—was grim, rather embittered. Like she'd only done it because she ought to, not because she wanted to. If I'd been thinking clearer, I'd have gotten worried about that.

But too much was still happening. The creature was continuously advancing, careless of our firepower. The gun I'd been handed gave one final rattle, then went silent in my grasp. I tossed it aside and drew my Smith & Wesson instead, for all the good that that would do.

Something else was going on around me in the darkness. It took me a couple more seconds to see what it was. Some of the people firing at the thing were no longer in uniform. The ordinary civilians had at last come forward. The fact that we were in real trouble had doubtless inspired them. They'd understood they could not merely stand back any longer. Even the guy with the hammer was in among us, swiping at the massive head each time it gave a thrust.

And I was grateful they'd joined in—don't get me wrong. But it was making very little real difference. If we couldn't stop it, how much damage could this creature do? If it just kept pushing on like this, unchecked . . . ?

It was progressing ever northward. If it carved its way through Garnerstown, and then straight up between Tyburn and Greenwood, that route would take it into the center of the town.

There was no way that I could see to win this. Any moment now, we were going to be forced to turn tail and withdraw. I glanced across at Saul, and saw he understood that too. And he hated the idea of giving up completely, just as much as I did.

A new sound came to my ears. So soft that—above this uproar—it shouldn't properly have been audible. But magic sometimes works like that.

A gentle thrumming. It was coming from the west.

Against the stars, there was a dark smudge moving, high up in the air. Not any pall of vapor, this time. Far more like a thumbprint on the canvas of the sky. A thin bolt of lightning accompanied it, although there was no thunder. And it was moving even faster than the snake had.

It dropped in our direction, hurtling swiftly down. Reached the ground several yards to my right.

And then resolved itself into a human form.

It was Judge Levin.

By the tightness on his face, he knew exactly what had been going on. His chin was raised, and he was holding himself very stiffly. His eyes glittered with a small, cold inner flame his glasses only magnified. He had his robes on . . . he always wore them when performing magic. There was still a breeze, and the hems fluttered, giving him an almost medieval look.

His arms were by his sides, his fingers twitching. He was getting ready to do something big. I knew him well enough to see that.

The monster was reflected in his spectacles. He stared at it with open disgust.

"I don't think that this is Millicent!" he told me, his voice raising itself above the din. "Or Hanlon!"

"What is it, then?"

"How the hell would I know?" he snapped back at me.

Then he started shouting to the rest.

"All of you! I need you to give that thing another solid blasting!"

Once again, it was the case that they shouldn't have been able to hear him with this racket going on. But something about his tone of voice embedded itself on the air around us, so that every nearby face swung toward him. He was using his powers, I understood. We could have heard his words inside our skulls even if our ears had been plugged up.

"Make the damned thing fly apart again!" he called out. "All I need is one brief second!"

I took aim. So did everyone around me. From the corner of my eye, I could see Cassie clamp her weapon to her shoulder, her whole face scrunched up. Then Saul barked out the order. And everyone let fly at once. The guy with the sledgehammer even threw it, in an almost mythic gesture.

When the beast dissolved a third time, Levin murmured something quickly. A brightness appeared between his outstretched palms. Merely the tiniest flicker, at first. But it spread out within an instant. Was composed of light so brilliant I had to look away.

The judge didn't even pause. Peering at the cloud of vapor, he curled back his upper lip.

"Reveal yourself!" he bellowed.

And he flung the searing ball of light. It kept expanding as it went. Washed through the gray cloud ahead of us before it had a chance to return to its original shape. That broke it apart again.

This time, it burst out wider, rolling away from us like a great cloud of dust. It spread much thinner than before. I could see right through it. And it did not start changing back into that reptile shape. Instead, a huge human face became apparent at the center.

It was merely in outline, monochromatic. The eyes were

still pale gray. But the features . . . they were pretty damned alarming. It looked like a madman's face.

The mouth was stretched inhumanly wide, like it was perpetually screaming. The teeth were broken and uneven. And there were folds in the skin in places where there ought not be.

The features were framed by wild, unruly hair and a thin, straggling beard. Impossible to tell what color they had been. No sound emerged from the open mouth. The dead gray eyes stared down at us.

And then, the face collapsed as well. And the vapor was there again. It didn't stick around, this time. It lifted, and started hurtling away from us, soaring high up and shooting off westward, the same direction that the judge had come from. Was it possibly going to Sycamore Hill? Levin and I exchanged worried glances.

At least the immediate threat was over. I doubled over, pretty shaken, sucking air into my lungs. Every guy around me was the same. Only Cass looked like she'd been enjoying this.

"The Light of Truth," the judge announced, explaining what he'd done to the people near him. "Always an excellent weapon. You would do well to remember that."

I could scarcely remember my own name. I went across to Lauren, who was slumped against a lamppost. She was barely on her feet by this stage and it would have been kinder to let her rest a while. But I had to know what we were up against, and wasn't prepared to wait.

I asked her sharply, "Was it Hanlon?"

After all, I'd never even seen the man. She took a moment trying to collect her thoughts. Then she shook her head.

That was when a deep voice, coming up behind me, called out, "I know who that was."

I turned and saw the guy who'd thrown the hammer stepping up, a grim expression on his stubbled face.

"That was Langham Tavitt. The guy's lived round here his whole life. And I always knew that creep would bring down trouble on us, one of these fine days."

CHAPTER 25

He introduced himself as Nick McLeish, holding out a faintly grimy hand. I was a little puzzled under the circumstances. This didn't seem to be the occasion for hospitable politeness. But I shook it all the same.

He was—as I had already taken note—a burly fellow around five foot ten, who'd run slightly to fat down his forty or so years. He had darkly curly hair cut short, and was dressed in his undervest, a pair of stained chinos, and carpet slippers. So obviously, he'd had to leave his place in a big rush. His deep brown eyes were wide, his face a little ashen. But otherwise, you'd have thought that oversized mutating reptiles turned up on this block most weeks of the year.

And he turned out, over the next few minutes, to be a pretty verbal kind of guy as well. He was in construction, he explained. That was what the hammer was about. His home, he explained, was one of those that had been wrecked. He and his family had barely gotten out in time.

"Sorry to hear that," I told him, looking at the scattered ruins.

But the only thing he did was shrug.

"Only sticks and stones," he told me. "Main thing is that we're okay. You can always replace a house."

I was quickly coming to understand that Nick here was the kind of solid citizen who took everything that life threw at him in his stride. What remained of the street lighting cast his face into stark relief, and there was nothing cowed about it. You find a lot of folk like that in the Landing. This place breeds survivors.

He had retrieved his sledgehammer, but set it down against the curb. Then he led me over to another house that had been turned into matchwood.

"This is where he lived, just three doors down from mine. Inherited the place from his ma, who was a good old soul. Hell, he could never have afforded it."

We stopped at the edge, and he kicked some broken planks away.

"Street sweeper, that's what he was. Only job he could hold down. He was . . . what's the word I'm looking for?"

"A loner?" I suggested, beginning to get the picture. On closer inspection, the place looked like it had been a wreck even before it had been dismembered.

"Not just that. Tavitt was plain anti-social. 'Misfit,' that's what I was trying to say. Hated other people, all the ones on this street for sure. Shouted curses at us from behind his fence. We've had vandalism on this block for years, and we know it's down to him."

"Sounds like a charmer," I came back at him. "Ever think of calling the police?"

"We tried. He wouldn't talk to them. And we couldn't prove nothing, so . . ."

His big round shoulders shrugged again.

I was starting to notice more about the mess this place had been turned into. There were chunks of furniture strewn around, the torn upholstery on them stained and greasy. And Tavitt seemed to have collected quite a load of empty wine bottles. Cheap brands, without exception. Dozens of the things. From my years on the force, I knew precisely this guy's type.

Then my eyes alighted on the garish, battered cover of a book. There was another underneath it. In fact, dozens scattered around.

All paperbacks, with the same type of illustration on the front. Horses cantered across red-brown deserts. There were tall cacti, and men in big white hats.

"He was into Westerns?" I asked.

The man's gaze went where I was looking. And then his expression crumpled up.

"Never knew about it until now. But heck, it certainly looks that way."

He bent down and picked one up. It had been purchased secondhand. The cover was worn like old tissue paper, and there was a handwritten sticker on it. He glanced at the blurb, then turned it over.

Again, there was a mounted cowboy. But the guy's horse was rearing back on its hind legs. Away from a rattlesnake.

In which case . . . Tavitt's reading habits and what we'd experienced, what he had been changed into, were somehow linked. Except there was no telling in what way. My mind reeled perturbedly.

"How exactly did this whole thing start?" I asked Nick. "Did you see him turn into that monster?"

His head shook with frustration. "First thing I knew about it, there was this almighty crash. I looked out my window, and that goddamn snake was breaking out through the front wall here. The entire house collapsed around it, but that didn't even slow it down. After that? We didn't have time to really notice much. We were too busy running."

More people were drifting in around us, the inhabitants of the nearby streets coming across to see what had happened. There were gasps and murmurs of surprise. And a family had appeared, a good deal further down. A slim woman, her hair copper in the artificial light, with three small kids clinging tightly to her skirt. They were staring nervously in our direction. McLeish spotted them and raised a hand.

"And that about sums up what I can tell you. If you don't mind, I have to be going."

He headed off toward his wife and children. When he drew up closer to them, the three kids ran up and hugged his legs.

I was pleased they'd got through this in one piece. But I have to admit something in me—something pretty massive—envied Nick McLeish.

* * *

I headed back in the direction of the rest. The cops were inspecting their damaged vehicles. Several of them were totaled, and there were bullet holes in most of them where shots had gone astray. There was glass everywhere, crunching underneath our shoes. And a lot of tires had burst. The whole place smelled of rubber.

Cass was reloading her Mossberg. She did it with mechanical zeal, clicking in one slug after another. Lauren was now sitting on the curb, her blond head down.

A couple of ambulances had arrived, the paramedics spilling out and hurrying to the bodies on the verge. Which seemed rather a waste of effort. None of them were moving.

Saul was on his cell phone, saying, "Yes, Reverend. There's about four families who'll need shelter for a while."

So I suppose he was talking to his friend Dr. Purlock, at the House of the Good Word on Savory Street.

Judge Levin was still around, though standing at a distance from the others, taking in the whole scene sternly. He had his robes pushed back, his hands thrust in his pockets, which was never usually his style.

"What is this, Devries?" he asked me.

I explained what I'd found in the ruins of Tavitt's house.

"And how does that make any sense?"

It was not like he was asking me. More like he was wondering out loud. I wasn't sure, but pointed out the plume of vapor may well have been headed toward Millwood House. He chewed his lower lip musingly.

"I suppose, under the circumstances—if Saul reapplied— he might just get his warrant."

I didn't think it wise to tell him I'd already been inside the place.

"And what are you planning to do?" he asked me.

I was just about to respond when one of the uniformed men started yelling out for Saul. Who ran across to his own car and talked quickly on the radio. When he looked back around at us, I could see how astonished he was.

"There's another one appeared!" he shouted. "It's over in Greenwood!"

* * *

Except it wasn't any kind of snake, this time. I'd drawn up beside Saul's car, and was peering at it through my windshield. And from the glimpses I was getting, I had real trouble understanding what it was at all. A lot of streetlights had been broken, like the last time. And the thing was keeping to the deepest shadows, the same way its predecessor had. I was reminded of the main fact about magic. It and its practitioners preferred to cling to gloomy places, avoiding direct bright light.

The ironic thing was, Greenwood was the dullest district in the entire Landing. Nothing dramatic or outstanding ever seemed to happen here. We were on Oak Tree Avenue, and there weren't even any oak trees in sight. Single-story houses stretched around me for as far as I could see. The place was as flat as a pancake, and considerably less interesting.

But in front of us, there were more wrecked homes, about a dozen of them this time. More corpses were strewn along the sidewalk, one of them a local cop. And at the heart of this destruction?

I climbed out, my gun already in my hand, and got a short-lived look at the creature as it slid along from one street to the next. Except that mostly, it defied description. It appeared to be composed wholly of tentacles, no main body visible. The elongated limbs, hundreds of the things, were mostly narrow. Some of them seemed to have curving talons at the end. And each of them was moving independently, coiling up then straightening. Watching them could make a soul feel giddy, but there wasn't even time for that. I got one last impression of the beast. And then it vanished into the darkness, making a strange whirring, lashing noise.

There was a wail from that direction. And no trick this time. As I watched, a man was lifted high into the air, a strange silhouette above the rooftops. I wondered if I could shoot him down. The tentacle grasping him was thin enough.

But I quickly forgot that idea. He was already gone.

A load more cops had shown up here. Presumably, the dispatchers had been calling the whole dayshift back. And the fire department boys had decided to join in as well—the cops were issuing them with riot guns. A whole crowd of them went forward. Weapons' fire started to wash across the street again.

The judge reappeared. His pale gaze battened on the area the fight was breaking out. He seemed to understand it might be far more difficult this time. I could see that by the way his face went even harder. Then he marched off in the same direction as the rest.

I was just about to join him, when I caught a glimpse of something in the corner of my eye. Another shadowy figure. My aim came up toward it. But then I realized it was a man, huddling in the shadows of a nearby porch. I went across to him. And when he cringed back, I could see he hadn't run away because be was too scared to move.

But I got him calmed down and talking. And it turned out he'd seen everything that had gone down before the cops arrived.

"It came out of Willis Penn's house!"

He pushed the words out anxiously, his body shaking. I was listening to him very carefully, desperate to figure out exactly what was happening.

"Which one's that?" I asked him.

He pointed to a ruined shell.

It turned out Penn had been another lousy neighbor. Little kids were his pet hate. He harassed them mercilessly whenever they came near his place. The folks here would have loved to see the back of him, except that he was penniless and had nowhere else to go.

It wasn't the same kind of creature, then. But it had been the same kind of man. I couldn't claim to understand it, but at least I had something to go on.

I tried to think what to do next. This was utterly crazy. But then I remembered . . . there was one person I knew who saw the world in such chaotic terms. If madness was being visited on us, who better to go to for an explanation?

Cassie's shotgun was still thudding in the distance. And when I finally went toward the racket, I saw two things more.

Lauren was in the thick of the fighting this time, really

going at it. Like I said, people adjust. And the judge was trying to use a Spell of Binding, his palms held out flat. A spider web of yellow sparks was pouring from them, but they couldn't seem to find a proper target. The beast, barely visible, kept on sliding out of reach. I got a glimpse of another eye, as pale as glowing fog. And that confirmed that this was, once again, bound up with Hanlon. But beyond that, I was completely stumped.

I hurried across to Saul, who was standing near to Cassie. He had his sidearm in one hand, his cell phone in the other, and was talking on it, looking like he'd just been slapped around the face with a wet towel.

"East Crealley!" he snapped at me, by way of explanation. "A third one!"

That was the next district up from here. This seemed to be happening in a steady counterclockwise progression. Hanlon and Millicent must have gone from one place to the next, drifting along in vapor form.

I touched Cassie on the shoulder. Her head jerked around.

"Can you keep a handle on things here?" I called above the gunfire.

She peered back at me cockeyed, like I was trying to insult her somehow. Then she got the fact that I was not planning to stick around. I felt a little guilty heading off like this. But one more gun wasn't going to make an awful lot of difference. What we really needed now was solid information. And the look on her face informed me she got that. She had always trusted me, in that respect.

"Where are you going?" she yelled back.

"The last place you'd ever want me to!"

"Which means either the Girl or Raine, right? Up to you! But best of luck!"

CHAPTER 26

Some instinct made me avoid Plymouth Drive again. Going that way would have taken me directly past Millwood House. And I wasn't sure that I wanted to get that close, in view of what was happening below me. That smoke-ghost I'd seen headed off in this direction might be present, after all. And capable of turning back into its serpentine form? I wasn't sure.

There was another route I knew, a track through the dense timber on the western slope of Sycamore Hill. It was barely wide enough to let my car through. Branches scraped continuously against the paintwork, and rocks grumbled underneath the tires. But I made it to the summit with my Cadillac still in one piece, although I'd have to get the chassis looked at.

Then I was making my way on foot to the Manor for the second time in twenty-four hours.

The moving window was no longer there. So—whatever it had been in the first place—Raine had given up on the idea. There was only bare brick in the space that it had occupied, no windowpane remaining. Above it, a couple of the gar-goyles on the roof had woken up. But they weren't doing too much. Just sitting by the guttering and peering at the stars, for all the world like a pair of old men entranced by the night sky's mysteries.

I did my level best to ignore them. Finally went up onto the porch and rang the bell. Then, when I got no answer, hammered on the woodwork. There was not a sound inside. No indication anyone was there. I understood that couldn't be the case. Woodard Raine was agoraphobic, hadn't stepped outside in years. And Hampton—loyal servant that he is— never leaves his master's side unless he absolutely has to.

But it wasn't just the noise that I was making. Raine has a keen inner eye. He had to realize I was out here. For some reason best known to himself, he was taking no notice of me.

I stepped down again and walked along the front of the house, trying to peer in through the windows. Which was as hopeless a task as any I could think of. The moon was out again, reflected in them, like on a series of dark, rectangular ponds. I knew that there was furniture inside the place—I'd seen it. Ornaments, paintings and stuff. And I ought to have been able to make out some outlines.

However hard I peered, I could not see anything beyond the panes of glass. Not even from this close up, with my nose almost pressed against them. Pure unblemished black returned my gaze. I already knew no light ever got into the place. Maybe that worked in reverse as well, and none could get out either.

I tried one of the frames, but it didn't budge. Didn't even tremble, like it was nailed to the surrounding wall. I took out my pocketknife, unfolded it. And, slipping it through a gap, felt around for where the catch ought to be. There seemed to be none. There was nothing physical holding this pane shut.

The same happened with the next one I tried. My temples began pounding with frustration. Then a sound came from above that made me suddenly look up. The two gargoyles on the roof were watching what I was doing. Maybe they'd never seen anyone trying to intrude on Woodard Raine this way.

I knew that I was taking a big risk here. But I couldn't see any other course of action. If Woody thought he could just sit in there and sulk while the whole town was torn to bits, he was mistaken.

Desperate measures, and all that. I went back in among the leafless trees and rummaged around a short while. Came back clutching the kind of object I'd been looking for.

It was a mossy, muddy rock, about the size of a sourdough loaf. I stopped a yard from a window, my lungs feeling heavy and my heart banging against my ribs. This was taking one hell of a chance. I understood that fully.

What finally made me do it was . . . I couldn't see the town from here, there was too much in the way. But I could hear the whine of sirens from below. They seemed to be heading in every which direction. And when I glanced across, I saw two more gray smudges drift through the night sky toward Millwood House, looking like the sails of old-time ships against the glittering blackness. The cops and their allies had managed to stop a couple more of the creatures. But mayhem and then some was still breaking loose down there.

I turned back, hefting the rock. And flung it at the glass.

It shattered easily enough. So I'd been right about it being mostly normal. Big shards and smaller fragments tumbled to the dirt beneath the sill.

I kicked away a few jagged edges at the bottom. Then I started climbing up.

But halfway through, I saw that I might just have made a really big mistake. Because the pieces on the ground were floating up again. The glass was putting itself back together, taking shape around me.

Quickly too.

I yanked my hand away as a section moved in underneath my palm. And then a long shard came swinging up and snagged on my pants leg. The cuff tore as I pulled it free. Panic swept across me. I hurled myself forward, slamming to the floor inside. All the breath was knocked out of me, but considering the alternative . . .

I lay perfectly still, trying to get a sense of my surroundings. Couldn't. It was totally dark in here. Everything seemed to have a floating, weightless quality, so that I wasn't even sure which way was up.

But I'd thought to bring a little flashlight with me and I clicked it on, then got up to my knees.

When I looked back at the window, it was exactly as it had been before the rock had gone through it. There was not the smallest crack visible. But the really weird thing . . . ?

I could see the view outside it perfectly. The tangled woods and the star-filled firmament. And if no light got into this place, how was that even possible?

It was best to simply try and forget it. So much around Raine defies explanation. So I looked away, and almost gasped. This was August Raine's old study. There were snapshots from his college days, up on the wall. And a photograph of his wife on the huge mahogany desk. I played the circle of light across them gently.

This was where he'd shown me the Thieftaker, during the course of one of his numerous garden parties. I'd felt honored at the time.

I got the rest of the way to my feet, still playing the beam around. There was a brass and crystal chandelier overhead. And a stuffed bear in one corner of the room, exactly as I remembered it. But I wasn't here for any of this, so I went into the corridor outside.

A different kind of light came bobbing up to me as I emerged. A candle, in a white porcelain holder. Behind it, I could see Hampton's face, his mismatched eyes glinting annoyedly.

He was far more used to living in this all-consuming darkness than I was. He'd had years to adjust to it. And as the distance closed between us, he must have seen the look on my face, and slowed down sharply. He's not a bad guy, and I didn't want to hurt him. But I wasn't about to let him get in my way.

His expression phased through from astonished to noticeably scared. And then he seemed to reach a quick decision, disappearing through a nearby doorway, blowing out the candle as he went.

That was the last I saw of him. I headed for the ballroom, which was where Woody was usually holed up, passing numerous examples of the family crest and antiques hanging from or clustered by the walls.

My soles finally clacked on parquet flooring. Several more candles on tall, thin holders had been lit in here. Given the size of the room, their glow was not particularly bright. The shapes around me were uniformly indistinct. There was a massive crystal chandelier above me, five times the size of the one back in the study. Huge portraits of Raine's ancestors dominated most of the paneled walls. But on the furthest one, his family tree had been engraved. It stretched right back to Theodore Raine, the founder of this town. And immediately after him, his son, Jasper. Who had married Sephera McBryde, the leader of the Salem witches.

Of the current owner, there was not a sign. But that's far from unusual. Woody acts like he's doing you a favor when he bothers to reveal himself.

I was opening my mouth, about to yell his name out. But then events went and beat me to it. Two things happened, one hard on the other's heels.

The door behind me suddenly slammed shut, with a resounding thump. It did that on its own, since there was no one standing there.

And then, the air around me started moving. Sucking inward fiercely. Gusting up around me. I could feel the hair lift on my scalp, and the loose edges of my clothing flapped.

The wind rose to a steady shriek, becoming so intense that I could scarcely breathe. It plucked at me like a giant hand. The bottoms of my shoes lost contact with the floor a second.

Then I was lifted completely off my feet and carried up into the air.

My first instinct was to grab hold of the chandelier. But I decided that was a bad idea. Staying calm, whatever might be going on, was always the best policy. Except that it was pretty hard under these particular circumstances.

And then—damn—I dropped the flashlight.

"Woody!" I barked. "Cut it out!"

A pair of dark gold eyes with slitted pupils came open below me. And they stared up at me balefully.

*   *   *

The main thing about Woodard Raine—however crazy he might get—is that he's always clung on to his father's values. He'd been taught them at such an early age that they were etched into his brain, I guess. And they included civility. So long as you were a guest in his home, he would never harm you.

Except on this occasion, I didn't exactly count as that. This wasn't a social call. I hadn't been invited. Quite the opposite, in fact. The word was "intruder." I'd committed B&E. And so, how'd he react to that? Maybe the old rules no longer applied.

The air continued to push in around me, streaming across the contours of my face. It was really hard not to surrender to panic. I had to be twelve feet off the ground, and that bronze-tinged gaze was still fastened on me.

Raine blinked slowly.

"Put me down!" I shouted at him, gulping as I did so. With the wind pushing against my features, it was hard to draw in any air.

I went up a little higher. There was a gleam of sharpened teeth as he finally replied.

"You have some goddamn nerve, sport! Smashing up the place? And scaring Hampton? Just because we've been on good terms in the past, that doesn't allow you to take liberties."

I'd no idea what "good terms" meant. I'd put up with his quirky behavior, that was all. Done it from expediency and little else. The less time I spent in his company, then the happier I was. But Woody's always had his own distorted way of seeing things. He looks at them through the eyeglass of his own imagination—realism barely played the slightest part.

Back before the magic had completely taken over, he'd been little more than a rich spoiled brat. Slim and blue-eyed, with a permanently cocky sneer imprinted on his face. His parents' influence had kept him out of trouble. Now that they were gone, he kept on finding brand-new ways of getting into it.

I kicked at the air defiantly, trying to show him I was not

afraid. Which wasn't wholly true. He'd never done anything like this before, and I was concerned how far he'd take it.

But, as I've said before, dealing with the adepts is a matter of not being intimidated by them, or their conjuring tricks.

"It's not me taking liberties!" I managed to shout down at him. "How can you ignore what's happening?"

His gaze narrowed, and I thought I could detect a hint of puzzlement.

"What exactly do you mean?"

"You must know what's been going on?"

"You mean the creatures in the suburbs? There've been monsters in my town before, old chum."

Which was how he thought of the whole Landing, in a patriarchal and possessive sense.

"They're being taken care of adequately. I don't see there's any need for—"

"These aren't the usual kinds of conjuration!" I broke across him. "There's a lot more to it this time. Something genuinely weird is happening. And it's partly down to Millicent Tollburn!"

"Milly?"

The twin bronze glows vanished. He'd either shut his eyes, or dropped his head. And, when they appeared again, their brightness was far less intense than before.

A pale, slim hand with long, narrow fingers like a pianist's became apparent. He stretched it out at me.

And when his palm moved downward, I did too. Relief washed through my entire frame.

CHAPTER 27

I settled to the parquet floor a couple of yards in front of him. The wicks of a few more candles sprang up with fresh flame, which danced but made the scene a little clearer.

He had changed since I'd last met him. It's like he keeps on reinventing himself. The sallow, sharply structured features were the same. And he still had the leaf-shaped ears that were the mark of all his family. But—apart from the darker eyes—the beard of before was gone. His hair was shorter than it had been. You could see the little scar on his chin where he had fallen over drunk one time, in college.

He seemed to be wearing pure black robes on this occasion. They were plain matte ones, and did not throw back a scintilla of the candlelight. His head looked like it was floating independently because of them. Whether that was an intentional effect or not I'd no idea. I'd better things to do with my time than try to figure out what was going on in that bizarre jumble inside his head.

But I needed his help, and didn't let myself forget that.

I explained everything that had been going down. Not merely the creatures, but Hanlon's arrival here, and the whole business at Millwood House as well. I left Lauren Brennan out of the equation, since I didn't want him taking too much of an interest in her. She'd already gone through quite enough, without being subjected to Woody's weird attentions.

I wasn't quite sure how much of this he was really absorbing. It was a whole big load of information, even for a saner mind. And I knew how Woody's focus kept on going off in strange directions.

He did look concerned, however. And kept making funny little noises, clucks and gulps and thoughtful humming sounds.

He broke across me only once, to explain about the Wand of Dantiere and what it did. The way that it turned human bodies into clouds of vapor, which could enter other people and affect their minds. Which was pretty much as I'd expected. I continued to the point where the last creature had appeared.

"Does the wand do that too?"

"Not that I was ever aware of," he came back at me.

The candlelight was leaving shadowed hollows in his face, so it looked partway like a skull. A few crystal beads on the chandelier tinkled softly above us, in spite of the fact the door was closed.

"I need to get an idea what's been going on behind the scenes," I told him. "What Millicent and Hanlon have really been up to."

He blinked at me again, but didn't move.

"That would mean looking back into the past. Which I can't do, old chum."

His mind was like a junk heap. So much garbage kept getting poured across it, he could no longer sort out what was valuable from what was not. His memory was shot to pieces. So I reminded him—gently—he could do precisely that.

He squinted at me, still not getting it.

"The Eye of Hermaneus, Woody. You know where you've put it, right?"

"Oh!" He suddenly brightened. "One of my most precious artifacts. Ah, yes! I think I know where it is!"

He held out his right arm, the hand closed to a fist. And when he opened it, the large white jewel was lying in his palm.

"What precisely are we looking for, sport?" he asked me for the umpteenth time.

He kept on getting distracted by the tiny, detailed scenes that were unfolding in front of us, and forgetting what this was about.

"Langham Tavitt, just before he turned," I reminded him wearily.

"In Garnerstown?"

"That's right."

"I really ought to do something about that neighborhood. It's honestly a bit of an embarrassment."

I had to fight hard not to let my irritation show.

The Eye of Hermaneus was floating six feet in the air. Brightness was churning at its heart, intensely as a tiny sun. A cone of light was being projected down from it. And, within that steady glow, images from this evening were being replayed in miniature, in full three-dimensions, but devoid of any sound.

There we were, shooting at the snakelike creature. There were Saul, Lauren, and Cass, arriving at the scene. Events were going backward here. It seemed to be the best way to discover the correct moment in time

The snake let go of a passer-by that it was clutching in its jaws, then went in reverse through the wall of Langham Tavitt's home, which promptly became whole again.

"We're getting there," Woody murmured.

Then we were inside the house. My God, it was an awful mess. Everything looked grimy. A huge pile of newspapers over in one corner looked like it went back a couple of decades. And three plates were lying on the dining table, each of them with leftover food.

The elongated black form shrank away to reveal Tavitt himself, sprawled back in a rocking chair. There was a bottle of wine gripped in his fist. And in his lap was the same paperback I'd seen in Garnerstown.

Despite the fact he was indoors, he still had his coat on. It was a thick woolen number with big buttons down the front, the kind of thing they used to wear in the trenches in the First World War. He had on big scuffed boots as well. And fingerless gloves on his grimy hands. His hair and beard both needed cutting. There was nothing clean about him, when you studied him properly.

Nick McLeish hadn't been joking. This guy was a total wreck. His eyes were closed and he was mumbling to himself. Of course, I couldn't hear a word that he was saying. The magic of the jewel, so far as I was aware, didn't allow for that.

But—I practically jerked when I saw it—he was not alone in the room. The ball of vapor was hanging over him, a gray miasmic pall like an embodiment of his own thoughts.

We went further back, to the point where it had first arrived. It came seeping in under the front door, for all the world like normal fog. Woody made a sudden motion with his hands. The scene stopped running backward, and we could see what had happened after that.

The vapor didn't pour into the man. It merely swirled above his head, looking pretty harmless. Then it densened a little, contracting.

Tavitt sat up alarmedly—although, curiously, his eyes did not come open. He tipped his head to one side, like he was listening to something. Then his mouth began to work again. Whatever he was hearing, he had decided to answer it.

But this was no real use to me. I turned frustratedly to Woody.

"This isn't helping."

He looked perplexed, and a strange buzzing noise echoed between the paneled walls. I was used to things like that, since I'd heard similar stuff on previous occasions. Sounds that manifested his troubled state of mind.

"It was good enough before," he argued.

He was referring to the time when he had helped me outwit Saruak. But that had been a completely different set of circumstances. I was pretty certain—whoever was in that ball of vapor, he, or she, was saying things to Tavitt. Things that could make him change shape physically. A spell?

It was the reason I'd come here. I just had to find out what it was. "Ached" was not too small a word.

"This is really important, Woody."

"I'm not sure that I agree," he stuttered.

He'd forgotten part of what I'd told him, and was wandering from the point again. I wondered what could bring him back. Appealing to his finer feelings? "The whole town's counting on you," I reminded him. "Your town. Your people, right? How can you let them down?"

His expression became far more sober. And he nodded, seeing I was right.

And once that was agreed, I gave him some elbow room. When the Master of the Manor turns to stronger magic, then it's not overly wise to get too close.

He spread his arms out to the sides. Thanks to the robe, the only way that I could tell was by the white blobs of his fingertips. He closed his eyes again and tipped his head back. Then he started muttering.

I couldn't make the slightest sense of it. Adepts use a range of languages when they're invoking the dark forces. Kurt van Friesling uses Dutch. The McGinley sisters, Gaelic. Latin plays its part, of course. But the stuff that Raine was using sounded like English that had gotten drunk, and then fallen over and started mumbling to itself in a gutter. Some old dialect from a place like Cornwall, England, maybe? It's believed to be the home of Merlin, so that's not impossible.

The scene inside the cone of light started running in reverse again, back to the point where the mist appeared.

And suddenly, almost miraculously, there was a blurt of actual sound.

"Yes."

That was Tavitt, his voice whiny, like he had a bug caught in his throat. The man looked attentive, for all that his eyes were closed.

"Yes, you're right. I can see that."

He tipped his head to one side and his features started creasing up, his expression becoming angry.

"It's true. I've always known that, really."

This was merely one half of the conversation. So I returned my attention to my host.

"This is single speaker, Woods," I told him. "I need stereo."

Woody's eyes came open a slit. They'd gone an ever darker shade of gold, and were glowing in an edgy, rather feverish way. But then he applied himself harder to the task.

I had to wait another full minute before a second voice came oozing out. As I listened, I could hear that it was actually two voices, speaking in unison and overlapping.

One of them, I recognized immediately. Those cut-glass tones were Millicent Tollburn's. The deeper accent had to be Hanlon. He sounded like a loud and fractious child.

So it had a weird, distorted echo to it. Rather like listening to the Little Girl, to tell the truth.

"None of these people understand you, Langham. No one in this whole town does."

"I've always suspected that."

"Look how you've been treated your entire life. All you're fit for—so far as these people are concerned—is sweeping up the filth they leave behind."

"You're right. I had dreams, once upon a time."

"And they've denied you that. They even teach their children to hate you, so it'll be the same for the next generation. Your life will never change. It'll be this way until the day you die. Do you deserve that?"

His face was growing angrier.

"They want to make you suffer, can't you see that? Want to keep you poor and on your own. Why should you accept that, Langham? Why don't you fight back?"

The man's eyes snapped open at last. And they were not gray as yet. But a strange murkiness had begun to swirl across their glassy surface. I stared at it, amazed. The pall of vapor was still hanging over him. Had not taken possession of him, the way it had with Karl. The whole transformation, this time, seemed to be coming from inside the man.

"Show them they can't get away with it," the voices urged. "They've hurt you so very much. Now, it's time to hurt them back. Make them regret what they've done."

When he nodded, it was sternly.

"Yep. I think I'll do precisely that."

The cloud had still not touched him. But his eyes turned a glowing gray from lid to lid all the same.

There was a sharp crash as he let go of the bottle. His hands dropped into his lap. Then they started melting into his body. Which was lengthening, and turning black.

I could have let it go on, but I got the general picture. Woody seemed to think so too. The cone of light, the scene inside it, vanished. The glow inside the jewel diminished, and it floated back into its owner's grasp. He slipped it quickly underneath his robes, then turned around to face me.

His features looked even more sickly than they'd been before. He was genuinely shocked. That was a rarity. Nothing seemed real enough to him for that reaction, most days. Which told me this was a very exceptional day indeed.

His lips were pressed together. And his golden gaze shimmered like a pair of distant lamps.

I still wasn't sure I wholly understood this. If the cloud had not possessed the man, exactly what had happened? I looked to my host for an answer. And was pretty astonished by what finally came out.

"I really had no idea," Woody murmured, "exactly how far reaching the wand's powers were."

Which didn't make things any clearer. But I sensed that he was getting to the point, and so I waited for him to go on. He raised his fingertips to his chin, growing lost in anxious thought, and not his usual batty kind.

"Normally, by means of magic, change is imposed on an object or a person. But this . . . ?"

He seemed aghast at such a concept.

"This is transmutation brought on by consent."

His eyebrows were lifted as high as they could go. And he stared at me like I was lucky that I didn't fully understand it yet.

"Tavitt became that creature because he wanted to. It was within him. I'm willing to bet the other man—"

"Penn."

"—was the same. They weren't turned into monsters, no. The monsters inside them were released. They were in there the whole time, Devries. Just hidden, until tonight."

I still wasn't sure I got it. Woody stepped in, getting so close up to me that we were almost standing face-to-face.

"Think about it. Can you really not see the big picture? Milly and Hanlon didn't change those men. They simply released their inner demons."

And that hit me like a blow, taking the remainder of my breath away. What he was suggesting wasn't possible, was it? I didn't see how that could happen.

I had watched it, though. I'd seen the process. There was no use trying to deny that.

"So . . . they're seeking out misfits, and what? Letting loose the bigger creep inside of them?"

But I still had not got it completely. Raine shook his head, looking very subdued. He seemed—for the moment—utterly sane.

"It's not only misfits who are vulnerable, old chum. We all have monsters trapped inside us, I'm afraid."

He saw the question spark in my gaze.

"Even me, remarkably," he nodded. "Even you."

CHAPTER 28

By the time I'd got back to my car, I could see clustered bursts of small bright flashes, far off in the distance most places I looked. More gunfire. There was plenty of it, both sides of the darkly gleaming river. And patrol cars were rushing from district to district. It seemed like what had gone down in Garnerstown and Greenwood was happening in East Crealley and Pilgrim's Plot as well. So I'd been right—it was counterclockwise. One by one, the outer suburbs to the east were being hit.

I climbed in and tuned my radio to a police channel. There was a load of shouting going on, several dozen voices competing for air space. If this went on, Cassie's neighborhood would be next. Then mine.

I should have gone down straightaway. But I noticed something, shortly before I set off.

The flashing in East Crealley died away abruptly. So the beast down there had been stopped in its tracks. Another cloud appeared above the roofs' dark silhouettes. It rose into the night sky like a misshapen balloon. And then it seemed to swell.

I understood it wasn't that. The thing was simply heading my way, getting closer, and at speed.

I tensed up. But the thing never reached the crest of Sycamore Hill. Like both the others, it turned at the last moment, plunging down to Plymouth Drive. And disappeared behind a spreading clump of elm trees, shortly before it reached Millwood House.

What would I find if I went down there? I reversed onto the main road, then headed down the gradient with my lights off.

Which practically turned out to be a very big mistake indeed. As I rounded the final bend before Ms. Tollburn's residence, a middle-aged man in expensive-looking sweats stepped out right in front of me, not even seeing I was there.

I stamped on my brakes, squealing to a halt mere inches from him. He glanced at me through the windshield. But then seemed to forget about me. He was more concerned about something else, apparently. His eyes had a haunted look. His face was damp.

He was silver-haired, distinguished-looking in a slightly paunchy way. Had a thin spike of a nose, and lips with a patrician twist. Most probably a local. There were big gold rings on both his hands, a chain of the same around his throat. And the watch that he was wearing hadn't come exactly cheap. By the sweats, he might have been out running. He could have been using one of the woodland trails up here, and not even noticed what was going on.

My gaze wandered past him down the wide, shadowy avenue.

There were more people standing on the asphalt. They all looked as if they lived here too. They'd come wandering out of their homes, a few of them in shorts or even housecoats. And were staring blankly at Ms. Tollburn's place.

I squinted across at it, and felt my face go slack. There'd been a high brick wall with spikes before. And a wide flat roof beyond it.

They had completely disappeared behind a barrier of plain, featureless gray that rose some thirty feet into the air. It was the same down the left side of the property, the entire mansion sealed from view, as if a huge box had been placed across it.

My heart sank even further. I couldn't remember ever

seeing anything quite so ominous. It looked genuinely threatening, sitting there like a steel fortress. I could only wonder what was happening inside.

As I watched, another ball of vapor arced across the sky, rushing in its direction. Which told me what precisely about the situation we were in? The creatures that had invaded our town were being dealt with, for sure. But they weren't being destroyed in any meaningful way. They were simply retreating here. To regroup? If so, for what purpose?

I watched it drop down to the barrier, then disappear behind it. And felt my heart sink to rock bottom. How many more were there going to be?

By the time that I'd rejoined the others, the attacks had spread up to East Meadow. Further mayhem had broken out a couple of blocks from Rowan Street, where Cassie had her home.

And that really ticked her off. Her dark eyes blazed, her lean face was white with fury. And she laid into this brand-new creature with a vengeance that was startling to watch.

It wasn't anything gigantic, this time. Everybody had their own particular size of inner demon, I supposed. The thing was roughly my height, although far more densely muscled. And retained a vaguely human shape. But it was really much more like some massive ape, the same silhouetted black as the others, with the same gleaming eyes. Fur hung from it in ragged tatters, swirling as the creature moved. It had a wide mouth with pointed fangs. Lengthy arms with sharp nails at the fingertips. And legs as powerful as springs.

And it was moving at a truly unbelievable speed. Even the fastest of us could barely keep tabs on it. One second, it was up in front of us and we were trying to take aim. And the next, it was on a roof in one huge bound, and hurrying around to flank us.

We were on a street where some developer, a while back, had had the brilliant notion of tearing the wood-built houses down and replacing them with tightly lined apartment blocks. It didn't make the place look any better. It simply made the shabbiness appear more permanent.

We kept on swinging around, trying to find our target. But we had to be careful where we opened fire. The people in the blocks around us were keeping themselves out of sight, of course. But a few times that a gun went off, a bullet sailed in through a window. Nobody was going to approve of the P.D. doing that, especially if some tenant caught a ricochet.

Cass, naturally, had no such qualms. She had her Mossberg out again, and was pumping at it furiously. She almost hit the creature twice, except it dodged away just in time. I wasn't quite sure which was louder—the repeated blasting of her shotgun, or the stream of curses that she let out every time she missed.

Both of them finally trailed to a halt. Because this new demon had simply vanished.

"Where'd it go?" somebody asked.

We peered around cautiously.

The thing had been up on a cornice to our right. Except it was no longer there, or anywhere else we looked. Maybe it had given up, turning into a cloud of smoke and heading up the hill like the others.

There were a dozen of us here. Half were cops, the rest were firemen and civilians. There'd been more outbreaks back the way we'd come. So groups like this were spread thinly across the whole eastern side of town.

An adept would be here soon—we'd been assured of that. The main thing was to simply hang on. Everyone around me looked exhausted and unsteady. I glanced across at Saul, who was perspiring heavily. But he didn't lower his piece. He stayed alert. And, following his example, the rest of us did the same. That thing could come at us again in the blinking of an eye. And so we kept on staring off along the rooftops, waiting for another glimpse of it.

There was a sudden blur of movement from an alley to our left. We started to turn, but far too slowly. The thing went ramming into a uniformed cop, knocking him to the ground before we'd even taken in what was happening. It ducked its head over his throat an instant. And then it was gone, retreating back into the alley, leaving us with no time to react.

It had happened so terribly quickly. I took a glance at what the thing had done, then grit my teeth. The cop on the ground was Colin Trent, the brand-new rookie. And he wasn't getting up any time soon.

Steam was coming from his open windpipe. I took that in, then looked away. Hobart dropped his head and swore. How many people had he lost in ways like this, during the years he'd been in charge? Yet another of his people reduced to a photograph in Sam Scott's Tavern, next to Davy Quinn's.

A second swiftly moving shape went past me, heading for the alley too. But it wasn't any demon, this time.

"Cassie!" I yelled out.

She must have heard me, but she kept on running anyway. I took another deep breath, then went after her.

East Meadow was holed like a Swiss cheese with alleyways like this. It was only about four feet wide, and half filled up with trash cans. It smelled foul. Spilled refuse crunched underfoot. You couldn't see the far end, since there was a right-angled bend halfway along, and that made the sense of being shut in even worse.

Something small and not too clean had died here recently—I couldn't see it, but my nose made up for what my eyes were missing. The night sky was a narrow strip above us, and looked very far away, almost unreal.

Cassie was moving far more slowly by this time, her Mossberg out in front of her and her left arm suspended at shoulder height for balance. She was trying to walk quietly, but that was plain impossible in here. A rusted tin can spun away from her boot and something crackled when she stepped on it.

Our eyes were darting everywhere.

"Where's Levin, by the way?" I whispered.

"Dealing with another one, out on the edge of Pilgrim's Plot. And Gaspar Vernon's shown up too."

There was no love lost between me and that particular adept, but I still considered it good news.

"What are these things anyway?" Cass asked me.

"To sum it up, the darkest side of our own natures."

At which point, she let out a groan that seemed to swell in the fetid darkness.

"You're not serious?"

"Afraid I am."

"Why can't anything be simple round this place?" she complained, continuing to move forward.

"Next time," I promised her, "I'll try and find you some nice, uncomplicated monsters."

Her head gave a tiny nod. "Appreciate it."

Then our talk went out the window. Just as we were getting near another clump of trash cans, they exploded like a bomb had gone off in their midst. Lids and cylinders went flying everywhere. And what we'd thought was merely a shadow resolved itself into a now familiar shape, which came rushing at us again. It was snarling furiously, despite the fact it hadn't made a sound before.

It was on me before I had time to move. One lengthy arm came swinging out. I tried to block it, but the thing was moving much too fast. Its knuckles caught me on the jaw. I flew back, slamming hard against a wall and scraping down it.

Then it turned on Cassie, and she disappeared beneath its jet-black silhouette. Its head ducked toward her neck.

I felt my heart almost stop in my chest. Had visions of her with her throat torn out, like Colin Trent's had been.

I hadn't counted on her resilience.

When the creature bit down, its fangs closed around her Mossberg. She had brought it up to shield her windpipe just in time. As its face pulled away, she swung the gun butt— really hard—into its cheek. The thing let out a yelp and staggered off from her.

She was back on her feet in the next moment, pushing herself after it. But it bounded away before she could hit it again. It bounced off the surrounding brickwork like a rubber ball and came caroming back. Both of its hands grabbed at her. But Cassie simply used its speed against it.

She swung her body around to the side as it made contact, pivoting from the waist. The beast lost its grip again, and went sailing past. Slammed into the wall behind her with a resounding smack.

Cass didn't even pause. She aimed and fired from the hip. There was a cloud of dust, a hole appeared. But, once again, the demon had escaped before the charge struck home.

It picked up an overturned pail and came hurtling back at her. Swung its weapon forward and down, trying to smash her in the face with it.

Cassie simply fended off the blow, crossing her arms in front of her. And then lashed out with her right boot, kicking her attacker in the stomach.

It let go of the can and doubled over. At which point, she drove her knee into its chin.

The apelike thing went down, landing heavily on its back. She calmly stepped onto its groin. And when its mouth came open—which was pretty much inevitable—she shoved the muzzle of her shotgun into it, and put a slug into its skull.

The whole thing dissolved into a large swirl of vapor, drifting upward and then disappearing past the rooftops. I watched Cass's body stiffen, and could almost feel the tremors of frustration rising off her.

"Goddamn it!" she protested loudly. "How's that fair? I won!"

It wasn't too much longer before I found myself doing battle in my own neighborhood . . . although not near Kenveigh Street, I'm glad to say. Some people were working as runners by this stage, resupplying us with ammunition, since everyone was getting low. We managed to defeat the creature there, but then were called down through Vernon Valley and West Meadow, almost to the edge of Marshall Drive, before being forced to turn around and head back the whole other way again. Why didn't the attacks continue down the west side? Well, the Little Girl lives in Marshall Drive, so maybe that had something to do with it.

Most of the information I was getting, by that stage, was from other cops or from the babble on my radio. I learned that the rest of the major adepts had put in an appearance, and was relieved to hear that. But there was an even more significant development. Once news of what was happening had really got around, whole droves of ordinary people started showing up, armed as best as they could manage and eager to help.

I started passing them as I drove from one neighborhood to the next, the suburbs around me becoming a seamless blur. You couldn't even call them a militia. It was too spur of the moment, too unplanned for that. But I watched them pitch in fiercely, throwing themselves into the fighting shoulder to shoulder with the uniformed guys. And it wasn't just the men of this town either. There were women too. A few of the older cops tried turning them away at first, but simply got shouted down.

"It's just as much our home!" was the constant yell I heard.

Cassie would have approved, but I didn't see too much of her for quite a while after the alley. So much was going down that we kept heading off to different places. There was no choice in the matter. Creatures were appearing in a constant flow. And all through the small hours till the crack of dawn, we battled with new demons of every shape and size. There were a few more huge ones, including one so shapeless that I still cannot describe it. But a lot of them were man-sized, and as fast and deadly as the first had been. Some of them were heavily scaled. Most had fangs and talons.

I spotted her again, and a lot of other people that I knew, during the very final battle of that night. We'd all got concentrated in one district—Pilgrim's Plot again—since there were four separate demons roaming it. We beat each one, thank God.

The fighting started to die away around me as the first couple of shafts of sunlight leapt up at the far horizon. By which time, I was so weary I could barely think. Christ only knew what was keeping me up on my feet. But I remained in that position long enough to look around. And I did that bleakly, with a feeling of despair.

The full light of dawn revealed a very sorry state. Several plumes of smoke were rising—you could smell it everywhere. A few houses had caught when they'd been ripped apart; those had burned to cinders, since our fire department had been occupied elsewhere. Everywhere I looked, I could see damage. Roofs were crushed, walls had collapsed. A good number of cars were overturned, and some were leaking gasoline. Still, as Nick McLeish had pointed out, it was replaceable.

In fact, I could still see Nick McLeish, a long way from his own neighborhood. He was sitting on the curb about ten feet away from me, still in his undershirt, a hunting rifle across his knees. He had his head in his hands, his eyes closed. And he looked desperately chewed up and wasted. So did everyone around me.

A short way further up, a pair of college girls—dressed in faded jeans and brightly patterned T-shirts—had their arms wrapped around each other and were crying on each other's shoulders. There'd been three in their group when I'd first noticed them. Damn. My heart went out to them, not least because I'd been to the place that they were visiting this morning. They had lost a friend.

Cassie had climbed back on her Harley, but only so she could sit down. She was slumped over the handlebars, and didn't look like she was going to move from that position any time soon. Other people were wandering around, their mouths hanging open and their eyes completely glassy.

I was aching too, from the constant exertion, and my eyelids kept on rasping every time I blinked. But I wandered across to Saul, who was talking on his cell phone yet again. He'd been doing that continuously since the fighting had stopped.

"How've we done?" I asked him.

And he peered at me unhappily.

"Twenty-two dead, so far. Four of my people, and eighteen civilians. Not the worst night we've ever had in the Landing."

And I knew exactly what he meant. Saruak and his creature, the Dralleg, had killed dozens more.

"But not the best one either. With how many more to come, I wonder?"

That was the real question, wasn't it? I stared around again. The adepts had gone by this hour. The dead had been carried away, and the injured taken to hospital.

But something else was happening. I started noticing that as well. The people who'd been driven out of their homes were returning to them. Some of them started picking dismally through the wreckage. Others just sat down heavily in their litter-strewn front yards, their legs going out from under them. It was mostly shock, I knew. Give them time and they'd get over it.

But I hadn't counted on the other townsfolk, those who hadn't lost their homes. They began emerging from their own front doors and moving among their stricken neighbors. Blankets were being thrown over the shoulders of those who were still shaking. Others got offers of help, or simply reassuring hugs.

Then people started to emerge with thermos flasks and mugs. They began handing out coffee to those who'd spent the whole night fighting. A few hip flasks were being passed around as well. Cotton wool and bandages appeared, and minor wounds were dealt with on the spot.

That's the thing about the Landing. It can be a pretty scary place to live in, sure. But what makes it bearable is its everyday inhabitants. I've seen them go through the worst the supernatural can throw at them, and still come bouncing back.

Watching the hushed activity around me, I felt pretty proud to live among them. Not that I had a lot of choice.

My own cell phone went off in my pocket, and I wondered what needed my attention now.

CHAPTER 29

I listened carefully as Judge Levin explained the new developments to me. The adepts were regathering at the McGinley place, to discuss what they ought to do. And they wanted me in, since I'd been useful in the past. But I decided to drop Lauren off at my house first. No one had forced her to stay here, or asked her to join in with the fighting. So it was the very least that I could do.

The only thing that seemed to be keeping her awake in the slightest was the memory of what had happened. Her skin was like bleached parchment in the morning light. Her eyes were marbled and glistening uneasily. She kept on rubbing her lips together, like she was struggling to remember how to speak.

"You live with this the whole time?" she asked me at last, gawking at me from the passenger seat.

I rounded a corner, going past a small truck that was headed back the other way.

"Of course not. How could that be true? Most of the time, the Landing is like Sticksville anywhere you'd care to mention. People mow their lawns and wash their cars and get on with their ordinary lives."

She looked unconvinced. The sky was turning blue again. The air was warming up. But that was lost on her. She still appeared to be reliving the past few hours, and I couldn't blame her. So was I.

"But sometimes?"

"Sometimes," I conceded, "things come busting out at us. And then we have to deal with them, because running away isn't an option."

In the outside world, I knew, there was a whole big load of refugees. But the concept didn't apply here. It's not a term we ever use.

She lowered her head, trying to take that in. And then she stared at me again.

"Incredible though it might seem . . ." Her voice had turned to a dull whisper. "I've been doing some thinking. In the lulls between avoiding getting killed, you understand. And I've figured something out. Your wife didn't leave you, did she? She couldn't leave town. Is she . . . ?"

I shifted in my seat. Although she hadn't meant to, her words burned like acid. We were on Colver Street by this time, and entering Northridge. I stared out through the speckled windshield, trying to ignore the heaviness that had begun to pull inside my chest.

"How long ago was it?" Lauren asked.

More than two years, but I didn't say that.

Instead I answered, "She's not dead."

Lauren looked genuinely surprised. "What, then?"

"I'm not really sure."

Which didn't help her.

"It was magic too?"

For all her numbness and tired disbelief, she seemed to catch on pretty quickly.

"Her and my kids. Two of them. Yes," I said.

"And . . . ?"

I still couldn't look at her. I just kept staring at the outside world like it was a series of disjointed pictures.

"I'm waiting for them to come back."

And I have to admit, I felt pretty awkward saying that. But it was the truth. I'd seen no proof that they had died. They had simply disappeared. And there were other planes of existence out there, other dimensions—I already knew that from the adepts' talk. Was it possible that they were trapped in one of them? I hoped so, because the alternative . . .

Lauren's face filled up with sympathy. She reached out to touch my arm. But then, looking at how rigid I'd gone, she decided not to.

The silent houses drifted by. None of them were damaged, here. Looking at them, you'd scarcely believe anything bad had happened. Except there was no one out on the sidewalk this morning. Even the little kids had stayed indoors.

The motor of the Cadillac continued its low thrum. And the unspoken question hung between us. If they don't come back?

Lauren cleared her throat uneasily, then ducked her head again, glancing away from me.

The thing about the McGinley sisters—Cynthia and Dido— was they put up a refined, genteel appearance, but were in truth nothing like that.

But the illusion was an impressive one. Who better to create such than a pair of sibling witches?

They occupied a massive Gothic residence at the far end of Billings Avenue from the judge's house. And it might have looked grandiose and threatening, the way that kind of architecture sometimes does. Except they'd done it up like something from a happy fairy tale.

There were bright floral drapes at the windows, red, yellow, and blue. Nesting boxes had been nailed below the eaves—there was the constant stir of finches for part of the year. There were rows of huge sunflowers in the borders around the house. And the lawns were strewn with decorative statuary, all in animal shapes. The March hare romped. A tortoise ambled.

You're always welcome, read the mat on the porch. That was a lie, and everyone knew it. Over to my right, a little plastic windmill whirred. You practically expected to see gingerbread in the walls if you stared hard enough.

The door itself was open, so I wiped my feet and then went in. And the truth of the sisters' nature was revealed.

There were lights in the ceiling, attractive ones with frosted glass shades the shape of buttercups. And they were switched on. But they seemed to cast barely any glow. It was like moving through an early twilight.

The brass engravings on the walls were tarnished with age, darkened. On them—when I squinted—there were devils depicted. Creatures with the heads of bulls and stallions. Numerous satyrs, doing things to nymphs. There was something deeply unsettling about them, an unconcerned malevolence.

The carpet was dark too, and had that kind of overly intricate pattern that makes you unsure of your footing. What made it worse was that the wallpaper was the same. There were display cabinets on view, with all kinds of junk behind the glass. Ancient bones, with mold in their crevasses. Shrunken body parts, some of them not human. One shelf just had teeth on it, in various shapes and sizes.

A dented skull stared at me from another, with its jaws partially agape.

A second door swung open in front of me. So I went through that, into what appeared to be a hidden corridor. There was no decoration here. It was far more narrow, and completely bare, the ceiling so low my hair almost brushed against it. But I kept on going.

I finally emerged into a small, entirely circular room. And, given the general shape of the house, that didn't make any sense. There were no windows. And the curving wall was painted with a vast, surreal mural. Jaws gaped and eyes stared. It extended, as though spilling down, across the stone-tiled floor. And that made me feel even more unsettled. Like I was entering the mouth of madness.

The major adepts were waiting for me.

The first thing that I sensed, when I stepped in, was a pair of gazes battening on me, emerald green and predatory. The sisters themselves. You'd have taken them for twins, but they'd been born a year apart. They were almost identical, hatchet-faced, in their midforties, with their dark hair piled up on their prematurely aged heads. They were both in black flowing gowns. The only way of telling them apart was that Dido, the slightly older one, had suffered a mild stroke a while back, which made her left eyelid droop.

Levin was here, of course. Standing next to him was a huge, barrel-chested bald guy with a long off-white moustache. Gaspar Vernon was very rich, but always insisted on dressing like a simple workingman. He came from humble woodsman stock originally, and never let anyone forget it.

Kurt van Friesling was the opposite, and wearing a tuxedo even at this early hour. In his youth, he had run wild with Raine. But he'd gotten more mature since then. His very pale blue eyes were pinned on me as well.

Martha Howard-Brett looked like she wanted to smile at the sight of me. Only the seriousness of the occasion stopped her. Unlike some who were gathered here, we'd always got on very well. She wasn't nearly the most expert of this crowd, but she made up for it with her warmth and her intelligence. An absolutely stunning woman, tall and shapely with long auburn hair.

Her gaze—a lustrous hazel—was sparkling in spite of what we'd been through. I'd once referred to her as the Good Witch of the North. And I'm glad to say it made her laugh.

Cobb Walters was in his waistcoat and bow tie, as usual. Most adepts seemed to be particular about the way they dressed. He stood only slightly taller than Levin and was scrawny, with slumped shoulders and a pronounced stoop. His black hair was thinning. His nose was so oversized that, combined with his sad expression, he looked like a basset hound. Which only really goes to show that you shouldn't judge someone by appearances. His sorcery was very strong.

Mayor Aldernay was there as well. He had no magic, despite his lineage. But I supposed they'd felt obliged to include him. He'd known Lucas Tollburn very well, and remained our town's titular leader. He was flush-faced, and had an embattled, angry look. But that was usual for him. I'd not noticed him among the fighting.

There was one thing missing. I couldn't feel the normal animosity from the sisters or Vernon. The three of them nodded at me mildly. Maybe they were starting to accept me a little better.

Gaspar Vernon let out a slow breath. The fringe of his moustache was gently tinged with red. I knew that, in private, he was a connoisseur of most fine things. So maybe he'd been sampling some claret before all of this had started.

"You must be tired, Devries," he rumbled in that big, gruff voice of his.

"That's true of everyone," I pointed out.

"It's been quite a night," Levin conceded wryly. "And a pretty damned confusing one. I'd ask you to bring us up to speed but . . ."

He glanced over to his right.

"Cobb can do it for us quicker."

I glanced at the little man. Cobb Walters didn't say a word. He simply raised his right palm. Stretched his fingers apart as wide as he could. There was no time to get out of the way. I felt a sudden tug inside my head, as if the balance of my inner world had shifted. And then the eyes of each adept became a good deal wider. There was something shining in them.

I wasn't exactly pleased about that. I hated magic being used on me, and knew what Cobb had done. He had plucked my recent memories directly from my head, and then passed them on to all the rest.

Vernon gave a low hiss.

"I knew Lucas fifty years. He never mentioned anything like that."

"Hardly surprising," Kurt van Friesling pointed out. "If you owned such a thing, would you?"

"I always thought he was a far too clever S.O.B.," Dido McGinley put in. "Now I know it."

And then it was Levin's turn.

"But why would Millicent do such a thing? Do you suppose she's fallen under the influence of this madman, Hanlon?"

Gaspar Vernon grumbled at him. "You don't know that girl the way I do."

The judge's eyes became pained-looking behind those rimless spectacles of his.

"She's still one of us—still part of this community. Why would she want to tear it up? We should at least find out what her motives are."

I was going to point out she'd turned her home into some

kind of fortress. But then I remembered they already knew that. They'd taken it from my own memories. And glances passed between them.

"Sam's right," Martha Howard-Brett said. "If we can somehow make her see sense . . ."

And after that, no one said another word. It seemed to be agreed on, simultaneously and without further discussion. The adepts sometimes work like that.

They moved up close and linked hands. And Martha stretched her free one out in my direction, smiling gently.

"Come along, Ross. We need you too."

Which made me pretty uneasy. But we were in a desperate situation here, and so I stepped across in spite of my misgivings.

As soon as her palm closed around my own, the room started to melt away around me.

The murals slid together, merged.

And then the house was gone completely.

CHAPTER 30

I'd only seen them in the darkness, up until this point. But in clear daylight, the barriers that had formed around Millwood House looked even more forbidding than they had before. They were the same color the sky takes on shortly before the sun begins to rise. As if dawn hadn't come to this particular spot. And they had a gentle luster to them, a platinum shimmer. You could see vague shapes in them, dim reflections of the world outside the walls. The other houses, and the trees around them. Except that world was noticeably changed from yesterday.

It wasn't only the scene below, the plumes of smoke still rising and the big crowds massed at certain points. This whole area of Sycamore Hill seemed different. Even quieter than it had been, so that every faint sound seemed to echo. Apart from us, there was no one else around.

This street had been full of people, last time I'd been here. Where had they gone? As I gazed around, the truth sank slowly in. Cars had been parked on the surrounding driveways, last night. But they were no longer present. There was no movement at any of the windows. In fact, some shutters were closed. The big, wide yards sat empty and abandoned.

No one born here could actually leave town. I already knew that. But the residents of this immediate district had moved out, for fear of what was going on. I wasn't sure where they had disappeared to. But the folks around here had plenty of cash, so they'd obviously made arrangements.

I looked back at the barrier. It was perfectly smooth, with not the tiniest flaw along its length. The sun, beyond it, only served to make it look a little darker, a soft pewter hue. Off in the far distance, the forest that surrounds most of our town looked blurry and unreal, another vaporous figment, except green this time.

"Do you think that you can get inside?" I murmured to Levin.

He didn't take his eyes from it when he replied.

"We tried last night," he told me, "within half an hour of it appearing. It was like trying to get through stainless steel by pressing your face against it."

Gaspar Vernon and Martha both stepped out ahead of us, the latter puffing up his chest.

"Millicent!" he bellowed. "We know you're in there! What the hell do you think you're playing at?"

"We only want to talk, dear," Martha added, in a more placating tone. "We're not sure what's upset you. But whatever it is, we've come to put it right."

They stood there waiting. We all did. But there was no response. The breeze had grown a little stronger, making the shrubbery around us rustle. That was when I noticed there were not even any birds left. Not even any insects that I could make out. Every living creature appeared to have fled.

Vernon's cheeks were growing more richly colored by the second, anger overtaking him. Which—to my mind—wasn't what you'd call the best approach.

"Do you even understand," he demanded, "what it means to be an adept? The duties and responsibilities that befall you, in that role? This community has quite enough problems, without its natural leaders turning on it. How can you justify what you've done?"

His annoyance sounded generalized, not merely about last night. I remembered the hard time Millicent had given the Vernon clan, and wondered how much of this was personal.

Levin seemed to think so too. It was his turn to give it a shot.

"I don't believe you're thinking very clearly, Milly," he called out. "So I urge you. Take a moment, please, to reconsider what you're doing."

And that finally seemed to have an effect. Because a bulge started appearing in the surface of the barrier, directly in front of us. It took us by surprise. Everyone around me took a sharp step back.

The bulge lengthened, stretching down until it reached the ground. And then it began rearranging itself, taking on detail. The outlines of a face and body came in view. But they did not detach themselves, remaining half-embedded in the wall.

I could see immediately who it was. And so could everybody else.

Millicent Tollburn remained where she was, like a stone frieze of a woman, the same pale hue as her background. Her eyes flickered across us, shimmering the way the barrier did. Then they settled, at last, on Gaspar Vernon.

Her lips parted. You could see the edges of her teeth.

"Still making demands, Uncle? It didn't work back then, and it won't work now."

Vernon looked shocked and slightly mollified. A little of the red drained from his cheeks. He sucked in a breath, ready to answer back. But Martha got in before he could mess things up.

"No one's your enemy here, Milly. And there's no point opening up old wounds. We're trying to understand what you've done, and why."

"Do you know how many people are dead, this morning?" Levin asked. He was trying to keep the anger out of his tone, and not wholly succeeding. "Ordinary people too, not adepts. If you have some kind of grievance with us, then why take it out on them?"

We were all making the same assumption. Since she never had dealings with ordinary folk, they ought to be beneath her notice.

It was pretty weird, watching that outline smile. I've seen a lot of bad things, but it shook me all the same. The cruelty and malice in her grin were unmistakable. She knew precisely what she'd done. It didn't seem to bother her.

"You're right, Judge. Astute as ever. My main grievance is with you—my grandfather's loyal friends, who smiled at him and clapped his back and kept on telling me what a fine man he was."

They looked mystified, and I could hardly blame them. What on earth was she yammering on about?

"And I'll get to you eventually," she went on. "But I want to make you suffer first. This town you claim to care so much about? I'm going to destroy it before your very eyes. How powerless you'll feel, when I do that."

She paused.

"Just as powerless as I felt, once."

I had no idea what that meant. And neither, apparently, did any of the others. Cynthia McGinley stepped up fiercely, her green gaze blazing.

"It's Hanlon talking, don't you see? It's him making you this way. You're in cahoots with a lunatic, young lady. If you thought about it clearly, you would see that."

The face turned to her. And the smile grew even broader, with a genuinely vicious edge.

"That oversized child? How little you know me."

Her attention went back to Gaspar.

"I'm the strong one, Uncle. You understand that."

He edged back a little further underneath her stare.

"And once I've started something, then I finish it. I promise you."

And with those words, her shape began withdrawing, sinking back into the wall, her features shrinking, flattening out. But she still had time for one final threat.

"Once I've finished with the town, I'll come for you. Don't say you haven't been warned."

Which was too much for Vernon. He lurched forward, trying to grab hold of her.

Another bulge started appearing in the barrier, off to the side of Millicent's vague shape. That set off alarm bells, and I ran across. I grabbed Vernon by his shoulders, hauling him back just in time. The outline of an arm came snaking out.

Clasped in its fist was a knife. It swiped, missing the man's stomach by barely an inch.

He let out a noise like a punctured ball. And then we were stumbling away to a safe distance.

I turned and stared back. Millicent's face was still there, very indistinct. Her lips parted again. And before she disappeared completely, she let out a delighted laugh.

The barrier became flat and featureless, the sound that she'd made clinging to it for another second. The sun lifted slightly higher, and the wall began to gleam like beaten steel beneath its rays.

Vernon shook me off.

"My God!" he thundered. "What's happened to her?"

We were silent until Levin pointed out, "What's been done to her, more like. She didn't get that way by accident. Could it possibly be we're guilty of wrongdoing, in some way we don't even understand?"

No one had an answer to that question. Every face was blank. We were as empty of ideas as this part of the hill was of life. But we knew one thing for certain.

Whatever her motives, we had better start preparing. The same was going to happen again. Or maybe even worse.

CHAPTER 31

She hadn't deliberately conjured up the barriers. They seemed to have sprung, fully formed, from deep in her subconscious mind. But everything had changed completely inside Millwood House since they'd appeared. It wasn't merely that the sunlight didn't reach the windows any longer. The only thing that did was a pale dull sheen a little lighter than the walls. No, it was rather that the whole place had been bled of substance.

Nothing looked entirely solid any more. No surfaces stopped you when you pressed your weight against them and there was no longer any point in using the doorways. When you walked up to a wall, you sank through it painlessly. And it reformed once you had passed. If you wanted to sit down, you merely sat—the thin air supported you. This was the way ghosts had to exist. The normal rules were gone.

Millicent had found it unsettling at first, although her companion seemed to be enjoying everything about it. He kept on ranting about "getting all the powers he'd ever wanted." Whereas she . . . she felt she'd gained a lot, but lost a lot as well. She prized the furniture and ornaments in this place—she'd chosen them personally. But now, was it even really there? Her wealth had given her life permanence and certainty, both of them qualities she badly needed. And by this time, it was all diminished. She had taken quite a while adjusting to it.

Her recent confrontation with the adepts had lightened her heart a little. She'd dreamt of facing them down ever since her early teens. And now, she could savor it for real. She thought about the looks on their faces, Uncle Gaspar's in particular. She'd been in control completely. That made her pulse quicken. There'd been nothing they could do to touch her.

Other matters were still bothering her, though.

The horses in her stables had not taken the new changes well. They'd whinnied frightenedly the whole night, beating their hooves against their stalls. So those had remained solid. She'd been able to hear the racket in her head, even from the other side of town. Been too busy to return to them, at first. And when she'd finally come home, she had felt too preoccupied to go and calm them down. She'd hovered above the rooftop of her house instead, watching the destruction unfold below her. That horde of monsters she'd let loose. She could see perfectly clearly through the barrier.

In the end, the shrieking from the stalls had died away. The animals were still alive, but utterly worn out.

And then there was another matter. She had always had this mansion to herself. And by this time—not counting Hanlon—there were twenty-three additional guests in here. Considering the sort of people they were, she was not inclined to play the gracious hostess.

When she'd moved through the suburbs last night, she had chosen those who were the easiest to turn. Folks whose dark side was already near the surface. There were plenty of them, when you really looked. People so sodden in alcohol they could barely remember who they'd once been. Ones who'd grown up with so little in the way of social skills they cowered from the world, reacting to it angrily when it came close. A few people who simply hated everyone and everything, but couldn't even tell you why. Magic had distorted some of their minds—she could see that.

One by one, she'd talked to them, cajoled them, until she had freed their dark sides. And one by one, the authorities had stopped them. But they could not be destroyed completely that way. When she'd worked her spells upon them, they had become an elemental force.

Once subdued, they had come here. And by this hour, they were roaming right across her mansion. They didn't even have the saving grace of being smoke-ghosts anymore.

As she watched, a wall buckled and then parted. And a grotesquely overweight woman came stumbling through. Millicent was appalled by her. She wore a dirty floral smock, which halted just above her knees. There was so much fat on her legs that great folds of it were trying to slide down them. Her face was as spotty as an adolescent's. Her mouth, which was remarkably small, kept chewing around the same few words.

"Where d'you get a drink round here? What kind of place is this, where a decent soul can't even get a goddamn drink?"

A belch followed. Millicent cringed.

Then a loud caterwauling erupted upstairs. Two of the others had started fighting. A volley of approving yells told her that more of them had gathered around to watch.

This wasn't what she'd planned. Not how she'd envisioned things. She'd fantasized her revenge a million times since her early years, and never once had it involved this ragged band of maladjusted deadbeats.

And she decided she was sick and tired of it. This was far too high a price to pay. So she raised her free hand. Murmured a spell quickly.

The lumbering woman halted. Grunted and looked down. Something in the middle of her chest had started to revolve. And was spinning—faster, faster—until it resembled a tiny cyclone.

It began to suck her in. She yelled out a frightened protest, tried to get away. But it was part of her, and she could not escape it. She shrank rapidly, and then disappeared from view. Shrieks and wails throughout the mansion told her that the same was happening to the others.

"What did you do that for?" snarled a voice beside her ear.

The momentary sense of triumph went away immediately. There was still this other problem. There was no way she could think of to get rid of Hanlon. He still had hold of the other end of the Wand of Dantiere. And, so long as he kept it in his grasp, they were inseparably conjoined, the most unlikely pair of Siamese twins.

Was she still, to his gaze, "Ma"? She'd given up on that pretense a good while back. But his mind seemed to work very differently than other people's.

Whatever, he seemed to be enjoying this alliance considerably more than she was. He had even started to complain to her occasionally. And—infuriatingly, to her way of thinking—that was what he was doing now.

"They were our guys," Hanlon snapped in her ear crossly. "On our side, and ready to do battle on our behalf. Why treat them like that?"

He'd killed and tortured harmless families in the outside world like they were nothing, but had sympathy for these dregs? God, it repelled her even to be near him. But, until the chance presented itself, there was no alternative.

"They were merely for starters, an hors d'oeuvre," she told him. "I'd no more rely on them than on a piece of mud stuck to my shoe."

Hanlon squinted at her puzzledly, a strange light shining deep within his eyes.

"Then what?"

"It cost this town, but they defeated everything we threw at them last night. So we change tactics. Now that we know exactly how to go about it, we choose better subjects, and we turn them far more carefully."

He didn't know what she was talking about, but tried to look like he did, and nodded.

"Why, exactly?"

"Nobody will know where the next threat is coming from."

Hanlon turned that over. Then his gaze brightened and delight gleamed in it.

"I get it—we turn the adepts. That uncle of yours? I'd really like to nail his pompous ass."

But Millicent shook her head.

"No. That's not what I had in mind. It's not even them that really bother me."

This was confusing the big lunatic, and he didn't look the least bit pleased by that. She was reminded of how potentially dangerous he was.

"Then who?" he spat out.

She stayed calm when she replied.

"That plainclothes fellow or whatever he is. Devries. I know of him. He's been all over town. He's been consulting with Raine. And he was even there with my uncle and his friends."

She paused and stared at the opposite wall.

"I get a feeling about him, and not a good one. He's stood in the way of trouble before. Managed to stop it when no one else could."

"He has some special kind of magic?"

"No." Millicent's cheekbones turned a few shades darker. "I'm not sure what you'd call it. But he's a threat to us, and we are going to have to deal with him."

"He has a dark side, like anyone else," Hanlon suggested, peering at her mischievously. "Why not simply turn him?"

Millicent's response was to close her eyes. She reached out with her inner senses, trying to detect what she was really up against. She trusted her own instincts, and they told her to be cautious.

"Again, no. The man has rigid self-control, and that would be a big mistake."

"Then what?"

And she finally grinned.

"I have a plan."

CHAPTER 32

Sitting in the darkness, he had watched the events of last night unfold in his mind's eye, his pupils glowing even more brightly than usual, almost incandescently. Plenty of disaster had been heaped on this town during the years he'd been here. But what he had been watching—the awful, grinding horror of it—shook him to the very core.

Once the sun had risen, Lehman Willets had attempted to lighten his mood the only way that he knew how. The record on his turntable was by Milt Jackson, live at the Museum of Modern Art in 1965. The percussionist was in full swing. The lilting, madcap tones of "Flying Saucer" echoed around the upstairs room. The doctor certainly did not feel happy about returning to his basement yet.

He was sitting on his camp bed, trying to lose himself in the jollity of the tune, when his head came snapping abruptly up. His vermilion pupils burned like tiny twin furnaces.

He snapped his fingertips. The record stopped.

Despite the fact that it was dim in here, he could make out something moving on the air. A faint smokiness. A texture, rather than anything tangible. But he could definitely feel a presence. Someone else's consciousness was trying to invade his own.

He saw who. And straightened up annoyedly.

"Do you know exactly who I am?" he barked.

The small creatures who were watching him scuttled for cover, when he did that. And the presence immediately vanished.

Saul Hobart was driving into Garnerstown again. He was not in the easiest of moods. The town had managed to survive last night, but, to his mind, it was more by luck than judgment. The whole thing was sure to start again as soon as darkness fell. So, if the ordinary civilians wanted to help—and let's face it, he didn't have enough men to cope on his own—then there were better ways that they could do it.

He had used up a good part of this morning going around the neighborhoods, organizing their inhabitants into proper militias rather than the unformed mob that had rushed in to help a few hours back. Most people had warmed to that idea. Last night had been chaos. And who wanted that?

He spent so much time in his car these days, it was almost like a second office. There was a small heap of files on the passenger seat. A pine-shaped air freshener and a string of worry beads hung from the rearview mirror. He'd never used the latter—he just liked the way it looked. And there was a half-used-up pack of gum in the well beside his seat. He never chewed in front of his men, but liked to when he was alone. There was a wad in his cheek right now.

The other thing down there, of course, was a snapshot of his wife and daughters. Saul never went anywhere without that. Like a talisman, it gave him extra strength.

He had one hand on the steering wheel, and the other clasped around his cell phone. Time was short. He wanted to discuss a few things in advance of his arrival. Nick McLeish sounded worried on the other end.

"The way you're describing it, this could happen to pretty much anyone."

"It looks that way."

"My friends? Even my family?"

"Which is what we have to be prepared for," Saul said, trying to reassure him. "The better informed about the danger everybody is, then the readier they'll be for it. I'm pulling onto Greenwood Terrace, Nick. I'll be there in about two minutes."

This route was familiar to him, and he negotiated it almost automatically. But as he was hanging up, he noted a faint mistiness on the air ahead of him. It didn't surprise him too much. It was not unusual, even this late in the morning, for patches of fog to come drifting in from the surrounding forest.

He continued onward, thinking that he'd pass right through. But it was inside the car in the next moment—despite the fact his windows were shut—and hovering about him. Voices started chanting in his head. And one of them he recognized as Ms. Tollburn's.

"Why are you bothering? You know that you can't win."

He pulled over to the curb before he lost control of his Pontiac. And then tucked his head down against the steering wheel. Fear was coursing through him like a second bloodstream. Could he even fight against this thing?

"You work all the hours God gives, protecting this town. And to what end? Nothing ever changes. No one really cares."

"That's not true! I know what you are!" he yelled back.

The voices kept on battering at him. And he started to feel another cloud—a black one of despair—begin to settle over him. But he ground his teeth and struggled against it.

He thought of the job he had to do. About the people who were relying on him. Most of all, he thought about his home, his wife and his daughters.

He kept on clinging to the image of his family until the voices went away.

The fighting had not come near here, and so he had not gotten caught up in it. Which was just as well, since he was not a violent man. He was a pacifist, if anything. Studying Chinese philosophy had made him so.

But Lawrence L. DuMarr was aware of everything that had been going on—he owned a TV and a radio. And wished that he could have helped in some way. If only he were more robust in his approach to life. If only he was a little bit more like Cassandra Mallory. He was friends with Cassie, and Ross Devries, and had come to admire her.

He was sitting in the office at the back of his apothecary shop on Exeter Close, where Marshall Drive sloped up to meet Sycamore Hill. As was his custom, he had lit an oil lamp, preferring its glow to the electrical variety. It had more depth, and gave things proper texture.

Its ochre flame illuminated the charts on his walls. They were of pressure points, meridians, running in lines across a human body. Lawrence was a practitioner of acupuncture, oriental medicine, and a whole lot more. His main business was healing people, by channeling their life-force in beneficial ways.

Like anybody else born here, he had never left this town. But objects from the outside world arrived, and they included books and magazines. Pretty early on in life, he had become fascinated with Eastern culture. He had become an expert on the Tao, the I-Ching, Confucius, and Buddha. And had chosen a profession which made use of that compendium of knowledge.

Except that . . . no one who'd been injured, even slightly scratched, had come to him this morning. Now that the chips were really down, no one had thought to make use of his services. They'd all gone to a regular doctor or a hospital.

Did no one trust him anymore? He felt rather abandoned and betrayed.

Lawrence sighed, and brushed his prematurely white hair away from his temples. Then his goateed face tilted up a few inches, his eyes narrowing behind his gold pince-nez.

Was the oil in the lamp burning inefficiently? There seemed to be a hint of smoke on the room's still air. The furniture around him—cabinets and shelving, all constructed of dark wood—seemed to be casting extra shadows. He suddenly took in the fact that he was not alone.

"Here you sit, discarded and forgotten," murmured a voice in his head. "No one really wants what you have to offer. No one understands the wisdom you possess. When they come to you at all, it's out of curiosity. They think that you're an absurd crank."

He should have gotten up and walked out of there. Didn't even understand what this voice was. But it seemed to have a grip on him. The words that he was listening to fixated him. And he waited for them to continue, his lower lip dropping nervelessly.

The smoke moved around him, filtering through his white mane of hair. It hung around for a good while.

Then it lifted from him, left the shop, and moved away.

It was heading northeast this time. To the district of East Meadow.

CHAPTER 33

Cassie was physically as shattered as she'd ever been, her brain teetering on the edge of sleep. But adrenaline and anger wouldn't let her go there.

She was in her living room again, on the couch, her boots on the cheap upholstery and her head pressed to her knees. A shudder ran through her occasionally. That was just her nervous system, trying to quiet down. She never liked to show it, but she was sore and aching after the fights last night. The fact that she'd won them didn't mean she wasn't hurt. She felt like she'd been tenderized.

Cleveland kept on moving up to her and dabbing at her elbow with his nose. But she ignored him. There was more than just the damage to her body, since her thoughts were painful too.

When the fighting had finally stopped, what had Ross gone and done? It still bugged her. He'd barely said a word to her. Simply wandered off with that new woman again.

She could scarcely lay claim to him. Not in any romantic sense. Their relationship wasn't in the least bit like that, never really had been. And she wasn't under any illusions, when it came to that side of his character. She knew what the score was with Ross. He'd never try to come on to Lauren, or give in to her advances. He was—unlike the men she generally chose—one of the straightest arrows that had ever flown, still devoted to his wife. It was one of the reasons that she genuinely liked him.

But . . . they'd been through so much together, side by side. Become so close. Good friends, but something more than that. They worked together as a perfect team. Matched each other like two pieces of a jigsaw.

Now she felt this Brennan chick was pushing them apart.

Memories came rushing back into her mind, the walls between the present and the past dissolving. She felt almost like she'd been abandoned, and she'd known that feeling once before. It had been when she was seventeen, and her folks had died in a road accident. She knew they had not left her alone deliberately. But back then, it sometimes felt like that. And she had wandered on her own for months, until she'd met up with the motorcycle gang.

Even they hadn't accepted her unanimously.

It had been in the washroom of the dingy basement bar they hung out in, The Hole on O'Connell Street. She was standing in front of the smeared mirror, admiring her tattoos. She'd got them very recently, since she had only been in the gang a week.

The door suddenly swung open behind her. Another girl member—Sheba —walked in, followed by her two inseparable buddies, Ursula and Vixen. They saw how she was admiring herself, and smirked sarcastically.

"Well, look at you looking at you. You really think you're some kinda big deal, don't you, bitch?"

She tried to pull back from the memory, but it wouldn't let her go. Her first real fight. The savagery and heat of it. She had been scared, but had come out the right end of it.

Her first taste of blood, then. It had been one-on-one, which was the rule. Sheba's friends had stood back and watched. And Cass had wound up with bruises and scratches, even a bite mark, sure. But it had ended with her slamming Sheba's forehead into a washbasin until the blood began to flow.

"Look what you've done to my face, you crazy bitch!"

"Well, look at you looking at you."

The others had stepped out of her way quickly when she'd

headed out of there. And none of the girls in the gang had picked on her much after that.

She tried to pull back from the images again. She didn't act that way these days—at least, not to human beings. Hell, she wasn't that scared, angry teenager anymore. She'd behaved like that because she had been cut adrift, was terrified the world would notice just how vulnerable she was.

Since those days, she had turned herself around completely. Become self-reliant. Got herself a family.

Except that . . . where was it all now? She'd worked so hard to keep herself on the straight and narrow. And everything had simply dissolved like bubbles in her grasp.

The memories kept flooding through her.

She'd cornered a drunk in an alley behind O'Connell once. He seemed to have got lost down there. Tall and strong even at that age, she'd pushed him up against a wall and held a small knife to his throat.

"Watch! Wallet!"

"Yes, miss," he had blurted.

And she'd liked the sound of that, being called miss for once, instead of kid or junior. It sounded like . . . respect.

Another evening, she stole a postal truck, and drove it in through a storefront window, just to make the rest of the gang laugh. Had felt slightly bad for the owner of the store. But she'd do anything for their approval.

No! Cut it out! That wasn't her! She was . . .

She was . . . ?

Her eyes came open and her head lifted. She gazed blearily around her living room. The ancient TV and the crummy furniture stared back at her. The pink walls that had needed repainting years back, and the tacky nylon drapes. A pile of motorcycle magazines sat on the low table in front of her. The acoustic guitar that she occasionally strummed was propped beside the couch. She couldn't even play it properly. None of this was worth an awful lot. The only things that genuinely mattered were the snapshots of her vanished kids.

It had happened two weeks before Christmas, practically two years ago. Cassie peered bleakly at the tinsel tree still standing in the corner. She ought to have gotten used to her circumstances by this time. But how could you honestly, really? Moisture started filling up her eyes.

Perhaps because of that, the air in the room started looking rather blurry. Cleveland hissed, then jumped off the couch and scuttled away.

She peered after him dazedly. Then a voice seemed to ring inside her head.

"Foolish girl!"

And that had to be the tiredness, right? She was so exhausted that her mind was talking to itself.

"You made your life better. Built up your business, like a good citizen. Had your children. And then?"

It began to weigh down on her massively, how damned hard everything was. And it all seemed to hit her at the same time this particular morning.

"This town took everything away from you when you were seventeen," the voice continued. "But you didn't give up, Cassie, did you now? You really tried. Made a new life for yourself, that you were very happy with."

She felt her chin duck gently. Yes, she had been that.

"And then, what did this town do? It took everything away again. Everything you'd worked so hard for. Everything you loved."

It paused a moment, and then asked, "So tell me . . . what exactly do you owe Raine's Landing?"

This didn't seem right. God, she was thinking crazy stuff. She wanted to ignore it, push the words out of her mind. But she was so horribly drained, her thoughts a hazy blur.

So she tried to find an answer to that question. But could think of absolutely no way to respond to it.

Cassie listened as the voice went on.

CHAPTER 34

There was nothing more that I could do among the adepts. So I got my car, and headed for the Marshall Drive area of town. Found the street and house I wanted. Went in through the door, which was ajar, as usual. And then headed up the stairs.

I went into the nursery. It was pretty much, I supposed, like the nursery of any little girl in any town in Massachusetts. Dolls were scattered everywhere, and there were plastic homes to put them in. There were fluffy toys as well, ducks and rabbits and a rather battered teddy bear. The wallpaper depicted a cartoonish stretch of sky, with white clouds, songbirds, and a rainbow. A mobile dangled from the ceiling, cows jumping over silver crescent moons.

The drapes were firmly shut. And so were the Little Girl's eyes.

What was she?

Nobody on Bethany Street even remembered a family living at number 51, much less that they'd had a daughter. There were no public records for the place. Cass and I simply stumbled across it one evening, drawn to her room by the bright blue glow.

And once I'd come to understand exactly what her powers were, I'd kept on coming back here. You could even say she was my oracle.

She saw everything. More than even Lehman Willets.

More than even Woodard Raine. She could stare beyond the limits of this town, and occasionally gaze a little way into the future. She'd foreseen Hanlon's arrival, after all. And neither of the others could do that.

The problem was, as I've already said, she sometimes spoke in riddles.

That's the trouble with the Little Girl. She poses far more questions than she actually answers. But I really needed her tightly focused insight today. When I walked in, it was halfway to noon. The sun was a pale smudge behind her curtains. It looked feeble compared to the glow that she put out. The walls were washed in electric blue light, which was emanating from her tiny body.

She was hanging at the center of it, her feet in their white buckled-up shoes dangling more than yard off the carpet. She had on her usual blue gingham dress. And was rotating in midair the way she always did, as though she'd gotten caught up in some invisible eddy.

Blond hair framed her face. I got a look at it each time she turned. And, in spite of the fact that her eyes remained closed, her expression was deeply troubled.

I stood there, waiting for her to speak. The energy that she was putting out washed around me, making my clothing stick to me slightly.

"Good morning, Mr. Ross," she said.

"Not so very good, in point of fact."

She thought about that.

"No. You're right."

Her expression screwed up a little more, her eyeballs moving swiftly underneath their folded lids. And, for the briefest instant, there seemed to be half a dozen faces up there, each of them overlapping. Then they faded. She went back to normal. But her voice had an echoing quality to it when she spoke again.

"I'd like to help if I can. It feels good to help."

I agreed with her on that.

"What is it with Millicent Tollburn?" I asked. "Why would someone of her breeding go hooking up with a psycho like Hanlon?"

That's another thing about the Little Girl. She can see into people's minds as well, far more deeply than the other adepts. She could hear what I was thinking at this very moment. I found that unsettling—who wouldn't? But I'd gotten used to it.

"Despite their differences, they have things in common, Mr. Ross. They were both damaged, very early on. Cornelius Hanlon, when he was young, was made to feel smaller than small. In trying to make himself a larger man, he overshot the mark and became grandiose, an obsessed monster."

I got that, although it didn't make me feel in the least bit sorry for him. But there was still the question of Ms. Toll-burn.

"Millicent, though? What damaged her?"

The Little Girl stopped turning, with her back to me, so that I couldn't see her face. And I didn't think that was a particularly good sign. Something's usually really bothering her when she stops spinning.

"I cannot tell you that," she muttered

Why? I wondered.

"You can't see it?"

"Yes. But I can't tell you!"

And I practically jumped back, my heart beating double-time. The Little Girl had never shouted at me before. But now, her voice was loud and harsh, insistent. So whatever she had looked at, it was something that upset her badly.

I struggled to think what that might be. What would genu-inely upset a little child of first grade age, if that's what she really was? Something truly nasty, perhaps. Something dark and even . . . shameful?

I began to suspect, even more than ever, that whatever was up with Millicent, it might have a great deal to do with her past. Her family? Old Lucas? The worst in our society are usually the ones who hide it.

Except I seemed to be the only person who suspected any-thing like that.

What Cass had told me once came back again. That whole speech about my new sense of perceptiveness. It was bound up with Amashta, I knew. All of it tied up with this "Defender" business. I seemed to have changed in certain ways, once my family had disappeared. And I knew that it was in part the shaman woman's doing. Other than that, it mystified me. I'd never thought of myself as special. And the idea that I might be didn't comfort me too much.

I tried to get some more out of her. But the Little Girl didn't even seem willing to address the subject any longer. She couldn't be budged from her insistent silence. So I was finally forced to give up.

Which—it appeared—pleased her. She began to rotate again. And when her face swung around, it was back to normal. Her features were relaxed, her brow uncreased. And she turned smoothly as clockwork. She'd apparently put whatever she'd seen right out of her mind. Erased it.

But the whole business had left me unsettled. And my next question rasped in my throat.

"How exactly do we stop them?"

"You cannot. The Dantiere wand is terribly strong. And with two people wielding it, both of such bloodthirsty intent . . . ?"

"What are we supposed to do, then?"

"You'll have to ride it out," she told me flatly.

I didn't like the sound of that one bit, and shoved my hands into my pockets. "That's your best advice?"

"It is. They cannot be defeated, but they can defeat themselves. They are not sane. They are not rational. Sooner or later, all their plans will fall apart."

Which sounded slightly better. Except that it still left this town with an awful lot of pain to go through.

"And until then?" I asked, as measuredly as I could.

"Encourage them to turn against each other."

My mind was whirling slightly. "How?"

The Little Girl looked thoughtful for a while.

"You're a clever man, Mr. Ross," she smiled. "I'm sure you'll figure something out."

I freed my hands up, put one to my chin, and asked her, "Any more advice?"

"The attacks, when they come tonight, will come from where you least expect. You can trust no one."

I waited for her to expand on that. But there were times when she just stopped talking. Was this one of them? The light from her continued to wash over me. I felt a strong twinge of impatience.

And she must have detected that, because her nose creased up.

"I'm not done."

"Sorry," I told her. "Please continue."

"Miss Cassie. She's getting back to her old self."

And what kind of crazy warning was that? Cassie had seemed out of sorts for a while now, that much was for sure. Even more prickly and hotheaded than was usual. But she'd get over it. She always did. So how was that a problem?

"No, Mr. Ross. You're not listening properly. Miss Cassie is getting back to her old self."

I stared at her. She had begun spinning a little faster.

"The way she was before she started working with you," she went on. "The way she was before she had her children. She's getting back to her old self, Mr. Ross. Before she turned into a good person."

The fact was that I didn't really know too many details about Cassie's past. She never talked about it much. But I couldn't imagine any worse news. For the first couple of years after her parents' deaths, Cassandra Mallory—I was aware—had been a rather different person from the one I was familiar with. There was darkness in her background. A fair deal of it. And this new enemy of ours . . . it thrived on darkness, didn't it?

Yet what I'd been told simply couldn't be correct. Cassie was the strongest person that I knew, and nothing in the world would make her . . .

I halted, my thoughts churning over furiously. The truth was—and I'd always understood it—that for all her courage and her inner strength, Cassie had her vulnerabilities, her weak spots. But could danger really come from her direction? I just wasn't sure.

I thanked the Little Girl for her help, which was something that I always do. But a sense of urgency had gripped me. I went quickly down the stairs and out onto the sidewalk.

I seemed to be on a whirlwind tour of our town, this particular morning. And my next port of call was Rowan Street.

It was empty, when I finally rolled onto it. A wide but uninspiring avenue lined with rather old, dilapidated houses, many of which were curiously shaped without being in any way picturesque. Cassie's Diner was halfway down. It was flat-roofed, with a big glass front. I slowed down and stared at it as I went by.

A while back, the place had been torn to pieces. Half the plate glass windows had been shattered, and a lot of chairs and tables had been blown apart. She'd told me that she'd fix it up. And I could see that she'd been as good as her word. The damaged furniture had been replaced. The hole in the back wall had been plastered over, so you'd never even guess that it was there. And the glass had been refitted.

The odd thing was, there was no real need to bother. No one used the diner anymore. But I suppose she was the same as me. She wanted everything the way it had been, just in case her family came back.

My frame of mind was grim and dull. Had she changed? I was praying that, for once, the Little Girl was wrong.

I drove around the back, and parked in front of her apartment door. When I got out, a dog started growling behind a nearby fence. The chickens in her neighbor's yard began kicking up their usual fuss. There was little greenery around this district, an odd, tangy odor to the air instead. Some dust kicked up around my shoes as I moved forward.

I went across and rang the bell. After a while, Cleveland's head poked out through the cat flap. His amber eyes shone gently as he took a good hard look at me.

Then he disappeared inside again. It seemed that no one else was home.

CHAPTER 35

She was woken, once again, by the ringing of the doorbell.

Lauren Brennan shifted on the small bed she'd been given. Its mattress hadn't felt right, even in her sleep. Her whole body smarted, and her mouth tasted like something that she'd swallowed last week had made a reappearance. She couldn't even lift her head from the pillow properly. A green triceratops stared back at her from the crisp fabric.

For a few seconds, she prayed that everything she could remember since she'd got here was a dream. But the memories simply kicked in harder. Especially last night's. That made her feel even worse. How in God's name had she gotten involved in a screaming nightmare like this one? It was practically beyond imagining. Except this lunacy had substance. It had claws and fangs, and hurt the human beings that got near.

She was already sick and tired of it, and weary beyond belief. The only thing she really wanted was to get her cuffs on Hanlon and then go back home.

The doorbell made her jerk again.

Lauren got up awkwardly. Since she only had the one set of clothes, she'd stripped down to her underwear and put on the robe Ross had lent her. It tried to trip her over as she moved. She was forced to hitch it up around her as she went to answer the front door.

When she opened it, Cass Mallory was standing there. The

woman was dressed from head to toe in black. Black T-shirt, black jeans, and those motorcycle boots of hers. As tall as a shadow before evening fell. She was still wearing her side arms. Man, a pair of Glocks like those looked pricey. Excellent tools for the job in hand, though.

The woman's arms were folded. Her expression was unreadable.

It seemed to be early afternoon, by the position of the sun. The street was still bright—which she was pleased to see after the hours of darkness she'd endured—and the trees along it trembled in a gentle breeze. A few leaves had already dropped off them and were skimming along the curb. The approaching fall . . . that was something pleasant and normal to concentrate on, and she tried as best she could. The colors of New England at that time of year—a natural marvel.

Then she came back to the present sharply.

"Hi," she mumbled, rubbing at her mouth.

Cass's gaze dropped to her robe. She asked, "Is Ross back yet?"

"Er . . . I don't think so. What do you want, Cassie?"

"There's something new you ought to see, regarding Hanlon."

Which woke her up a fair amount.

"Okay, then. You'd better come inside."

They hadn't exactly gotten off to a good start. She understood that. And the woman seemed unfriendly because of it. But she remembered something else. Cassie grabbing her by the collar last night, dragging her out of harm's way. So maybe there was still a chance for them to connect. She never liked to be on bad terms with anyone she had to work with.

So as soon as the front door was shut, she came out with, "Hey, I never got the chance to thank you. That thing with the snake, I mean."

Cassie blinked at her, her features passive.

"Don't mention it."

At which point, Lauren became worried there was something genuinely wrong with her. This was like trying to hold a conversation with a speak-your-weight machine. Cassie seemed so rigid and unyielding. And her eyes looked slightly darker than they had before. She didn't understand how that was possible, since her irises were already black. But there seemed to be a strange gloss to them that made them look bottomless.

This wasn't fair either, she realized, being critical and finding fault. Cassie had to be exhausted too. She'd fought harder than anybody else last night, throwing herself into the battles with a total disregard for her own safety. If she'd been on the force and behaved like that, she'd have gotten either a medal or a reprimand.

But Cassie wasn't any cop. Which made what she'd done all the more remarkable.

Turning it over, she found that she was starting to admire the woman. Which made her feel increasingly awkward. That first encounter between them had been a mistake, an accident, she kept telling herself. They'd just got off on the wrong foot.

"Are you going to get dressed?" Cass asked, a little sarcastically.

Good point. Lauren went back on through but left the bedroom door ajar, so they could still talk while she smoothed out her crumpled clothes and pulled them on.

"I didn't get time to apologize for the way I acted when I first arrived. I'm really, genuinely sorry about that."

Cass's voice, from out in the hallway, was as flat as a slab in a graveyard.

"You were doing what you thought was right. Easy enough mistake to make."

But she didn't sound particularly convincing. Is she going to stay pissed at me forever? Lauren thought. She yanked her pants over her hips and zipped them.

"I'd like to make it up to you. I'm simply not sure how."

"Dressing faster would be a good start."

Lauren frowned and did up the last buttons on her shirt, then slid her shoulder holster on. She checked her Walther, and then slipped her jacket over it. She was acutely aware she hadn't showered, still felt very tired. And didn't appreciate Cass nagging her. But if this was to do with Hanlon, if it brought her closer to her goal.

She went back into the hallway, smiled briefly at Cassie and said, "Mouthwash, at least." Then disappeared into the bathroom, where she quickly swilled between her gums the contents of a mint green bottle. She took a glance in the mirror, saw how drawn she looked, but did her best to ignore that.

Cass's gaze was still strange when she finally emerged. The bulb out here was not particularly strong, and made her face look shadowy.

"You done?" she asked.

"As ready as I'll ever be."

Then Cassie led the way.

The sunlight outside made Lauren squint. It seemed so bright and clear, in view of everything that had been happening. Heavy cloud would have been more appropriate. The Harley was parked on the drive, a big red beast with narrow black stripes down it, its thick body shining like an insect's carapace.

"Ever ridden pillion before?" Cass inquired, climbing on.

"Sure. Got a helmet?"

"No."

She ought to have expected that. Goddamn, talk about reckless. But she climbed aboard anyway, gripping Cass around the waist. The smell of hot machinery and fuel eased up around her, bringing back an image from her past.

"My first boyfriend had one of these," she said into the woman's ear.

"Me too," Cassie answered without looking back.

"He turned out to be a total asshole. But I've always liked bikes, ever since."

"Same here, on both counts."

And Cass let out a brisk, sharp laugh before turning the ignition. That made Lauren smile gently, with satisfaction. The bike shuddered underneath them, and its twin-cam engine roared.

See, they did have things in common. There was the potential for a bond between them.

She saw no real reason why they couldn't be good friends.

* * *

They appeared to be heading north. She wondered what lay in this direction. God, but Cass rode this beast hard. Ross's neighborhood sped by her, mostly in a blur. But she managed to pick up enough detail to understand what kind of place it was. Everything was simple, unpretentious, even humble. But properly looked after to the smallest detail. All the homes were freshly painted, and the lawns around them neatly mown. The cars on the drives were mostly older models, but were clean and shiny. There was no mess or disrepair, anywhere she looked.

A plain but entirely wholesome neighborhood, in other words. The kind of place her own folks would have loved to move to, if they'd ever been able to afford to leave their cramped, noisy apartment in South Boston.

They began to slow after a while, a thick row of trees coming in sight. It was the forest she had passed through when she'd arrived here. This was the first time that she'd seen it in the light. It looked dense and almost endless, and she supposed it played its part in keeping Raine's Landing hidden from the outside world. A whole ocean of tightly packed trees. And this town was like a raft on it, drifting a good distance from the shorelines of normality.

Cassie drew the bike to a halt a few dozen yards from the tree line, and they both got off.

"Municipal limit," the woman announced.

And then she simply walked across it. What about the curse? Lauren froze for a few seconds, but then followed her.

"I don't understand." She hurried up to Cassie's shoulder. "I thought you guys couldn't leave here."

"Hell, we can do that. We simply can't get anywhere else. Somebody born here could walk a week, a month, a year, and never glimpse another rooftop, never see another town. Or another person."

Lauren frowned uncertainly. "I'm not sure I get that."

"Lucky you," was the only response she got.

They headed in among the trees. The odors of the forest swept across them. Some finches noticed them and danced up to the higher branches, but nothing else happened. Lauren really felt that something should.

"There's a turnpike a couple of miles from here," she pointed out. "You don't even see cars?"

"Not a one. What's a turnpike anyway?"

Which made her fall silent for a while. She'd never really understood, up until this point, what it meant to be this isolated.

They kept marching steadily along. Cass apparently knew where they were going. Some kind of natural path opened up ahead of them. When Lauren looked closer, she could see that it had heavy drag marks on it.

"Logger's trail," Cassie explained. "There's a big lumber mill east of here. If this was a regular town, then we'd be famous for our furniture."

They left the path after a while, turning left and heading through deep undergrowth. Fallen twigs and dead leaves crackled underneath them. There was a rich, dank stink, like compost. It was dimmer here, the sunlight filtered. Pretty quiet as well, besides the noises they were making. Occasionally, a larger bird would call briefly, flap its wings, then disappear. Otherwise, they were completely on their own.

Lauren was still trying to get her head around this whole business of Regan's Curse.

"So you can come wandering out here? And, besides not getting anywhere, there's no effect?"

"Not exactly," Cassie answered, rather tersely. "Once you cross over the border, the forest gets pretty weird. Everything around you bleeds of color."

She raised her head and stared about, as if to confirm that.

"And it all goes very quiet and still, like you're not really in the world at all."

But Lauren could hear sounds and see movement. And the colors around her were the same as they had been before. So she wasn't in the least way affected by the curse. She ought to feel relieved, she told herself.

"Isn't that rather scary?" she asked, trying to imagine what it had to be like.

Cassie dropped her gaze, and mulled the question over.

"No," she announced finally. "I don't mind it too much, to be honest. It may be odd. But it demands nothing of you. It's peaceful."

Except it didn't sound that way to Lauren. Moving through a bleached-out, hushed-down version of the world? That seemed awful to her. But she reminded herself of the way this woman lived her life. The violence and the urgency of it. Primed for action, constantly. Always there on the front line. She usually thought of herself as being pretty tough. But she couldn't do that, not twenty-four seven.

So if Cassie found the curse relaxing, who was she to argue?

They were starting up a gradient. Lauren thought she could make out a hill, maybe a hundred yards ahead. It was difficult to be certain with so many tree trunks in the way.

But it turned out that the ground did begin to slope up. They pressed on without another word until they reached the top. Went a few dozen more yards down the other side. Then Cassie drew to a halt. It was practically pitch-dark in this part of the woods, and full of the humming of insects.

"We're here."

Where exactly? Lauren wondered. Where was Ross? Or Saul? Or anyone, in fact? She stared around blankly.

"Okay? So what am I supposed to be looking at?"

"You can't tell?"

Lauren turned around on the spot. The only things that she could make out were the outlines of more trees and branches, exactly like the ones they'd passed through. A shape whizzed away from them that she supposed might be a rabbit.

Faint annoyance began to seep up underneath her skin. She had been woken up and dragged along for this?

"You still don't get it?" Cassie asked.

"I'm not in the mood for playing guessing games all afternoon," Lauren replied.

Which was when she heard a sharp rustle behind her, so sudden it made her jump. She swung around.

Cassie had picked up a stout length of fallen branch. And her eyes had turned completely gray.

"Absolutely right," the woman grinned. "No guesses left."

And then the branch came swinging—hard—at Lauren's chin.

CHAPTER 36

I had no idea where Cass was. I'd been looking for her most of the afternoon, with no result whatever. She wasn't at any of her usual hangouts, and she wasn't even answering her phone. I knew that there were times when she just cruised around for hours. It didn't seem like much to do, but it was better than being at home on her own, with those dozens of photographs staring at her.

With everything that had been going down, though, you'd have thought she'd stay in touch. Which bothered me badly. It was rare as hen's teeth for the Little Girl to make an inaccurate prediction. But it didn't stop me praying that she'd made one this time.

Evening was closing in on us once more. The town was darkening, its avenues becoming gloomy. The streetlamps came on, trying to alleviate that, but not succeeding the whole way. And the emptiness of the place made matters even worse. It's strange how the night changes everything, turning the familiar into the opposite of that. Shadows cast across your backyard make it a faintly unreal place. And the street you live on . . . What else lives there, once the sun has gone?

Most folk who weren't in the militias had disappeared indoors. And the breeze had dropped away completely, as if the world around us was holding its breath. My fingers had begun to itch. The demons could start showing up any time, in any place. But where?

On an instinct, I swung my Cadillac around and headed back into Garnerstown. I'm not sure why. But the place seemed to be a magnet for trouble. Saul Hobart was of the same opinion, since I found him there. We were a little west of Keane Street this time, on McAdam.

There were two uniformed cops with him, three firemen, and a band of armed townsfolk. I squinted at them curiously in the fading light. This was the militia Saul had organized. One of the women was in her fifties, and one of the men beat her out by roughly twenty years. Nick McLeish had finally put on a proper shirt, and appeared to be in charge of them. Most of their expressions were anxious and strained. Which reminded me that being brave did not mean being unafraid. In fact, the reverse is usually the case.

Saul could see what I was staring at. Or rather, the lack of it . . . the shortage of properly trained peace officers.

"I've had to post men in every part of town," he told me, bringing me up to speed. "We're stretched as thin as taffy here."

Then he peered across his shoulder.

"And we're short a man as well. Matt Chalker hasn't shown up."

He was obviously puzzled as to why. I recalled the way that Matt had been when I'd last met him, sullen and detached. But he wasn't the kind of guy to go abandoning his colleagues and his duties. It seemed ominous . . . but then, so did almost everything this evening.

A sudden angry, blatting noise announced the arrival of a Harley Davidson, and my heart jumped a little. I looked around to see a cyclopean headlamp coming down the street. Well, Ms. Mallory at last. I wondered what she'd been up to. And felt slightly unsure, watching her ride up.

And where, for that matter, was Lauren? She couldn't still be asleep. And if she wasn't with Saul any longer . . . ?

I kept a careful eye on Cass as she climbed off her bike. She looked very drawn and moody. Somewhat diminished from her usual fiery self. But that was hardly odd, under the circumstances. There were no real signs that she had changed.

She came over to me, thrusting her hands in her back pockets.

"Where were you?" I asked her.

And I studied her reaction.

She cocked an eyebrow at me, like she was wondering what business it was of mine. Pretty typical of her. And then her face relaxed.

"With friends. I dropped in on Pam." Who was her half sister. "And Bella. And I wanted to see how Ginny and Karl were, and their kids, of course."

Her expression grew slightly darker.

"Then I dropped over to your place. And guess what? I bumped into Lieutenant Brennan, headed off the other way."

"What?" Saul asked. He'd moved up to my side.

Cassie looked down at her boots.

"She's left town, and in a hurry. Told me that she couldn't take it any more. Can't say I blame her—she's not used to any of this. So it's probably for the best all round."

I knew she didn't care for the woman. And noticed a faint hint of triumphalism in her tone. But for myself, I felt astonished. And Saul looked dismayed.

"She was so determined to get Hanlon," he blurted. "She didn't look to me like she was going to quit."

Cassie looked at him rather sardonically. The tired edge that I'd noticed before had dropped away completely. She was showing us a harder, slightly meaner aspect of her nature. Maybe that was what the Little Girl had meant.

"After last night?" she asked. "Are you kidding me? One-way ticket to Boston, I'd say."

And when I thought about it closely, well, she had a point. But it didn't stop me feeling disappointed. Without Ms. Brennan, we were alone once more, the outside world lost from view completely.

I decided to put it out of my thoughts, since there was no sense dwelling on it. Leaving here was not a luxury that the rest of us had. The only thing that we could do was wait for whatever came down on us tonight. Saul stayed by his car, busy on his radio, coordinating everything. The rest of us were left to hang around at something of a loss. Our talk was stilted, coming out with difficulty across the swelling tension on the air. The police department had already checked around, of course, seeking out the few obvious misfits still remaining, and then making sure to keep close tabs on them.

Apart from those, we had no idea who might transform next.

Woody's words came drifting back to me. "We all have monsters trapped inside us."

This area hadn't picked up too much since Saruak had been here. There was still a lot of rust and shabbiness, and dandelions poking through the sidewalks. People from my neighborhood view Garnerstown with plain disgust.

After a while, I found myself talking to an older cop called Harrison Whitby. In the time that I'd been on the force, we'd not had much to do with each other. But he'd been in the department nearly thirty years, and had known my father well.

"He was a good man. A really first-class cop." His pale, nicotine-stained moustache screwed up. "I felt real bad about what happened. In fact, the last time you and me talked, it was at his funeral."

And I remembered it, that long, rainy day in late October, years back. Harrison had looked marginally taller then, his hair and moustache still shiny black.

Neither of my folks had been around to see their grandkids born. They had passed away within eight months of each other. My mom went first—bone cancer. After that, my father—who had been such a strong presence in my life— simply crumbled. It was like watching a statue fall, or a cliff-front slipping down into the ocean.

It wasn't that depression made him quit his job or hit the bottle. He'd never have given in to anything like that. He just stopped eating very much, his health began deteriorating. And after a while, the precise same kind of cancer began eating at him too. It was like he'd rather share Mom's fate than remain in this world without her.

I still missed them, and could feel their presence sometimes. But maybe that's the kind of wishful thinking that we're prone to when there are questions of mortality around.

The sky was fully black by the time we'd finished talking. And the stars were out again, bright specks like grains of sand. I knew how far away they were . . . but, this night, they really looked it. The air was minty clear, and even misting up our breath a little. The figures around me were reduced to silhouettes. Cass was standing by her Harley like a piece of solid shadow. Normally, she is the last word in impatience, and unable to keep still. But I guessed that this uncertainty was getting to her just as much as anyone.

On a more normal evening, the homes around us would be full of light and muffled sound. Dinners being cooked and eaten. Toddlers bathed and put to bed. TVs—and, in a few cases, pianos—gathered around. But not tonight. Most windows were dark, although there were definitely people in the houses. You could see a glimpse of movement occasionally.

"What the hell are they waiting for?" I heard one of the militia women grumble.

She meant the demons, naturally. Anybody in this town could turn into one, and we all knew it. But I had no idea how conscious a process that might be. Could it even be me? That made me really start to worry. How to tell exactly?

Footsteps started coming up behind us. And we swung around, aiming our weapons.

But a badge flashed, the next second, on a dark uniform shirt. It was Matt Chalker. I got a better look at the man as he passed under a streetlamp. He didn't have his cap on, and his brown hair needed cutting. His face was down as he came along to join us. And he seemed horribly robbed of energy, his gait a shambling one.

None of which got any sympathy from Saul.

"Where the hell've you been?" he demanded.

At times like this, I knew, he expected the utmost from his men.

"Sorry, Lieu. I overslept," Matt came back at him.

He was still moving in our direction when I took in the fact that there was something very odd. Matt Chalker lived in Vernon Valley, not too far from Saul's house. Which was a good way to the north of us, a further journey than my own place.

Had he walked the entire distance?

He was a dozen yards from me, and getting closer. Two of his colleagues stepped across to greet him.

That was when his head came up.

His eyes had turned completely gray.

His uniform melted away, revealing a far more profound darkness underneath. And then his shape began to alter.

His torso swelled and stretched. His whole body broadened, taking on extra swathes of bulk. His shoulders grew wider, his chest stretching like a barrel.

Then his legs bent backward, the knees reversing on themselves, the feet swelling to a massive size. His arms grew unnaturally long. And his hands had claws on them, with curving tips.

His face changed too, the features stretching out to create a lupine muzzle. Matt's ears lengthened to narrow points. When his lips parted, his mouth was full of hungry, pointed teeth. He stared at us balefully, then snarled. Was this the inner darkness he'd been carrying around inside him?

When his good friend Davy Quinn had been killed, the Dralleg had been in town. And that creature had been wolf-like too. So maybe it had stuck with him, a constant presence in his nightmares.

One of the militia people drew a bead on him. But Harrison Whitby reached across and knocked his aim off.

"He's one of ours!"

Matt abruptly rushed forward. Grabbed the cop nearest to him. And plunged his talons into the guy's chest.

"Not anymore, he ain't!"

Harrison stumbled back, his expression crumbling. Nick McLeish ran up and started shooting, and the civilians around him followed his lead and did the same.

Matt howled and thrashed as the bullets struck him. But he showed no sign of going down. I remembered how it had been with the beast that had inspired him.

"Aim for the face!" I yelled. "The mouth and eyes!"

And everyone did that. The creature moaned and shook its head furiously, staggering off to the side. But it still didn't look like it was going to come to pieces. Where was Cassie, with her heavier ordnance?

The beast lurched to our right with alarming speed. It reached a parked black-and-white, then bent down and grabbed its lower edge. And flipped the whole thing over on its side with a huge crunching sound. It had a metal shield now, to deflect our shots.

A grating noise reached my ears after that. The car had begun to scrape across the ground in our direction, the creature shoving it along. Both the carbine and the Mossberg could shoot through several layers of metal, couldn't they? So I glanced across, again, at Cassie. Felt amazed by what I saw.

She was standing next to her Harley, her arms by her sides. Watching everything as though from a tremendous distance—a spectator to this, and nothing more. And she never acted that way. She was always where the action was the thickest. What on earth did she think she was doing?

"Hey!" I yelled.

But she didn't seem to hear me. The upended car was getting closer. The only thing she did was blink, her gaze strange-looking in the dim electric light.

I wasn't sure what was wrong with her, and didn't have time to find out. There was another patrol car next to me. Its doors were open, I could see the key in the ignition. So I went across and yanked the seat belt on. Started it up and then swung it around.

Got it pointed at the upended car approaching us, then jammed my foot down on the gas. The prowl car surged ahead and hit the other vehicle with an almighty crash. The black-and-white went over on its roof, with the creature underneath it.

But I didn't stop at that. I kept pushing my car forward, shunting the upturned one over the rough asphalt.

If there'd been a man underneath, he'd have been ground to paste in seconds. But Matt wasn't that thing, not any longer. There was a burst of vapor up ahead of me. It drifted above the pavement for a few seconds, then soared away, heading up into the darkness and retreating from us quickly.

I undid the belt, feeling my body go a little slack.

The general mood on the street, by the time that I climbed out, was one of shock and absolute dismay. Of all the places danger could have come from, the last that we'd expected was another cop.

I could hear Harrison Whitby murmuring.

"Any of us? Any of us could go like that?"

I swung around angrily, looking for Cassie again. What did she think she was playing at?

But her bike had disappeared from view. I'd not the first clue as to why.

That was when I noticed Saul was gesturing to me. He was on his cell again. And when I walked across to him, he squinted at me frozenly.

"You're not going to believe this," he said.

"Try me."

There was an awful lot I was prepared to believe, these days. Except it still turned out that he was right.

CHAPTER 37

The dragon was some forty feet long, and stood nearly three stories on its narrow, sharply angled legs. There were no cadavers in its wake, so it didn't seem to have killed anyone yet. Let's face it, you could see it coming from a mile off, and had plenty of time to get out of its way. And besides, this was a shopping street, empty by this hour.

But it had wrecked most of a block of Exeter Close, right up on the edge of the Marshall Drive area. The town's practitioners—which included most inhabitants from time to time—would have to go elsewhere to get their magic supplies for a while.

The stores here were devoted to the sale of such goods— or at least, they had been. A lot of the buildings had been wholly or partially demolished. Front walls had collapsed. There was not a single window left intact, and most of the streetlamps had been knocked over.

Among this ruin, thousands of scattered crystals flashed. There were pendants and amulets strewn in the gutters. And the whole place had an awful perfumed reek—the contents of smashed bottles intermingling with each other. There were books lying everywhere, many of them with black leather covers.

My gaze went to Lawrence L. DuMarr's oriental clinic, which had been destroyed completely. The furniture had been turned to kindling, and there were broken jars all over the place.

Then the dragon held my attention again, its tail sliding off across an intersection. The thing was starting to climb the gradient of Sycamore Hill itself.

Every person here was shooting at it. But it barely even seemed to notice. Looking at its size, I doubted it could feel more than a very mild discomfort. Not even Cass's weapons would have changed that very much.

The moon had reappeared. Two dark, blurred shapes— they were not vapor—showed up against it and came hurtling down. They reached the ground either side of the great reptile and resolved into human form, Judge Levin nearest me, Kurt van Friesling on the other side.

Both the adepts held their palms up, and two nets of glowing sparks shot out. They wrapped themselves across the lizard, winding along its body and then tangling around its legs, its massive claws.

It simply snorted, gave a shake. The webs broke into shining pieces. Well, so much for that.

It was headed for a row of large houses some quarter of a mile up. There didn't seem to be anything special about them, but it was striding at them with that purposeful manner reptiles often have. I watched it carefully as it climbed away from us.

It was relatively narrow for a thing that size. Looked less like a St. George type of dragon than a snake with legs. There was a pair of leathery wings behind its shoulders, but they were small and pretty useless-looking. Big, soft spikes ran the length of its back. And hanging from its chin were several flopping whiskers, like a beard.

I began understanding what it really was, my mind digging back through things I'd read, from books that had been loaned to me. And it took me a few seconds more, but I finally got it.

This was a Chinese variety of dragon. The kind they believed in across the whole Far East. And it looked as strange—on a Massachusetts hillside—as a statuette of Buddha would on a Christmas tree.

My head went darting back toward the ruined medicine shop. And I realized who had transformed this time. He'd loaned me that particular book. Usually so gentle-natured, he liked doing things like that.

A thing this size didn't need to have been ill intentioned. It could have caused that wreckage simply climbing out of there. And trashed the other establishments merely by turning around on the spot.

It hadn't hurt a single person, and wasn't attacking anyone.

So I looked back at it with a revised opinion.

DuMarr?

I still found it hard to believe what he had turned into. But most of the destruction seemed to have been accidental. Then I took in something else.

People were still firing at him. And both adepts were trying to snare him with their nets again. But he ignored that.

He went a little higher up. The moonlight caught him fully. Something else became apparent. He should have been completely black. The other creatures had been. But in this case, there was a little color trying to break through, a faint blush of red underneath the darkness. And his eyes were pale gray, sure. But there seemed to be a shifting glitter to them, as if they were trying to alter that.

In which case . . .

It had not occurred to me before but . . . if a person could be turned toward his dark side, maybe he could be turned back?

It was pretty hard to imagine how, confronted with a creature this size. Lawrence had reached a line of trees and was trampling over them like they were buttercups. I struggled to think what might stop him.

Cassie, it occurred to me. Lawrence thought the world of her. Would he back off for her sake?

But she wasn't here, and I wasn't even certain that she was still on our side. I hurried across to the judge, explained my theory to him. Kurt appeared and listened too. The dragon had climbed even higher up the slope, a few of the militia guys still following it and firing. I could make out reinforcements arriving, drawing up in cars above us. A new cordon was being formed in front of the houses. But that was useless—I already knew it. They didn't have the faintest chance of slowing something that size down.

Judge Levin could see it too. His eyes became thoughtful and he bit his lower lip, then nodded quickly.

"Yes, you're right." He looked at Kurt. "We could create a real-seeming illusion, couldn't we?"

They both turned around to face the hilltop. Raised their hands again.

A perfect image of Cass blinked into existence in front of the dragon.

It stopped dead.

It lowered its head. Its muzzle edged slowly closer to the tall figure in front of it. I started climbing further up to get a better view.

There was something about its face that was rather placid, more like a horse than a creature with scales. So I struggled to remember what I knew of Eastern dragons.

They weren't merely dumb brutes, were they? They were rumored to be very wise. And that proved to be exactly the case. Its muzzle sniffed at her audibly. Then it reared back, and its jaws stretched wide.

A huge jet of water shot out of its throat and washed over the image. Which dissolved.

My mind was working overtime. Chinese dragons did spit water, not fire. They were generally peaceable, which gave me some degree of hope. Lawrence hadn't transformed into anything crazed or murderous. Darkness might have claimed him, but his good side was still there. He simply wasn't thinking all that rationally by this stage of the game. If we could only get to him, make him see sense . . .

The great dark beast moved off again, its tail leaving a deep, wide furrow in the dirt.

There was a sudden tug at my sleeve. I turned around to find myself facing Martha Howard-Brett.

CHAPTER 38

When I explained to her what was required, she didn't hesitate.

"You understand you have to actually change shape?" I asked her. "An illusion won't do it."

After all, the shadow show that Kurt and Levin had created hadn't fooled DuMarr in the slightest.

"No, that's fine."

She smiled again, then muttered a stream of foreign words. Her silk blouse, linen slacks, and high heels rapidly gave way to ripped jeans, a T-shirt, and tall black boots. Her face grew longer, narrower, with a squarer jaw. Her irises turned black. And then her hair turned the same color, starting to shrink back. Faded tattoos came into being on her upper arms, a scorpion and a broken heart.

"You understand this might be dangerous?" I asked.

She stared up again. DuMarr had passed through the cordon, hardly noticing it was there. He'd reached the row of homes, and was trampling a pool house, although whether on purpose or not was impossible to tell.

"I know how dangerous it might be if nothing gets done," she told me.

Even her voice was different. Her enunciation was not so crisp and had a distinct throaty burr to it. And before I even had time to respond, she had turned to a murky outline that swept away uphill. My gaze followed it. The dragon had gone through one side of the main house and had disappeared from view.

I went quickly up myself. Not that I could do much good, but I didn't want to leave her coping with the thing alone.

When I got there, nobody was firing anymore. The cops and militiamen were still hanging around, but they were looking unsure what to do. We were on Covey Avenue, and none of its inhabitants had stuck around to watch. Which was a shame, since they were really missing something.

The dragon had lain down in the center of the road, its tail following the broken white line. Its massive head was resting on its claws. Martha—still a doppelganger of Cass Mallory—was stroking its muzzle, whispering in its ear. And the darkness of its body was fading away. Its eyes were not as colorless as they had been before.

As I watched, they turned to a pale brown laced with tiny flecks of gold. I felt the tension lift out of my body as the shape subsided and the man came back in view.

His bell-bottom pants. His velvet smoking jacket. His pince-nez and his knitted skullcap. His prematurely white hair and his goatee beard. He'd not turned to a cloud of vapor like the others. So we'd pulled him out of the spell's vaporous grasp.

He staggered slightly. Martha grabbed his shoulders, steadying him. And then she turned herself back to her normal shape as well.

"Oh, my good Lord!" DuMarr gasped.

His legs went out from under him. He was lowered gently onto the blacktop.

"I am so, so sorry."

He tried to peer back at Exeter Close, but it was lost behind the row of houses. The damage that he'd done the nearest one was pretty bad, though, and it made him look even more apologetic.

"I don't know what came over me."

But I did. I understood it all too well, and felt a mild tingle of satisfaction. Lawrence was an easy touch, admittedly. But he was a start.

Another pair of shapes moved up beside us, Judge Levin and Kurt again. They peered around curiously, taking in the fact that the dragon had vanished.

"Everything's under control at last," Levin commented. "Well, that's a relief—or at least, a partial one."

I could see what he meant. Because from this high up, I could see more flashes. Firefights were starting up in other parts of town again. I could only stare helplessly as a roof about a mile away imploded on itself. The judge didn't seem aware of that, and beamed warmly at Martha.

"Well done."

Then he turned his gaze to me. "So where's the genuine Ms. Mallory, Devries? Isn't she usually with you?"

Which was the biggest question so far this evening. Where exactly had she gone, and what precisely was she doing? The patrol cars had started to move away. Past the wrecked walls of the house behind us, you could see some shattered woodwork floating in a swimming pool.

"I don't have a clue," I told him. "I was kind of hoping you could answer that."

He closed his eyes, and focused inwardly for a few seconds.

"I can't find her anywhere," he grunted. "Very odd."

No—it was more than that. She had no way to leave this place, and ought to have been easy to detect. But then something else came to mind, with an urgency that almost shook me.

"How about Lauren Brennan?"

The judge concentrated. "I can't find her either."

But then, as I watched, his small fists clenched.

"I've found her car, though."

Which made little sense.

"It's in an alley behind Colver Street. The driver's door has been left open. So it seems that it's been dumped there."

I took that in quickly and then turned to Kurt van Friesling.

"Do you still have that compass? The one that detects supernatural forces?"

His pale eyes sparkled, his mouth twisting gently out of

shape. He didn't seem sure what I was getting at, but took it with his usual casual wryness.

"Yes, of course. But she's not . . ."

"I know that. Could it be adapted to find someone born outside this town?"

He considered that.

"I would suppose so."

"Can you bring it here?" I asked.

"By magic? No. A magical object is, in itself, immune to witchcraft."

Which was one of the numerous rules of magic. I'd forgotten about that.

"If you want to use it," he said, "then we'll have to go and fetch it, I'm afraid."

He was already there—naturally—by the time that I pulled up outside his place. It was only a drive of a couple of minutes. He was waiting at the front door, with the lights turned on.

Like Millwood House, his home was purpose-built. I suspected he'd modeled it on photos from the canyons in Los Angeles, a very modernistic style. Most of it was open-plan, and two of the outer walls were glass. The furniture was mostly Bauhaus. There were paintings and sculpture most places you looked. His Porsche was sitting on the drive, next to a brand-new Lamborghini. You could make out a huge illuminated pool out back, much larger than the one we'd left behind. And stars hung around the place as if he'd placed them there as backlights.

It was the best bachelor pad in the Landing, I knew. He had a good number of female visitors, but had remained resolutely single.

He gestured to me hurriedly. "It's ready."

So I followed him inside.

The compass was laid out on his enormous blue-glass dining table. It was exactly as I remembered it, a black stone disk with a needle in the shape of—of all things—a thin golden dragon. Cabalistic symbols were engraved around its edges. Kurt bent across the thing, but did not touch it.

"What do you want it to find?"

I explained it to him again.

He murmured what sounded like a rather complex spell, in Dutch. Then, before my eyes, the symbols in the stone began to move, becoming fluid. Slithering around until they'd taken on completely different shapes.

The pointer immediately lurched to the northeast, then swung about crazily before returning.

"What's this?" Kurt muttered unhappily.

I could see what was happening almost straightaway. We had asked it to find somebody not born here. So the compass had pointed, first, at Lehman Willets. And then it had attempted to track Hanlon before going back. We needed to be more specific.

"So how should I word this?" the guy asked me.

"How about 'a brand new friend'?"

Which was what he did.

The needle immediately pointed slightly to the right of north. Toward my neighborhood, in fact.

CHAPTER 39

Back when we'd last hung out together—if you could sensibly call it that—I had gotten to drive his Porsche. And I'd enjoyed it. But we took my car this time. If Lauren was hurt in any way, we'd need a vehicle with more room than a sports model.

Before much longer, we were speeding through my neighborhood. It was pretty much like every other one I'd visited. The streetlights cast an amber glow. But again, there was far less illumination in the windows than you'd normally expect. A good few people from around here had probably gone out with the militias. We're a hardy bunch in Northridge. But a good deal more were probably just scared, staying put and laying low, trying to avoid drawing attention to themselves.

The last intersection slipped by. We reached the town's border, and drew to a halt. Kurt and I glanced at each other. We'd been in this same situation once before.

But he's a resilient type himself, in his own unique way. Nothing ever fazes him, or genuinely slows him down.

"It looks like we're going for a walk," he commented. And he looked slightly intrigued by the idea of it.

We got out. In the darkness, the massed trees ahead of us looked like huge old men in shaggy coats. I recalled there was a logging trail somewhere around this region. Kurt brought the compass with him. I fished out a larger flashlight from the trunk. I had to let him lead, of course. We set off through the forest.

As soon as we crossed the town line, the usual happened. Although I'd never experienced it before at night.

Leaves crumpled under our tread, surely. But that was the only sound. The trees around us looked like merely shadows, robbed, somehow, of their reality. Nothing made the slightest noise. There was no scampering through the undergrowth. And even the moon, when glimpsed through the branches, looked paler and more distant than it previously had done. A ghostly afterimage of a mottled silver coin. It seemed to me we'd not stepped out into the real world. Just its afterthought.

"What the hell?" Kurt muttered, peering down between his hands.

At which point, I glanced over. And saw what the problem was. The needle on the compass . . . it had stopped pointing at anything, and was teetering around slackly on its axis. I remembered something else about Regan's Curse. If you're born here, then your magic doesn't work beyond the borders either.

Which left us completely stranded. Damn! We conferred quickly, and decided there was nothing else to do but continue down the logging path. I kept on swinging the flashlight around me as we went, searching desperately for anything that might tell us where we should be headed.

Finally, I saw it. A great mass of rotted leaves had been disturbed, off to our left. Two pairs of shoes had gone right through it. Breathing heavily, we went in that direction, and were going up a slope before much longer.

And at last, we did hear a sound ahead of us. We both froze, listening carefully. What was that? It seemed to be coming from beyond the crest of the hill that we'd been climbing. And it was very muffled, no real shape to it at all.

We pushed on quickly, reaching the top and heading down the gradient on the far side. I had my gun out. My beam kept on sweeping through the big dark trunks in front of me . . . until it picked out something pale.

Blond hair.

* * *

Lauren had been chained by her wrists to the base of an ash tree with—presumably—her own handcuffs. And a thick hank of cloth was knotted over her mouth, gagging her.

Her arms were stretched out painfully behind her, the shoulders so tense they looked like they were going to break. She was sitting down on the leaf-strewn dirt with her knees pressed up against her face. And I thought at first she'd assumed that position out of sheer despair. Until I saw that she'd been trying to protect herself.

Her drained face came up startledly in the yellow circle that the flashlight cast, her blue eyes opaque with fright. There was a bruise on her chin, and some fresh bloody scratches on her forehead. Some creature, a night bird maybe, had been trying to attack her eyes.

She jerked and struggled violently when we first reached her. But then I took in that the beam had to be blinding her. I angled it away. She seemed to recognize me, or my silhouette at least, and stopped fighting. And we crouched down to help her. She seemed far more focused by this stage. Remained entirely still and let us work at getting her loose. Her chest was pumping like a big steam engine all the same. A lot of the moisture on her face was perspiration.

Kurt began untying the gag. I fumbled in her pockets until I found a little set of keys.

"It was Cass!" she blurted, as soon as her mouth was free. "She had gray eyes, like the others!"

Her voice sounded fuzzed up, and I wished I'd thought to bring some water.

As for what she'd said, it hurt to hear it, but I'd mostly figured that one out. I knew how strong-willed Cassie was. If she'd been turned toward her own inner demons, they were likely to be something pretty powerful and nasty.

"Some kind of animal came at me," Lauren was explaining as I got her wrists unlocked. "And there were eyes staring at me from the undergrowth, just before you guys showed up."

It must have been damned terrifying for her. I could scarcely believe Cassie was capable of this, whatever condition she was in. The New England woods are not a desperately risky place, but even smaller predators sense when a person is completely helpless. And they just don't care how much they hurt you. To their minds, you're simply food. The Cassie that I'd always known would turn her own guns on herself before subjecting anyone to that kind of pain and terror.

But we were dealing with a Cassie that I didn't know at all, by this stage. I kept reminding myself that.

Something else occurred to me. We were right on top of Lauren, close enough that we were touching. And an outsider, beyond our borders . . . ?

The curse meant that we shouldn't have been able to get anywhere near her. That was the way it worked, keeping us isolated from the normal world. So the question raised itself. Had its grip relaxed a little? Or was she becoming in some way one of us, a part of our community?

There wasn't time for those kinds of questions, so I put the thought aside. Inspected her injuries instead. None of the gouges were particularly deep. Most of them had already stopped bleeding, dark red gummed around their edges. But they'd get infected if they were not seen to. I understood that much about animal bites.

Kurt looked rather subdued. Because—even if we got her back across the border—it's the one thing that most adepts simply cannot do. They can transform themselves, hurl themselves across great distances. Conjure up almost anything you'd care to mention. But they can't repair a human body. Only Lehman Willets ever managed that.

"You could take her to Raine General," I suggested.

Which would be a very busy place right at the moment, with the night's new battles in full swing. He pulled a face.

"Pullman Cedars would be better."

Which was the finest private clinic in town. She deserved it, so I nodded.

Except he couldn't even transport her the way he usually would have. That's another thing about the curse. We had to make it the whole way back to the car, supporting her between us, before Kurt turned himself and her into blurs and whisked away.

* * *

I couldn't see the fighting from out here, so I called Saul while I was driving back.

"Where are you now?" I asked.

There was firing and yelling, a great deal of it, going on in the background once again. And his voice was strained when he replied.

"Halfway down River Avenue!" he yelled. "And things have gotten really bad, Ross! You need to get down here, as fast as you can!"

Why me especially? I opened my mouth to ask him, but the line went dead.

I took the next right, and started heading for West Meadow. There were no other patrol vehicles headed that way, so far as I could see. Each team had been assigned its own district and charged with the job of defending it. Which meant, whatever the people down there were facing, they were going to have to deal with it alone.

Saul had sounded more stressed than I'd heard him in a good long while. And he'd been badly stressed the whole time for the past couple of days. So he'd be grateful for an extra pair of hands, at least. I turned onto a straighter road and floored the gas.

Reached River Avenue and swung south onto it. It was appropriately named, leading the whole way down to a reed-filled bank. The Adderneck gleamed softly beyond that. There were mostly taller houses around here, old and genteel-looking, ringed with trees.

But halfway down, clusters of shots were going off. I couldn't see what they were being aimed at, but they were all over the place, the cops and militia people swinging around wildly.

As I got closer, I could see that none of them were taking cover. And no barrier had been set up. They were standing upright, with their weapons lifted high. Shooting in the air, the whole bunch of them. So what exactly—this time—were they trying to fight off?

I skidded to a halt some thirty yards short of them. Then, ducking slightly, I got out, my revolver in my grip again. And scanned the skies, trying to see what was attacking us.

The darkness made it difficult. A few more clouds had drifted across by this hour, breaking up the constellations into scattered patches. I jerked as something shot across my field of vision. It was moving so fast I could not make out a proper shape. Just a general impression of a creature, long and dark, with hugely spread wings. It was lost behind the rooftops before I could pick out anything more. My breath hissed between my teeth, and I peered at the spot where it had vanished, waiting for it to come back.

But it had to have circled around very quickly. Because, when it came in view a second time, it was from the direction of the river. It sailed high at first, its wings making a heavy beating sound. But then it folded them partway and suddenly swooped down, the way a hawk might. The men below kept firing, but it was descending too fast.

They all had to duck as it buzzed them. And, when that happened, I heard a high-pitched wail. The back of someone's shirt had been ripped open, and the guy was bleeding badly. He was still alive, although writhing on the ground and yelling, his friends trying to help him.

The creature soared up and was gone again in barely a second.

Keeping low, I moved in their direction, trying to catch sight of Saul. He was over by a municipal pickup truck. Was hunkered down, his own gun clasped in both fists. And his expression was desperate when he noticed I was there.

There was something strange about the look he had. He appeared to be concerned as well as scared, a strange combination under circumstances such as these. My heartbeat kept flipping over. What exactly were we facing this time?

The sound of beating wings pulled my attention over to the left. The creature had appeared again, and was landing on a tall rooftop. Its wings—I could see—were leathery and batlike. And vast, with a span of several yards. The thing had huge talons at the ends of its long legs, two pointing forward and two back. And it gripped the narrow ridge of tiles with those.

Apart from that, its shape was mostly human. It was

wholly black, the way the others had been. The eyes were a glowing misty gray, of course.

But I immediately recognized the weapons hanging from its long-limbed grasp. The hairline cropped closely to the skull. That long face with its rectangular jaw.

Every ounce of strength drained from my body in an instant.

Cassie.

Or at least . . . what she'd become.

CHAPTER 40

That moment of recognition seemed to hang on the air for the longest while, like a massive echo that kept resounding through the dark. It could only have been a few seconds in reality, but seemed to last a whole lot more than that. I don't think I moved during that period, or even blinked.

Considering what had happened to Lauren—well—I should have been expecting something like this. But I still couldn't quite believe what was in front of me.

Except that—in a strange and awful way—I could.

Don't get me wrong. Next to my missing family, Cassie is the most important person to me in this whole peculiar little world of ours. She cares about people, and has limitless courage and strength with which to back that up. She doesn't merely feel, in other words. She does something about it. And I've lost track of the number of times she's saved my hide, not to mention dozens of other people's. I'd always been able to rely on her.

But there's been a savage darkness in her for a long while now, ever since her children disappeared. A brooding anger, and a restlessness that nothing seems to satiate. The world was never right for her, after that happened. And she reacts to it angrily sometimes.

It had come spilling out, becoming physical. Just like it had in all the other townsfolk who had turned. Except that this time, it was happening to someone that I genuinely cared about.

The house below her appeared to have been abandoned. It was just a lifeless silhouette that she seemed to sprout out of the top of, an extension of its shadowy mass. I watched her hunker down slightly, her wings folding behind her with a papery rustling noise. Had her mouth come open slightly? I thought that I could make out the jagged glint of teeth.

Several of the militia guys began shooting at her again, hoping they'd have more success now that she was not a moving target. And I have to admit, something in me wanted to yell, "Cut that out!"

I stayed put and watched, though, seeing what would happen next. I didn't think that their bullets would hurt her. And it turned out I was right about that.

Except it wasn't quite like with the other creatures. The shots didn't ricochet off her or pass through her darkened frame. It was hard to tell precisely in the poor illumination, but they seemed to change direction slightly, skimming off around her.

She'd despised magic for a good long while, the same way I did. But now, she seemed to have acquired some powers of her own.

I heard her let out a furious hiss. Insensate. The kind of noise an animal in a trap might make. And then the weapons at her sides both started lifting.

Which was when I got another shock. I'd thought that she'd been simply holding them. But as the moonlight caught their edges . . . could that possibly be right?

The carbine and shotgun seemed to be growing directly out of the ends of her arms. There was no sign of her hands. I couldn't even see how that was possible. What the hell had she been turned into?

It was one of the hardest things I'd ever done, but I fought to keep a level head. Tried to assess the situation clearly. As she brought her firearms to bear, I saw the danger we were in. There were people scattered right across this street, most of them out in the open. And I knew what a dead shot she was. If they stayed there, they were in real trouble.

"Everyone take cover!" I started yelling.

Hobart, thank God, did the same. A sudden urgency infected the people in my line of vision. And the next instant, they were running for the nearest piece of cover, diving out of sight.

I knew the Mossberg and the Heckler & Koch could both punch holes through my Cadillac like butter. So I turned around on my heels and sprinted, heading for the side wall of the big house nearest me.

As I ran, I could hear gunfire breaking out. The thud of the pump-action, and then distinctive whizzing noises as some carbine slugs went by. Something hot whirred past my cheek.

When I finally found a place to shelter, my heart was thumping furiously, my chest rasping like a barrel organ. Cass had nearly shot me once before, but this was different. Wilder. Less discriminate. I took a few seconds to compose myself, then looked back out, expecting the worst.

My own car had barely been touched. But most of the vehicles further up the street were shot to pieces. Windshields had been turned to glistening fragments. Doors had been blown right off their hinges. Several hoods and trunks were open, and gas was spilling out across the blacktop.

Although there were no dead bodies that I could see, I couldn't be certain, without leaning further out. But everyone seemed to have gotten to safety. Except . . . how much longer would that last? The saboted slugs in the Mossberg could shoot straight through ordinary brick, I reminded myself uncomfortably.

But this lack of casualties . . . I thought it over as best I could, and it didn't tally. A terrific shot like Cass? There should have been at least a couple of corpses lying out there.

So, bearing that in mind, I stared at her again.

She was standing at full height, an arrogant, aloof figure against the purple-black of the sky behind her. Smoke was drifting from the muzzles of her guns. I couldn't tell what the expression on her face was—probably there was none, only that dark oval. But the set of her body was imperious and proud.

I thought I understood what she was up to, at that point. She'd merely been showing us who was in charge. Exerting her authority rather than trying to kill anyone. The real fireworks were still to come.

Her huge wings came back open, with a massive rushing noise. They started beating slowly at first, and then churned faster. And she lifted herself off the roof again.

She hung suspended for a couple of seconds, and then swooped down to the middle of the street, and landed there.

Her claws made an abrupt, harsh rattling as she hit the pavement, the kind of sound that had a dreadful impact to it, practically making me flinch. She was balancing on the talons easily enough, like she had always owned a pair. She paused, then swung from side to side, her weapons at the ready. Everyone still partially in view shrank back when she did that.

Was she recognizing any of them as the townsfolk who she usually defended? Did she even know that I was there?

The details of her body were still hidden underneath that shroud of blackness. But her eyes were clearly visible. They glowed like opals in the sparse street lighting. Except that, once more, there was something odd.

They appeared to be flickering very slightly, instead of remaining as a steady monochrome. And as I watched, they wavered momentarily, trying to go back to normal.

Which put me in mind of Lawrence. I had seen the same from him not long ago. He'd had misgivings about the whole process. And maybe—I clung to that hope desperately—maybe she did too. Could that be why she hadn't actually shot anyone, when she could have done it so terribly easily?

She moved along a few yards, clacking, so I couldn't see her properly from this point any more. And I wanted to keep an eye on her. Needed to see what she was going to do next. So, holding myself steady, I began to edge a little further out.

She noticed that, and swung around. The arm with the Mossberg on it straightened up. There was a lethal-sounding boom, and I ducked back. Barely in time, was my first thought. But it turned out that she wasn't aiming at me. The corner of the house four feet above my head exploded into broken chunks of masonry. A warning shot.

So perhaps I was right. She could have killed me, and she hadn't. Maybe I could work with that.

Very carefully, I eased my face out again, ready to duck back. But Cass had already turned away from me. I'd been forgotten, in favor of someone else.

She was headed for the shattered vehicles. There was a large amount of fluid pooled around them by this time, the smell of it powerful even from this distance.

Then I caught a glimpse of something moving in among the cars. Pale and smooth and round. I couldn't figure it out, at first. But then I realized it was the big crown of a head, a bald one.

Not everyone had made it to cover.

Saul Hobart was still out there, directly in her path.

CHAPTER 41

Her pace slowed and her lean frame stiffened. She was staring right in his direction, I could tell, but only by the angle of her head. I couldn't see her face at all. And felt pretty glad of that. Because as soon as she spotted him, she took on the stealthy manner of a hunting dog that had spotted something close by it could snatch between its jaws.

Saul had been crouching behind a departmental pickup truck. But when he saw the game was up, he tried to make a break for it.

You'd have thought that such a cumbersomely large man would move awkwardly, but there was none of that. He began heading swiftly to the nearest brick wall on the street. But only got halfway.

The shotgun boomed. A cloud of dust and debris flew up in front of the lieutenant, where a section of asphalt had been. He skidded to a halt, and then was forced to go the other way.

Disappeared behind the back end of the truck again, and started edging toward its cab.

Cassie let out a hoarse bark of a laugh, then marched forward. A deadly game was being played here. And I couldn't see what to do about it. I kept on wondering for how much longer she'd resort merely to warning shots.

Some people emerged from cover and started firing at

her again. But—exactly like last time—none of the shots seemed to touch her.

"Hey!" I yelled at them. "You're going to hit Saul!"

They seemed to get that, and the shooting died away. Which left only that stark rattle of talons, still closing in on the vehicles.

I had to do something. Couldn't simply huddle here and watch. So, steeling myself, I did the only thing that I could think of.

I stepped out in the open.

Then I shouted to her.

"Cass!"

She stopped again, and turned to face me.

Looking at her when she'd been high up on a roof was one thing. On the ground, so much closer up, the whole experience was very different. Far too close for comfort. Too immediate to be ignored. The shock of it struck me harder than I'd thought it would, and that was to put it mildly.

Her eyes that way? That blank, black face? It was like my friend and closest ally for the past couple of years was dead. The only things left were this shell, this dark mask. Where had all the goodness and self-sacrifice in Cassie gone?

She stared at me, her weapons still partly raised. Then cocked her head slightly. It was like she was having trouble even recognizing me. Her eyes remained an even gray, no flickering in them any longer. And her mouth came open. The jaw worked gently, but no words came out. Yes, her teeth had become jagged. They were the same black as the rest, but with a faint sheen that made them stand out.

Couldn't she even talk anymore? None of the other demons had, it occurred to me. Just maybe, the darkness that had enfolded her was so primal it went right beyond anything like that. I knew how much rage and pain she carried around inside her. The mourning for her family and the way her life had been. So perhaps it went beyond mere conscious thought, and she could only express herself through violent action.

I spread my hands out to my sides, showing her that they were empty.

"Cassie? It's me! It's Ross!"

Her lips slid shut. But her pale eyes glowed a touch more fiercely. I could feel everybody gazing at us. So the game I'd been watching? I was part of it by now. And could just make out Saul beyond her. He was tensed like a spring, uncertain whether or not to make a break for it again.

I looked away from the man, not wanting to draw attention to him.

"Cass, this isn't you," I said.

I was having to talk loudly from this distance, which made it difficult to sound exactly calm. She stared at me the way you might do at a curious-looking stain you hadn't noticed until this point.

"I know what's inside of you." I took a few more steps toward her, gently. "I'm the same, remember. But this isn't you. You have to see that. There's a whole lot more to you than this."

I drew to a halt, gazing at her steadily. She was more immobile than I'd ever seen her, not responding to my words in the least little bit. But I wasn't giving up. I kept on trying to reason with her.

"Look what you've done for this town the past couple of years," I reminded her. "The people that you've helped. The lives you've saved. We owe you a great deal. Don't make us regret it now."

I could see that I'd been right before. Her eyes flickered again. And this close up, I could see what it really was. The whites showed up momentarily and there was a fleeting glimpse of her dark irises. Cassie's normal eyes were fighting with the gray ones she'd been given, the better aspects of her nature trying to push back through to the surface.

All of us have inner darkness, sure. But inner light as well. Except it was obvious the spell she'd been subjected to was suppressing that fiercely.

Her gaze went pale and dull again. Her black lids batted, and her eyes turned noticeably glossy. But it wasn't dampness. They had become glazed. She looked further away from me than ever, like I'd only made her whole mood worse. I saw what was happening. She didn't want to think about this. Didn't want to face the truth. She was caught up completely in her own inner turmoil.

It was like she had been swallowed by the deep shadows inside of her. The Mossberg came back up, its muzzle aimed directly at me. And Cassie's lip curled.

"What do you think you're doing?" came another voice.

Saul Hobart had reemerged. Like me, he'd put his gun away. He started edging carefully in the direction of her silhouette. His step was nervous, his big brown shoes coming down uncertainly on the blacktop. But he didn't let that show on his broad face. If anything, he looked quite angry.

"I can't believe you're doing this," he told the thing that had been Cassie.

She swung around once more.

In the corners of my sight, I could see fresh heads bobbing up. Nobody seemed sure how to deal with this.

"We're your friends, Cassie," the lieutenant said. "I don't have to tell you that. We've never done you any harm."

He stopped, and I could see his eyebrows draw together.

"What happened with your kids? We're genuinely sorry, but this won't fix it."

My God no, he was getting this wrong. My frame seized up, the breath turning solid in my throat. He was referring to her one Achilles heel. The subject I had always skirted around, even back when she was normal. Bringing it up now was taking a hell of a chance.

The entire scene—the houses, the trees, even the river in the background—seemed to all be locked behind a massive plate of glass. I felt dislocated from the world around me, captured in a frozen moment. Nothing seemed to move.

Cassie remained still for several breathless seconds.

Then she raised the strange arm with the carbine on it.

And shot Saul in his chest.

CHAPTER 42

All that I could do was watch him hit the ground. His big feet flew up as he bounced. And then he was extremely still, his arms splayed out and his legs lying crooked.

Dull noises started resounding in my head. It was the rushing of my blood, at first. And then, there were sharper sounds. I might have been turned to stone—the other guys had not. They had opened fire massively again, unafraid of hitting the man this time.

Cassie paid them no attention whatsoever. Her wings unfolded almost casually. They stretched out to their full span, then became a racketing blur. I could feel the wind they made. It carried scraps of dust with it, but I didn't look away. And she was gone in the next instant, spiraling high into the air and hurtling off.

I didn't even take note in which direction. I just stared back at Saul again.

Do something! my mind was telling me.

My limbs unfroze, and then I was charging forward. Every second was vital. I knew that. I sprinted across to where he was sprawled out, knelt down beside him and pressed two fingers to his throat. And at first, I couldn't find anything. Helplessness swept over me. But then . . .

"He's got a pulse!" I shouted.

And I started yelling for a medic. Which was pretty much

a waste of breath. Two guys with blue bags on their shoulders were already hurrying our way.

Lamp-lit dimness gave way to a cold, bright glow—the fluorescent lighting of a hospital corridor. It was outside an operating theater at Raine General. There were plenty of chairs, but I didn't use any of them.

A few cops had accompanied us. Then word spread, and more started showing up. Despite the fact that they were stunned by what had happened, none of them could stay for very long. The reason for that was obvious.

The operating theater was at one end. At the other was the waiting room for the ER. A double set of swinging doors shielded us from some of the hubbub. But they had windows, and we could see right through them. It was like a scene from Florence Nightingale in there.

People were bandaged up and creased over with pain. Many had their families with them. More were coming in. New battles were breaking out across the town, and an awful lot of ordinary folk were getting hurt. Saul wasn't the only one.

And so these guys were needed elsewhere. They looked shame-faced all the same, fingering their caps and mumbling apologies before heading back out into the fray.

"He'd want you to," I told them. "Hell, he'd do the same."

His wife, Amelia, turned up several minutes later. He likes to keep his work and family separate, so I'd only met her once before. She's a tiny, pretty, fine-boned woman, barely five foot two. I almost laughed when I first met her, standing by a man that size, but there were no smiles on this occasion. When I went across to talk to her, she had real trouble listening. Her eyes wouldn't focus, and her head kept moving around in a peculiar way.

Finally, she settled down in one of the plastic chairs, an unnaturally stiff expression on her face. Making a supreme effort just to hold herself together. Her eyes were fixed on the opposite wall, except I wasn't even sure that she was seeing it.

She'd not had time to leave her kids with anyone, and had

been forced to bring them with. Which, perhaps, explained why she'd not broken down yet. She was trying to be strong for their sake.

Saul had married late, had children even later. So the oldest of his daughters was only six. The youngest—at two years old—had no way of understanding what was going on. She was simply upset because her sisters were both crying. She pushed her head into Amelia's blouse and whimpered bitterly.

The other pair clung to her skirt and were making noises like their grief was strangling them. That ground at me, and I looked away. Lord, they were so small and frightened. Of all the places that I really didn't want to be, this had to be at the top of the list.

Lauren arrived, with her face patched neatly up. Kurt, she explained, had taken her back to her car after the clinic. She'd heard what had happened on the police band while she'd been heading back in.

Her manner was one that I was unfamiliar with, rattled but still businesslike. So I supposed she'd been through stuff like this before.

"How long's he been in there?" she asked, her voice noticeably tight.

At least half an hour, I guessed. But I wasn't sure. I hadn't thought to check my watch, and it felt more like half a year.

Jenny Pearce put in an appearance after that. There was a rip in one of her uniform sleeves, and some heavy grazing underneath. But otherwise she looked okay. She hunkered down in front of Amelia, talking with her for a while. They seemed to agree that she should take the kids away. But good plans and small children do not always mix. None of them would let go of their mother. And their misery got so intense that, in the end, they were allowed to stay.

A weight had settled in my gut, and kept on increasing. When I did look at my watch again, another twenty minutes had passed. No one had emerged from the operating theater. And we didn't have the first clue what was going on in there. Jesus Christ, I couldn't believe I was just standing here, completely useless.

I took it for five more minutes. Then I pushed on through into the little anteroom, and stared into the theater through the plain glass in the doors.

Saul was mostly covered up—you could barely see him. A tent of white cloth had been raised above him, centered on his chest. The surgeons and nurses were clustered around the table, each absorbed in different jobs. Except that they looked more than simply busy. They seemed frantic. There was a tangible sense of panic in that room.

And blood everywhere. All over the surgeons' gloves and aprons. Hard to believe that a single body, however large, could contain that much.

I tried to fight against my next thought, but it wouldn't go away. They were going to lose him. I was watching Saul live out his final evening.

A young blond nurse looked up at last and noticed me. Her smooth brow furrowed above her surgical mask. Then she came over and pushed one of the doors halfway open.

"Sir, you can't wait here. If you'd . . . ?"

"How is he?" I cut across her.

Her gaze became more sympathetic.

"We're doing everything we possibly can," she said. "But there's a great deal of internal damage. We're still trying to stop the bleeding."

Words seemed to fail her at that point. Her head dropped, then she finished up with, "We're doing our level best for him. I'm just not sure it's good enough."

She was about to let the door drop shut, when a sudden, loud commotion broke out to the back of me. It was coming from ER. People began yelping, even screaming. And I heard a crash as something hit the floor. My first thought was, another demon, right here in the hospital. My hand went to my gun. And I'd already started moving in the direction of the racket . . . when the sound of a familiar voice stopped me dead in my tracks.

"Doctor coming through!"

The tone was deep and slightly gravelly.

"Out of my way! I've no time for this nonsense!"

He wasn't that kind of doctor, of course. But Lehman Willets stepped into view, everyone else scrabbling to get out of his way.

Willets never left the building where he lived, not willingly anyway. I'd dragged him out by the scruff of his neck once, but that had been on account of a very different kind of threat. Otherwise, he had been holed up in there ever since the disaster at the Iron Bridge . . . his powers had overwhelmed him, twelve people had died. Which was the cause of the reaction I was looking at right now. I knew he was more controlled these days, okay to be around. But most of the people in town were still terrified of him.

The point of his being here, though? So far as I knew, he was the only adept who could heal injuries.

What had drawn him here? And why to Saul specifically? There were loads more townsfolk hurt. Lord, you could see them all around him.

Then it occurred to me. I was the only person in the whole Landing who ever dared to visit him. Usually it was for advice. But a bond had grown between us, of a kind. So maybe he had heard my anguished thoughts, decided to respond to them.

When he came bursting through into the corridor, he was wearing the same floppy denim hat I'd given him last time he'd been out. I'd intended it as protection from the sunlight. It was night this time—he didn't need it any more. But maybe he'd come to think of it as his outdoors hat, or something of that nature. He's not nearly as bad as Raine, but can still go off at curious tangents sometimes.

Amelia Hobart looked up startledly, breaking out of her trancelike daze. Even her daughters stopped crying. Their faces lifted and they gawped. Willets's features had an utterly determined set. His pupils shone like molten metal. He marched straight past the huddled family, then went by me and Lauren too, not even acknowledging that we were there.

When he burst into the operating theater . . . you'd have thought that educated folk like surgeons would have acted far more calmly. But he got precisely the same reaction as he had outside. They yelled and shied away like the crowds in the ER. Forgot about the lieutenant in their care, and began retreating.

I headed in there hard on his heels, and passed most of them on the way.

"Not you!" he was shouting at a terrified nurse, the same blond one who'd spoken to me. "I need you right here!"

She came to a rigid halt, her face a bewildered oval. And eyed him like he might be planning to devour her.

"But . . . what do you want me to do, s-sir?" she managed to ask, each word a fragmented stammer.

Under the very bright lights in here, he looked larger than he normally did. Fierce, almost imposing.

"Find something nice and heavy," he told her. "Stand behind me with it while I work. And if I start to lose my mind again, please feel free to slug me on the noggin. I insist on it, in fact."

Then he noticed I was standing there. He swung around, looking affronted.

"I don't need an audience, man."

What? I peered at him blankly.

"There a saying, Devries," he explained quietly, "which goes 'let not too much light in upon magic.' In other words, thank you for calling me here. But I'd like some privacy, if you don't mind."

I got that, and was happy to oblige.

Just before I turned away from him, I saw the redness in his pupils swell out to fill both his eyes.

It was another quarter hour before he resurfaced. By then, the panic of before had slackened off. The ER had returned to what passed—tonight—for normal. In fact, the surgeons that he'd chased out were helping other patients. Amelia Hobart was looking anxious and pensive but fully alert, whereas she had been completely out of it before. And her daughters hadn't made another peep since they'd seen Willets walking past.

Like the small animals in his home, they seemed to be fixated by him. The three of them were staring in the direction that he'd disappeared, with a special brightness in their gazes.

When he finally came out, there was not a trace of blood on him. Which was no surprise—at least, not to me. I already knew he didn't need to touch people to heal them. But he looked exhausted all the same, his face even more creased than usual. Sweat was beaded on his rumpled brow, and his jowls seemed to sag.

The nurse came out behind him, peering at him like he was a ghost. She was holding a metal canister, the type that they keep oxygen in. And was clutching it so hard that all her fingers had turned white.

Willets didn't look too pleased with himself, and that bothered me. He's never the most cheerful type. But he was genuinely somber by this stage, so something had apparently gone wrong.

He took off the hat I'd given him, and mopped his temples with it.

"I've stopped the bleeding, and the damage is repaired," he told us.

Although he still seemed unhappy. If he had saved Saul, then what was that about?

"But the one area of medicine I could never get to grips with," he continued, "is the human nervous system. Lieutenant Hobart will live, for sure. But I'm afraid he's in a coma."

CHAPTER 43

The memory kept on slamming at her. Yet another one from her unhappy past. And why, at a time like this, did she keep thinking about a very different evening from so many years ago?

They'd disabled the alarm first. It had taken them a good while, after that, to prize open the metal door. But finally they'd got it hanging loosely from its hinges. Viper, Slam, and Vixen clustered around the opening, behind her. And her boyfriend these last two years, Rooster, shone his flashlight inside . . .

Cassie had not headed west, like any of the others who had changed. After all, she'd not been beaten. Not been turned to vapor. She was still in silhouette, her wings folded behind her. Perhaps out of instinct, she had flown back to her own neighborhood, although she had not gone home.

At the top of East Meadow, almost at the border with the commercial district, lay the sprawling expanse of Greenlea Cemetery. Half the town was buried here. There were headstones going back the whole way to the seventeen hundreds. And they looked it too, badly weathered, mossy, patched with lichen. The names on a lot of them could barely be read.

The ground was not flat anywhere around these parts. It continually rose and dipped, and was covered in a mass of tangled shadow. There was moisture in the hollows, nettles in the damp places as well.

Cass stumbled among the markers like an angry drunk. Waves of pain and fury kept on rushing through her, although she wasn't even certain what was causing them anymore. Confusion was creating violent eddies in her mind. She was not sure what she was doing, where she'd been or how she'd gotten here.

But however much her memory had broken up, she couldn't shake that solitary, insistent one. Her last night with the motorcycle gang. It kept on flooding back.

"Sweet!" Rooster whispered, grinning at her.

They were at the rear of a small clinic not far from their usual bar. Their bikes were parked in a nearby alley, hidden out of sight. Bringing them here would have made too much noise. But they were smirking now, delighted with themselves. Because the flashlight's beam was sweeping across rows of shelving with jars lined up on it. Some of them were translucent—you could make out the shape of pills and capsules stacked inside.

"Here's the really good stuff," Rooster murmured. "Booze and weed? That's for kids. This is where the real fun starts. Like stepping off a cliff, not knowing where the bottom is."

And she wasn't sure about this. In fact, she felt pretty nervous. Cassie had a fairly good idea what drugs this strong could do to people. And they were addictive, weren't they? But ever since she'd joined the gang, she'd fallen in with their plans unfailingly, whatever her personal misgivings.

So she did that this time. She smiled wider and said, "I can't wait."

Despite the pleasure on their faces, they were hanging back uncertainly. There was still one question hanging on the air between them. Which of them was going to go in first? Cassie understood that—if she did it—she'd gain even more respect from them.

Something inside her badly needed that. So she drew herself up straight, then went in through the doorway.

Her life would change completely from this point, she knew. Except she had no real way of telling how . . .

Her surroundings came back. She'd been stumbling blindly, her boots catching on the longer strands of grass. Why this particular recollection? Why tonight? It made her even angrier.

A life-sized marble angel loomed up directly in front of her, its face partly smoothed out by a century of New England weather. Its expression had become mild and bland because of that. But its pale stone eyes seemed to gaze at her accusingly.

Cass let out a howl of rage, and swung at it with her right arm. There was still no fist on the end of it, however. And the barrel of her Mossberg connected instead. The head of the statue shattered like a gourd. She watched the pieces fall. And then she was pressing on again, the scene from the past still grinding at her.

Once she'd reached the shelves, she stopped. She had hold of the flashlight, by this time. She squinted at the labels ranked in front of her then, without turning, whispered to the others.

"Hey, guys? All this stuff has really weird, long names."

But nobody answered her. So maybe they'd not been expecting that.

She wet her lips. "Which ones do we want exactly? Guys?"

She turned around . . .

She did the same in the cemetery, present and past becoming fused. Then she kept on lurching past the headstones. They were every shape and size, great rows of them, punctuated by the occasional small tree. The lopsided symmetry of it confused her.

It was like she couldn't stop. As if the only thing that she could do was keep on moving, while the thoughts in her head went rushing back. The graves went by in a haze, a multitude of carved inscriptions passing across her gaze. These had all been people, once. But now they were here, reduced to memories themselves, if even that. She was alone, and became horribly aware of that.

Why was that one evening so important? She didn't understand it in the least bit. Her head pounded furiously, and her eyes felt weird and sore. She wanted to rub them, and clutch at her temples. But her hands were still missing. There were only the steel weapons. So, in spite of the new power she had, she felt pretty helpless.

Tremors ran up through her body, almost as if she was going to explode.

When she looked back at the doorway, there was nobody in sight. None of the gang was watching her any longer, not even Rooster. And she couldn't hear a sound outside.

She realized there was something wrong, her voice remaining at a harsh, low whisper.

"Guys?"

There was still no response.

She dropped to a slight crouch. Her hand went to her back pocket, and came out clutching a knife handle. The blade dropped out when she jerked it, six inches long with a serrated edge. The rubberized grip felt damp in her palm. Cass edged slowly forward.

The primal senses that she'd honed over the last couple of years were reaching out, trying to get a feel for what was happening. But she still couldn't tell what was waiting for her in the alley. Maybe this was just a prank, the others doing this to spook her.

She reached the doorway, paused for breath. Then, when she still heard nothing, she went slowly out. The knife preceded her.

A hand appeared and closed around her wrist, yanking her violently the rest of the way into the open. She got a brief impression of a dark blue uniform, the metallic flash of a badge.

Dammit! She tried to wrest her arm free, but the man was stronger than she. He pressed his thumb down hard on her wrist. Pain flared through it and her hand opened involuntarily. The blade dropped away.

Cassie tried to fight back all the same. Tried to lash at him with her free fist, and kick him at the same time. But suddenly, he was applying a different kind of pressure, twisting her around. And before she knew it, she was in a rigid armlock.

"Let me go!"

His only response was to start pushing her back to the opening of the alley. She let out a stream of curses.

"Heard it all before, kid," said the soft voice behind her. "Call me names till Sunday next, and it won't change a thing."

His car was waiting by the curb. The rear seats were caged off. And right here was the thing she'd always genuinely feared. She was going to be locked away, and that thought petrified her.

Cassie squirmed and struggled, but could not break the patrolman's grip.

When he took her up to the passenger side, though, she stopped and went slack with amazement. He wasn't putting her in the back after all.

The cop pulled the door open, started guiding her inside.

She finally looked around at him. He was tall and muscular with big wide shoulders. His light brown hair was cropped very short. He had to be in his midforties, deep lines on his solid face. And he was wearing dark glasses, even at this hour of the night. Like he preferred to keep his eyes hidden at all times, giving away little to the outside world.

"Get in and sit still, young lady," he told her. "We need to have a serious talk."

She'd gone another distance through the cemetery without even knowing it. When her surroundings came back this time, she was in among the small copse of lime trees at the very center of the grounds. They rustled as she passed between them, their branches casting striped shadows across her. She was panting heavily, and felt off balance. Tried to grab hold of a nearby trunk. But was reminded, again, that she no longer had fingers.

She felt like she'd run a marathon, when the only thing she'd really done was walk across some open ground. It wasn't effort making her this way. It was the turmoil going on inside her.

The edge of one wing snagged on a low branch. It yanked her to the side, practically making her stumble. She righted herself and pulled at it furiously. There was a rip as it came free, but no pain she could feel.

She couldn't seem to block out the confusion churning through her mind. Felt like she was drowning in a storm of violent emotion. She'd never known anything quite like this since the first few days after her kids had disappeared.

Then something flashed, without any warning, on the edge of her surroundings. When she looked in that direction, she could see that it was a bright point of light, a good long way away. It had just passed by the cemetery walls. And kept on flashing as it moved toward her. It was bright blue. So Cassie thought at first that it might be some kind of beacon on a vehicle.

But no—it was moving unimpeded through the tightly clustered headstones. And so that couldn't be right.

She straightened up as it approached her, wondering what this was about.

As the light got closer, she could see that it was floating, about six feet off the ground. And was rotating too.

And when she finally realized what it was, Cass cringed back with terror.

A small shape was approaching her.

The Little Girl.

CHAPTER 44

Lying immobile in his bed, all hooked up to tubes and wires, Saul Hobart reminded me of Gulliver tied up by the Lilliputians. And it wasn't just his size. This was a man of massive spirit, although he kept it hidden most of the time. Which only made the sight of him this way harder to bear.

A monitor was beeping by his side, lights flickering on it. They had moved him into a private room, dimmer lit than the corridor we'd been in. Everyone else had filtered away by this hour. Willets, I knew, was still in the ER. I had persuaded him to stick around a while and help. Most of the injured—unfortunately—were too scared of the man to let him near them. But a few had accepted his assistance, out of desperation more than anything else. He seemed to understand their feelings, and had tended to them gently and solicitously, his normal abruptness gone. And I felt good about that. He needed to be back among the human race.

The only people with Saul now were me and Lauren, and his direct family.

Amelia was on a chair beside him, with their youngest daughter still in her lap. She was rubbing gently at his knuckles, and gazing at his face like he was simply sleeping. The two older girls were standing by the side of the bed and taking turns to nudge him.

"What's Daddy doing there?" the four-year-old asked. "It's too early."

They couldn't really figure what was happening, in other words. And maybe that was for the best.

Me and Lauren stuck around a few minutes longer, but were forced to make our own excuses in the end. We both felt guilty about that. But there were still plenty of battles raging, and an enemy to be faced down. And we weren't going to do that hanging around here all night.

"Any idea what we do now?" she asked me wearily, as we went out.

We were heading down a corridor in the direction of the car park at the rear, the clamor of the emergency room finally behind us. There was an odor like formaldehyde on the air, and a ringing sound as our footsteps echoed. That's the thing about hospitals. Parts of them are far too busy. Other parts are far too quiet.

"I've been giving it some thought," I told her.

Which was not entirely true. My thoughts had been focused elsewhere for the past couple of hours. But a plan can form without your even knowing it. The human mind can churn notions around pretty well under its own steam.

"And . . . ?"

I was recalling earlier this evening. That dragon on Exeter Close, and how it had been overcome.

We emerged into the open, and there was no fighting visible from here. The clouds had melted away again almost entirely. The stars were very bright, above. The shadows of the forest out beyond the edge of town were visible. Which must have brought back nasty recent memories for Lauren, but she didn't show it.

The air was very fresh and clean, and smelled of the approaching fall. We'd taken precautions against house fires this evening, at least.

"I think another trip to Sycamore Hill is called for."

"Okay."

But she said it without enthusiasm, and I could understand what that was about.

"Some of the people up there are a lot better than you'd imagine," I told her. "Get your car and follow me."

Martha Howard-Brett's house was one of the first you reached beyond the first wide stretch of open ground, if you ascended the hill by way of Plymouth Avenue. It was nothing like her family's grand, palatial mansion up near Gaspar Vernon's place. She'd moved out of there when she'd been nineteen. And was already, by that age, a far subtler and more clever adept than they'd ever be.

There'd been conflict between them, I was pretty sure. The rest of her clan were a pretty snobbish, disingenuous bunch. The women were attractive, and she'd certainly inherited that. But Martha was remarkable for more than simply her looks. She was a spirited individual in her own relaxed and gentle way. And she got on with plain anyone, from the most aristocratic to the lowest.

Some of that was obvious from the place where she lived. It was remarkable, on Sycamore Hill, for being one of the few wood-built homes remaining. Almost all the rest of the houses up here had been rebuilt in brick or stone. But her place looked like a larger version of my own, except that it was on two stories and with dormer windows in the roof, a low fence around the whole structure.

Maybe she was still away helping the townsfolk. There were no lights visible, at least not out front. But then, as I walked down the garden path, a glow sprang up behind the frosted glass pane in the door and it swung open. Martha's shapely figure was framed there in silhouette.

My step faltered and I stared at her, feeling a twinge of apprehension. Had she changed as well? But then her face tilted a few degrees, and light washed across it. She looked normal, and was smiling. And it wasn't just her mouth. It was her eyes as well.

"I sensed that you were on the way," she told me. "That's why I came back here. And you have a plan? Lord knows, Ross, we need one."

Not that she could read minds, the way the more powerful

denizens of this town could. But she's massively intuitive, and usually picks up on stuff like that. She'd probably got it off my bearing and expression.

She greeted Lauren warmly, and then ushered us both through into her living room. You'd have expected a preponderance of fancy decor, damask, silk, and lace, but there was none of that. The place was prettily but simply furnished, floral scatter-cushions on the chairs and couch. Delicate porcelain figurines on the mantelpiece. A small fire was burning in the grate beneath them. It had to have been lit because she liked the way it looked, since there was no need for it at this time of year.

In fact the flames, as I got closer, seemed to cast not the slightest particle of heat. I'd come across magic like that before, and it didn't surprise me too much. The lights in here had been turned down. But, as I've already pointed out, sorcery and shadows cling together. The only thing that you can ever do is hope that your eyes properly adjust, so you can see what's really going on around you.

The paintings on the walls were by local artists, exactly like my place. And there was a large bowl on a plain round table in the corner, with a pair of tiny bug-eyed goldfish swimming around in it. Maybe they imagined they were trapped there by a curse as well.

The smell of recent cooking was still wafting from the kitchen. She'd been doing something with cinnamon and ginger. I could see a row of copper pans in there, and a long rack of spices.

Her hospitality was impeccable, as usual. She didn't take too long over it, realizing how serious the situation was. But she got us both sat down comfortably and offered us a drink. And then, when we declined it, took a tall chair facing us, crossing her legs neatly, folding her hands in her lap.

Sitting down, she had the bearing of someone riding a show horse. It was all part of the way she looked.

She listened intently as I outlined my idea. And when I produced the Thieftaker from my pocket, her nose screwed up a little and her mild gaze narrowed.

"I haven't seen one of those in quite a while," she said.

"But you can use one, right?"

She gave a brisk, stiff nod.

She didn't feel entirely comfortable—and I understood that—using a device that was not her own. Such things often carry the peculiar vibrations of their owners with them, and can throw you all kinds of unexpected curves. So she knew what the risks were. But she would do it for the town's sake.

It wouldn't work on Millicent, she went on to explain. Ms. Tollburn was the wand's rightful owner, and nothing could change that fact. But Hanlon was still vulnerable. The two had merged into a single entity . . . so drawing him to us would, doubtless, bring them both.

Then I went on to ask her about the way she had changed shape this evening.

"Can you do the same to someone else?"

An alarmed gleam sparked up in her eyes, but she stayed motionless.

"You mean yourself?"

I stared back at her and nodded.

"But I thought you hated magic, Ross?"

And was not even supposed to use it—Amashta had told me that. But magic could be used on me, by a third party. I could be a conduit for it. That had happened before.

So I carefully explained to Martha what I wanted her to do.

CHAPTER 45

With so much rage pouring through her, you'd have scarcely thought that she was capable of fear. But if there was one thing that terrified Cassie, it was the sight of the Little Girl. The creature—and that was how she thought of the apparition, not as a genuine child—frightened her even worse than Lehman Willets.

She had only met her once. It had been on that first evening she and Ross had come across her. Nobody in Marshall Drive had told them anything about her. They had simply noticed a strange blue glow coming from behind the drapes of a window, and followed it. And when they'd stepped into the nursery room . . .

She'd been aghast, plain horrified. Every fiber in her body seemed to rear away. Partly because the Little Girl resembled one of her own missing daughters, though with lighter hair. But mostly, because she got a real peculiar feeling.

Cassie knew her, on one level. She was positive of that. There was a sense of recognition. And that disturbed her on a profound level, because she was absolutely certain they had never met.

So how could that be possible? Instinct and reality did not match up. Her mind had struggled with the problem for a long while before giving up on it completely.

In the end, she'd told herself a trick was being played.

Because of that, she'd never gone back. Felt far safer, staying away. Ross didn't seem to share her misgivings. And that was his business, she supposed. But, so far as anyone knew, the Little Girl never left her nursery on Bethany Street.

So what was she doing out here? Was this some new kind of illusion?

Her tiny form was floating nearer, her electric blue glow lighting up the tombstones as she passed across them. She was still revolving in the air. Her eyes—like they always seemed to be, from what Ross said—were closed. Her pale blond hair fluttered gently, despite the fact that the breeze had died away to nothing by this hour. So it was being caused by her own motion.

Cassie stumbled back among the trees and tried to think straight. It was almost impossible under these circumstances. But she knew that—several times in the past—the Girl had managed to communicate with Ross while he was in another part of town. She had projected herself into his mind. Was something like that happening now?

The child reached the edge of the copse. She paused a moment, hovering. And then continued inward. And she wasn't moving in a straight line any longer. She was changing direction constantly, slipping around the tree trunks rather than passing through them. Did that mean that she was really there, or was it merely some more general deception?

Cassie started backing away again, petrified the Little Girl would get too close. Although, however quickly she retreated, it didn't seem to make the slightest difference. This was taking on the surreal quality of a bad, anxious dream. She couldn't seem to put any distance between them. It was like the child was tethered to her invisibly, and the rope was getting shorter the whole time.

The infant rose a few inches higher in the air, and Cassie went stiff with fright and stopped.

When the Girl was a few yards away, she finally—out of desperation—resorted to violence. Cass raised her arms and fired, using both her weapons. There was enough discharge to blow a full-grown man apart.

It had no effect. The Little Girl kept moving in, until her buckled white shoes were spinning around slowly, practically in front of Cassie's face.

She lashed out at them. The muzzles of her weapons passed right through the small, pale ankles.

So perhaps she was not really there. Was it possible that she was still back in Marshall Drive, and this was just an image of her?

Cassie didn't care. She simply wanted this to go away.

But nothing she could do was going to make that happen.

"Why did you try to hit me, Miss Cassie?" the Girl asked, in that high-pitched voice of hers. "I'm only here to help."

Cass didn't answer. She went stumbling back again. The image of the Little Girl turned blurry for an instant, then resolved once more in front of her.

"Why are you running away from me? I'm not going to hurt you."

Cassie reached out for a tree trunk again, to support herself, then took in the fact that there were none. She had retreated the whole way through the clump of lime trees and was back on open ground. It was flatter here, and neatly mown. Some gravel scattered in the grass crunched underfoot. She had wandered into a wealthier section of the graveyard, the shadows around her larger than they previously had been.

A few more steps, and she was among the mausoleums. Some were square, and looked like bunkers. Others were more Byzantine in design. Many had statuary on top or in front of them. Lions, favorite pet dogs, and yet more angels, spectral figures in the gloom. And there were studded doors and iron grilles barring the entranceways. Quite a few had arcane symbols carved on them or welded to their frames.

Many of these were dead adepts. She'd never wandered into this part of Greenlea before, although she'd skirted around it many times. It was wise to avoid places like this. Dark forces still lingered here, or so was the general opinion in town.

None of which seemed to bother the Girl. She kept on

drifting forward at the same unbroken pace, a delicately sad look on her tiny features.

"Why are you following me?" Cass howled at her. "Leave me alone, goddamn you!"

"God would curse me if I stood back and did nothing," came the echoing reply. "You are Mr. Ross's friend. I owe it to him to help you."

"I'm nobody's friend! Don't you understand, you stupid brat?"

The Girl's expression didn't flicker.

"You don't mean that, Miss Cassie. It's the darkness in you, talking in that way. It has a very strong grip on you at the moment. But it did once before, and you defeated it."

Her head reeled again. She hadn't the tiniest idea what the infant was referring to.

"You turned back to the light that time. And I know that you can do it again."

Cassie tried to clutch her forehead, but her arms were still the same. Her skull was pounding furiously. What was this mockery of a small girl trying to tell her?

"You were already halfway there," the infant told her sharply, making her draw back. "Complete the memory."

Cassie turned and tried to run, but stepped on a damp patch of earth instead and stumbled. Wound up on her knees and elbows, the blue glow hovering above her and washing down.

"You were already thinking how it happened. But you didn't finish. It is time, Miss Cassie. Do it now."

Cassie let her eyes slip closed. And the whole encounter came rushing back.

"I know who you are," said the cop.

They were pulling slowly away from the curb, leaving the alley behind them.

"You're Cassie, right? Gus and Joanne Mallory's kid?"

What of it? The only thing he wanted to do was to put her behind bars like some kind of animal, so why pretend to be concerned? Cass stared out through the windshield and said nothing in reply.

"Never met your ma," he continued. "But your pop? I knew him well. He was a great guy, quite a character. I was sorry as all hell to hear what happened."

It had been twenty months since her parents had died. But her eyes still began to prickle. And she turned her face away to hide their dampness.

"Must've been pretty tough on you, since then."

"I've been fine," she answered tersely.

"Yeah? How do you figure?"

"I've got a whole new family now."

She could feel him staring at her with open disbelief.

"That bunch of jokers you've been hanging out with? Good God, family? They're not even your friends. They lit out when I showed up, didn't even try to warn you. Genuine friends don't do that, Cass. They look out for each other and they watch each other's backs."

Had they genuinely just run away and left her? When she thought about it, she could see no other explanation. But she'd spent most of the time since she had joined the gang trying to hang on to their approval. So she shook her head and set the thought aside.

"What do you even know about it?" she said. "Think you're smart because you got a badge?"

He laughed.

"You may be right."

And then, as if she had said absolutely nothing, the man kept talking to her quietly. Telling her how proud her Dad had always been of her. How he'd shown around photographs, and talked about her the whole time. Was this what cops did when they caught someone like her? Did they try to worm into your head and make you easier to handle? Another trick? Another lie?

"That's not true!" Cass retorted. "He didn't even really want me. He wanted a son."

She'd been trying to tell herself that for months, to make herself feel better about the fact that he was gone. But it only got a grunt from the man beside her.

"You mean the shooting lessons and the judo stuff?" he answered. "Hell, all he wanted was to know that you'd be safe."

And she'd always suspected that, whichever way she tried to twist it. Cassie found she had no comeback, and lowered her head.

How would Gus feel—the cop continued—if he knew what she was up to these days? What would his opinion be of the kinds of people she was hanging out with now? And if he ever found out she'd been trying to steal drugs . . . ?

She couldn't even speak. Could feel her insides drawing tighter, her whole body clenching in upon itself. Other memories came back to her, from the time her folks had still been alive. The warmth and security of those years. And it seemed to have all happened in another lifetime. Something that was practically a physical pain ran through her, because there was no way back.

"Cat got your tongue?" the cop finally asked.

She hated the way he'd gotten to her. Felt that she was being undermined. But she couldn't seem to help herself. The words came rushing out.

"I've nowhere else to go!" she blurted.

And there, she'd said it at last.

"How's that?"

"I can't seem to go forward, and I can't go back! There's nowhere else but where I am!"

The cop peered at her.

"In the gang, you mean? Explain that."

"I was never any good at school. And the only jobs for me in this town all come with a hairnet or a paper hat. I'd rather . . ."

And she didn't say the last word. But she thought it, loudly.

The cop pulled a sympathetic face.

"There's an alternative."

And now he was really messing with her, wasn't he? She was qualified for nothing, and so how could that be possible?

"You inherited your folks' place free and clear, right? And it's all paid up? That's called an asset, Cassie. You could raise money against it, start up on your own."

Which made her thoughts whirl slightly. No one had explained that to her before.

"You could be your own boss. That was Gus's dream, one he never lived long enough to turn into reality. But how proud do you suppose he'd be if you did that?"

The car finally drew to a halt, and she became aware of her surroundings for the first time in a good long while. They'd not stopped outside any station house. They were almost back where they had started, out in front of the alley where the bikes were hidden.

"You'd better be getting along," the cop told her, smiling gently.

He was . . . letting her go?

"That's right."

But—?

"I've a son about your age," he told her. "And every time I look at him, I know he's going to turn out right. I get the same feeling off you, Cass Mallory. So why don't you just go home?"

Her head was still reeling when she got back out onto the sidewalk. She couldn't seem to get a grip on any of this. Was he playing some kind of game with her? But he seemed genuine enough.

At first, she felt deeply relieved. But then, as she walked away, some of her earlier attitude returned. Stupid cop, she started thinking. Who did he imagine he was dealing with?

Maybe she'd wait until he was gone, and then go back and steal some of those drugs anyway. That would be a tale to tell the others when she got back to The Hole.

She rounded a corner, then stopped dead. There were only bare brick walls in front of her, nothing else in sight.

The noise of an electric window made her look back the way she'd come. The cop was gazing at her, with a sad expression on his face.

"Those 'friends' of yours came back and took your bike, right? Didn't think you'd need it anymore?" His lower lip came jutting out. "I kind of figured they'd do that. And I'm sorry, Cassie. But some lessons are only learned the hard way."

She stared at him, feeling the breath leak out of her body.

"Need a lift?" he asked.

She shook her head. He seemed to understand that, shrugged.

"A good long walk'll give you time to think. And I guess you've not done much of that for a while. Good night then, Cass."

On an impulse, she asked him, "What's your name?"

She was not sure why. It just came spilling out.

He adjusted his shades a touch.

"Most people simply call me Frank."

And then he turned his head away, and the car drifted off . . .

The Little Girl dropped back a few feet. Cass stood up abruptly. The mausoleum walls around her were washed with blue light, making them look eerier than ever. But the child—or whatever it was—was no longer revolving.

She was hanging limply in the air, her small face tilted down. Her eyelids were still closed, the pale, fine lashes quivering.

"It wasn't easy," she was saying, "but you did it once. You rediscovered the brightness in your life."

And that had grown more intense down the years, once she'd started having children.

"You can do it again, Miss Cassie," the girl said urgently. "You must."

But the only thing she felt was renewed panic. Where was the sense in trying to change back? It was better to stay the way she had become, wasn't it? Nothing could really hurt her this way.

"Get away from me!" she howled.

She began stumbling between the mausoleums. The Girl kept following her from a safe distance.

"You know who Frank was, don't you?" she asked.

Cassie tried to cover her ears, but there was still the problem with her hands.

"Francis."

"Shut up!" Cassie yelled.

"Blane."

"Stop this!"

"Devries."

It hit her like a bolt of lightning.

"It was Ross's father who helped save you from the darkness, Cassie. It was he who pulled you back from the abyss. You and Mr. Ross are joined together, riding on the same river of destiny. You should be with him, helping him. Not turning your back on him like this."

The words seemed to be making her skull burn.

"I don't know what you're talking about!" Cass bellowed.

She began to run. But only got a dozen yards before her boot tip caught on an exposed root. She fell heavily, facedown. And lay there as the bright blue glow moved up behind her.

The voice reached her ears once again, paining them.

"If you don't turn back, Cassandra, everything might well be lost. You see, you are a part of the prophecy too."

What the hell was she talking about? She rolled over angrily. Then froze, consumed with utter shock.

The Girl's face seemed to have split up into dozens, each of them translucent and overlapping. Most of them were children's too. But there was one set of features that stood out amongst the rest. That of a very aged woman, wizened, craggy, gaunt. Her hair was gray, and her nose was hooked. She wore bone earrings and a strange double scar was visible on her withered neck.

Her lips moved, in time with the Little Girl's.

"A prophecy is not law, you see. No future is set in stone. It can be altered by free will. So, Cassie, you must decide. Can I trust you to choose wisely?"

Cass stared up numbly, lost for words.

And then, when she blinked . . . the Little Girl was gone. The glow had vanished. And the dimness of the graveyard settled around her again.

Her head went from side to side confusedly. She was well past the mausoleums by this time, and seemed to recognize this place.

Cassie started getting up, before coming to another rigid halt. There were two headstones in the thick grass in front of her, planted side by side. They were small ones, very plain.

Her parents' graves.

For a while, it was like she was seventeen again, and staring at them for the very first time. Shock and guilt ran through her. Her mind had been a maddened blur, until this point. But it began to clear. And when that happened, she started to remember everything she'd done.

Hitting Lauren Brennan. Attacking the cops.

And Saul Hobart facing her, his lips moving. She couldn't really hear what he was saying. But she knew that she'd been angry with him. Terribly so.

There'd been a sudden flash, and . . .

Oh my God! What had she done?

The wings on her back shrank away to nothing. Her feet and arms returned to normal, the weapons dropping away with dull thuds. Her usual skin tone and dark irises returned.

Cassie put a hand across her mouth, stifling the noises that were trying to push their way out.

And, sitting there on the damp grass, she rocked back and forth for the longest while, overcome by what had happened to her. What she'd brought down on the people that she cared about.

What she had let herself become . . .

CHAPTER 46

"We'll make it happen here," said Martha, once that I had outlined what I wanted her to do to me.

I looked around her place again, and didn't like the sound of that. And so I told her so. Once set in motion, this could turn extremely violent. And I hated the idea of her peaceful, pleasant home getting damaged.

"So one more house gets wrecked," was her brisk, unconcerned reply. "That's happened enough already, and most people don't even have the powers and resources I do. No, Ross, it's worth the risk. We've no more time left for delays."

Lauren had been looking at me strangely for a while. Silently, with her brow creased. I supposed that, up until this point, she'd been seeing me merely as some kind of ordinary detective, simply trapped in extraordinary circumstances And trying to make the best of it. But now she was beginning to understand that I got involved, myself, in the arcane on some occasions. Sometimes right up to my neck. If she thought that I was happy about it, she was very badly wrong. But if you want to deal with certain situations in the Landing, you are sometimes left with no alternative.

I wondered briefly if I'd raised her opinion of me, or lowered it. But Martha was exactly right. There was little time left for considerations of that kind.

So I stared back at the lovely female adept. "I'd still hate to see this room smashed up."

"Actually, I was thinking of my studio out back."

I hadn't known about anything like that. And wasn't sure which kind it was until she led us there, opened the door, and flicked on the lights.

Me and Lauren followed her in, stepping into a white-walled area some thirty feet by forty. The floor was of very pale wood, and rang under our tread. Except it almost felt like floating, so light and airy was the space she had created.

There were no shades on the lightbulbs in here. Practically no ornamentation of any kind. Just paleness, like a blank sheet of paper, waiting to be written on.

But not completely that. At several points around the room, easels were set up. And there were bright spots of dried paint in a variety of colors spattered on the floor around them. The frames themselves were empty. And so . . . where was all her work?

Directly across from us was a massive picture window, spanning most of the length of the opposing wall. Set up in front of it was the only other large object in the room. A brass telescope on a wide tripod. It was pointed not at the sky, but at the town below.

What exactly did she paint? I began to wonder. Whatever it might be, it could only ever be viewed from a distance.

It occurred to me how lonely the life of an adept could become. She was a beautiful woman, brimful of vitality. But this home, when I really thought about it—pleasant to visit though it might be—was the tidy, comfy residence of a solitary spinster. Nothing more than that.

I liked her a lot, but felt very slightly sorry for her. Like many of her kind—when you looked at them closely—she seemed slightly distant from the world, regular life lost to her.

"Can I see what you paint?" I asked her quietly.

"Don't we have other, more important things to do?"

But I persisted. At which, her cheeks became a little flushed. She walked across to the bare wall on our right.

And when she pressed her hand against it, the top half of her arm went through.

There was some kind of secret area back there, the surface simply an illusion. And I'm pretty used to things like that, but noticed Lauren's shoulders bunch.

When the hand came back, it was holding a small canvas by its wooden frame. Martha kept it turned away from me at first, but then pulled out another couple. I watched her take a deep breath. She wasn't too comfortable doing this, it seemed. But then she walked across, and showed the paintings to me.

They were portraits. And I guessed, not of anyone she knew. She'd obviously got them from the telescope. But they still took my breath away.

The first was of an old man sitting on a bench by the lake in Crealley Street Park. You could see the personality etched into each line of his tired and largely shapeless face. The decades lived, for good or bad. The strengths and weaknesses that made up what he had become. It was all there, in colorful oils that seemed to transform themselves into a whole lot more than that.

"It's wonderful," I told her.

But her only response was to look away.

The other two were of a teenage girl, about thirteen, and a young mother with a baby. One was launching herself into her future, delighted but slightly scared at the same time. The other had set aside ambition, and was thinking only of her newborn child.

Martha remained distinctly edgy, although she managed to look back at me again.

"Apologies. I've yet to finish one I'm genuinely pleased with."

Which was what made her such a damned good artist. But telling her that would have only embarrassed her more. So I handed them carefully back, and watched as she hid them away again.

It was time to get on with what we'd come here for.

The lights were on dimmer switches, and she turned them to their lowest point before she started. The night seemed to press through the window and close in around us. After a few murmured words, the segments of the Thieftaker began to rotate, their shifting facets throwing out sparks of brilliance against the walls. The device started making a faint cranking sound, like a chainsaw in the distance.

"Time to work your magic," I told Martha.

"But to take on that particular form . . . ?"

"A theory," I told her.

It was more an instinct, really. But I knew she trusted mine.

"You think she'll be glad to see him?"

"Precisely the opposite, is my guess."

Creases appeared in her temples. She had no idea what I was talking about. But she had the sense to give me the benefit of the doubt.

"We'll be waiting in the next room," she told me. "I can cast a Spell of Shielding, so we shouldn't be detected."

"One more thing," she added. "If it does get violent, you're on your own on that score, I'm afraid. I'm no use in the slightest when it comes to that."

I doubted that was entirely true. This was someone who could manage pretty much anything she wanted, if she really needed to. But just past her shoulder, Lauren was checking her Walther. So we had that angle covered, and I didn't need any more help in that regard.

"You're doing enough already," I assured her.

"I hope so," she answered slightly ruefully. "There's no point in my staying here. I'll work my magic on you from the living room."

She went out, Lauren following her. The door banged shut behind them.

Alone in the dim, echoing space, I could feel my heart racing a little quicker and the lines on my palms getting damp. Oh boy, here we went again. As I've pointed out, I had been used as a conduit for magic before, and the experience had left me shaken. Disconnected, torn apart from who I really was. My body kept on trying to clench up at the memory of it.

Except that, by this time, I was already altering.

I could feel my fingers stretching, my whole body narrowing and then stooping over. My hair was growing longer, tickling at my neck. Even my clothes were changing, getting darker. Finally, the vision faded in my left eye until the only thing that I could see there was a milky fuzz.

I should have been expecting that last transformation, but it startled me worse than anything else. I turned around and walked to the big window. It was highly polished, very clear against the darkness of the night. And slightly reflective. Peering through my good eye, I could see my image in it.

I was shorter than I had been, with my back severely hunched. And a good deal thinner too. I had a black suit on, which hung around my frame like a wet rag. My hair had turned pure white, sprouting in every which direction. And the same was true of my eyebrows.

My good iris was a weird, gleaming turquoise. This was simply a disguise, but a pretty convincing one.

The Thieftaker continued to grind away, casting out swift, glinting scraps of light. It was the only movement in the room, apart from my own breathing. Dozens of little pale specks continued to sweep across the shadowy walls like a planetarium gone rather wrong.

But nothing else was happening.

"Gonna keep me here all evening?" I murmured impatiently, under my breath.

Then I took in what the problem was. I'd never once seen any of those balls of vapor move through an obstruction. So I went along the picture window, found a catch at the far end, and slid a section back.

The night air—beyond the opening—seemed extremely heavy, laden with ugly possibilities. The town's streetlamps and a few windows glittered far below. It looked wide open and very vulnerable to my protective gaze. And battles were still taking place.

Could I see something else moving out there, very faintly? Something closer up? I wasn't sure. My hand clenched a little.

When the ball of pale vapor came surging into the room, there was no real warning. I didn't even see the thing approach the glass. It seemed to come rushing inward out of nowhere.

I stepped back to the center of the room. It hovered a couple of yards in front of me, like it was giving me a good hard look. Its edges boiled briefly. Was it surprised?

It was seamless at the moment, a featureless cloud of pallid gray. There was no way to tell where Hanlon started and Millicent left off. In all the time that I'd been fighting magic forces, I had never before faced anything like this.

The thing to do, I guessed, was to try and take it off balance, before the people in it figured out what was really going on. I tried to straighten my bent back, then decided it was better not to.

"Milly! What do you think you're playing at, young lady?"

I had to hand it to Martha. She had worked this spell just as thoroughly as before. It wasn't only my appearance that had been altered. My voice was wheezy, croaky, exactly like Lucas's had been.

I stooped a few inches lower and patted one bony knee-cap.

"Come to Poppy," I said softly, with a quiet, cruel undertone.

If I was right, then I felt pretty awful, goading her this way. But too much was at stake by this stage of the game. Far too many lives were hanging in the balance. And survival can be a ruthless thing, any way you care to cut it.

The ball of vapor drifted closer. Then it narrowed down its middle. It was starting to divide into two separate parts.

This seemed to be working. So I kept it up.

I dropped my voice to the gentlest croon that I could manage. And made sure that it retained a faintly mocking undertone as well. If I wanted to get under her skin, this seemed the right way to do it.

"Be a good girl, Milly. Do as Poppy says, like you did when you were little."

The vapor separated almost completely into two sections

of equal size. Only a thin strand, darker than the rest, was joining them together. It didn't shift or waver, the way the mist on either side did. And so . . . was that the wand? It occurred to me that each might be clutching one end of it.

I'd have to make her let go, in that case. And still felt pretty bad doing it this way. But I could see no choice.

"Did you think that death would stop me, Milly? Did you think that you were free of me at last? Well I'm back, and ready to start again where I left off. I've still got so much to teach you. Thousands of new wonders and horrors that you ought to know."

Which was what—I had already guessed—had made Millicent turn out the way she was. Being introduced to Lucas's world at far too early an age. If she'd been thinking sensibly, she would have seen through this. But I was plucking at far deeper and more primitive nerves than that. Wounds like the ones I believed she'd suffered never properly healed up. And when they were reopened, surely rational thought dissolved? That was precisely what I was counting on.

The ball of vapor to the right resolved itself into a vaguely female form. It remained monochrome for a few heartbeats. Then its details and full range of colors suddenly became apparent.

Millicent's features were drawn so tight, they barely seemed to fit across her skull. Her mouth was pulled back like an elongated knife mark. And her turquoise eyes were blazing.

"This can't be!" she bellowed. "How can you be here again? I saw your corpse! This simply can't happen!"

All I did was favor her with a smug, sickly grin.

"Anything can happen, if you want it enough, Milly dear. And I want to be with you again *so* badly."

Which finally broke her. She let out a strangled yell. Barely human. Utterly confounded.

Then she let go of the wand, and threw herself at me.

CHAPTER 47

She came at me with such tremendous fury that—I have to admit—I wasn't properly ready for it. Ought to have been, God knew. I'd faced enough that was destructive and malevolent the past couple of days. But I was only thinking of her size compared to mine, and had underestimated the extent of her bottled-up, bottomless fury. It struck me with the force of a tidal wave, exploding over me.

I raised my arms to fend her off. Easily outweighed her, and my reach was longer. But she just ploughed through, clawing at me, her fingernails as sharp as scalpels. And they tried to rip my neck first, before heading for my face.

I tried grabbing at her wrists, and only partially succeeded. Her hands kept slithering out of my grasp and attempting to savage my cheeks again.

When I finally got hold of them both, she let out another howl. Then started kicking at my shins with her high-heeled pumps. It hurt like hell, but I hung on.

Millicent came to a halt next instant. Went completely still, like stone. Her eyes grew even wider, and I thought I'd managed to subdue her. Then I saw the truth.

I'd made a big mistake here, hadn't I? Her grandfather had been a very old man, strong in sorcery, but physically feeble. In which case . . . ?

Her head cocked at an angle. And a gleam of recognition sparked up in her blue-green eyes. Her inner senses had most probably taken over, I imagined.

"You?" she blurted abruptly.

She had seen through the illusion.

Her whole mood changed in less than a second. The heat in her dissipated. It was suddenly like holding on to a big block of ice. Her entire body became stiff. And her strange, feline gaze felt like it was trying to drain the warmth out of mine.

Understanding she'd been tricked, she looked at the remaining ball of vapor. But if she was counting on Hanlon's help, she'd got that completely wrong. He was now the sole owner of the wand. And was already retreating through the window. Even I was startled at the speed with which he'd turned his back—if you could call it that—on her.

The last of the gray mist disappeared as we both watched. She had not only been fooled, this time. She'd been betrayed as well. She gave her wrists such a savage jerk they slipped free of my grasp again.

Her shoulders hunched forward, like those of a cornered beast. And when she spoke again, she literally spat the words out at me.

"Do you think that you can stop me? You forget what I am, even without the wand!"

Millicent took a quick step back, and raised her flattened palms in my direction. Her lips formed around another word, a silent one this time.

The air directly in front of me seemed to thicken, coalesce. It was still transparent but looked wrong, distorting the dim light passing through it. The woman looked misshapen on the other side, like I was staring at her through a poorly fashioned lens.

Which was growing thick appendages, like stumpy limbs. I thought to move. But too late.

It suddenly lurched at me and grabbed hold. Then it was folding across my shoulders like some vast amoeba, tightening around my head and pressing in against my face.

Christ, it might have still been air. But it was so intensely thick that my lungs couldn't draw it in. I couldn't breathe. I struggled to push it off. But some of it slid further down my body, pinning my arms to my sides. I didn't give up, shoving at it with my elbows. But it was like pressing them against foam rubber . . . the stuff merely sprang back.

Blood rushed up into my head. I was still attempting desperately to fill my lungs, and couldn't get so much as half an ounce of oxygen. I started to become dizzy, then went down on my knees.

Couldn't even shout for help. Where the hell were Lauren and Martha? A burning had started in my chest. My pulse was banging against my skull, and I was vaguely aware that it shouldn't have been up there. I fought to get free again, but it was a much weaker effort this time.

Through the distortion around me, I could see Millicent's face. It was hanging above me, staring down as though from some enormous height. Totally out of proportion, centered around a prominent sharp nose.

Her smile was a gloating one. And her pupils glittered with a cool, vicious delight. It occurred to me that I had brought this on myself. I'd pushed her much too far, and knew it.

But it was all academic now. My vision started blurring. The whole room seemed to tilt abruptly, but it wasn't that. It was me, going down on my side. The fire I'd noticed a few seconds before was really taking hold of my insides.

My face didn't go the whole way down against the floor. The hardened air around me kept it clear by several inches. And I was just beginning to pass out, when I heard a soft thump from above.

The air promptly lost its density. My cheek banged against smooth wood. I hardly even noticed that. Just sucked in one of the most grateful breaths I'd ever taken in my entire life.

It made a weird ratcheting sound, going down my larynx. But it felt really wonderful, so I decided to try another.

The room started coming back to me as my head cleared. And I could see exactly what had saved me.

Millicent Tollburn was lying on the floor not far from me. She was sprawled facedown, both arms flung above her head. Her left shoe had come off, which made her look rather less stylish than she'd been. Behind her was a pair of legs in charcoal pants. So I looked higher up.

Lauren Brennan had her Walther in her right hand, and was holding it by the muzzle. She'd simply walked up behind Milly—who'd been too preoccupied to notice her—and cold-cocked the woman.

A smile managed to work its way onto my throbbing lips. Magic can be impressive, yes. But sometimes, it's the simpler methods that really make a difference.

Martha came back through the door. Her expression grew quickly shocked when she saw that I was down, and she hurried over to me.

"Are you all right?"

I coughed. "I suppose I'll live."

I struggled back up to my feet. Martha offered to get me a chair, but I told her no. My surroundings remained a little swimmy, but I returned my attention to the figure on the floor.

She was motionless at first, then started coming around a little. Her teeth parted a small gap, and her sharply pointed fingers twitched. Lauren turned her gun around, and Martha drew her body straight, holding herself ready. If another surge of magic came, she'd do her best to counter it.

But matters didn't get that far. Because the woman only partially revived. A strange murmur escaped her throat, the kind of sound a child makes when it's having a bad dream.

Then her frame suddenly convulsed. She curled up into a tight ball, and began wailing in a high-pitched, anguished voice.

"No, Poppy, please! Don't make me into that again!"

She whimpered.

"I'll be good, I really will! Just don't use any more magic on me! Please don't! I don't like it!"

So I'd been right the entire time. But it was still news to the other two. Neither of them looked pleased about it, as the truth sank in. Martha's face especially was sickened.

They were still looking grim when the cops arrived to take Millicent away. I suppose we all were. She was back on her feet by then, but still caught up in that half-dreaming state. Kept on murmuring to herself as she was led out through the doorway. And she no longer seemed conscious we were even there. God only knew what kind of hell her grandfather had put her through when she'd been small. Magic should never be used that way, and I felt genuinely sorry for her.

"What'll happen to her now?" Lauren asked me in a brittle tone. "Lock her up, throw away the key, and that'll be that?"

Which exasperated me, and I saw no reason to hide it.

"We might not be big-city folk," I told her, "but we're not savages either. She'll spend some time behind bars . . . no different from Boston, I'd suppose. But we've got good doctors, and she'll get the help she needs."

Which made her back off a way and look apologetic.

"At least we've solved half the problem," Martha pointed out.

But half wasn't good enough. I understood that only too well. We still had a lunatic running around out there. One who had the power to do a lot of things he'd always wanted.

And none of them involved world peace. We were still in an awful lot of trouble.

CHAPTER 48

Hanlon was back in Millwood House, and blissfully starting to absorb the fact that it belonged to him alone, as if he
had inherited it. There were no other claimants left. No one
remained to hold him back or tie him down. It was simply
himself, his feverish plans, and the tremendous power that
the wand imparted. When he genuinely thought about it, he
could see the plain reality of what had happened. The Old
Ones had wanted it this way the whole time, perhaps even
conspired to make it come to pass.

He felt vaguely sorry for the Tollburn woman. She had
taught him so much, after all. Opened up new doors to him,
showing him aspects of the world he had never previously
known existed. But he had found it distasteful, to be quite
honest, being connected with her so closely. He had begun
to hear some of her inner thoughts. And there had been some
very dark, unsettling stuff in there.

Wasn't that true of the whole human race? Yes, he could
see it for a fact. Humanity had been around too long, had
grown corrupted, and needed cleansing. Well, the End of
Days would see to that.

The wand in his grasp murmured to him quietly. Its voice
was inside his head. It had been talking to him since he'd
had it to himself. And finally, Cornelius understood.

His eyes went very wide at first. And then his whole face

became suffused with joy. He could see—at long last—what the Old Ones genuinely had planned for him. It wasn't merely his job to survive the End of Days. No, his purpose was to bring it on.

He held the wand between his palms, and could feel fresh power surging through them. The thing seemed far heavier than it had been, but his hands tingled and quivered all the same. He knew it with absolute certainty, by this time. With it, he could do literally anything he wanted. He had the power in his grasp to crush this entire seething planet.

He headed for the back of the house, several figures passing by. And they were not the kinds of wretches who'd been gathered here that first night. These were people of a stronger nature, even if they had a powerful dark side. Hell, there was even a cop among them, and he usually hated those.

If he led them out there, as an army . . . ? But no. Hanlon reconsidered that. They'd only get blown to smoke again. He needed a better plan.

Something that could tear this place apart completely. And then, once that was accomplished, begin ripping down the very fabric of reality, allowing the outer darkness to come spilling in.

He was back in the room where he had first met the Toll-burn woman. Cornelius strode over to the window, gazing out. Only the gray barrier met his gaze.

But then he heard a faint whinnying, and his eyes went to the stables. The wand spoke to him once again, a small but urgent voice inside his head. It was reminding him of things he knew. Suggesting where he took that knowledge.

End of Days. The Apocalypse. That was his goal. And what precisely was supposed to herald them . . . ?

It came to him in another flash. Pure inspiration.

Yes, of course!

He went to fetch three of the others. Stood them side by side, then swept the wand across them.

They started to transform, changing shape completely. And then, using the wand on himself, he followed suit.

* * *

How was the Big Guy holding up?

There hadn't been a ten minute span—since he'd heard about the shooting—when he hadn't spent a part of it thinking about his colleague Saul.

Richard Vallencourt—called Ritchie by anyone who knew him—was brand new to the rank of Detective Sergeant. He'd only been promoted last month. Heidi, his wife, had shrieked and hugged him when he'd come home with the news.

"The youngest ever? Hon, you're kidding me?"

And he had swelled up with quiet pride. "I'm not."

Some of the cops around him, let's face it, were old enough to be his dad. And here he was, officially their superior. He could see what an honor it was, to have risen through the ranks so quickly. But it had its downside too.

Some of the guys looked at him a little cockeyed before following his orders. "God, you're nothing but a kid." He could see it on their faces. And the fact that Big Saul was amongst the fallen only made things slightly worse. The lieutenant had commanded their immediate respect, attention. Those were qualities you earned. He hadn't nearly got there yet. And now, the whole burden of this nightmare had fallen directly on his shoulders. He kept on wondering—did he have what it took to cope?

Vallencourt was twenty-eight. Only five foot seven inches tall but built like a professional boxer. Brown-haired and almond-eyed. Darkly handsome and intense. He'd worn sharp suits since he'd been seventeen, and had a deep scar running through one eyebrow, which he'd gotten in a fistfight, long before he'd joined the force. He'd grown up in East Meadow, just a few streets from his wife. But they lived in Clayton these days.

He mostly worked the west side of the town because of that. His own neighborhood and Marshall Drive were both peaceable districts, and didn't cause him too many headaches. West Meadow was slightly worse. But the real problem was Tyburn, off to the extreme southwest.

It had had a reputation as long as he'd known about it. Since he'd been a little kid, in fact. The area looked reasonably normal, but could turn into the weirdest place. It was one of the oldest parts of town, the streets narrow and heavily lined with trees, the houses tightly packed. Shadows clustered there in dense, long pockets, even on the brightest days. But it wasn't just the district's atmosphere. It was the folks who lived there.

They'd evolved into a tight, enclosed community, almost a separate town within a town. Had their own ways of doing things that went right back as far as Regan Farrow. And—whereas most people in the Landing only used magic occasionally—they practiced it all the time. Which meant constant trouble for him. How exactly could it not?

But he'd stuck with it for four whole years, the longest anybody had policed that part of town. And he'd earned his promotion. Lord, let no one be in any doubt of that.

But look where it had brought him?

He was up on the Plymouth Drive, outside what had been Millwood House. He'd heard the news about Ms. Tollburn's arrest, of course. And a good thing too, Ritchie thought. Hell, he hated those rich nut-jobs. And so far as he was concerned, it was a relief to see one put out of the way at last.

There were other people in the house, though. He'd been brought completely up to speed on that. He stared, frustrated, at the glistening gray barriers. Ever since they'd first appeared, a few cops had been assigned to staking them out. And they'd reported new balls of vapor entering the premises, not long after twilight had fallen. He still found it rather hard to get his head around, but . . . fresh recruits to Hanlon's insane army, he supposed.

Ritchie had a powerful hunch about this whole business. Everything that had gone down so far? Yes, it had been pretty awful. But he'd been on the job long enough to get the feeling that this wasn't the whole story. This was simply magic flexing its muscles. Terrifying and impressive, surely. But the real battle? Well, it might be still to come.

He sighed, peering around bleakly. He'd brought twenty people from the department up here, acting on that suspicion. They looked tired to the last, but were still in the game. And just as well. A greater challenge was awaiting them. He felt it in his bones.

A breathless silence hung about the neighborhood. There were no other signs of life. All the houses in this district were deserted, he already knew. But it was more than that. Not so much as a night bird flitted. Everything had fled this place, acting on the self-same instinct he was feeling. Which made him even more apprehensive. What exactly was going to be unleashed on this already sorely battered community?

And what would the Big Guy do? He constantly asked himself that. Saul Hobart was watchful, very patient. So the answer might be, wait and see . . . do nothing beyond that.

Except that Ritchie found that very hard, preferring to keep on the move. He paced a lot, and his fingers kept on twitching. For want of anything better to do, he called a uniformed sergeant called McKendrick over, who'd been talking on his radio.

"How's it going in the rest of town?"

"It's starting to quiet down, sir," the burly man with silver hair replied.

His mouth said sir, but his eyes said sonny. Vallencourt was used to that.

"Maybe we should do this in shifts, and give some of these guys a break?"

The sergeant shook his head, looking a touch affronted.

"Every one of these men is defending his community. They'll stay here till it's over, one way or the other. You can be sure of that."

Ritchie stared at the uniformed figures. They were spread out evenly along the drive, the whole length of the barrier's frontage. Their faces were reduced to smudges in the dimness. Their hands were either on their hips, or hanging by their sides. Their expressions were wary, but determined too. And he felt a quiet pride when he saw that. A Raine's Landing cop didn't scare off easily.

There was a sudden noise from behind the barrier. And that got a reaction from them. Side arms started being drawn and shotguns clacked. Ritchie's gaze went darting around, hunting for the source of the sound. It had been extremely faint but . . . had he heard a scream, in there?

No, it hadn't been quite that. His mind was still struggling to identify it.

The center of the wall began to shift before his very gaze, the sheen on it distorting. A small bulge appeared at about chest height, then spread out in the shape of a wide circle. Another followed, and then several more. They were concentric rings, like ripples. And they kept on coming faster as he watched.

Ritchie drew a breath, then pulled out his Browning.

There was another, slightly louder, shriek. But definitely not a human sound. Given what had been showing up the last couple of nights, he reckoned that was hardly a surprise.

A hole appeared at the center of the ripples. And, like them, it started spreading, growing vastly wider. He could see it was a portal opening.

Well, here we go, Vallencourt thought.

He thought briefly about his home and Heidi, and then put images like those aside. Gazed down his muzzle. Then his shoulders gave another jerk. More high-pitched sounds were drifting out, and he recognized them this time.

It was whinnying. Horses.

A clattering erupted, sharp and heavy. The beating of hooves. And it was getting swiftly closer.

CHAPTER 49

Maybe I needed to go into business as some kind of low-rent lawyer, the kind who chases ambulances. Because I'd been following sirens and flashing lights almost since this thing had started. And tonight was no exception.

I was heading back to my car, Lauren right behind me, when a couple of them went howling past us, casting the whole of Plymouth Drive in pulsing shades of red. They were headed up the gradient, toward the richer sections again. And the last time they'd gone there it had heralded disaster. So I couldn't see how it was going to be any better this time.

I went after them, the headlamps of Lauren's Focus bringing up the rear.

My heart sank when I saw where the paramedics had drawn up. Another scene of devastation, right outside Millwood House. And the dead scattered around it were, to the last, wearing blue uniforms.

But a few had made it through. The cops who were still alive were helping with the wounded. And there was a young plainclothes man sitting on a car hood, clutching at his upper arm. I'd only met him a couple of times, since I don't go into Tyburn much. But this guy was something of a legend on the force. Detective Richard Vallencourt. Young and smart, and with an attitude like Cassie when it came to danger. I'd heard he'd been promoted recently, and so he had to be in charge. The expression on his face told me he wished he wasn't. He was dressed in one of the nattiest looking suits I'd ever seen . . . or it would have been if it wasn't damaged. A cream-colored shirt and a canary yellow tie. And as I watched, he slipped the jacket off.

A paramedic started cutting away the sleeve of his shirt and inspecting the wound beneath it. He seemed to take that in his stride. I went across, made myself known. And he recognized me, nodded.

"Hey, Devries." He looked very pale indeed, his gaze extremely troubled. "How about this, huh? It couldn't get worse, dammit."

There was genuine emotion in his tone, though he was trying to clamp down on it. Dismay for the most part. His first time in command, and what had happened? These men had been his responsibility. I knew how I'd be feeling, like I had failed them and their families.

A few more ambulances were arriving. We have plenty of them in the Landing, precisely for incidents such as this. In fact—after Saruak—the mayor had ordered their numbers doubled.

By the corpses and the body bags, at least a dozen cops had died. I took that in, appalled. Then I asked Vallencourt what had happened.

"Hanlon and his pals, what else? Except he don't look human now, and neither do the others."

I waited for him to explain. He seemed to be having real trouble putting it into words.

"Four riders came out of there."

Millicent had horses, I remembered. But it turned out they had been transformed as well. They'd had jagged fangs and blazing eyes when they'd emerged. And then he started describing the riders.

"One of them, its face was shriveled. I think it was wearing some kind of crown. It was carrying a bow and arrows. Another had its face, like, all screwed up with anger. And it had a sort of . . . burning sword."

I sucked in a breath, recalling what Lauren had told me when we had first met. Hanlon's obsession with the Apocalypse. And my mouth felt dry when I asked him the next question.

"The third was emaciated?"

"Skinny, yeah."

"And carried a pair of scales?" Lauren asked from behind my shoulder. She sounded pretty troubled too.

His wound was being stitched up, but the man didn't even flinch. Instead, he looked at us both strangely, wondering what we were talking about.

"No," he replied. "An ax with a short handle, double headed."

And an ax wasn't traditional. But it was close enough, the same general shape.

"The fourth one had a skull for a face," he continued. "And a couple of the horses were weird colors."

"One was white," I put in quickly, scarcely believing what I was being forced to spell out. "Another was pure jet black."

"The third was red," Lauren added. "And the fourth, the final one, was a pale, sickly green."

I turned to look at her. How had she known that?

"Catholic school," she told me.

She had a perturbed look on her face, like she wished she'd never learned about such legends. Much less find out that they'd been turned into actual fact. But that seemed to be the case. A powerful sense of urgency overtook me.

"Which way did they go?" I asked the young detective sergeant.

He pointed with his good arm, and I could make out hoof marks trailing off downhill across a stretch of open ground.

"But what are you guys talking about exactly?" he asked.

My face was becoming increasingly stiff, like a freezing wind had blown across it. You see, he hadn't been describing any four horsemen.

These were the horsemen. The four in Revelation.

And if they were loose in Raine's Landing, then this might turn out to be our personal Apocalypse.

We'd been fighting demons this whole while. But now, the very worst were here.

CHAPTER 50

I wanted to set off after them, if "wanted" is the correct word. In spite of the vast variety of curves our town can throw you, I had never expected anything like this. But an instinct made me look a little harder at the young man sitting in front of me. And I decided to stick around a while.

His wound was stitched up. But he was still looking pretty gray about the gills. I didn't believe it was shock—there were none of the usual signs of that. So something else was wrong.

An idea occurred to me. A pretty awful one. But then— if the Horsemen were here, things were going to get worse than they had ever been, from this point on.

"Was it the one with the ax who cut you?" I asked him.

Vallencourt gave me another odd look, still not properly understanding what this was about. But then he nodded.

And began to double over, his brow creasing up.

"Man!" he muttered. "I just feel . . . completely hollow."

The shouting of a paramedic brought my focus lurching to the right. There was something wrong with another cop who'd recently been bandaged up. I couldn't be certain in this lack of light, but it looked like he was succumbing to some kind of disease. Boils were appearing on his cheeks. A few more of the cops who'd only been mildly wounded were wobbling and lurching too. There was a lot more wrong with them than simply being cut or punctured.

"Oh my God!" Lauren yelped, bringing my attention back.

Vallencourt's lean, handsome face was doing more than furrowing. It was growing visibly thinner. Withered lines had appeared on his cheeks, and as I watched they began sucking inward.

The one with the ax, I knew, had been Famine on its tall, skinny black stallion. The detective's lips drew back from his gums, and his clothes started looking baggy.

He seemed to grasp the fact that there was something badly wrong with him, and peered up at us in a startled fashion. There were gaps appearing in between his teeth. And his eyes were sinking away into deeply shadowed hollows.

He clutched at his stomach . . . it looked like that whole part of him was drawing back as well. And then asked in an anguished whisper, "What the hell is wrong with me?"

It wasn't merely that I didn't have the heart to tell him. I wasn't quite sure how it worked. Either some kind of poison had seeped into him, or he'd been subjected to a spell. But either way, Famine had touched him . . . of that there could be no doubt. He was starving to death because of that. And I didn't know what could be done to help him.

A moving smudge in the corner of my vision told me Martha Howard-Brett had arrived. I stepped away, taking her with me. And she listened again as I explained the situation.

Her lovely face went blank, at first. But she recovered quickly, handling it better than I'd thought she would.

"I might be able to do something," she said. "You'd better get going, before there are more like this."

I hated leaving Vallencourt this way, but understood that she was right. He was becoming more emaciated every time I looked at him, and getting pretty frightened too. Had already lost most of his strength, his body slumping. Martha went and bent across him, talking to him soothingly. Then she put her hands on his shoulders, and her palms began to glow. Like the others, she couldn't heal injuries, but could assuage sickness and try to counter spells.

She glanced at me again, mouthing the word "Go."

Except I had no idea how we were going to deal with creatures like these.

I knew one thing for certain, though. We had to try.

"You still in?" I asked Lauren.

"Have been up till now."

"Then we'll take your car," I told her.

It was smaller than mine, you see. And if we were going to follow the Horsemen, then we needed something that could go down narrow routes.

We wove between the residences to the right of Millwood House. None of them were as big as Ms. Tollburn's mansion, but they were still pretty large. Most of them had palatial grounds. You almost expected to see peacocks on the lawns. There was not a light on anywhere—no one had remained at home. And it felt genuinely odd, seeing a district that had had so much money spent on it lying empty like this.

Then we headed further down, through small clusters of trees and open stretches of grassland, my heart pounding the entire way. The car bucked over bumps and dips. There was not so much as a footpath around here. But we didn't make it as far as the bottom. Other habitations came in sight. They were not quite as impressive as the ones we'd left behind, but pretty decent places. Five or six bedrooms, and big, wide yards.

These ones were far enough away from the gray barriers they hadn't been evacuated. Not until recently, that was. And as we drew closer, we could see the inhabitants had paid a savage price for that.

Fences lay ahead of us. The hoofprints went right up to them, then started again on the other side, trampling across lawns with not the slightest damage to the intervening woodwork. Clods of turf had been thrown up. But the rear walls hadn't been affected either. Even the windows were intact.

Although we could make out a jumble of smashed furniture beyond them. And a few dead bodies too. Apparently, these riders could just pass through solid barriers. It was something that I'd come across from supernatural beings in the past.

The worst of the carnage by a long shot was out front. Most people had managed to get that far before the riders had caught up with them. Corpses were scattered all over the road. Some had actually been killed with a blow from a weapon. Others had much smaller wounds, but had perished all the same. Disease had taken some. Starvation others. My heart sank, looking at them. Sooner or later, we were going to catch up with the things that had done this. And I wasn't looking forward to that.

One middle-aged man was sitting on the curbside, with a black-fletched arrow poking from his shoulder blade. It was nothing fatal in itself. But his face was covered with huge welts. Lauren went to stop the car and get out, but I wouldn't let her.

I felt really sorry for the guy. But pretty helpless too. We couldn't go to his aid, since we didn't even know if this stuff was infectious.

As we watched, he slumped over. It tore at me, but I pulled my gaze away and kept on studying the scene around me. Trying to remain objective. Understand what we were really up against.

A few of the cadavers looked like they'd been not so much as scratched. In fact, they looked like they had still been running when they'd dropped. Between one heartbeat and the next, they'd simply fallen dead. And what exactly did that mean?

"Oh, my good God!" Lauren breathed, just as shaken up as I was.

But He had nothing to do with the horrors around us. We were at the mercy of far crueler forces by this time.

The hoofprints ran away from us along the wide verge opposite. And when we looked in that direction, we could see the distant flags on top of the Town Hall.

These new visitors of ours were headed downtown. Straight into the Landing's heart.

If you're headed in from Sycamore Hill, then the first major avenue you reach is O'Connell. It's mostly lined with cheap stores, eateries, and bars. And, thank heavens, nobody was in the mood for socializing this particular evening. Because— if it had been busy—then it might have made what we'd left behind look like a good-natured picnic.

Few folk actually lived here, so there was no militia in this part of town. There'd been a scattering of people on the sidewalks, though. They were still there, mostly on their stomachs or their backs. Disease had eaten away one whole side of a woman's face. Lauren hissed, and we both looked somewhere else. Anywhere.

Jesus Christ, what were we getting ourselves into? My breathing was coming with difficulty, and the skin across my face felt very tight.

The neon signs that lit up the place had been smashed for several blocks. And parked cars had been trampled on. So it appeared the riders and their mounts could be very solid when they wanted, the same way the previous demons had been. That was less than promising. Union Square lay up ahead of us, and we could see dark flickers of movement there.

Lauren killed the headlights, without needing to be told. We drove to the last intersection, then got out as quietly as we could and went on foot the rest of the way.

We clung to the shadows. Crouching low and panting slightly, our guns out in front of us. Although I doubted that they'd be much use. A quiet dread had filled me by that time, and I'm not ashamed to admit it.

The beat of hooves kept ringing out. It sounded like thunder. The tall buildings around the square amplified it, making it echo. And there was something like a painful shriek. Was that human? It was hard to tell.

We reached the final corner. There seemed to be far less lighting in the square than was usually the case. Maybe I was simply imagining that. The dimness yawned in front of me. I didn't want to go any further. Every instinct held me back.

But that was not an option any longer. So, very carefully, I poked my head around.

Felt my eyes widen. The riders were there, for sure. But some smaller figures were visible too. They were crouched and cowering while the huge stallions lurched around them.

Mayor Aldernay and about a dozen of his staff had been herded to the center of the flagstoned space, the bronze face of our founder staring down at them.

CHAPTER 51

They were still alive so far, which made the situation rather different from the ones we'd left behind. Maybe the riders had plans for them, although there was no telling what exactly those might be.

What were these people even doing here at this time of the night? I glanced at the ornate, darkened frontage of the Town Hall, and got a partial answer. A lot of windows in the second story were still lit. That was where the mayor and his staff had their offices. They had apparently been working late, helping to coordinate the defense efforts. And I have never cared much for the long-serving mayor of our town. Edgar Aldernay can be hostile, unreasonable and—quite frankly—a pompous ass. But he takes his job extremely seriously—there was no doubt of that. If he was here this late, then it was typical of his persistence.

But how'd the Horsemen even gotten to them? Then I got a startling demonstration of the abilities they had.

The four of them were riding in broad circles, hemming in the panicked workers, keeping them all trapped. A lot of the globe lighting around the outskirts of Union Square had been smashed. They seemed to have a real love of destroying things, although that shouldn't have surprised me. As I watched, one of them—War—rode straight at the bronze statue of Theodore Raine. The creature and its horse went straight into the huge square plinth. Then reemerged smoothly on the other side.

I stared at them, horrified. We'd had some pretty dreadful things appearing in this town before. You'll never really know what fear feels like until you've faced a Manitou or a Dralleg. But the forces of darkness had outdone themselves this time. The sight didn't merely take my breath away—it didn't want to give it back.

They're not the real thing, I kept trying to tell myself. They're only imitations. But it didn't really feel like that. More like I was watching Chaos and Destruction rendered into living flesh.

And besides, I wasn't even sure that was completely true. How far did the powers of the wand extend?

The riders were wearing flowing black robes. There were wide hoods pulled up almost to their temples. Only their hands and faces were on view. And those had a slightly ethereal look, as if they existed somewhere between being mist and being solid.

War had an expression like a thunderstorm, his grim features twisted up. His eyes were narrow orange slits that seemed to leave impressions on the night air as he moved. His brow was creased like corrugated metal, his mouth set as firmly as twin plates of steel. Muscles were shifting underneath his cloak as he swung his great sword around. Flames were springing from it, leaving marks against the darkness too.

Famine—far narrower—looked even more ghostly. The eyes in this case were dead white, like tiny fluorescent lamps. They gleamed from deeply sunken hollows. The cheeks were concave. And the mouth was one big pucker around a sparse few rotted teeth. The bony hands looked barely strong enough to keep a hold of the horse's reins. But it was managing with one of them. In the right was the ax that I'd been told of.

As for Pestilence . . . I don't think we need to go there for too long. I'd already seen a couple of its victims. The creature was similar, an insubstantial mass of pus and scabs, barely any clean flesh visible at all. The lesions shifted as I stared at them, as if they didn't have a fixed position. That was the one armed with the bow and arrows.

And the steeds that they were mounted on were genuinely alarming too. Great dark slabs like something from a quarry that had come alive. Their hooves set up a terrible percussion. Their skulls were oversized, even in comparison with their huge bodies. It was a wonder that their necks could bear such massive burdens. Each face was covered with bony protrusions. The skin on them was twisted. I had never seen a horse with an expression before. And I suppose these had none really—but the flesh was so deformed it looked that way.

Where there should have been wide, flat teeth, there were jagged fangs instead. Their eyes burned like hot metal, with no pupil remaining.

My gaze darted to the final rider. Oh Lord. Death himself. He appeared to be more solid that the rest. And I supposed this one was Hanlon, in all his demented glory. Just looking at him, I felt exhaustion creep over me.

Skeletal hands gripped the reins, in this case. Merely bones, with nothing holding them together. The face was a bare, tissueless skull, with a bony ridge of temple and a crescent of discolored teeth. But like the horses, it seemed to contain emotion in its structure. Not just vicious, this time. Pleased with itself. Gloating.

Its eye sockets were hollow, but there was a gleam in them. A laughing one, of victory assured. The thing carried no kind of weapon. Didn't even need one—that was what I figured out. Blades and arrowheads were merely paths for it to travel down. I remembered the people at the bottom of the hillside who had simply fallen in midstride.

The figure noticed me, and drew its stallion up. Plumes of steam came billowing from the horse's nostrils, and it pawed with one hoof at the flagstones, making sparks.

The three other riders drifted to a halt as well. Silence pressed down over everything. Even the trapped folk at the center went extremely quiet.

Deal with this, I kept telling myself. At least their attention had been diverted from their prisoners. And that was some comfort to me, although not an awful lot.

There was no further point in trying to stay hidden. So I stepped fully out into their line of sight. Lauren tried to follow, but I signaled her not to. And she took notice and stayed put, thank heavens. There was no sense in both of us getting directly in harm's way.

Death's hollow jaw dropped open. There was no tongue, but a voice still came ringing out.

"Devries?"

It was so loud it hurt my ears.

"I know about you!" it went on.

The words thundered around me, echoing between the buildings. I tried to remind myself this was not the true figure of Death, not really. Just some lunatic who wanted to be that.

"You've saved this town before, or so I understand. Demonstrate that to me now. Save one single inhabitant."

He turned his massive horse around, and began trotting over to the captives. I could only watch him frozenly, wondering what he was going to do.

Aldernay and his people were huddled in a tight mass, many of them kneeling. As the Horseman drew closer, the whites of their eyes expanded. The mayor was shaking visibly. Mrs. Dower—his assistant—looked almost on the point of fainting. As for the rest, they were mostly young interns, volunteers. I recognized Joe Norton's daughter, Iris. She'd just turned eighteen, and lived a few houses away from my own. She gawked up helplessly as Death's shadow crept over her. A tight fist clenched around my heart.

What exactly could I do to help them? This was on a different plane to anything I'd ever encountered before.

Hanlon stopped before the cowering people and reached down. And I thought at first that Iris was his intended victim. I took a step forward.

But he grabbed hold of the collar of the slim brunette directly next to her instead and hauled her into view.

He lifted her into the air, turning around in his saddle to show her off, the same way that a hunter might show off a trophy. Her limbs flailed frantically, and both of her shoes dropped away. But she was so petrified that when her mouth sprang open, there was only a thin creaking sound.

"This one, for instance?" Hanlon called out. "Are you going to rescue her?"

His empty gaze fastened on me again. And the smile beneath it was more horrible than I could bear. What could I do against something like this?

He extended the index finger of his free hand. And then began to move it to her cheek with a deliberate lack of haste. I knew what would happen when it touched her. All those victims with no wounds? The blood surged in my veins.

"Take me instead!" I heard myself shouting.

Which was, realistically, a damned fool thing to say. But it stopped him for a moment. He considered my proposal.

"Why should I do that?" he said. "I'll kill her, then the rest of them. And then I'll kill you too."

His hand started moving toward the girl's face again. And she finally found a proper voice. A high-pitched wail of terror rang across the square.

And that was just too much for a person to take. I held my pistol out in front of me and tensed my legs.

But I didn't get the chance to move. Because a massive thump rang out.

Hanlon's whole arm exploded into fragments. And the girl who he'd been toying with dropped, unharmed, to the flagstones.

CHAPTER 52

She scrabbled away to safety on her hands and knees, heading for the side of the Town Hall. And would have been easy enough to catch up with. Except none of the riders were watching her any longer. They were staring around, trying to make out where the shot had come from.

I was the only person in the entire square who understood what was going on. In fact, my heart lifted a touch. A Mossberg 590 shotgun had made that sound, firing not pellets but saboted slugs. Which meant that not only was Cassie here, but she was back on our side.

She didn't show herself, at first. Those angry, spectral faces kept on searching for her in the gloom. The rest of the mayor's party was still huddled in the same spot. But they'd gone motionless, their heads anxiously raised.

Then Pestilence swung its horse around and, taking out an arrow from the quiver on its back, started trotting up warily toward the north end of the square.

I took another glance at Hanlon. His shattered arm had turned to a vapor gathered around his shoulder. And it was reforming.

There was a sudden movement in the corner of my eye, below the Town Hall's clock. My sense of relief started to evaporate immediately. Oh my God, was she back there?

While everything else had been going on, Cassie had

obviously snuck, unnoticed, right across the frontage of the building. And was now behind one of the stone lions at the entranceway. The Horseman was headed directly at her. And when it found her, there would be no place left to hide.

But Cass is never stupid in a fight. She saw that there was no point staying where she was. She lifted herself smoothly into view. The wings were gone. Her arms were normal. She was back to her old self.

And she wasn't nervous about these creatures either, the way I felt. Her attitude was the same with anything that threatened our town. She threw herself directly at the rider, running flat out at the thing.

But . . . did she even understand what she was up against? Fear tightened its grip around me as I watched her.

Her face was contorted, and she kept on firing as she ran. Her aim was as good as ever. Every single one of her saboted slugs struck home. They could have felled a medium-sized tree. But when they hit the rider, they blew clouds of vapor straight out through its back. Which promptly returned to the thing's body.

As I watched, it drew its bow. I fired a few shots myself, but was too far off.

The string was let loose with a singing noise. Cass didn't even try to duck. She held the Mossberg up in front of her, sideways. When the arrow struck, it hit the metal, burying itself in one of the holes in the gun's heat shield.

The Horseman paused, apparently surprised. But then it started tugging at the bow again.

This was going to be a test of speed. Cass was still going as fast as she could. But the rider had already put a new notch to its bowstring. Was taking aim. She wasn't going to make it. And I was too far away to help.

But I hadn't reckoned on Ms. Mallory's quick thinking. She yanked the first arrow out with her left hand. Then she swung the shotgun back, and hurled it with full force.

It didn't do the rider any harm, of course. But that was not what she'd intended. She managed to knock its aim off, and the second shot flew wild.

Cass was right up to the stamping, snorting white horse in another instant. It shrieked and reared over her.

She ducked around the side of it. And drove the arrow she was holding into Pestilence's thigh.

Time seemed to stand still, for a moment after that. The faces of the other three were all suspended, facing north.

Pestilence's face was so covered with shifting sores and welts that it was hard to tell exactly what was going on. But the creature's eyes got noticeably wider. And its mouth clamped shut—a ridge of pain.

It reached down for the arrow, but did not complete the motion. Abruptly, it was toppling sideways. Coming loose of its saddle, then dropping to the ground.

It tried to push itself back up. And got halfway before it started getting weaker. Dozens of ugly bulges pushed out through its cheeks, its forehead. And the sores and welts were spreading, eating the last scraps of faded flesh away.

It went down a second time. And then its body started falling apart before our very eyes.

Its horse vanished completely.

At least I now knew how they could be beaten.

One down. But still three to go.

War went howling after Cassie, furious and vengeful, the burning sword in its grip held high. She could see immediately this wasn't going to be as simple as the first time, and she scrambled back to the Town Hall's front steps. Reaching them, she scaled a drainpipe. And barely got up high enough in time. The blade lashed at her, narrowly missing her heels.

Famine turned its emaciated face to me. This was the same creature that had done such harm to Vallencourt. Its flesh clung to its skull like thin tissue paper. Its mouth dropped open in an uneven circle. Then it gathered up its reins, and spurred its horse in my direction.

I stared at the ax clutched in its narrow grasp. That was what Cass had figured out. Use their own weapons against them. Then everything came back in much broader focus.

The stallion had crossed most of the square before I'd even had time to react.

It was on me. Its massive hooves lashed at my face. I lurched to the side, lost my balance and fell. And that was probably what saved my life.

As the rider went by, its ax came swinging down, making a strange murmuring as it split the air. And it would have sliced my head in two. Its aim was deadly accurate. I felt my hair being ruffled by the passing gust of wind it made. But the blade missed me . . . barely.

I hit the ground and rolled away. By the time that I was back on my feet, the rider had swung around.

Lauren was still against the wall. It hadn't seen her yet. She had her own gun out, and was trying to take aim. But everything was happening too fast. And I doubted that a handgun would be any real use, even at this distance.

She hadn't seen what Cass had done, I realized. There was no view of the north end of the square from where she'd been hiding.

The rider came at me again, leaning over in its saddle this time. It was not going to make the same mistake twice.

But I'd a few more tricks of my own. I waited until the beast was practically on top of me. And when I did move, it was not away from the weapon but toward it.

I threw myself into the broad arc of the rider's swing. And grabbed the Horseman by its black-cloaked elbow.

Its arm slammed into me. The impact knocked the breath from my body. I felt my feet leaving the ground. But the horse continued forward. And gravity has the same effect, whatever kind of creature you are.

The rider parted company with its saddle. I crashed to the ground a second time, Famine coming down on top of me. For something so ethereal-looking, it landed on me heavily enough to make my ribs flare with agony.

Although what really caught my attention was the sharp metallic clatter that I heard at the same time.

This thing might still have the upper hand. But I had made it drop its weapon. I started feeling around blindly, but I couldn't seem to find it.

CHAPTER 53

I tried to see what the rider was doing, but a mass of billowing black put paid to that. The folds of its cloak had dropped across me, covering my face. I struggled to get free of them.

The weight on my rib cage became more compressed, narrowing to two sharp points. And I knew what that meant. The rider had already got part way up, and was kneeling on my chest. I tried to shove it off me, jabbing blindly through the cloth. But had no success on that score either.

Both its narrow hands bore down and closed around my throat. And the look of the thing belied its strength. It began to squeeze with awful power and ferocity.

I tried to knock its arms away, throwing punches near its elbows. But the blows felt spongy, ineffective. And its grip didn't relax even a little bit. Some of the cloth parted finally. I caught a glimpse of its lean face looming over me. And that was when I saw my chance.

I didn't even hesitate. Held my right palm flat and straight, and drove the tips of my fingers as hard as I could into one of its deathly eyes. That really hurts when you do it to a human. But the figure on top of me wasn't that.

There was the same lack of solidity again. Although its head did lurch back a few inches. And the pressure on my throat eased off a touch. Which was—I could see—all the chance that I was ever going to get. I immediately began to roll, pushing myself over. That threw it off balance, and I didn't stop. I went onto my stomach, sucking in breath like there was no tomorrow.

The Horseman's weight slammed into me again. It might be less than whole flesh when I tried to hit it. But that didn't seem to be the case the other way around. One of its hands grabbed a fistful of my hair. The other began sliding around my neck, trying to throttle me from behind this time.

I put one of my forearms in the way, to stop that happening. And the creature got really annoyed when I did that, shoving at the back of my head, slamming my face hard against the paving stones. Colors flared behind my eyelids.

Then they slid back open. And locked on something that gave me a slim hope I could still prevail.

The ax was lying right in front of me, gleaming on the sidewalk.

I reached out for it. But the rider had noticed it as well. We lunged for the weapon at the same time, our hands clashing. The ax skittered away. When I tried to grab it a second time, it had gone several inches further than my arm could reach.

The thing on top of me attempted to get hold of it. That gave me the chance to throw it off balance again. It was forced to let go of my hair. I lifted my upper body, and then sent an elbow slamming back.

The Horseman paused a second. Then it began pounding furiously at my shoulders and my back, its knuckles driving into me like cannonballs.

Two shots rang out. The rider paused. Whoever had fired, I didn't think that it was Cassie. Lauren had let go of the wall, and the muzzle of her gun was smoking.

But the thing had been no use at all.

"The ax—use that!" I yelled out to her.

But there was a real big problem. The thing on my back had heard as well.

I felt the whole direction of its body shift. As it tried to scramble over me, I brought my head up sharply. The back of my skull connected with its chin. Again, to lack of any real effect.

I reached around and grabbed its robes. It reacted to that by landing another punch at the center of my spine. The pain was so intense that something in my nerves seemed to short out. I could feel my body going slack. My grip loosened. Then the rider went across me.

My vision had faded momentarily. I could only make out a fuzzy shadow up ahead of me, a darkened blur that turned out to be Lauren. And she did three things in one continuous motion. She rolled across the last few feet of sidewalk. Snatched up the ax as she went past. And then, coming up on her knees, she slashed the rider across its open palm, just as it was reaching for the weapon.

A flesh wound—that was all that she inflicted on it. But it stopped the creature dead. I struggled out from under it and pushed myself away. I had a pretty good idea what would happen now, and didn't want to be touching the thing when it started.

The rider was huddled on the sidewalk, a look of astonishment on its ravaged face. It was staring at its injured palm. There was only the narrowest cut, a thin trickle of colorless goop easing out from it. An injury that should barely even hurt. But the effect was considerably more dramatic.

Even the parchmentlike skin seemed to be getting thinner. And the skull underneath started melting away. The rider shrank before my gaze, hunching over and then folding in upon itself. When its mouth came open again, the gums were receding. And the few remaining yellowed teeth dropped out.

The glimmer of its eyes was getting tinier as well, like lights moving away from me. A hand came up, and pawed at its retreating features. Then it all began to fall apart. The whole body was doing that. There didn't seem to be enough strength left to support its own weight.

The rider collapsed in an untidy heap in front of us, its pieces held together only by the tangled folds of cloth. One finger gave a final tremble. And then nothing moved in the slightest.

A rather nicer-looking hand reached down. Lauren helped me back to my feet. I felt like I'd been trampled by a team of oxen. But I got up all the same, although I couldn't stand entirely straight at first.

"You okay?" she asked me worriedly.

It depended on how you defined that. I gazed at the mess on the sidewalk, then across at her again. She was out of breath, but otherwise unharmed. Pretty startled, it was plain to see. The creatures of last night—viewed mostly from some kind of distance—had been one thing. But this fight had been altogether far too close for comfort.

"Congratulations," I said quietly, trying to think of something that would cheer her up. "You've just killed your first real demon."

She tried to smile, but it was pretty unconvincing.

"The nuns would be proud of you," I added.

Catholic school, right?

But I was jumping the gun, wasn't I? This wasn't nearly over yet. Another whinny and a harsh metallic clatter brought our faces swiveling around.

Cassie was still up there on the front of the Town Hall, still clinging to that drainpipe. And the Horseman with the flaming sword had nowhere near given up on trying to bring her down from there.

I stiffened with renewed shock. He was halfway to succeeding.

CHAPTER 54

Cass was only just out of reach of the warlike rider's burning sword. She hadn't managed to climb any higher, and a quick glance upward told me why.

The section of drainpipe above her had buckled, dragged out of shape by the weight she'd brought to bear on it. The bracket that was keeping it in place had torn loose of the brickwork. If she tried to head further up, then there was no doubt that it would rip free completely. And the fact was, she had nowhere else to go.

She was dangling, and looking pretty worried. That look is unusual for her. But there are no circumstances under which she won't fight back. Her free hand had a Glock in it, and she was firing down at her attacker. She was hitting the thing more often than not. But normal bullets were still little use. Her Mossberg was lying on the flagstones where she'd thrown it, right out of her reach.

As for Hanlon? He had remained over by the statue, and was watching the events unfold from there. He seemed to have lost any interest in me and Lauren, his focus moving wholly to the front of the Town Hall. He was taking in the scene almost detachedly, waiting to see what would happen. His robes billowed gently. And his sickly horse had gone as still as he was.

He hadn't even noticed that the mayor and his people were

getting away. Aldernay scrabbled—hunched and crablike—off into an alley on the east side of the square, then disappeared into its shadows. Mrs. Dower, following along behind him, did the same.

A loud clash brought my head swinging back. The warlike rider had come up with a new plan. It had given up on trying to hack at Cass, and was attacking the drainpipe she was clinging to instead. Its first blow made the whole thing rattle. And the second time, an entire lower section fell away.

Which forced Cassie to holster her gun and concentrate on simply hanging on. There was a row of window ledges above her. She stretched for them, but couldn't reach them either.

The horse reared up below her. It was as ugly as its master, its hide the same red as dried blood. Its mane was a series of high, rigid spikes. And all these beasts had sharp fangs, surely. But this one was saber-toothed.

It stretched as high as it was able. And then pounded at the next section of pipe. Cass kept hanging on like grim death. Except—by this time—there was very little to hang on to.

Me and Lauren were both running. I still wasn't quite sure what difference we could make. Perhaps if I got the shotgun and distracted the thing for a few seconds . . . ?

But if we didn't have a proper plan, then Cass apparently did. Before we reached her, she had set both of her booted feet against the wall. I watched her body go tight. Her back arced, her arms stretching to their full length.

And then she did something that I'd never even thought her capable of, before tonight.

She let go. And, at the same time, pushed herself away with her legs, as hard as she could manage.

She performed a back flip in the air.

And when she landed, it was on the horse. Behind the rider.

The only thing that we could do was stumble to a halt and gawk. I'd watched Cassie do some crazy things in my time. But was pretty sure this topped them all.

There was a maddened logic to it, on reflection. If you've

only got one place left to go, then why not go there force-fully? And once she had landed, she didn't even hesitate. Her left arm went around the rider's throat. She wasn't trying to strangle the thing—it was simply the best way to hold on. The stallion started to buck furiously, bellowing with mind-less rage. Its neck craned around. Its long teeth snapped. But its jaws couldn't reach her.

Cassie tried to grab the rider's sword. I thought at first that she was going to manage it. But then the Horseman saw what she was doing, and snatched the weapon away from her.

They were flailing around in circles, the steed going up on its muscular hind legs. Clattering and braying echoed in between the empty buildings. And my bones seemed to shudder with the sound.

Cassie's face was hard, determined. Set like rock, her eyes twin spots of anthracite. She grabbed for the hilt again. And this time, her fingers almost closed around it. But the Horse-man proved to be a good deal stronger. One sharp yank, and it was clear again.

This couldn't go on too much longer. Human beings, however tough, are only made of flesh and blood. The horse lurched up so fiercely all but one of its hooves left the ground. Cassie yelped. Lost her grip, starting to fall. But just as she was sliding down, she managed to grab hold of the black robes in front of her.

She clung to a double fistful, setting her teeth grimly. And, thank God, the fabric didn't part. But she was dangling pre-cariously. And she'd already done enough of that to last her several lifetimes.

The rider turned around in its saddle, twisting its shoul-ders as far as they could go. The bright blade plunged in her direction. Cassie swung off to the side. The tip of the sword almost grazed her arm. And one tiny cut would have been enough to finish this. A sharp tremor ran through my body.

She tried to right herself, but couldn't do it properly. Her balance was off, and she kept on wobbling and slipping. I raised my firearm, trying to take aim at the rider's head. But couldn't manage it without risking hitting her. Lauren, with her Walther raised, could see that too.

Cass was losing her grip.

I started closing the distance again. Perhaps I'd get a chance to drag her out of there. But she wasn't finished yet.

She let go of the cloak with her right hand. What exactly was she doing? She was yanking at the wide folds, gathering up as much of the black cloth between her upper arms as she could manage.

The blade came hacking at her again, its edges still on fire. But instead of drawing back, Cassie shoved her arms toward it, pushing the wad of cloth into the dancing flames.

She was leaping clear in the next instant. Sailing off behind the horse, where its hooves couldn't reach her. She hit the flagstones badly, on her shoulder. But that didn't slow her down. The next moment she was back on her feet, and sprinting out of reach.

A silent prayer of thanks went through me. Then I looked at what she'd done.

Fire had spread across the Horseman's back, and was climbing up across its neck. Its steed was still turning in circles, faster than it had before. And shrieking at a higher pitch. It was trying to throw its master off, and looked completely terrified.

Orange flames started crackling fiercely, all over the black-clad body. As I watched, they engulfed the hood. The creature tipped its face back and let out an anguished howl that seemed to split the air in half.

When the figure finally dropped from its saddle, it fell like a burning branch. It kicked furiously for a while, its limbs diminished to thin, flickering outlines.

Then it went completely still, although the fire did not go out immediately.

An awful stench began drifting to us. The horse, like its brothers, disappeared from sight. The front doors of the Town Hall seemed to tremble in the shifting light.

I would probably have let out a long, slow breath at that point. But there was nothing resembling that still remaining in my lungs.

CHAPTER 55

But by what means exactly were we going to defeat Hanlon? I couldn't imagine how that could be done. There weren't any weapons to use against what he'd become. There was only the creature itself, possessed of its deadly touch.

I looked back where he had been sitting. But he was no longer there.

Was nowhere to be seen at all. He had simply watched his comrades being vanquished, and then gone away, presumably to hatch some new plans.

Where to? That was pretty obvious. But it was a reprieve of sorts, and I was grateful for that. My bones ached.

The square was completely deserted apart from us three, where there'd been such sound and fury before. The shadows of the buildings hung around us. And the big bronze statue—it continued to gaze down. Did old Theodore approve? I glanced across at Cassie, who had gone off to the left side of the building and was rubbing at her injured shoulder.

There seemed to be something odd about her. Nothing as serious as before. Her eyes were back to their normal shining darkness. But a strange, ominous sense began to overtake me at the sight of her.

I simply knew it, staring at her. This was not quite the same Cass Mallory I had come to know and rely on. She might have returned to help us, and in a more than usually impressive fashion. But something was off center.

Normally, she'd look pleased with herself. But this time, there was none of that. She looked hunched and shrunken, pretty miserable in fact. And she was keeping her distance from us, in spite of the fact that the danger was gone.

She didn't look like she knew which direction to go. There was something almost waiflike and disoriented about the way she was standing. I kept peering at her through the broken dimness. What the hell was going on?

She looked like she'd lost a fight, rather than winning it. Something had obviously changed, inside her. Been taken out of her, perhaps?

I stepped in a little closer, holstering my gun. Some glass from a broken lamp skittered away from the tips of my shoes. And Cass tried to shrink back from me a little, before deciding to stay where she was. There were emotions in her eyes that I wasn't familiar with, not from her. And not simply sadness. Could I make out shame? Perhaps a trace of self-disgust? The battle, her victory, seemed to mean nothing to her. Maybe she'd been fighting on some kind of automatic reflex, since it looked as though her spirit had been broken.

"Cassie?"

To my astonishment, she took two paces back. She was holding her body stiffly by this time, the way a child might when confronted with an angry grown-up.

"I'm sorry, Ross," I heard her say.

And I tried to put this right, before it got completely out of hand.

"What happened before—it wasn't your fault."

"That's not true!" she came back at me.

What on earth was she talking about?

"I've tried to make it right," she went on, "best way I know how. But I can't do any more, understand? It's up to you to finish it."

I opened my mouth again. But she simply turned away, and began loping off into the darkness, growing smaller as I watched.

I was so astonished I remained stock-still, instead of trying to follow her.

* * *

"What just happened?" Lauren asked me quietly.

She had come up, and could see how stunned I was. Her hand went to my arm, but I barely noticed that, my thoughts a dense muddle.

"I'm not sure," I heard myself say.

"Does she do that kind of thing a lot?"

The answer was . . . never. We still had a final battle up ahead of us, and Cassie knew that perfectly well. And she'd never backed down from a fight before.

I couldn't get a handle on any of this. What exactly did it mean? I had always been able to depend on her, no matter how bad things got. To lose her at a time like this was like having one of my own legs chopped off.

"Does she think Saul's dead?" Lauren suggested. "Maybe she's in shock, or denial?"

Which would account for a hell of a lot. And I wished Cass were still here, so I could set her straight on that. But it was too late, and might not even have made a load of difference. She seemed to have gone into a state of mind a long way beyond that.

A moving smudge flitted across the corner of my vision. And then Martha Howard-Brett appeared in front of us. Her face was drawn, like she'd been deeply worried, or else working really hard, or both.

"How's Vallencourt?" I asked her quickly, glad to change the subject.

"I almost lost him, to be honest. But then, a few minutes ago, he suddenly revived."

That had to be have been when Lauren killed the Horseman. And was some cause for celebration, at least. The thought of losing a third good guy in just one evening . . .

But Martha was still looking pretty darned unhappy.

"Hanlon's back at Millwood House," she told us. "I watched him ride in. That was quite a sight."

"And?"

"Something else is happening. You'd better take a look."

CHAPTER 56

The barriers were still there, at the same height and extensive breadth. But something had definitely changed about them. They didn't have a glossy tinge to them any longer, and had turned a darker shade of gray that blended more readily into the surrounding night. In fact, it was much harder to see them. Was the whole thing going to vanish? I could only pray that was the case, although I doubted Hanlon would give in so easily.

Glancing further up the street, I spotted Ritchie Vallencourt. He was active again, half hidden behind the topiary on somebody's front lawn. And had Paul McKendrick with him, who had also managed to survive the first assault. So I headed over to them, feeling very glad the young detective was still with us.

It had been a real ordeal for Ritchie. I could see it in the dark shadows around his eyes, the startled gleam in them. His skin still had a sallow look, despite the fact that he'd recovered. He appeared to have aged several years since the last time I'd talked with him. Roughly half an hour ago.

The Landing can do that to a person sometimes. Leave you older—and hopefully wiser—between one moment and the next. What must it have been like for him, feeling his whole body waste away? I couldn't even imagine.

He was trying to put a brave face on it, standing squarely, issuing orders through his phone. But when he finally got to bed—if any of us ever got there—what would it be like for him? What kind of dreams would he descend into once sleep had claimed him?

"Hold your positions," he was saying. "And stay out of sight, for Pete's sake."

So he'd brought more uniforms up here. I wasn't sure if that was the right move, after what had happened to the first batch. But I wasn't in charge, and had to accept that. A careful glance along the length of Plymouth Drive revealed the snouts of rifles poking out from behind walls and protruding from rooftops.

He noticed me, and gave me a respectful nod.

"You got them?"

Martha appeared beside him in the shadows.

"All but the important one," I told him. "What exactly are you doing now?"

He glanced around the same way I'd done.

"Containment."

"Yeah? I don't think it'll work."

Annoyance spread across his face. Which made me see that his reputation as a tough nut, fairly volatile, was warranted.

"Then what exactly would you have me do? Christ, Devries, I'm just an ordinary man. If you want something better, ask the adepts. Where the hell have they all gone?"

And that was a good point. Martha had been helping us, of course. But Vernon? Levin? The others on the hill who were possessed of really serious magic? They'd come to our assistance readily enough last night. But they were no longer in evidence.

There had to be a reason for that. I glanced across at Martha, who looked puzzled too.

"Okay, I'm on it," she told me.

Then she turned into a smudge, and vanished.

The rest of us took another hard look at the barrier across the street.

"What is that?" the uniformed sergeant murmured.

Something seemed to be happening to the wall. It had turned an even darker gray since I'd arrived, and parts of its surface had started shifting. Not in any pattern, as had been the case before. This was more like watching water being sloshed around in a rectangular tub. Entirely random, with no proper direction to it. Sections just detached themselves and flowed across each other, merging constantly and changing pace. It was happening to the whole expanse. And could have been mesmeric, if it wasn't so damned threatening.

"What do you suppose is going on in there?" Vallencourt wondered.

But the barrier was still opaque. What Hanlon had planned was anybody's guess.

Martha came back. This time, she had Judge Levin with her. She looked upset, apologetic. And the judge was so dour and unhappy he could barely raise his narrow head. He was still in the same brown suit, but had put on a fresh white shirt. Except he didn't have his robes across his shoulders. Which meant either he hadn't been planning to use magic, or else things had become too urgent for that.

I couldn't see his eyes behind those rimless spectacles of his. The angle was wrong. But what was bothering them both? We'd faced a lot that was pretty dreadful in the past couple of days. Could there possibly be something worse?

"Where are the others?" I asked.

At first, there was no response. Martha seemed to have lost the power of speech, and Levin looked too overwhelmed to answer.

He finally pulled himself together. He had dignity, when everything else failed. As he lifted his face to look at me, his glasses tilted, clearing. There was genuine regret in his pale gaze.

And something else. Genuine fear as well. A horror that was swallowing him.

"The rest aren't coming," he informed me.

His voice was so diminished I could barely make it out. Not even a whisper, really. Little more than an exhaled breath.

"And in point of fact," he continued, "I have no business being here either. There is absolutely nothing any of us can do."

I got the rest from Martha, who'd recovered her senses a little by this stage. She had gone to the Vernon residence, the judge's, Kurt van Friesling's, and found each of them empty. Then she'd headed for the McGinleys' home. And found the whole load of them in the inner sanctum, that strange circular room that I had visited before. They'd been pensive, barely moving. Almost dazed, in fact.

"We came to a joint decision several hours ago," the judge broke across her. "Our involvement last night helped to save the town, for sure. But we could see that picking off these individual demons wouldn't solve the central problem."

"Hanlon?" I asked.

"No. Not him, but what he stole. At the center of this nightmare lies the Wand of Dantiere itself. Of course, we didn't even know of its existence until recently. So we decided to combine our powers and delve into its origins, its past."

And this sounded familiar. Magic left footprints, I already knew. It left a trail on the night air. If you had sufficient spells and knowledge, you could follow it back to its source. And find out how and why it was created. Its strengths and limits, and intended purpose. Willets did it the whole time. It was how he'd clued me in on Saruak.

The fear was growing stronger in the judge's gaze. And the blood was draining from his lips.

"It was created to do all of this. And ultimately, one more thing."

I didn't like the way he said that. He paused briefly, drawing his thoughts together before going on.

"The wand was created back in the ninth century by an alchemist and necromancer by the name of Emile Dantiere. The man was privately wealthy, but also eccentric and obsessed with darkness. And he chose to make his home in one of the filthiest slums in Lyon, a place so dank and dangerous even troops thought twice before going there. He hoped that way to keep what he was doing hidden from the outside world."

Levin stared across at the barrier, his face seeming to draw in traces of its shifting darkness.

"For four decades he lived and worked there. And we're talking about an era when the average lifespan was less than that. There's little doubt he used his magic to prolong his years. He used it for a lot of other things as well."

"What exactly was he doing?" I asked.

"What any sorcerer of his kind does. He was searching for ultimate power."

It had been practically the turn of the ninth century—the judge explained—when Dantiere started to make the wand. And by that time, he had gone completely mad.

"I think that's part of the solution to all this, and why it's happened now. Whatever else Lucas might have been, he was not clinically insane. He must have used the wand thousands of times, without ever once understanding the kind of brutal force that he was holding in his grasp. He probably thought it was a conjuring device like any other. But he couldn't have been more wrong."

"You're telling me," I asked him, "that its real power can only be got at by a man like Dantiere himself?"

"A raving lunatic. Exactly."

"Hanlon."

"Yes." The judge straightened up a little. "That's what we've been seeing this entire time. It's not that our visitor's been growing stronger. More likely, the wand has been opening up to him, revealing itself in its true form."

And to me, that sounded like the same thing as . . .

"It likes him?"

Levin nodded stiffly.

"You're talking about it like it was alive."

"It is, Devries."

That staggered me. Despite which, I could see that the judge wasn't finished yet.

"Okay," I asked him. "What's it really for?"

His gaze became extremely distant. And his face went slack.

"Emile Dantiere was killed before he ever got to use it, thank the Lord. One of his neighbors realized he was up to something truly evil, and so crept into his home and stabbed him while he slept. The wand got passed on from hand to hand—after that—without anyone ever recognizing its true potential."

He stared around at us.

"By the time he created it, Dantiere had grown so violently insane that he had come to hate all living things. The ultimate purpose of the wand is to bring on the end, the Apocalypse."

"The end of everything we know," said Martha.

And it was now in the grip of a modern-day madman who really wanted that.

CHAPTER 57

Almost as soon as she had spoken, Paul McKendrick mouthed a curse, his thick silver eyebrows coming up. And our attention swung to the point where his gaze was fixed.

It wasn't a matter of tight focus either. The whole barrier was changing shape.

The front section was no longer rectangular. Its outer edges had become distorted, shapeless. And the central part, where the gates had been, was growing taller, oozing upward as I watched. The whole thing seemed to have taken on a life of its own. I reminded myself there was a consciousness behind it.

"What's it doing?" Martha blurted.

Except if she didn't know by this stage, who else was supposed to?

The distorted mass became slightly translucent. And, for the first time since the walls had gone up, the outlines of Millwood House became vaguely apparent through them.

I squinted, trying to understand what I was looking at. It didn't make any sense, at first. And then I finally got it. I'd been trying to pick out proper shapes. The truth was, there were none. I was looking at a tangled jumble, nothing more than that. We hadn't heard the tiniest sound. But the whole mansion had been demolished. There was not an intact portion standing anywhere.

Not a wall still upright, even part of one. The place had been ripped apart completely and reduced to shattered rubble. The really strange thing was, it wasn't strewn around the way you might expect.

This was not mindless destruction, like we'd seen throughout the rest of town. There'd been planning behind it once again. The wreckage was piled up in a solid block, some fifteen feet in height. And at the very top was a deep indentation. I struggled to figure out what I was really looking at.

The barrier was pulling itself into an upright shape, some kind of irregular column. It dwarfed by far the pile of shattered bricks behind it. And it kept on growing, so tall that my neck practically creaked. A dark gray pillar, maybe forty feet from top to bottom. It reached high enough to blot out several stars.

Then it started to resolve into a different shape. One that I recognized almost straightaway. I had seen this before, and not so long ago. Massively enlarged—but it was Hanlon, still transformed into his Death persona. I think I cursed as well, at that point, sick to my stomach of this maniac.

The bare skull was there again, its sockets peering down at us, the fixed grin still in place. The bony fingers and the black robes too, the whole thing vastly magnified. But there were a few differences.

Where there'd been lightless hollows in its eyes before, there were now flames. They burned a ruddy crimson color. You could practically feel the heat from them the whole way down here.

Where there'd been bared teeth, the canines had extended to long, sharply pointed fangs. There was a fluid dripping from them that I didn't doubt was venom.

There weren't merely bony fingertips this time. Long, curving nails protruded from them, cruel-looking, like talons. And—between the thumb and index finger of the right hand—I could see the Wand of Dantiere, as tiny as a toothpick in that giant grasp. It looked insignificant from this distance. But I'd been around magic long enough to not be fooled.

The moon was up behind him, like some muddled reflection of his face. At first, Hanlon merely stood there, casting his massive shadow across us. But I didn't imagine that would last for very long. My gaze swung to Levin.

"Is there nothing you can do about this?"

Fear and sadness jostled for position on his features. I had never seen him look so helpless.

"Once begun, this can't be stopped," he said. "Only the person holding the wand can control events from this point onward. Dantiere intended it that way."

"I can't accept that!"

But his shoulders slumped.

"You might have to, I'm afraid."

I thought of everything we'd been through. And it had been full of pain and loss, for sure, but we'd come out the right end of it. Found solutions to each problem. So I wasn't about to accept that verdict. There had to be some way to prevent this.

Then I remembered who else was here, and my attention went across to Lauren.

"You're not bound by Regan's Curse," I told her. "You can still get out of here."

I had already started wondering—if the End of Days was coming, then would it be confined solely to the Landing, or would it spread out to the normal world? At least, if it was the former, she still had a fighting chance.

There was a strange thrumming noise above us. That was the creature moving its cloaked arms, the air around them being pushed aside. The wind from it brushed across our faces and made the shrubbery around us clash.

She could still get to safety. Or the hope of it, at least. But Lauren shook her head. She kept on staring at the skull above us. Her own face had taken on a peculiar glow.

"No, Ross. I told you—I'm not leaving without him."

Which was pretty crazy, given what was happening. Except . . . I understood craziness of that kind, and respected it. She was still as determined as she'd ever been, and even tougher-minded than she'd been a bare few days ago.

"If you stay, you might not be leaving here at all," I pointed out.

A stern expression crossed her features. "There's always that chance."

Okay then. I kept on staring at her.

"Any ideas?"

"Me? 'Fraid not."

Me neither. I peered back at the enormous figure.

Maybe it was the fixed grin, the kind that all skulls have. But it looked delighted with itself, like it had done something exceptionally clever. My flesh crawled. Who was this really? Some nut who got his jollies bringing suffering down on innocent folk. Whatever he had turned himself into, that was the image I held in my mind. I wasn't going to back down from him, the way the adepts had. Like most bad guys, he relied on that.

He thought he had already won, and I could see that clearly. He looked down at us again, every motion languid. Then, with a decisive air, he settled onto the pile of rubble. That was its purpose, I could see. It was intended as some kind of throne.

He sat perfectly upright, his off-white, bony chin raised. I suppose the word for it would be "imperiously." The flame in his eyes seemed to burn a little brighter. Then he raised the wand. Its tip winked in the moonlight.

"Jesus Christ!" I heard Vallencourt murmur.

The figure lifted its arm as high as it was able. And drew the wand across the night sky like a pencil. It couldn't be actually touching the heavens—anyone knew that. But it still left the faintest mark. A thin line, traveling downward. A barely visible abrasion on the purple darkness, almost like a narrow scar.

I was trying to work out how that could even be possible, when it deepened and then split open. A strong, moaning wind began to push out through it, carrying all kinds of odors. Foul ones. Most of the guys around me ducked their heads.

Then something started shifting in the bottomless darkness beyond the gap. And when I looked closer . . .

No, not simply one thing.

A load of them. An amassed army.

CHAPTER 58

I glanced back around at the judge. His spectacles had turned glossy in the white glow of the moon, making it look as though the things that he was witnessing had blinded him. And his mouth had dropped to a wide oval, showing off his teeth and tongue. His normal dignity had vanished. He was too amazed to even begin showing signs of fear. Although I didn't doubt that that would come.

"What's happening?" I asked him.

He didn't even seem to hear me at first. And didn't turn to me when he finally replied.

"I didn't think that this could happen! It's completely beyond anything we know!"

"What is?"

"He's torn open a barrier! Between our dimension and another!"

He'd explained to me once that there were literally thousands of them. Multitudes of states of being, invisible walls holding them apart. Some were pleasant. And some rather less than that. There was no need to guess which kind this was. There was the smell, for starters. And the shapes behind the opening seemed to be writhing.

The stench was mostly rotting flesh. But there were other odors in there too. The pressure of the wind increased around us.

The rest of the night sky was normal. But the hole gaped across it like an open mouth.

Something pushed its way out from the bottom edge and dropped the twenty feet or so to the ground with no apparent injury. It lay there for a few seconds, curled up on its back. It was some kind of mottled brown hue, and I thought I could see folded arms and legs. But it was hard to be sure. The thing was balled up like a giant wood louse.

Then it started to unravel. Four narrow limbs suddenly appeared. There were what looked like hands on the ends of each, except that they were flat and splayed. They waved for a moment in the air. And then the thing flipped over, righting itself.

It hunched down on its hind legs, gazed at us and snarled, displaying rows of pointed teeth. It looked like one of the gargoyles on the rooftop of Raine Manor, except furrier and larger. Standing at full height, I guessed it had to be about four feet. And its limbs might be thin, but they still looked powerful.

Its face was a grotesque parody of a human one, the ears going to tufted spikes, the mouth much wider than it should have been. The eyes were a bilious pale yellow, and the brow above them was heavily ridged.

Two more of the things came tumbling out. Lay beside the first a moment, in the same position. Then sprung up themselves. They were its exact brothers, identical in every way. And they peered at us balefully. One of them sniffed the air and hissed.

"Some breed of demon from the lower orders," I heard the judge say.

He had reached out with his powers, to understand them.

"They seem largely mindless, little more than animals. Though I'd imagine, pretty deadly."

His voice had changed, losing its urgency. Becoming far more measured, purposeful. This was push-comes-to-shove time, and he knew it. Everyone here did. And he'd responded to that by finding a little of his calmer self, taking in the fact that panic was useless.

There was so much hurried movement beyond the opening, it was impossible to make out individual shapes. A churning swarm of darkened bodies was the only thing that I could see.

"How many of them are there?" I asked.

"At a rough guess? Millions."

The first few had only been the vanguard. They were dropping to the ground in a continuous flow by this stage. First a small bunch at a time, then dozens. And the wind that accompanied them was getting even more intense, making it hard to stand up straight.

The creatures at the front got up from their crouched position and started to approach us. And the rest began to follow them.

They came on all four limbs, making no attempt to stand upright. Looked like they could move fast, but were closing in cautiously right now. This had to be as new to them as it was to us. Did they even know what a moon and stars were? Hills, trees, blades of grass?

Those yellow gazes swiveled around, taking in their surroundings in a slightly edgy manner. But then they fixed on us, trying to size us up. Trying to get the measure of the weapons in our hands especially. The creatures lurched and shuddered as they moved. The fur on their bodies was patched with dampness.

Ritchie Vallencourt yelled out, and the cops opened fire.

Chunks were blown out of the hunched shapes. Flecks of yellow goop began appearing on the ground. But it didn't seem to hurt them as much as it should have, even when small sections of their heads came off. I could see what the problem was immediately. They didn't seem to have vital spots the way that we did. This was like trying to kill insects with a needle. Which part of them did you hit to actually stop them moving?

Several of them started limping as a leg was blown away. But even those ones kept on trying to move in on us, hobbling on their shattered stumps. They were making high-pitched yowling noises, their jaws stretching open wide.

Levin squared his shoulders.

"If this is to be my final day," he sighed, "then I might as well make it a memorable one."

He stepped out smoothly from the shadows of the topiary. Extended his palms in the direction of the closing horde. Two beams of white light shot out from them, and a pair of the demons burst into flames and disintegrated.

Martha Howard-Brett stepped up beside him, doing the same thing. Which meant that they were taking four down at a time. But it didn't discourage the rest in any way. And there were hundreds more tumbling from the opening, falling so rapidly that they were dropping onto the backs of the ones that had preceded them. A huge pile of the things was forming, narrow feet and elbows thrashing everywhere you looked. And as soon as the creatures at the bottom struggled out, more came down to take their place.

I was firing furiously, and there was gunsmoke all around me. But you could shoot at these things for hours, and it wouldn't be any real use. How long would it be, I wondered, before we started to run out of ammo? And the adepts would begin to weaken as their powers were drained away.

I stared back at Hanlon. He still had that grin in place. And wasn't even looking at us any longer. He was peering at the gap he'd made, watching the creatures struggle through. His skeletal hands were on the move, like he was conducting a symphony. There was something almost dreamlike to the way that he did that.

My gaze went to the Wand of Dantiere, clutched between his massive fingers. If I could somehow get it away from him . . . ?

Last time we'd been in a hole like this, Amashta—the ancient shaman woman—had helped. Her dry voice had started ringing in my head, and then her powers had flowed through me. But there was no sign of that happening right now. If she was watching, she was standing back.

"Defender," she had called me. So was I expected to do this by myself?

I thought of maybe trying to shoot the wand, but there were two things working against that. In the first place, it was a good long way off and a moving target. In the second, I doubted that a mere bullet would work.

I stepped out into open ground myself. There had to be another way to get the thing from him. But how?

"Just grab it, while his attention is elsewhere," suggested an aristocratically toned voice, behind me.

Raine?

But when I whirled around, he wasn't there. Only the darkness of the house behind me met my startled gaze. No one else had reacted, so maybe only I could hear him.

"I'm still in the Manor, sport."

His voice was behind me once again. And so I didn't bother turning, this time.

"I don't need to go outside to talk to people. Surely you must realize that?"

I hadn't. It was a talent he had never revealed before. Although—considering how powerful he was—I suppose I should have really guessed.

So I said, "Woody, he's forty feet tall. What are you going to do, conjure me up a nice big ladder?"

And you'd have thought that nothing serious was going on, because he sounded breezy and lighthearted when he answered me.

"I picked you up before," he said.

He meant our previous encounter in the ballroom, when he'd swept me up into the air.

"And I can do the same again. I hope you're not afraid of heights."

The wind around me altered course, gusting up in the direction of the open sky. My coat tried to swirl around my face. My hair felt like it was being wrenched.

And then I was lifted off my feet again, rising toward the hand above me.

CHAPTER 59

From the start, I was amazed. Not simply that I was air-
borne. I wasn't claiming to like it, but I'd been there before.
No, I was astonished that the Master of the Manor was helping us in so active a fashion.

He'd provided a little assistance before, usually by means
of the Eye of Hermaneus. But a lot of the time, the worst
of perils could descend on this town, and he wouldn't lift a
finger. He'd express what sounded like genuine shock. And
then turn away, his deluded mind finding another matter to
fixate on.

Why had he jumped in with both feet this time? I decided
it was better not to ask.

As I lifted higher, my surprise gave way to growing
unease. I had to be some twenty feet clear of the ground.
And only Lauren seemed to have noticed I was gone. Her
face looked like a tiny upturned smudge.

I glanced around at the rest of the town—the avenues and
spires and leafy parks. Then my attention went down past
my shoes again. The cops were still blazing away, to limited
effect. And the judge and Martha were frying as many of
the scuttling demons as they could manage. But there were
already too many of them, thousands more flooding from
the hole. The narrow line of human beings was beginning
to fall back.

Which was a pretty alarming sight in itself. But not the

only reason I was getting scared. The fact was, I knew Woody. He had carried me this far, but how much further? He could suddenly become distracted. If that happened, I'd drop like a stone.

I held myself together finally by telling myself one simple thing. If I fell, then it would be a relatively quick death. Far better, probably, than what awaited me below. And there was nothing I could do about it anyway. No way left but up. So I kept my eyes fixed on the bony hand above me.

Hanlon didn't even see me coming. He was wrapped up in delirium, swaying to a tune inside his own crazed head. His fantasies had, at last, reached fruition. Which was the really bad thing about magic . . . it allows all the wrong people to do that.

I chanced a final quick glance down. The people and the other shapes below me had been reduced to moving dots. The smaller flashes were gunfire, once again. The larger ones were Sam and Martha, hitting the beasts with full force. It was an awful long way down by this time. But the distance between the two groups was getting even shorter.

Then I focused on the wand completely. The massive hand went skimming past my face. I stretched my arm out after it, and missed. And my first instinct was to go chasing after it. But I wasn't in control of this. Woody held me statically in midair, like a key suspended on a chain. The wind from the opening had no effect on my position.

Another instant, and the arm was coming back at me. And Cornelius still hadn't noticed I was there.

I stared at the black stick as it got nearer to me. Its tip gave another brilliant shimmer, for no reason I could see. Alive, I kept on telling myself. And as crazy and unpleasant as the person holding on to it. My first instinct was to shy away. But I hadn't come up here for that.

Another heartbeat, and it was right in front of me. I reached out as it hurtled past. Felt it brush against my palm, and closed my grip around it. Then I yanked the thing away.

As soon as I had hold of it, the enormous skull above lurched down. The flames leapt higher in its empty eyes. The jaw dropped wide—no sound came out.

An arm the size of a narrow tree trunk lunged in my direction, the folds of the jet-black robe swirling around it. At which point, conscious thought took a backseat, stronger instincts taking over.

"Woody!" I bellowed. "Time to leave!"

I went shooting backward, just as the hand started closing around me. It was an awful, gut-wrenching sensation, like a bungee jump but in reverse. Hanlon's bony fingers clacked together, missing me by barely a foot. The talons at the ends of them scraped across each other with a violent grating sound.

I continued drifting away from them, descending at the same time.

I closed both hands around the wand now. And took in the fact that it felt weird in my grasp. For a start, it didn't seem any cooler than my skin, which an inanimate object ought to do. So perhaps it was at body temperature, the same as my own palms.

Secondly, it was so light my senses barely registered it was there. And third . . .

I thought that I could feel a very gentle pulse.

Whatever, I had to destroy it. And the easiest way seemed to be to snap it. It was no thicker than your average pencil. But phenomenally rigid too. When I applied pressure, it didn't yield a tiny fraction. I couldn't bend it a little bit.

I had managed to annoy it, though. And the wand instantly paid me back.

A jolt of flaring energy ran through me. Felt like liquid fire sweeping underneath my skin. I howled. Couldn't help it. And dropped the thing. Panic rushed through me when I did that.

Except—for once—Woody was ahead of the game. He released me immediately, letting me fall after it. I managed to grab hold of it again.

Then the supporting wind came back. I was about twelve feet up by this time, and was drifting away from the battle.

A steady surge of creatures was advancing across Plymouth Drive. Hundreds were crowding in to take the place of those that had fallen. And the flow of mottled bodies from the opening hadn't stopped. If Levin and the others couldn't hold them back, then what chance did the rest of the town have?

I looked back up. The death's head was surging closer, very quickly. And its arms were reaching out again. Hanlon hadn't even left his makeshift throne. His whole body, below the chest, had become a misty blur that was stretching out like gray elastic.

"Faster, Woody!" I yelled out.

He turned me around, then began towing me along, parallel with the gradient of Sycamore Hill. I was headed for the very top, the moonlight making silhouettes of the large shapes ahead of me. A huge backyard, and then another, skimmed below. The battle was lost to my rear, and there was no one else in sight.

"Where exactly do you want to go, sport?" Woody asked. "I can't simply keep you buzzing around like a June bug on a string all night."

He sounded slightly peevish. Which made me suspect he was getting bored. I'd probably survive a fall of twelve feet. But, with Death on my heels, not for very long.

A broad, uneven shape became apparent up ahead. I was headed straight for it, and couldn't quite see what it was in the darkness. Then, "Tree!" I bellowed.

And I skimmed around it just in time.

"Well?" he asked me again, as if nothing had interrupted us.

He was starting to sound genuinely unhappy. And I knew what kind of trouble that could bring.

I fought to think straight—it was pretty hard, given where I was. The air rushed around me, and a stretch of woodland swept below. If I couldn't break the wand, then who could? Levin or Martha, it occurred to me. Except that getting to them would involve turning back the way I'd come. And that was not an option. I could try for the McGinley place, where the others were holed up. But that was off to my left, so I stood the risk of being intercepted.

Hanlon was still coming up behind me. Why would it be any other way? His skull was looming higher up, and both his hands were still stretched out. So much as a pause, and they would grab me in an instant. But I couldn't think where else to go.

What exactly did I know about the object in my grasp? I remembered what the judge had told me. And the main thing that he'd said came springing back to mind.

Dantiere had been a lunatic. He'd made that very clear. And if it took one madman to create the thing, then might the best person to destroy it be . . . ?

"Woody?" I yelled. "Keep me going in this direction! You've got it exactly right!"

"But you're headed for my own house, sport."

"Yeah! I need to talk with you, in person!"

"Really?" he asked, sounding pretty intrigued. "And why's that?"

You'd think that he'd have got it, but he simply didn't work that way. And this needed diplomacy—I could see that right away. Tell him the real reason that he was needed and he'd get offended. But flattery could get you everywhere with Woodard Raine, a fact that I was already aware of.

And I was putting together the right words in my head . . . when his voice rang out again, cutting across my train of thought.

"My, that is an interesting wand you've got there."

He made a soft humming noise, like he was musing to himself.

"I can feel this terribly strong aura coming off it. Rather a pleasant one in fact."

Which wasn't quite how I'd describe it. And I wasn't sure I liked the way that he said that. His tone had become deeper again, far more brooding and reflective than it had been.

When he spoke again, it was practically a rumble.

"In fact, I'd like to take a closer look at it. Stop dawdling for heavens sake, Devries! Good Lord, man, hurry up!"

I was lifted slightly higher in the air and began hurtling toward Raine Manor at twice the speed I'd gone before.

CHAPTER 60

Before too much longer, its unkempt grounds were rushing beneath me. A few large crows burst from cover, startled by the fact that I was at their height.

I dropped a couple of feet lower as I approached the house. The spindly, leafless branches of the trees kept trying to snatch at the soles of my shoes. They looked even weirder than usual from up here. As dark as the surrounding night, and impenetrably tangled—what you might get if you poured a pint of Scotch down Jackson Pollack and then handed him a stick of charcoal.

But they were not the half of it.

The high spire was already in view, with the W at its apex. But I could also see the rest of the roof, more clearly than I had before. The gargoyles had all come awake. They were clustered on the upper ridge, their backs hunched over and their deformed faces tilted, staring up at me. Then they saw what was pursuing me. And within another moment, they were scuttling out of sight.

The house below seemed to lurch crazily as I changed direction. I could make out the ruined west wing, and the covered porch out front. And in the latter case . . .

There seemed to be some extra shadow on it. It didn't look as empty as it normally did. I could scarcely believe what my eyes were telling me. But as I went lower, I got a better angle. And could see two figures standing there.

One was Hampton, a round, meaty bulk in the gloom. He was gawping at me startledly, his mismatched eyes shining with alarm. The other shape?

He hadn't exactly come out into the open. Was wedged back against the partly open doorway. But, considering how deeply terrified of the outdoors he was . . . this was the first time Woodard Raine had crossed his own threshold in years.

He looked like he was ready to retreat given the slightest reason. And his whole body was hunched. But Woods was staying put for the time being. So perhaps I'd underestimated him.

When I usually met him, it was in the ballroom and surrounded by faint candlelight. He was merely a vague set of features or a pair of glowing eyes in there. You never got to see the entire person. So I was looking at him clearly for the first time in a good number of years.

He was thinner than I remembered. Slightly shorter too. His shoulders were rounded, his posture awkward. I suppose the best word for him—and I puzzledly took this in—was "average." Pass him on the street, and you would give him little thought. Only his great powers and his even greater lunacy had made him someone to be reckoned with.

I was almost to the ground. And heading downward far too quickly.

"An easier landing, if you'd please?" I called out.

"Landing . . . ?"

I'd confused him.

"Slow me down!"

I decelerated at the very last moment. My heels skidded through a dense mixture of gravel and crabgrass all the same, before I finally came to a halt.

Then I was running up onto the porch, and waving the wand at the man's shadowy form.

"You need to destroy this, Woody! You might be the only person who can do it!"

He pulled an unimpressed face, then abruptly snatched it from me. Woody ran a finger down it, studying its markings. His eyes, which had been glowing yellow, took on a more amber shade.

"Why?" he asked me, sounding quite annoyed. "It seems a rather lovely thing."

Which was precisely the opposite reaction from the one I'd wanted. The kind of response that made your hair curl. Not for the first time when dealing with this crazy adept, I felt like I wanted to scream.

But Hampton beat me to it.

He was pointing out across the gardens, high above the wild, uneven line of trees. Me and Raine both looked in that direction.

Hanlon was catching up. His bare skull appeared at first. Then his black-cloaked arms rose into view, the claws still grasping, the rest of the vast, elongated body stretching in their wake.

"Sir?" the manservant yelped. "I suggest you do as Mr. Devries asks!"

But the look on Woody's face made my heart sink even further. He had a bland, detached expression now. So we were back to square one, weren't we? The danger we were in meant nothing to him, or so it appeared. Perhaps he found it all rather distasteful. Overly prosaic and—because of that—beneath his contempt. His eyelids fluttered briefly shut, and his lips pursed with disapproval.

"And now my own staff are telling me what to do," he sighed. "What is the world coming to?"

Except that Hampton was his only staff. There wasn't any plural. This was a fine time for him to go losing his grip on reality completely. I clenched my teeth, my breath seething through them.

"Woody?" I barked at him. "Don't you understand what's going on?"

He had to know about the battle. And I jabbed my index finger at the vast, approaching figure. But he wouldn't even look at it again. He kept brushing his fingertips along the wand, seemingly obsessed with it. And at that point, frustration boiled over in me. Otherwise, I wouldn't have done what I attempted to.

It made no sense to try and force him physically. If I'd

been thinking clearer, I'd have seen that. But the situation was too desperate. And so I lunged at him and tried to grab him by his robe, forcing him to look around.

But my palms had barely closed around the fabric when he saw what I was doing. And his eyes abruptly flashed. They went brilliantly hot for a few seconds, so vivid they dazzled me. When the glare shrunk back, they'd returned to the ugly orange I had seen several nights back.

The heel of his right hand brushed, lightly and deftly, against my chest. I could feel its pressure for the briefest instant. Barely a plausible attempt at self-defense.

But as it pulled away, it suddenly felt like an earthquake had struck me. My bones shook fiercely, and the flesh on them seemed to quiver.

The strength was sucked out of my limbs. And I didn't merely fall; going down I crumpled like a loose sack of coal. I tried to get up, found I couldn't. Not a muscle in my frame was under my control.

Out of the corner of one eye, I could still see Hanlon. He had already floated halfway across the grounds, and was drawing ever closer.

"Sir?" Raine's manservant moaned again.

But I heard no reply.

One side of my face was down on the porch's cold stone surface. It was a struggle to attempt it from here, but I managed to get another look at Woody. He wasn't looming over me, as I'd expected him to. In fact, he had forgotten all about me. He was bending over, studying the wand again. Touching it delicately with both his hands. And what was that noise he was making? A strange murmuring sound with no shape to it.

There was madness contained in that little stick. And perhaps, like Hanlon, he identified with that. The thing seemed to fascinate him like nothing else had ever done. As I watched, he stopped dabbing at it, and then gently tipped his head to one side.

Looked as though he were listening to something. And it didn't make me feel a whole lot better, seeing that.

Hampton had backed off, too afraid to venture close. I

doubted he'd ever seen his master in a mood like this, and he didn't seem quite sure how to handle it.

I tried to move again. Couldn't make so much as an eyebrow twitch. But if my eyesight was still working, maybe the same applied to my voice. Neither my lips nor my jaws were responding. But I could still push air up through my throat, then shape it lightly with my tongue.

I made a stab at it. "Woody!"

It came out more like "Oo-ee." And he didn't look around. So I tried again, more forcefully. He glanced at me with a peevish air.

"What's that, sport? Why does everyone mumble so much these days? Speak more clearly, if you please."

And he wasn't being spiteful or sarcastic. He seemed to have genuinely forgotten what he'd done.

He clicked his fingers suddenly. And my entire mouth started moving again, although nothing else did. If I was going to make anything happen here, then it would have to be with words, not actions.

"I thought you were going to help us?"

He looked distinctly puzzled, like he didn't recall saying that.

"Why bother to start, then stop again?" I went on.

His chin dropped slightly, and lines appeared on his brow. I could only pray that he was trying to think of an answer.

The death's head passed over the final line of trees and Hampton shrank away into the shadows of the hallway.

"I . . ." Woody muttered.

We were running out of time for little chats like this. But . . .

"Yes?"

"Though it might be a good idea."

"Helping us? It still is one."

"Really?"

"Look around you at what's happening."

His head came back up and he closed his eyes. But I knew that he was staring with his inner one. A tic appeared on one side of his face. What he was looking at was not making him noticeably comfortable.

"If those demons win . . . ? he asked.

"Uh-huh?"

"There'll be no one left, now will there? Nobody in my whole town."

"That's pretty much the size of it," I told him.

We only had a few more seconds. I could hear the noises of the battle faintly, drifting up the hillside. Woody was inspecting the wand again.

"And even if I manage to survive . . ."

Which was not impossible.

"I'll be . . . alone, won't I?"

He was that anyway most of the time. An almost total recluse. But I knew he reached out with his senses to the world beyond his mansion. Kept his eye on everything that happened down below this place, even if he mostly saw it as a fantasy, a half-formed dream. And so I held my tongue at that point. There are times when silence can be far more eloquent than words.

A much deeper shadow fell across us. When I swung my gaze around, the sky had been blocked out. The only brightness up there was the flame in Hanlon's sockets. He was looming right above us, one hand reaching down.

"Break the wand. None of it'll happen if you do that," I whispered to Raine urgently.

He applied some cautious pressure, and then went at it with all his strength. The wand bent slightly, which was more than I'd been able to make happen. But there was no sign that it was going to crack.

"Use magic, sir!" called Hampton from inside the doorway.

So he'd not gone very far.

"Ah. Quite."

And Woody grinned. But then he peered at me inquiringly.

"Devries, do you suppose there's such a thing as a Spell of Breaking?"

"You're a great magician," I hissed at him. "Make one up."

CHAPTER 61

Two of the uniformed cops who'd been standing near Lauren were already dead. They'd let the hunched creatures get too close. And she'd had some extremely ugly demonstrations of how these things operated. They could put on far greater bursts of speed than they'd originally shown. They'd get within a few yards, and then suddenly come rushing forward, swiftly as a closing trap. Several of them at a time would leap onto a victim, their thin limbs taking purchase. Then they'd start clamping down with their mouths as well, devouring their prey alive.

Not that that last word really applied for very long. Dozens of others would come surging in, drawn there—so she imagined—by the sight and smell of blood. Both cops had disappeared beneath a writhing mass of mottled brown and grabbing hands within a bare few seconds.

It was an awful thing to watch, worse than anything she had ever known. The screams, and glimpses of torn flesh. Lauren kept on fighting, but felt shaken to the core. And the hole in the air was still filled with the things. An unbroken stream of them kept on dropping down. What she'd been seeing . . . was this the fate in store for this whole town? For her?

There was little time, thankfully, for reflections of that sort. The line was falling back a few more yards, Vallencourt shouting out the order. They had almost reached the front walls of the dark houses behind them.

The pavement of Plymouth Drive was so solidly swamped with the advancing demons that you could no longer see it. And the ones at the front kept spilling across the curb ahead of her. A vast, lurching body of them. If it wasn't for their size, they would almost have resembled soldier ants.

She and the guys around her kept on shooting, and they killed three more. But another three hundred must have arrived by the time that they'd accomplished that. There seemed to be an inexhaustible supply of them. Lauren changed her clip, and kept on firing.

Levin and Martha were still blasting at the things. But it was like trying to stop a blizzard by snatching at individual snowflakes. Not nearly enough to do the whole job.

There were hundreds of yellow eyes fixed on her. Lauren tried to edge away and keep her distance from them. But her heel caught on a clod of turf. She practically went crashing downward, terror surging through her. If the demons saw her fall, they would be on her in an instant.

A big, meaty hand caught hold of her elbow, righting her.

She swiveled around, and found herself staring into an aged but robust face, its bald head offset by a drooping white moustache. This new guy—she had not seen him before—blinked at her solemnly, then raised his other hand, palm flat. A bolt of green-tinged light shot out. A demon that had gotten too close caught fire and crumbled.

Looking across, she saw that other figures had appeared. A younger man, blond and fairly handsome. A distinctly weedy-looking fellow in a bow tie and waistcoat. And a pair of fiercely glaring women who looked like they might be twins.

"At last!" she heard Levin shout.

So were these the other adepts she had heard about?

"We discussed it," the man who'd saved her grumbled. He was talking to the judge, not her. "And decided we at least had to try and stop this."

"Pleased to hear it," Levin came back dryly.

"Waste of time, if you ask me. But I'd rather die on my feet than sitting down."

All of them began using their powers. Blinding streams of light shot out. Most of the advancing front line went down, and the demons coming up behind it paused. But then they started to move again, like nothing had really happened.

"We need to find higher ground!" Levin yelled.

Which sounded like a plan. They were on a hill, after all. But when she glanced from side to side, she could see that they were being flanked. These beasts might be brutishly dumb, but even they seemed to know what a pincer movement was. Thousands of the things had swept out past the edges of the battle, scampering around to cut them off. And a few had got onto the rooftops, attacking the marksmen up there.

Lauren felt a crushing sensation in her chest, like a rock pressing on it. There was nowhere left for them to go.

The new front line was only about five yards off. There was another hurried surge from it and another cop went down. She drew a bead on the creature nearest her, aiming at its narrow legs. Blew one away. It didn't kill it, but the thing started going around in mindless circles.

Two more replaced it immediately. She did the same to the one on the left, then heard a clack that told her she was out of ammunition. And she'd used up the last of her clips.

More weapons were falling silent, the air becoming quieter as their echoes died away. She heard somebody curse, and a cop behind her muttered what sounded like a brief prayer. The hisses and snarls of the beasts seemed to become more insistent, pounding at her ears.

The adepts were still trying their level best. But the first two—Levin and Martha—were both looking pretty wasted, and firing less frequently. Would the same happen to the rest before much longer?

Something in her wanted to hunch down, just wrap her arms around her head, and wait there for the end to come. Why'd she even stayed here in the first place? What on earth had she been thinking of?

But she rebelled fiercely against that idea. No, she was damned if she was going out that way. Lauren held herself stiffly, refusing to back down.

The night's darkness seemed to fold across her, trying to distract her. Everything was happening so fast.

Three more of the demons, in a tightly packed bunch, came running at her. She gripped her Walther like a club again, setting her feet apart and holding her ground.

They were almost on her. Their flat hands were reaching for her legs. She tensed herself and swung the gun back, hoping that this would be over very quickly.

There was an unexpected but immense crackling noise off in the distance. She glanced up at the hilltop, just in time to see a brilliant white flash bring the mansion up there into sharp relief. Its bizarre-looking silhouette was burned into her retinas, that weird spire and the mass of trees around it.

The demons stopped, so close that they were almost touching her. The brilliant light flared up, then faded. Nothing seemed to move.

And then, the moment the hilltop went dark again, the wind that had been screaming around them this whole while . . . it changed direction. It reversed. Began sucking back into the hole it had emerged from.

At first, it looked like that might be the only thing that was going to happen. But then, the beasts in front of her were lifted off their splayed feet. They went hurtling away from her, and disappeared back through the opening. She wasn't affected, and neither were any of the others. But in a few more seconds, the massed ranks in front of them were disintegrating. Hundreds of the demons, and then thousands of the things, were being sucked away.

It looked like they were actually being siphoned back. And the more of them that disappeared, the smaller the hole was getting. The sky was returning to normal. And the road in front of her was becoming visible again.

Gratitude surged through her, and she almost doubled up.

It had to be Ross, she figured. Somehow, he had done it.

The hole shrank swiftly to a dimple on the air, the stars hanging around it like a great cluster of fireflies. It wavered there a short while longer, and then disappeared completely with the gentlest sucking noise. Lauren felt her body try to crumple in upon itself.

But this was not over completely, and she forced herself to stay fixed in the moment. The thousands of creatures might have gone. But there was still one apparition left in view.

The great, robed skeleton of Death had returned. Its massively extended body was shrinking back in the direction of the rubble throne. It didn't sit down on it this time. And was getting smaller as she watched.

It finally contracted to the size of a man. And then the skull and bones, the black swathes of cloth around them, melted from sight. Giving way to draw-stringed sweatpants and an old, stained polo shirt. A familiarly pudgy face was staring around with bewilderment.

She took in the unshaven jowls, and the deep shadows underneath the eyes. Hanlon. Lauren felt her shoulders stiffen. He'd been reduced to a human being again, the magic taken from him. And this was what had brought her to Raine's Landing in the first place. When she let out her next breath, it carried two whispered syllables with it.

"At last."

He seemed to be in shock himself. Was stumbling around beneath the piled-up wreckage, unaware that there were eyes following him. Well, that was something she'd be glad to change.

Sweat was running down her face, and her clothes were sticking to her body. Her limbs ached with exhaustion and were trembling. But Lauren paid no attention to that.

She tossed aside her empty Walther. Lying on the lawn in front of her was the revolver of a cop who'd fallen. She felt sorry for the man, but picked it up all the same. This was no time for finer feelings.

It turned out to be heavier than she was used to. But that barely even registered. She checked the chamber. There were two rounds left inside.

"Cornelius Hanlon!" she yelled out.

She'd waited practically a year to do that, and it felt good coming out. It had the desired effect too, lifting him out of his stupor. He stopped tottering around and looked up at her.

Then she saw his head cock to one side. And so she took a few steps in his direction, making sure that he could see her clearly.

"Face-to-face finally, and on equal terms!" she called.

Then she held up the gun so he could see that too.

"Or maybe not!"

Even from this distance, she could see the terrible emotions fighting for position on his face. Utter devastation. Failure. All his crazy schemes destroyed. His imaginings reduced to dust.

Then that slid away, revealing the bile underneath. Fury screwed his features up. He wasn't going to take this lying down.

His shoulders swung away from her. He was reaching for the pile of rubble. And he fished out something from it that flashed when he turned back around. It was a long shard of glass from one of the house's broken windows. He was grasping the base of it like a knife.

His mouth came open. And he started letting out terrible screams. His bulky frame began to move. He was running at her with considerably more speed than you'd give him credit. But not nearly fast enough.

The few uniformed cops around her hadn't even noticed what was going on. They were still recovering from the onslaught. Lauren gripped the gun in both hands, aiming it at Hanlon's chest.

She shouted out a warning, giving him one final chance. He didn't even seem to hear her. Just kept on coming at her at the same pace, howling like an angry child. The glass was cutting into his grasp. She could see his palm was bleeding. But he wasn't taking that in either. He had really lost it, hadn't he?

The fact was, he'd never had it in the first place. Lauren reminded herself of that, then squinted down the sight.

"Back to the shadows for you, Cornelius," she murmured.

Then she squeezed the trigger, twice.

CHAPTER 62

There was a lot of clearing up to do once . . .

But no. I'm getting ahead of myself here. I should tell it in the order that it happened.

I thanked Woody, once he'd got me back up to my feet. As soon as the wand had been broken, he had gone to his more normal self. If you could call it that . . . it was stretching the word "normal" well past its limits. But his eyes were yellow-gold again, the redness in them gone. His face was somewhat blank, apart from that. It was as if he was still having trouble remembering what had happened. God almighty, how could anyone forget?

I thanked him all the same. Rather grudgingly, I must admit. He'd taken his sweet time about saving us, taking it right up to the thin line between life and death. A few more people could probably have been saved, if he had acted sooner. And I still wasn't even sure he'd done it for any sensible reason.

But I didn't see that last part really mattered. Any way you cut it, he had spared us from a pretty dreadful fate.

"Splendid job, sir! Immaculately executed!" put in Hampton, who had reemerged, looking a touch embarrassed.

All Woody did was glance around nervously, as if he'd only just discovered he was outside in the open. Then, without a word, he turned away and walked back into his place. Hampton frowned, then went shuffling after him.

The door slammed shut. I rubbed my brow and sighed.

By the time I'd headed back down Plymouth Drive and found the others, it was perfectly apparent what had happened. The hordes of demons were gone. Some more ambulance crews had arrived. And Hanlon's corpse was lying there, sprawled out on the gradient. It had two bullet holes in it—I could guess who'd put them there—but otherwise looked pretty insignificant, the way most corpses do.

Millwood House was still a total wreck, and there seemed to be no chance of that changing any time soon. Maybe we'd just leave it there, as a memorial to madness. Lauren Brennan—her face the color of oatmeal—was sitting on a low wall next to Vallencourt. I went across to her.

"You okay?" I asked her gently.

"Define okay in a place like this?" Her head shook with confusion. "I just . . . it was . . . nothing here's okay. Don't you get that?"

I shrugged, and exchanged the briefest smile with Ritchie.

"Yes, I do. But you learn to live with it."

"How?"

"When you're born here and grow up with it, it's just the way things are. Like . . ."

I found myself struggling to find the right analogy.

". . . driving on the left in England."

Lauren dropped her head exhaustedly and mumbled, "Never been there."

"Me neither," I told her.

Vallencourt let out a weary laugh.

When she tried to get back to her feet, it wasn't easy and it wasn't quick. I could see that she was nearly dropping. I'd thought I was tired, but she couldn't even hold her head up straight. So I supposed it wasn't merely physical exhaustion. She was finally caving in from the pressure she'd been under for the last few days. Her mind must have taken far more strain than even her body.

So I moved in closer and put an arm under her shoulders. She did not object. In fact, she slumped against me. Which felt nice. How long had it been since I had felt another body's warmth against my own?

"Time to get some rest," I said.

Her eyelids fluttered shut, and only came halfway back open.

"That's it?" she slurred. "That's all we do?"

And I could see what she meant. After everything that had befallen us, the horrors of the past couple of days . . . ?

"Sometimes, that's the only thing there's left to do," I explained to her. "We made it through—that's the main thing."

Although admittedly, only just.

"The other guys'll take care of the rest," I added.

And I glanced across at Vallencourt. He nodded back, still smiling. Lord, the new top cop was certainly the resilient type.

Lauren was fast asleep by the time I pulled up outside my garage. I carried her in and set her down on Pete's bed. Removed her shoes, but nothing else. If she came out of this with just a crumpled suit to show for it, well, that was something to be thankful for.

I threw a sheet across her and stared down at her for about a minute. Then remembered I was really tired as well, and went off to my own bed.

I suppose I should have dreamt of Hanlon changing. And of demon horsemen. And of crouching things, and ones that scuttled.

But the only thing I dreamt about was my lost family, as usual. When I woke, it was with sadness clinging to me, as it always does.

It was shortly before dawn. I could hear movement in my living room.

CHAPTER 63

I'd fallen asleep in my day clothes too. They were snagged around me. It's something that I never did, back when my family was still around. But things were very different these days. I didn't bother to change, or even pat myself down before I went on through. Given the circumstances, a body could live with a little unkemptness.

Out in the hall, I paused by my answering machine. The light wasn't flashing. So there were no messages, not a peep from Cass. And that bothered me badly. Where'd she gotten to, last night? And after she had fought with the dark riders so very courageously. What was going on with her?

It was unnaturally quiet outside the house. Not the yap of a dog, nor the clatter of a trash can. Which I supposed was no tremendous surprise. Calms come after storms, just as much as before them.

Lauren was standing in the living room, a slender shadow by my coffee table. I'd expected her to sleep later than this. It was hard to tell exactly, in the predawn light. The scratches on her face looked to be healing up nicely. But she still seemed tired and unsettled. She had pressed out the creases in her clothes as best as she could. And had her small case in one hand.

"Looks like you're ready to leave," I commented.

And was she in a hurry to? I couldn't keep the sadness out of my voice. Her lips narrowed and she shrugged.

"Now that Hanlon's gone, I think the curse has really kicked in, Ross. I kept on hearing voices in my sleep last night."

So that was it. Goddamn that hex hanging about this town!

"What were they saying?"

" 'You're not welcome here.' "

"That's not in the least bit true," I told her.

And she finally managed a smile, although the rest of her body remained motionless.

"Any news on Saul?" she asked.

Which made it my turn to shrug.

"Or Cassie?"

"She's behaving like a riddle wrapped in a mystery inside an enigma at the moment."

"Churchill on Russia," she came back at me, recognizing the quote.

Which made me take a bet that she read a lot too. I was finding it a real struggle to stop liking her so very much.

I muttered, "She'll be okay. She's very tough."

"I noticed."

"Sorry that she hit you."

"Felt to me like she's had a lot of practice."

"That's the truth," I agreed.

We were trying to make a joke of this, and not succeeding very well. We both knew what was going to happen next. And was there any point in trying to drag this out? We stared at each other for another short while, separated by an invisible wall made up of circumstance and history.

Then Lauren started walking, and I followed her. As we went out through the front door, the sun came up. The yellow light struck her hair, making it shine golden. And in that instant, she looked more like Alicia than she ever had.

Emotion welled up in me, fierce and powerful. I wanted to ask her to stay longer. Wanted to tell her that she had a home here, any time she liked. Was there anything for her in Boston? In the time we'd spent together, she'd not mentioned family or friends, not even once.

And then my thoughts calmed, settling down. I saw that was not possible. This was not my wife, however she might look. So I held my tongue, and walked her over to her little car.

She seemed to be uneasy too, but kept on trying to make light of it. Before she got in, she grinned awkwardly at me and said, "I can't imagine how I'm going to write this up in my report."

"You won't need to," I told her.

Then I explained to her what we'd already figured out.

The truth was, people came here the whole time. Truckers, mostly. They brought stuff here, and carried it away. But they kept their heads down and their eyes averted all the while that they were in this town. And left as soon as possible. Part of the curse as well.

"Our best guess," I finished up, "is that, as soon as they're gone, they forget this place even exists. Or it gets tucked away at the back of their minds, which amounts to the same thing. The same'll most likely happen to you, once you're back in the normal world."

Lauren looked surprised, and then rather disappointed.

"Well, I'm sorry to hear that." And her head ducked down. "I don't want to forget you, Ross. I don't see how that's right."

"Right and wrong don't have much to do with it. It's like . . ."

"Driving in England?"

I took that in and smiled.

"Yeah. That."

She seemed momentarily bemused, uncertain what to do. But then, she suddenly reared up on her toes, and kissed me on the cheek. It seemed to be on impulse, and it took me by surprise. And it wasn't just a friendly peck. Stayed there longer than it should have done, the warmth of it seeping into my skin.

When she pulled back, her eyes had gone damp again. She looked like she wanted to say something more, but all she did was squint unhappily. The voices of the curse still had to be ringing in her head. And so she got into the car next moment, shut the door, then wound the window part of the way down.

"Take care, right?" She forced another tight grin. "I know it's hard round here but . . . don't do anything too crazy."

"Absolutely," I replied, stooping toward her.

But then the engine turned, making me straighten up again and step away.

I was still watching her car disappearing down the street

when my cell phone started ringing. I fumbled it out and answered it without looking away.

It turned out to be Ginny Graves, the woman who'd been rescued from her possessed, ax-wielding husband.

"I didn't know who else to call," she told me anxiously. "Something weird is up with Cassie."

"She was here five minutes ago. Turned up at my door, unannounced. Her face was set like stone. She didn't say a word, which isn't her at all. She had Cleveland with her, and just handed him to me."

I could hear a faint mewling in the background.

"Then she turned around, went back to her bike, and simply rode away," Ginny continued. "I wasn't sure what to do; frankly, I couldn't believe it."

Except that, after last night, I could. My pulse started thudding all over again. I thanked her for the information, and then hurried to my own car. My front door was still open, but that didn't really matter in a neighborhood like this.

Cassie's place was silent when I got there, not a light on anywhere. Her Harley was not in sight. I let myself in—we keep each other's keys, for emergencies. And practically tripped over something, just inside the porch.

Her carbine was propped behind the door. Why'd she left it there? And when I went through to the living room, both her Glocks were lying on the coffee table.

I immediately saw that there was something missing too. This whole room was full of pictures of her kids. But on the same table where the Glocks had been set down, there'd been her favorite one. A big framed photograph of all four of them—her, Kevin, Angel, Cassie Jr.—out in Crealley Street Park on a bright, hot summer's day. They'd been lying on the grass, shoulder to shoulder, with the brilliantly mixed hues of the floral clock behind them, the four of them smiling at the camera like, if they got any happier, they'd burst.

It was not there anymore. A thin ridge of dust sat where the photograph had been. But where'd she taken it, and why?

I went back outside. Mrs. Plack—her neighbor, the same one who owned the chickens—was emerging from her own

door. She was carrying a basket full of washing, had green
rubber gloves on, which she always seemed to wear, and a
cigarette butt screwed into the corner of her mouth.

"Know where Cassie's gone?" I asked her, over the low
fence.

Her lips puckered further, and she stared at me like I was the
cause of all life's problems. I was unshaven, a mess, and she
obviously didn't approve. But that didn't stop her answering.

"Saw her riding north, not long ago. And she looked in a
hurry. But then, that girl always does."

What was north of here, though? Only the commercial
district, and she had no reason to go there.

I kept searching for her as I headed up. My gaze darted
down every side street, every passing alley. There was not a
sign of her, no red Harley anywhere in sight.

When I reached the edge of town, I braked, and sat there
with the motor idling. Where had she gone?

An instinct took hold of me. I started heading west along
the narrow road that marked the Landing's upper limit. And
finally, a small shape came in view. I'd been right. She'd
gone back to the place where she had ambushed Lauren, the
old loggers' trail. She was sitting on her bike, just gazing out
into the forest. I had no idea what she was looking at.

I parked a few yards from her, got out. Wanted to walk
over to her. But something about the set of her body warned
me not to get too close. She didn't even look at me, although
she had to know that I was there.

She was dressed in an old blue T-shirt, black jeans, and her
usual boots. Was grasping the bike's handlebars, but leaning
slightly to the right, still favoring her injured shoulder. A ruck-
sack was strapped to her pillion, the khaki canvas bulging. I
thought I could make out the edges of a photo frame. What
was this? What the blazes did she think that she was doing?

Her head was tucked down. The Harley's motor was still
running.

"Cass?" I asked, raising my voice above the sound.

When she failed to respond, I took a gentle step in her
direction.

"Planning on taking a trip?"

Which was a ludicrous suggestion, factually impossible.
I'd only meant it as a joke. But she looked extremely determined when her face came up.

"I'm sorry, Ross," she murmured. "But I just can't do this
anymore."

I held myself still, trying to understand what I'd just heard.
And then I thought I got it.

"Is this about Hobart?" I asked urgently. "He's alive,
Cassie. You didn't kill him."

Which didn't seem to brighten her mood any, as I'd hoped
it would.

"Should I congratulate myself on that?"

And I could see what she was getting at, how much it had
to hurt her. I'd have felt the same. But what was done was
done, and she had to get past it. She had always managed
that before. I smiled at her gently and let my limbs relax,
waiting for the Cassie that I knew to re-emerge.

"Hell, is that all this is?" I tried to reason with her. "You
tried to shoot me, remember, back when Saruak was around?
Almost succeeded too. But I'm still here."

Her face dropped again, vanishing. All I could see was
her cropped black hair.

"That was different," she answered slowly. "Saruak had
complete control of me. This time . . ."

The world seemed very still around us, the forest shrinking off into the distance. She took a good while, finding the
right words.

"It was me. The darkness inside me, understand? The fury
and the helpless rage."

"We've all got that, to one degree or another."

"No!" she broke across me. "You still don't get it! Ever
since my kids . . ."

I caught a brief glimpse of her eyes. They seemed to be
leaking brightness.

"Ever since that happened, there's been such anger in me.
And I guess I've been trying to let some of it out by helping
you. Trying to blow off steam and let the pressure go. But it
just keeps growing, just keeps building."

I could see she'd started shaking. And that worried me
more than anything else had.

"And I've reached the stage," she went on, "where I can't
do this anymore."

My face had gone completely tight. I'd never heard her
talk like this. I'd known all along how badly she was suffering, for sure. But I was in the same boat . . . I had lost my
family too. And this was the right time to remind her of that.
So I did it, the words clogging up slightly my throat.

"You're different," she snapped. "You cope, Ross. With
everything. That's your talent. You always keep the darkness under wraps, control your inner demons. But me? What
if, next time, I do kill someone? Or a load of people?"

"That won't happen," I tried to assure her, although I was
finding it pretty hard just getting words out by this stage.

"Can you be completely certain?"

She stared into my eyes, looking for an answer. And
I couldn't hide the true one. You can never be completely
certain about anything, especially not here. We both knew
that.

"This is crazy," I pointed out. "Where do you expect to
go?"

She jerked her head at the trees. "Out there."

Which sounded so bizarre I thought her sanity had gone.

"Uh . . . there's the small matter of a certain curse."

"Regan's Curse means I can't get anywhere else. But I can
still go out into the woods. We do it all the time."

She was talking about . . . remaining out there? In that
awful quiet and stillness that enveloped us whenever we
stepped past the town limits? My sense of alarm increased.

"Alone out there?"

"Looks that way."

"You can't be serious?"

"Except I am."

This was just plain nuts. Had her mind broken down completely? I started to walk over to her, realizing I had to make
her see some sense. But she revved her engine, then the
Harley moved away from me in a broad circle.

"What are you doing?" I asked her, swiveling around. "You can't stay out there. We don't belong there!"

"Add it to the list of places where I don't belong!" she shouted back.

She had the bike pointed at the trees by this stage. And before I could say or do anything else, she opened up the throttle and went hurtling forward. I ran after her. Went over the border a few yards. Everything around me bled of color and went still.

Except for Cass, that was. She was roaring away along the logging track, moving too quickly for me to catch up.

I stumbled to a halt, watching helplessly as she dwindled. She was lost among the dense tangle of branches before much longer.

I could still hear the Harley for a good while after that. But then even its howling finally diminished, fading away to absolutely nothing.

There was utter silence, not even the whisper of a breeze. I stood immersed in it for perhaps an hour, waiting.

But Cassie did not come back.

CHAPTER 64

Forget everything that had happened to her in the past few days? The more Lauren tried to get her head around that concept, then the more it seemed ridiculous. She'd never been in such incredible peril. Never seen such startling, nightmarish events, or been so terrified in her whole life. She could no more lose those memories than replace her own head.

Still, she had come through it. That was a huge relief, and quite surprised her. But it was behind her now, just like the town was, physically. She'd gone past the final intersection a couple of minutes back.

It was turning out to be a very bright and pleasant morning, one of those last gasps of summer that were commonplace in this part of the world. No other cars were on this road. The sun shone through the foliage. Her window was still partly down, and she could smell the leafy odors.

A grackle sprang up from the road in front of her and soared away, a flapping dart of black and sapphire blue, rapidly diminishing against the sky. And was that some kind of good omen? Frankly, it didn't really seem to matter. Getting out in one piece was enough good luck for an entire lifetime.

She glanced in her rearview mirror. Raine's Landing had become merely a narrow strip of rooftops, glimpsed between a gap in the trees.

Forget it? Hardly likely. She'd recall it until her dying day. The only genuine problem was . . . would she ever dare tell anyone else about it?

She went around a bend in the road. And when she glanced up at the mirror again, the town was completely lost from sight.

It started fading from her thoughts immediately. She could no longer remember what the place looked like. There'd been a square, and a big hill near the center, hadn't there? Or maybe not.

She'd had some difficulties there. She remained pretty sure of that. But of what nature . . . ? Strange, unworldly figures flashed before her inner eye for half a second, then were swiftly gone. And just as well, since things like that did not—could not—exist.

Other faces started to appear. A black man. A short guy in spectacles. An attractive redhead, and a huge, bald cop. They hung in her memory for the briefest instant, and then faded too.

Who exactly had they been?

What was the place where she had met them even called?

Met who? she wondered finally.

One last face was hanging in her mind's eye, longer than the others had. A man's face, somewhat gaunt but handsome, blond hair thinning slightly at the front. Steel gray eyes peered at her. And there was concern in them.

His lips moved.

"Not welcome here? That's not in the least bit true."

Lauren pulled over abruptly to the ditch at the side of the road.

Who was that? She glanced back across her shoulder, but could see only the trees. But she had some kind of connection with this guy, a bond. She was positive of that. And she struggled to recall his name.

It came to her. She breathed out a soft syllable.

"Ross."

Yes, that was it. *Ross Devries.* And suddenly, the rest of it came flooding back. She remembered every moment, every footstep, every street. The whole of it. Raine's Landing.

In a lot of ways, it was an awful place. But there was an upside. In her few days there, she'd found herself among some of the hardiest, most resilient, bravest people she had ever known. And was that because they had no choice in the matter?

No, Lauren thought. You can fight, or you can fold. Everyone has that choice.

She'd started to perspire faintly, but was surprising herself now, thinking of the townspeople with fondness. Saul? Would he recover? And would Ross ever get his family back?

God knew, they had problems. But they'd protected her when they were able, in the time that she'd been there. And, once they'd gotten used to her, they'd treated her with kindness.

Raine's Landing. Lord, what a place. And—who knew?— some day she might even come back. Just to see how everyone was getting along.

That old saying was true, wasn't it? That which didn't kill you really did make you stronger.

A pensive smile flitted across her lips, then spread up to her eyes. Lauren put the car back into drive, and headed for the freeway.

CHAPTER 65

On the way back home, I stopped and bought some cigarettes. I'd given up the habit a while back, but to hell with it.
Just one more pack, then I'd be done. My thoughts were in
a total blur.

I had to stop again for a row of flatbed trucks, at the intersection just before my street. They were local, rather than
from out of town. And they were loaded up with cinder-
blocks, shingles, scaffolding, and lumber. Reconstruction
was already underway, all over the Landing.

A soft, warm breeze was blowing in from the west when
I finally got home. This might turn out to be one of the last
genuinely hot days before the fall set in. There was ham-
mering and the loud noise of a drill a couple of blocks away.
Maybe they were rebuilding Evan Cope's house, which I
knew had been partway flattened.

A few doors down from my place, some kids were playing on the sidewalk with a Frisbee. And somebody's old
lawn mower was setting up a whirring chatter on the gently
moving air.

I sat down on the edge of my front porch and lit a smoke.
But it didn't go exactly as I'd planned. I wheezed fiercely
after the first pull, and my eyes began to water. So I threw it
down and stamped on it, then tossed the pack away.

"You okay, mister?" came a small high voice.

The kids had stopped playing and were watching me. But I wasn't sure how to answer them. So I simply got up and went inside, their inquiring gazes still following me.

They were gone when I emerged again. It was late afternoon. What had I been doing all day? I wasn't even sure myself. Just hanging around. Thinking. And sometimes trying not to.

The memories came back to me, replaying for the thousandth time. All of those occasions Cass and I had fought against the worst effects of magic, shoulder to shoulder, side by side. The times that I had saved her skin, and the numerous times that she'd saved mine.

On the rooftop of my office building, not so very long ago, the thing called Saruak had lunged at me, trying to spear me through the gut. And Cass had aimed her shotgun and then stopped him in his tracks.

Her words, once she'd done that, kept repeating through my head.

"It's what I do. I watch your back."

And who was left to do that now?

More time passed, largely unnoticed. The light faded around me, and the west horizon turned progressively redder. Some denser clouds had started blowing in. We would be heading into winter before we even knew it. My mind was merely wandering, picking up on any vagrant thought.

Then the cell phone went off in my pocket. My heart leapt, and I fumbled to answer it.

"Cassie?"

"Huh?"

It was Vallencourt. He sounded harassed, and there was shouting in the background.

"I'm in West Meadow, Devries, on Parson's Avenue," he told me. "And I've got this situation here. Wondered if you might be able to help out?"

I listened to the problem, told him I was on my way, then

headed for my car. But climbing into it, I glanced behind me. Purely out of instinct.

It felt unfamiliar—and pretty damned unsettling—setting off into possible danger with nobody to watch my back.

But it sounded like they needed me out there. So I went anyway.